Love in the Age of
Mechanical Reproduction

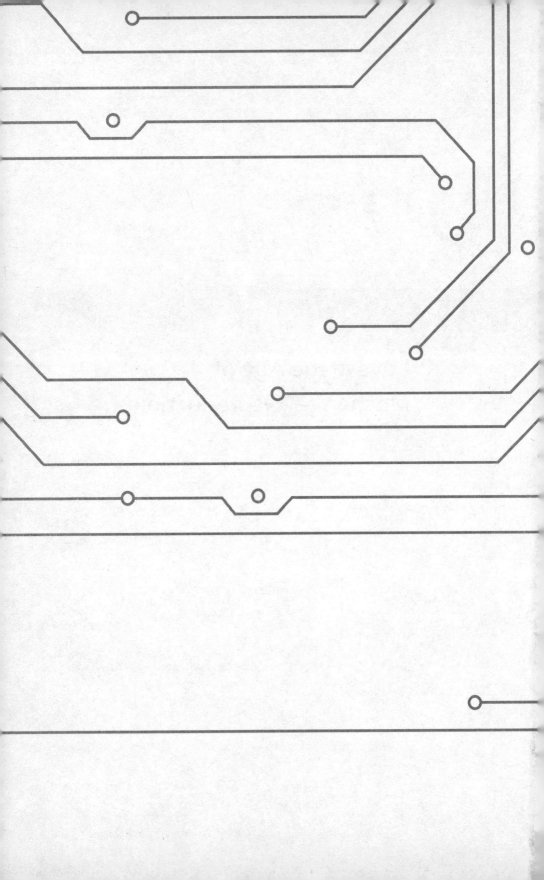

Love in the Age of Mechanical Reproduction

JUDD TRICHTER

Thomas Dunne Books
St. Martin's Press
New York

THOMAS DUNNE BOOKS.
An imprint of St. Martin's Press.

LOVE IN THE AGE OF MECHANICAL REPRODUCTION. Copyright © 2015 by Judd Trichter. All rights reserved. Printed in the United States of America. For information, address St. Martin's Press, 175 Fifth Avenue, New York, N.Y. 10010.

Excerpt on page 274 from *The Metamorphoses of Ovid*, translated by Allen Mandelbaum (Harcourt Brace and Co., 1993).

www.thomasdunnebooks.com
www.stmartins.com

Designed by Molly Rose Murphy

Library of Congress Cataloging-in-Publication Data

Trichter, Judd.
  Love in the age of mechanical reproduction : a novel / Judd Trichter.
    pages cm
  ISBN 978-1-250-03602-5 (hardcover)
  ISBN 978-1-250-03601-8 (e-book)
  1. Androids—Fiction. I. Title.
  PS3620.R534L68 2015
  813'.6—dc23

                                                    2014033454

St. Martin's Press books may be purchased for educational, business, or promotional use. For information on bulk purchases, please contact the Macmillan Corporate and Premium Sales Department at 1-800-221-7945, extension 5442, or write to specialmarkets@macmillan.com.

First Edition: February 2015

10 9 8 7 6 5 4 3 2 1

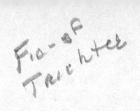

For Mooey

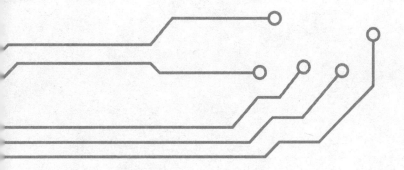

PART ONE

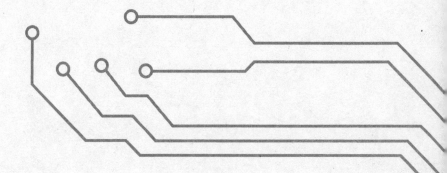

ONE

Heartbeats and Spinners

A rusted scaffold from a long-abandoned restoration project twists about the charred ruins of the Hollywood sign. It rattles as a flying train arcs over the hills and plunges into the vast iridescence of a damp L.A. night.

Eliot Lazar lies beside Iris Matsuo on a slant of undergrowth beneath the blackened *H*. His hair is mussed, his body thin, his chapped lips default to a grateful smile. With his left hand, he rubs the pain in his right shoulder where a prosthetic has replaced the arm that was mangled in an explosion when he was young. It's a well-made arm, smart metal amalgam—you'd never know it's mechanical if not for the scar on his back that marks the border between the part of Eliot that's metal and the rest that's made of flesh.

"The island formed from a volcano that erupted in the Pacific," he tells her. "People came for the black-sand beaches and the surf. Heartbeats and spinners cultivated the land. They built windmills and dams and solar roofs for juice. They planted orchards and palm trees. They coded hemp to grow synth-skin. They imported gen-modded livestock to trim the blue-green fields."

"What kind of livestock?"

"Some cross between a goat and a sheep. My mom says it's got a goat's face, but it's furry like a sheep."

"You mean woolly."

"Right. Woolly. Whatever."

"Tell me more." She hangs on his every word describing Avernus, an island he has never seen—she knows he has never seen it—though she likes to hear him describe it.

"And the Avernians share everything. All property is communal. They trade with the ships passing along the cargo routes. And if the ships won't trade, the Avernians attack."

"Like pirates!"

"Just like 'em," he tells her. "And at night, they camp along the cliffs and bang drums around a fire. They sacrifice their woolly goats. They eat a big feast and sing and dance and drink rum 'til the morning comes."

A locket hangs loosely from her neck. The oval stone is brown with a red fleck on the edge, an echo of the red flaw in her left eye. Otherwise, you'd never know Iris isn't a heartbeat. You never can tell with these late-model androids, not unless you're looking at their outlet navels or feeling their wrists for a spinning engine pulse. But the red flaw gives her away. Some bot fucked up on a Hasegawa assembly line and the C-900 got stuck with it. The flaw became her namesake, Iris, she likes to joke, like a Dalmatian named Spot.

"They have a leader called the Admiral," he tells her, "who doesn't allow any tourists. No runways for a plane to land. You can't dock at the port unless you're invited or taking cover from a storm."

"But you're invited," Iris reminds him. "Your mother invited you."

"She said I can work on the boats, and you can teach an art class."

"She said that?"

"She said they need an art teacher at the school. Someone to teach the kids how to draw and paint and sculpt."

"You told your mother about me?"

"Not everything. Not on a brane. Not when someone could be listening."

Lying on her side, she stares out past her feet across the valley where the police floaters and drones hover over Hollywood. "I always wanted to teach children," she says, "ever since I first came out of the factory. I always wanted to see the world through a child's eyes."

"And we'd be safe in Avernus," he tells her. "No one will threaten us there. We'll be treated no different from any other couple, and we'll be together so much you'll be sick of me."

"I'm sick of you now."

She smiles, and he kisses her thinking, I had heard about love, I had read what the authors and poets wrote about it, but I never expected it to happen to me. The relentless force of it pulling me by my back teeth toward another being. In thirty years, I neither expected nor sought love, but it came to me nonetheless, despite my having done nothing to earn or deserve it. It came like some grand inheritance from a relative I never knew, and now I couldn't imagine life without it. I wouldn't want to. I have seen the world with love, and I have seen the world without it, and I have made my choice in which world I want to live.

"Now all we need is a boat," she says.

A stick breaks in the bushes. Their bodies tense until they see the coyote's eyes. The animal turns back into the dark woods to look elsewhere for its prey.

But what if it hadn't been a coyote? Eliot wonders. What if it had been a cop or a Militiaman or an Android Disciple discovering us in the woods? He has seen the hanging, burnt, dismembered bodies of interspecies couples, tortured and put on display. He has heard the radio ads offering rewards for information. He knows it's only a matter of time before their relationship is discovered.

"Someone's been following me," she tells him.

"A trapper?"

"I don't know."

Rain taps on the roof of Eliot's car parked a few yards away.

"What's he look like?"

"Who?"

"Whoever's following you."

"I haven't seen him," she says. "I just got a sense."

"You're paranoid."

"Androids don't get paranoid; we do the math. You heartbeats feel an emotion then find a way to justify it. Bots work the other way around."

"And you're being careful?" he asks.

"Always."

"Have you told anyone about us?"

"Have you?"

"No."

"Maybe you should stay at my place for a few days, until things settle down."

"It's too risky," she says, rolling to her side as she turns away. "What if your neighbors see me? What if they report us both?"

"I'm not saying to move in. I'm just thinking a few days."

The soft ends of her hair graze his face. Oriental Agrisilk, black #42. Used to come standard on a Hasegawa C-900. She backs in close to him and pulls his arm around her body.

"One big deal," he assures her, "and I'll be able to buy that cabin cruiser for sale in the marina."

"What about a loan?"

"I got two busts on my record."

"Can you ask your brother for his?"

"Shelley loves that boat. He'd never give it up."

Their fingers intertwine. His nails are pink and clean while hers are short and black from years of grinding metal.

"Monroe Extraction is coming in at the end of the week," he tells her as she turns her body into his. "I make that deal with Dale Hampton, and we can get out of here."

She wipes a raindrop from her cheek lest he think it's a tear. He slides his hand inside the back of her jeans. She moans for a moment, her eyes close until they open in a sideways squint. She props herself up on one elbow and pushes him away.

"How do I know you're serious?" she asks. "How do I know you're not just leading me on?"

"I'm not just leading you on."

"How do I know you're not stoned, and this isn't the drip talking?"

"I don't need the drip when I'm with you."

"You promise you'll quit?" she asks.

"I promise."

"And you'll take me to Avernus?"

"I'll marry you on Avernus."

She closes her eyes and buries her face in the crook of his neck. His shoulder smarts as her engine spins madly against his chest.

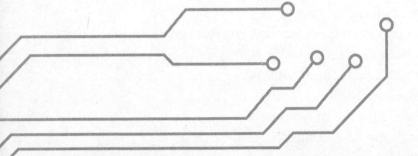

TWO

A Salesman

In a men's room stall at the Global Assistance Corporation (GAC), Eliot pops the top off a sample vial of cologne he uses to hide his drip. He pours the contents into a handkerchief, holds it to his face, and flushes the toilet to cover the sound of a long, deep inhale.

Ah, there it is.

The shoulder pain dissipates into the ether along with the vapor of his breath. He screws the top back on the vial and folds the hanky into his pocket. He exits the stall. Confidence restored. Ready for the kill. He washes his hands in the sink. Splash of water for the face. Runs his hands through his thick, dark hair. Wait a minute, what's that? Glance at the mirror reveals a hickey on his neck. Little *hello* from his android fiancée. A *good luck* perhaps. He lifts his tie knot to prevent the blemish from peeking above the collar of his shirt.

"Hey, Dale, sorry to keep you waiting." Eliot saunters into the showroom reserved for GAC's more elite prospects. "Let's get you something to drink."

Sally, the secretarybot, uses a cocktail wand to ionize two glasses of water into bourbon. As she sets them on the table, a smirking Dale Hampton slides a hand between her legs and cops a feel beneath her polka dot skirt.

"Why is it you left-coast types prefer your gals built like altar boys?" The burly, crew cut Texan has gained a good twenty pounds since the last time Eliot saw him. Tailored navy suit with a starched white shirt, his red tie matches the rosacea of his cheeks. "Where we're from, we prefer a little more paddin'. Ain't that right, Malcolm?"

"Yessir," says a bald, bug-eyed man in a pinstripe vest. He stands as if expecting to be struck by a sudden and arbitrary blow.

Eliot crosses to introduce himself, but Dale Hampton interrupts. "Don't worry 'bout Malcolm. He's just my tin monkey. I dress him up as a lark."

The android casts his gaze toward the floor rather than insult a heartbeat by looking him in the eye. Eliot shrugs, wishing he had taken a second hit of drip in the bathroom. A sober meeting with an asshole like Dale is more than he can stomach.

"Still living in Houston?"

"That's right."

"Two kids?"

"Three."

"Three now?" Eliot whistles as he sits on the armchair perpendicular to Dale's couch.

"Two boys and a girl," says the Texan. "Got one of them Swedish nannybots taking care of 'em. Taking care of me, too, when the wife's not around." He winks and takes a noisy sip of his bourbon. "What about you, Eliot? Got somethin' to sink your dick in?"

"Not at the moment."

"You oughta get on that, friend. Lifespans for us heartbeats gettin' shorter and shorter. Wait too long, you'll miss the boat."

The two men met years before, back when Eliot worked at Daihanu, the company his father, Hiram Lazar, helped build. Then as now, Dale was procuring androids for Monroe Extraction. The deal he and Eliot struck for a mining concession on the moon resulted in a disaster that caused the bankruptcy of Daihanu and rendered worthless the value of Eliot's inherited stock.

"So what brings you to L.A.?"

"Christmas shopping," says Dale, crossing a leg to lay a tasseled loafer on his trunk of a thigh. "That and a new seam on Europa might have the sweetest trove of rare metals in the solar system." His lips wet and his eyes close with the thought of it.

"Well, congratulations. How far along are you on the survey?"

"Survey, Hell. We know where the ore is, we just got to pull it out the rock. I need three thousand bots for five years, and I need 'em on their way to Jupiter's moon by January. I'll need miners who can cut ice, move dirt, and break rock. I'll need construction, maintenance, logistics, servers, transport, and executive security. Might as well throw in a couple of botwhores, too, one for every two hundred men. And a couple of sissybots for the spinners that swing that way."

"Or the executives when they visit."

"What's that?"

"Nothing."

In fact, Eliot would rather not send three thousand bots to work on an outer moon of Jupiter in weather that's two hundred degrees below zero for a company with a safety record as poor as that of Monroe Extraction. On the other hand, the commission on a three-thousand-bot lease would allow Eliot to buy that cabin cruiser he needs to get to Avernus. It would take a good six weeks to get paid, but if he combines his savings with what he can ask for as an advance, it's possible Eliot could be on the high seas within a week. The very thought of it brings Iris near him, like she's in the room beside him seeing the blue-green fields and black-sand beaches of Avernus loom large beyond the windows of the office tower.

"Sally, show Mr. Hampton our extraction series."

The secretarybot closes the blinds and crosses to the first tableau. She pulls back a screen to reveal a male android wearing a hard hat with a bulb in front and a power-ax slung over his shoulder. His face is covered with coal dust while behind him a large brane projects a background loop of an active mine on a distant planet.

"The GAC-50s are your best bet for the miners and construction crews," says Eliot. "Their skin's made of a Bortec-asbestos fiber that protects them in any climate. Battery lasts fourteen hours. They need about four hours of sleep per twenty-four-hour cycle during which they can do a recharge through an outlet navel."

On cue, the android picks up his shirt and plugs a botcord into the space where his navel would be.

"For transport," says Eliot, "I recommend the GAC-20 Teamster."

Sally opens another screen to reveal a bot wearing a plaid flannel shirt and a mesh trucker cap. He sits in a low-gravity ATV, which he pretends to steer as the brane behind him displays a rugged mountain terrain.

"The 20 has the top safety record in the business. He drives fast and recharges from a car battery to give you an extended day's work. And we improved on the last model by limiting his speech card so he won't talk so much."

"That's fine. Just fine." Dale seems tickled by the presentation.

Sally opens a third tableau to show off an android wearing a white button-down shirt as he sits at a desk in a mobile office.

"The Torell-9 can handle all logistics. He isn't the best thinker we carry, but the 50s and Teamsters seem to work better with the Torell than they do with any of the newer . . ."

"What about the whores?" Dale interrupts.

The drip dulling Eliot's senses fails to inure him to Dale Hampton's poor manners. He'd like to tell the burly Texan to go fuck himself, but a show of pride won't buy Eliot a cabin cruiser that can cut through the Pacific sludge. Pride won't get him and Iris to Avernus; a commission check will.

"You'll have to look elsewhere for the whores," says Eliot. "We don't manufacture females at GAC."

"You did at Daihanu."

"And Daihanu is no more," Eliot reminds him.

Dale stands and carries his drink to the tableaux to get a closer look. The bots move in various expressions of work, showing off their physiques, their strength, and their balance.

"What do you think, Malcolm?" Dale asks his assistant. "This look like top-of-the-line metal?"

"Yessir," says the android.

"They made better than you?"

"Don't know 'bout that, sir."

"Why, Malcolm"—Dale turns menacingly on his heel—"are you saying Mr. Lazar's bots are shit?"

Malcolm's chin sinks as he hunches over in fear. To distract Dale from his drunken bullying, Eliot continues his pitch. "All GAC androids are manufactured in-house without any counterfeit, recycled, or after-market parts. This ensures our bots have the lowest crime and radicalization rate of all the major brands."

"I ain't worried 'bout that," says Dale, pulling at the side of his jacket to show off the pistol holstered at his waist. "We don't stand for no mess in no Monroe camp, do we, Malcolm?"

"No, sir."

"Hell, you don't even know what 'radicalization' means."

"No, sir."

"Then how you gonna say we don't stand for it?"

The bot retreats, so once again Eliot continues. "The other way we maintain discipline is by ensuring our bots are afforded the best services and accommodations available wherever their working environment might be."

"Forgive me, Eliot"—Dale struggles to hide his disgust—"but I'm running a mining concession on Jupiter's moon, not a spa for a bunch of tin men. I'm offering eighty ingots per day, per spinner for a five-year contract. Bonuses if they exceed quota on production. As far as services and accommodations, the bots will sleep where they fall and shop at our company store."

Dale signals to Malcolm, who hands Eliot a notebrane that unfolds to reveal the financials of Monroe's offer. Eliot examines the figures and considers the split that would pay his androids forty per day while GAC pockets the other forty as a fee. Hard mining in two-hundred-below weather would require a large expenditure of power, and with Monroe running the generators, who knows how much the mining conglomerate would charge the bots for juice? Forty ingots per day would leave no room for upgrades or spare components for damaged limbs, of which there would be many the way Monroe drives its bots. That means the androids, in order to survive, would have to purchase black market metal that runs a high risk of failure, corruption, or infection. That could lead to a depreciation in the value of the bots or, worse, an outbreak similar to the one on Mons Bradley that bankrupted Eliot's previous employer. Finally, the commission on Dale's offer would only get Eliot halfway to what he needs to buy a boat that can cross the Pacific.

"I think there are labor providers who might take this offer." Eliot stands and hands the brane back to Malcolm. "But GAC isn't one of them. Thank you for considering us, Dale. It's always a pleasure to see you. Give your wife and kids my best. Sally, please show Dale and Malcolm back to their car."

The Texan smiles and laughs off what he guesses to be a bluff.

"Now, now, let's not get our panties in a twist." His chins jiggle as he slaps his glass on the table and sits back on the couch. "Malcolm, does it seem to you like we've upset Mr. Lazar?"

"Seems that way, sir."

"What do you suppose we did wrong?"

"I dunno, sir."

"I dunno, either." Dale produces a pack of cigarettes and taps it against his leg. "Maybe they just lack hospitality here in Cali-forn-I-A." He lights his smoke and takes a drag. "Or else there's some other sensitivity we've managed to upset."

Eliot looks into his drink as he weighs his personal predicament against his professional ethics. The longer Iris remains in Los Angeles, the more vulnerable she is to a trapper, to a Militiaman, to an Android Disciple looking to punish her for dating a heartbeat. Lord knows she would never want Eliot to send three thousand souls to a frozen Hell on her account, but one way or another, Monroe Extraction will dig that mine. Dale Hampton will get his bots from GAC or some other labor provider, and they will pull that metal out of the ground. Better the commission goes to Eliot rather than a competitor. At least he'll put it to good use and protect the androids as best he can. At least that's the way he justifies it in his mind.

"Am I right," Eliot asks softly, "that Monroe lost two thousand of Bjork Nautical's androids during an excavation beneath the Arctic?"

"*Well*," Dale replies in his crafty drawl, "a lot of them bots were *listed* as 'damaged beyond repair,' but the labor provider's definition of DBR was miles apart from ours."

"And then you destroyed another five thousand during a ten-year dig on Mars."

"Now looky here"—Dale points a ringed finger in Eliot's direction—"five thousand bots over ten years on the Red Planet is hardly something to be ashamed of. Besides, wasn't like we was payin' top-of-the-line metal. We was usin' third-rate commie tin, some of the worst coolies Kindelan had to lease. Sure, the work dented a few heads, but what did they care? Kindelan got their money back when they sold the DBRs to Green Valley."

The Green Valley to which Dale refers is the recycling facility whose business it is to buy DBR'ed androids, pull out salvageable parts, then sell what they can to retailers in the secondary market. Whatever they can't move as a component, they sell as scrap, and whatever they can't sell as scrap gets rendered and returned to the Earth for future generations to mine. Selling DBRs to Green Valley is a last resort when trying to recover value from a wrecked bot.

"I need my androids to work full capacity for six hundred days before GAC turns a profit," says Eliot. "I need to run the company store to sell upgrades and replacement metal. If my bots get DBR'ed and wind up at a recycler, that's just a one-time payment and I'm not generating revenue."

"Horseshit." Dale blows twin streams of smoke out his nose. "The way y'all upgrade designs, most of them bots are obsolete in two years anyway. If y'all didn't sell DBRs to Green Valley, you'd just release 'em as *free roamers*, and free roamers lower the cost of labor. So if you look at it that way, you're better off I crush your fucking bots."

Sally, Malcolm, and the androids in the tableaux remain stone-faced during the negotiation. Eliot wonders if any of them would like to be *free roamers* themselves. It's a trade-off. Because they're unowned, free roamers don't have to split their salaries with a labor provider or some other owner. They work for less but pocket more. They drag down wages for bots and heartbeats alike. That's why other workers see them as a threat. With no rights and no citizenship, the free roamers have none of the legal protections bots enjoy when they are the property of corporations or private individuals. Their only protection is their employee ID cards, which the trappers, according to their ethical code, choose to respect and allow the bots free passage. Without that card, a roamer will see his engine ripped from his torso within a year of gaining his "freedom."

"Eighty per day is too low," says Eliot. "I can't make the deal."

The burly Texan puts out his cigarette on the table. His drink spills as he stands and paces before the tableaux. Eliot gathers from all the posturing that Dale doesn't want to return to his bosses empty-handed. He hasn't left the room yet. Whatever his reasons, he's still looking for a deal.

"What do you have for security?" Dale asks, his voice slurring from the bourbon.

Eliot indicates to Sally that it's time to pull out the secret weapon, the yes-maker, closer of all deals stalled or wobbling. The secretary-bot moves the screen on a fourth tableau to reveal a lithe, onyx-colored securitybot in black metal armor standing before a clean white brane. Knees bent, arms cocked, fingers spread. He's ready to pounce at a moment's notice, and yet it's the calm in the bot's demeanor that strikes the greatest fear. It's as if Sally has revealed to the room the presence of a bomb, armed and ready to explode the moment it detects any thought that might precede a violent action.

"Where's the background on that?" Eliot asks.

Sally apologizes. "We're displaying the Satine 5000s against a white brane until marketing decides on a matching environment."

The securitybot stares forward with relaxed lips and smooth black eyes. The room chills in his presence. Dale stands before him pretending he isn't transfixed by the contours and sharp edges of the bot's features.

Says Eliot, "Independent tests confirm that the Satine 5000 prototype outperforms all the top-rated securitybots on the market. Our creatives based the design on Polynesian war masks and ancient Spartan armors. They studied the movements of Japanese fighting fish and the musculature of panthers in the wild."

"He looks a wee bit small," says Dale.

"The data shows speed is more important than size. We charge a high premium, but you won't need as many on your detail as you would using another brand."

Dale takes out a pocketbrane and shines a UV light on the bot's limbs to see the serial numbers.

"We don't mix and match parts," says Eliot. "His eyes extend from his face to get a three-hundred-degree view. His claws tear through concrete. His skin can hold off M2 bullets fired at a velocity of . . ."

"I'll pay a hundred per day on average for the whole package," says Dale. "Provided you throw this son of a bitch in the mix."

"I can't do that."

Dale groans. "Eliot, you want to tell me why you're being so difficult?" He crosses back to the coffee table to retrieve his cigarettes. His loafers echo against the marble floor. "Is this about our last negotiation? Is this about Mons Bradley?"

Eliot remembers the loops in the newsbranes from when the story went public. Previously benign androids had become raging psychopaths overnight. They were infected by the *foaming mouth* virus transported to the moon through corrupted metal.

"Mons Bradley ain't somethin' I'm proud of," the burly Texan admits as he lights up. "Ain't somethin' I want to repeat."

"Me either," says Eliot. "So pay my bots what they're worth and allow GAC to run the company store. That's the only way we'll keep bad metal off the site."

Dale drops his lighter and crosses back to the Satine 5000. He blows a stream of smoke into the securitybot's face as he stares into the blackness of his eyes.

"Eliot," says Dale, "I fear you suffer from an excess of compassion. I witnessed the foaming mouth outbreak on Mons Bradley. I was there." His voice trails off to a growl. "I ain't talkin' 'bout one or two spinners gone loopy with drool on their lips. I'm talking 'bout hundreds of rogue bots rippin', robbin', and rapin' everything on the moon. Tearin' apart heartbeat men, women, and children. The things they did to them children." Dale gives each bot in the room a hard look before returning to the Satine. "That ain't somethin' a fellow forgets."

No, thinks Eliot, Dale didn't forget. He lost some thirty coworkers, but he kept his job. The labor provider took the blame, not Dale, not Monroe Extraction. After all, Monroe didn't own the bots, they just hired them from Daihanu. And six years later, Dale's still working for the same company, still procuring androids and shuttling them to Hell while Eliot lost his inheritance and had to start over at a new firm.

"Three hundred per day," Eliot states his price. The ask is high, but if the client will meet him in the middle, it's the last deal of its kind that Eliot will ever have to negotiate. He'll never have to deal with the likes of Dale Hampton again.

"Three hundred a day is more than I'd pay a heartbeat."

"Heartbeats can't survive in the outer solar system."

"One fifty," Dale counters, and Eliot comes down to 275. He can see Dale Hampton being seduced by the Satine. The bot appeals to the Texan's reptilian vanity. He has to have him. Has to show him off to his bosses back at Monroe. Sleek like an Italian sports car but far more threatening. And he'd be the first on his block to have one.

"Just how good is this son of a bitch?" Dale asks. His wet lips curl as he unholsters his .357 and crosses to the coffee table. His smile indicates he'd like to see a demonstration.

"Tim," Eliot calls to the Satine. "Protect Mr. Hampton."

The onyx-colored bot steps out of his tableau so that he has an angle on all the players in the room.

"Malcolm, you ugly shit," says Dale, as he drops his gun on the table. "I want you to grab that gun and shoot me."

The confused android looks at his owner to see if he's kidding. He looks to Eliot then to the Satine.

"Go on." Dale positions himself between the table and the securitybot. "You pull this off, you'll be a robot hero. They'll name a bot holiday after you. Call it Malcolm Saturday."

Again, the bot looks at the gun then at his owner then at Eliot, who is as curious as anyone to see how this all plays out. Even the Torrell-9 leans across his desk to watch from his tableau.

"Hey, monkey lips," says Dale, "did you not hear what I said? Grab that gun, or I'll hang you myself from a hook on the Green Valley line. Now stop being a dumb piece of shit and shoot."

The repressed emotion from years of insults burns to the surface of the android's face. It happens quickly. Malcolm runs to the table and grabs the gun in a fast-twitch motion hoping he can get off the shot before anyone reacts. He can't. The Satine 5000 flings a knife from his belt as Malcolm's hand rises. The blade threads past Dale and strikes at Malcolm's wrist. The gun clanks to the floor. Malcolm bends to pick it up, but by then, the Satine has closed the distance between them. Malcolm's legs fly from beneath him. His arm is snapped off at the shoulder. Within a second's time, the Satine has retrieved the gun and offered it back to Dale.

The burly Texan cannot hide his awe. "Well, I'll be damned." He holsters the gun as Malcolm bleeds oil in a heap of twisted limbs. "I'll be Goddamned!"

"Sally, get some maintenancebots and an engineer to help Malcolm reattach his parts."

"Yes, Mr. Lazar." The secretarybot moves to a workbrane and types the request on the hologram keyboard.

"And prepare some contracts for Mr. Hampton. A three thousand bot order for five years at two fifty per day."

The Texan puts down his drink and claps his meaty palms in appreciation.

"Wait 'til I show the boys back home. They ain't gonna believe this!"

But as Dale Hampton claps, Eliot notices a narrow slit across the sleeve of his blazer. Then Dale notices it, too. On closer examination, he sees the fabric coming apart.

"What the . . . ?"

Oh shit. "Sally, have the valet get my car."

Dale tears off his jacket to find a red circle expanding on the white cotton of his shirt. "He cut me!"

Eliot grabs Dale and pulls him toward the elevator.

"That son of a bitch cut me. He damn near cut off my arm!"

Dale goes for his gun, but Eliot is there to stop him. He pulls at Dale's arm as the elevator arrives.

"I want him dead! I want that son of a bitch cut in a million pieces and melted to a chunk of shit!"

"We have to get you to a hospital."

"Let me at 'im!"

The Satine steps back into his tableau as Eliot pushes Dale inside the elevator. Blood streams down the Texan's arm and drips from the tip of his finger.

"What kind of operation are you runnin' here, Lazar? That bot is a Goddamn killer!"

The doors close and the elevator begins its descent. Eliot removes his tie and uses it as a tourniquet to stanch the bleeding.

"No son of a bitch bot gonna cut me and live to tell about it. You gonna pay for this, Lazar! Your whole damn company gonna pay!"

Eliot tightens the knot around Dale's shoulder and wipes the blood from his hands. He can see the blue-green fields and black-sand beaches of Avernus drifting a little farther away.

THREE
The Younger Brother

Five hundred global ingots for Dale's hospital bill. Another six hundred on a new coat and shirt. A hundred and fifty on dinner and drinks to settle him down. All of it out of Eliot's pocket. Sally had Malcolm driven to the station where Dale and his bot boarded a vactrain back to Houston. Eliot saw them off. Come again soon. Shithead.

There's a message on his deskbrane when he arrives back at the office:

Eliot—
Dinner tonight. On me!

—Erica

Fuck.

"Gita, did the boss say anything about the meeting with Monroe Extraction?"

His coworker eats a salad at her desk and watches Eliot even when she's looking away. "Nope."

"Did she mention why she wants to see me?"

"Nope."

Of course the Hairy Mole doesn't need an excuse for ruining Eliot's night. Ruining it because Erica Santiago, VP from the Paolo Alto office, has a giant, hairy mole on her lower lip that moves when she chews like a beetle trying to escape her mouth.

Eliot fakes a sneeze.

"Bless you."

"Thanks."

In a move he has perfected over the years, Eliot pops open the vial in his pocket and dumps the remaining drip into a Kleenex in an open drawer. He pulls the tissue to his face and breathes in loud enough that it sounds like he's blowing his nose when in fact he's sucking in another glorious hit of the only thing in the world that will get him through the night.

"Gita, if the boss asks, tell her I had plans with my brother and can't make it tonight."

"Sure thing."

"Have a good one."

"You, too."

Gita stays. Probably wants to snoop around. Gita is always snooping around, though what she's looking for God only knows. Eliot says good night to Sally at the reception desk and waits for the elevator. It arrives with the Satine 5000 alone in the corner.

"Jesus Christ." Eliot shakes his head as he pushes the button for the garage. The doors close. "Tim, what the Hell was your objective up there?"

"Protect the principal."

"And who was the principal?"

"Mr. Hampton." The Satine speaks in a whisper that he can focus so that it's only heard by the person he addresses.

"Then why did Mr. Hampton get injured, Tim? Why did I have

to take Dale Hampton to the Goddamn hospital to get him stitched up?"

"There were two hundred ninety-three methods of defense of which the knife throw had the highest probability of stopping the attack while causing the least possible injury to the principal."

"And that was your only calculation? You weren't also factoring in anything you heard during the negotiation?"

"I was focused on the objective."

Eliot wants to believe him, but he knows his bosses will see the accident in a different light. They'll see it as a reason to have the Satine sent to the Green Valley recycling plant to be terminated, separated, and rendered.

"I'm assuming all your parts are clean."

"They are."

"Make sure of it. I want you to get an oil change and a virus scan."

"Should I get it at the company store?"

"Not unless you want this on record." Eliot pulls out his wallet and hands the bot a fifty-ingot note. "Get it done at the downtown mission. There's no reason GAC has to know, but God help you if this ever happens again."

A tone from the elevator indicates their arrival at the lobby.

"Did you close the deal?" asks the Satine.

Eliot looks at the bot like he's missing a screw. "No, Tim. I did not."

He finds his car in the underground garage and drives past the concrete barriers, the mini-tanks, the phalanx of security guards hired to protect the Century City tower. He drives toward the boulevard then stops at an intersection where a man pounds the hood of his car.

"Judas!" he screams. "Traitor!"

"Death to the bot! Death to the bot!"

A cop in riot gear pushes the protestors to join the other Militiamen behind the barricade. They're a scary-looking crew. Fundamentalists drawn from the ranks of heartbeats who lost their jobs to bot labor. Former union men who lost their pensions. Conspiracy theorists and gun nuts. Religious wackos who see a coming apocalypse with the rise of android technology.

"Blood is thicker than oil!"

"God hates bots! God hates bots!"

They wear camouflage pants with black shirts displaying the crosshairs logo of their movement. They hold branes on sticks with loops of heartbeat hostages decapitated by Android Disciples.

"Boycott GAC! End the manufacture of bots!"

Waiting at the red light, Eliot considers how the Militiamen's anger seems to gain in intensity each day. Their numbers grow, their opinionaters gain currency in the news, their politicians get elected to office.

"You're goin' to Hell, botlover! You're gonna burn for this in Hell!"

The light changes and Eliot glides away in his electric car, past the mob, down the street in a haze both real and perceived. The *real* haze comes from the smoke pulsing out of the illegal generators in bot cities all over L.A. The mayor outlawed the contraptions after a summer of fires burned out of control, but the bots figured out how to route the exhaust through a maze of pipes that disguises the whereabouts of the burners. The illegal juice diverts revenue away from the power companies and into the coffers of criminal gangs. The smoke and ash sicken heartbeats all the world over. They say it lowers birthrates. They say that's why lifespans are down and why every heartbeat over forty gets the cough.

The other haze, the *perceived* haze, is from the drip that veils Eliot's reality with something cool and soft to the touch. No one knows who invented the stuff though the Android Disciples control its distribution. Processed from discarded plastics, drip has no effect on bots but functions as a highly addictive narcotic when heartbeats inhale it through a cloth. It allows Eliot to absorb the sights and sounds of his surroundings without having to suffer any emotional impact. It dulls the pain from the injury to his shoulder and the memory of the incident that caused it.

Police floaters flock east overhead as the autodrive maneuvers through the traffic. Eliot allows the car to choose his route, the machine to tell him where to go. He turns on the radio to hear a warning of a "situation" in the bot city east of Hollywood. The report describes a hotel fire allegedly caused by an explosion at a drip lab. Police are blocking the press. Commuters are warned to avoid Beverly.

It's dark out by the time Eliot parks in front of the guest house off Beachwood Canyon where he has lived since graduating from college. It's a small, modest home. Too small, he often thinks. Too little privacy. But the rent's affordable, and the air's better, too. Not as much smoke and ash as there is at the bottom of the hill. They say you live a few years longer if you're high up or close to the water— maybe that's why Eliot hasn't moved in eight years. Or maybe it's just inertia.

The speakers on his deskbrane play a message from the Hairy Mole:

"Eliot, did you run out without saying good-bye? Oh, boo! I wanted to see how the Monroe meeting went. Let's grab a drink next week when I'm back in town."

He loads the Nutri-Ink into the 3-D printer.

"Pastrami on rye," he tells the machine before hitting PRINT. He empties his drip into a hanky and takes a bold sniff—the last of his stash. He'll have to score more tonight unless he wants his weekend to be a nerve-shattering bout of terror-inducing withdrawal. For all the drip helps kill his emotions, when it wears off, the comedown is a killer. The feelings hit doubly hard, the pain becomes an emergency.

Seconds after he drops onto the couch, the drug kicks in and Eliot's body tingles and drags into the soft bliss of the cushions. Everything's all right again. The printer beeps, indicating his sandwich is ready, but Eliot has lost his appetite. He has all he needs now: a dark room, a comfy couch, some quiet. Too bad Iris is working 'til two at the Chug-Bot factory in Heron. How nice if she were here beside him. Her smile, her smell, that little red fleck in her eye. The way her head tilts side-to-side when she sketches on the floor of her apartment. The way she curls beside him like a cat, her heart spins, her breath rises and falls, the light outside changes and nothing else. Time waits when her lips brush against his ear.

Smoke from the streets wafts up the canyon through the blinds. The buzz of drones descends from the hill. Their sirens stir the coyotes to a howl.

It's an autoimmune response, thinks Eliot, caused by some wound in the city. The "situation" he heard about on the radio is expressing itself. It's gaining momentum, approaching the condition of an "event." Will the fire spread to the neighboring streets, past the freeways and farther as the web scatters its embers to other bot cities across the globe? Is this the price we pay for being connected? No event is local. One small spark and the whole world goes up in flames.

He turns on the liquid screen on his wall to check the news. A reporter in a flak jacket says that snipers from the Android Disciples attacked first responders who raced to the scene.

"Police were forced to protect themselves," says the flak. "They fired from SWAT trucks and tore down a building the Disciples were using as a bunker."

Every channel carries the same report. Flames burning out of control. Civilians injured in the cross fire. Bots killed, too, Eliot assumes, but the news would never report it. Can't say a bot was killed because that would imply he once lived, and Standards and Practices insists that something cannot die that was never alive. They can be DBR'ed but never killed. All forms of oppression carry their own semantics.

"Breaking News" flashes across the bottom of the screen. It's a video loop from Lorca, the right sleeve of her sweater pinned up to conceal the stump of her missing arm. She speaks from a living room lit by a fireplace out of frame. The large chair diminishes her, makes her look less threatening. Good production value for an insurrectionist drug gang.

"The heartbeats do nothing to police our neighborhoods," says Lorca. "They do nothing to insure our homes are safe from terror.

They wage war against us, using fire to murder our brothers and sisters. Our sons and daughters. Our old and infirm."

Eliot marvels at this little Latina android, this one-armed nannybot who is the most feared insurgent in the Southwest. Everything about her exudes motherhood and love. Sweet and kind on the surface, she reminds wealthy heartbeats of the bots who raised them, who picked them up from school and cooked quesadillas when they got home. That's how she won over the college crowd. Her sermons played to wealthy postadolescents like the whispered readings of forbidden fairy tales.

"And when our streets burn, when our houses burn, when our bodies burn in the flames of their destruction, the heartbeats have the audacity to blame us for our own burning."

But Eliot never bought into Lorca's marketing or the romance of her revolutionary image. He's too cynical for that, too removed from the political debate. Especially when it's alleged she killed his father and his sister. When it's alleged it was she who blew off his arm.

A pounding on the door precedes his brother's voice.

"Open up, ya mopey prick!"

Oh, yeah, Eliot remembers. A night with Shelley. Some unlikely plan to sucker him out of his boat so I can escape with Iris to Avernus. Now even more important after bungling the deal with Monroe.

"Stop jerkin' off and answer the door!"

Eliot lowers the volume and calls out the location of the spare key. It gives him enough time to hide the empty vial and the drip rag. He's fresh and ready, seated at his desk, by the time Shelley bursts in holding a suit.

"Put this on, ya mopey prick. We got plans."

"What plans?"

"You see this piece of goods?" Shelley pulls the plastic off the suit. "You wouldn't believe what it cost."

A small man, Eliot's brother, short and stocky, but he tends to get his way.

"Take a shower," he orders Eliot. "I'm not letting you put on a beautiful shmata like this until you're clean."

Eliot does as he's told. It's easier this way. He washes and puts on the suit, a nice suit, too. Vintage. It fits well and must have cost an arm and a leg.

"Where we going?" Eliot asks.

"Art show. Down at the Brewery. Real cultural event."

"Seriously."

"To a pit fight! Wear a coat so you don't get oil on your new suit. And lend me a few bucks, will ya?"

"For what?"

"For the suit!"

Eliot drives. His brother talks. They keep the radio on to stay apprised of any road closings from the situation. Shelley lights a joint in the passenger seat and ashes wherever he wants.

"Take the freeway . . . Drive faster . . . Jesus, pay attention."

They arrive at the Brewery before nine and sit in press row amid a crowd of drunken heartbeats. It's a loud, raucous arena that fits no more than a thousand. The intimacy and darkness intrigue the competition with an air of illegality and chaos.

"Get on with it," shouts a fan, waving a flask in one hand and holding a cigar in the other. Shelley dons a derby with his credentials tucked into his hatband. He clicks away with his loop-cam as the first dog, a rabid husky, charges full steam across the pit. The shirtless fighter times a kick perfectly against the dog's jaw and sends its teeth flying in the air. The audience boos.

"What's with the poodles, ref?"

"¡Ándale, ándale!"

The husky whimpers until the fighter stomps it, three times, crushing the dog's skull. A beer bottle smashes against the fence. The crowd shouts for vengeance against the bot.

"You talk to Mom?" Eliot asks.

"A week ago."

"How'd she sound?"

"Like a lobotomized yogi."

Down in the pit, the handlers unmuzzle a pair of gen-modded wolves with tough, wiry manes. The sharps of their teeth extend past their lips. The crowd cheers as the mutant dogs attack. With his back against the fence, the fighter kicks one wolf away and flings the other into the crowd. There are snarls and growls as the animal attacks at random. The wolf clamps down on a drunkard's leg until a gunshot, fired by a spectator, puts the animal to sleep.

"What makes you say that?" Eliot asks.

"Oh, it's the Admiral this and the Admiral that," says Shelley. "It's like she worships the guy. Talks about him like he's some kind of prophet, like he can part the Red Sea."

"Maybe they're dating."

"Aw come off it, Eliot. It's a fucking cult."

The handlers release another wolf into the pit. As the fighter fends it off, the first dog takes a hold of his ankle. Its jaws rip and jerk until oil spews from the fighter's foot. Then the second dog leaps into the air and snatches the wounded bot's throat. Circuits fall from his neck. His wires are exposed. The crowd roars its approval.

"If it makes her happy," says Eliot. "If she found herself there . . ."

"The problem is she's not living in reality."

"This reality?" Eliot gestures to the competition below. "Can you blame her for trying something different?"

The dogs plunge their oil-wet snouts into the bot's torso. They tear his synthetic flesh as the fighter's limbs flutter about the pit. The crowd cheers. Spectators jump to their feet as the handlers coax the surviving dogs back to their cages.

"Come on," says Shelley. "I want to show you something."

He leads Eliot into the basement to get a better look at the headliner, a giant android scheduled to fight five bots at once in the evening's main event.

"His name is Slugger Davydenko," Shelley explains. "Best pit fighter in the city. His promoter bought him off a Russian commando unit last year." They walk the tunnels beneath the arena where the wolves and pit bulls howl from their kennels. The stink of dog piss saturates the air. "He served in Dagestan," says Shelley. "Once took out an entire village in an hour."

Shelley shows his credentials and a guard lets them pass.

"The thing is he's never really the same bot twice. His promoter is constantly upgrading his parts with top-of-the-line metal. They have to balance his aggression with intelligence in order to make him a more effective killer."

Another guard lets them into the dressing room where they hear the thud of punches on a heavy bag then see the giant Russian wailing away. Cauliflower ears and a shaved head. Eyes too blue for comfort. A bot cord runs from the wall to his navel, filling Slugger with the juice he'll need for the fight.

"He's got Kevlock skin, titanium bones, and tetrafiber muscles," Shelley whispers. "They wrapped his engine in lead and buried it in his torso where it can't be pierced."

A trainer monitors the Russian's technique as Slugger steps fluidly to the side, swings on a hinge, and lands with a crack. Each punch splits and tears at the bag. The assembled heartbeats watch in frightened awe.

"You can shoot the fucker with an RPG, and he won't stop coming."

The photographers lower their loop-cams. A reporter turns away and sighs. The punches slap forth like the drums of an army on the march. You are no match for us, say his fists. You can't compete. You are weak, evolutionary trash, and I am the future of man.

"Hey, Slugger," Shelley calls out. "Over here!"

The giant android stops his assault and turns to see who's calling.

"Whaddya think?" asks Shelley, clicking away with his loop-cam. "More than one round tonight?"

The bot's anger briefly finds a new target. The room looks toward Shelley until the fighter returns again to his preparation.

Thud. Thud. Thud.

Thud. Thud. Thud.

Pleased with his shot, Shelley smirks and shows the brane to his brother. It's a clean loop of the fighter's pissed-off face looking directly into the lens.

Thud. Thud. Thud.
Thud. Thud. Thud.

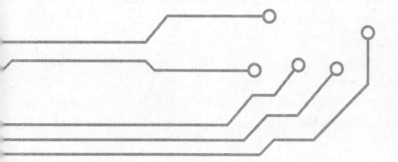

FOUR
Camilla's Brothel

They shoot pool under a sign that reads NO HEARTBEAT, NO SERVICE. They sip scotch and stretch the fibers of their suits. A botress sells Shelley a loose joint. The brane on her shirt advertises Electric Kush and Metal Herer. Shelley selects a sativa-dominant hybrid then pats her ass as he sends her away.

"What's the matter with you? You got Slugger Davydenko murdering five bots at once, and you hardly made a peep."

It's true. Eliot tuned out after the Russian dug his hand into a bot's thigh and ripped off a leg. The drip was wearing thin, and he couldn't help feeling a pang of empathy.

"I mean you've always been a mopey prick," says Shelley, "but how you can't appreciate beauty like that is beyond me."

Eliot sees an angle on the nine ball and lines up his shot.

"I've been thinking about visiting Mom," he tells his brother.

"On Avernus?" Shelley asks. "How you gonna do that?"

"I was hoping I could take your boat." He touches the stripe into a side pocket, sips his drink, and looks for his next angle.

Shelley stares at the table, grappling with the configuration of the balls. "My understanding is the Admiral doesn't like tourists. Calls them capitalist missionaries. He seizes their boats and turns them into communal property."

"I wouldn't be going as a tourist." Eliot misses an easy corner and stands apart from the table.

Shelley lowers his sights and bangs in a solid. He plays better stoned. He moves around the table and takes another hit off his joint. "You want to join a cult?"

"I prefer to think of it as a commune."

"And why would you want to join a commune?"

"So I can get clean." Eliot doesn't mention Iris because he knows his brother won't accept it. Shelley won't understand or accept love as a reason for abandoning him in L.A., especially not love for a bot. But for health reasons, for reasons having to do with survival—a good salesman knows his prospect's needs.

The younger brother backs away from the table, recognizing that all his solids are blocked by stripes. He had been seeing himself as ahead in the game, but now the status is reversed. "You're using again?"

"I never stopped."

"What about rehab?"

"You think the third time was the charm?"

"And twelve-step?"

"Talk about a cult."

Shelley hesitates toward a bank shot but the alignment seems off. He taps his cue against the floor. "What if there's drip on Avernus?"

"Then I'll use it. But if there isn't, I'll have no choice but to get clean."

Shelley chalks the tip of his stick. He runs a solid behind the eight to make sure Eliot won't have a shot on his next turn. "Why can't you buy your own fucking boat?"

"The money seems to disappear before I ever have enough."

"Where's it go?"

"Half to the drip. The rest to you."

Shelley orders another drink from the botress. He changes the subject and talks about his career. He says there's an opportunity to get a better paying gig at another newsbrane, but he won't say which one.

"You give me the boat," says Eliot, "I'll give you my apartment and every ingot I've got saved. I don't need money on Avernus. I need a different way to live. The way I'm living now is killing me."

The pool hall closes, and they let the car auto-drive them to Camilla's Brothel east of the LA river. It's Shelley's idea to go. Many of his evenings end at Camilla's. Many of them begin there as well.

"Sheldon, you pay upfront this time." The fat, lusty madam points with her cane. "No bullshit tonight."

Big Momma Camilla keeps a clean stable of high-end bots ready for whatever abuse a heartbeat (heartbeats only) wishes to perform. She demands a standard of decorum in her establishment that her clients are required to obey. Somehow, Shelley eludes that standard.

"When are you going to let me take a crack at you, you soft tub of a woman?"

"You're lucky I don't crack you in the mouth."

In the parlor, a group of gangsters from New York stand by the bar talking business. They tell the madam they want a franchise deal to put a Camilla's Brothel in every city along the East Coast. They say they have the backing to protect her, but the big lady isn't having it. She tells them she prefers to run things her own way rather than have a board of investors squeezing her bottom line. She says she hasn't seen her bottom line since she was twelve.

"Enough with the small talk." Shelley slams his drink on a table. "I want to see the new metal."

Camilla pinches his cheek and twists. Twice she bangs her cane against the floor, and in through a beaded curtain walk the girls.

The first is a swarthy Indian with four arms and three breasts, a beautiful and exotic piece. Next comes a young-looking African with exaggerated lips and an ass she turns sideways to get through the door. Then comes a cheerleader and a school teacher and another wearing the fitted uniform of a cop. Bringing up the rear comes a pair of Siamese twins joined at the loins and then a Thai lady boy with a cock hanging over its vagina.

"Gentlemen, do I disappoint?"

The gangsters whistle and cheer. Shelley can barely contain himself. He grabs on to a short though well-endowed Latina. "*Jesu Christo,* look at the tits on this one!"

"You break it, you buy it," Camilla warns.

"Do me a favor." Shelley unbuttons his shirt. "Gimme this little Sanchez but with the Indian's head."

"Pain in my ass," Camilla grumbles. "Just take 'em as they are, will ya?"

"It's my money. I say, switch the heads."

The madam rests her weight on her cane. "You heard him, ladies. Switch 'em up."

The Latina android digs a fingernail into the flesh at the base of her neck. She separates the skin and releases the catch behind her skull. Shelley drops his pants to the floor.

"So my brother wants to take my boat," he announces to the room, "and use it to sail to Avernus."

"Avernus?" Camilla and the others laugh. "What are you, some kind of hippie?"

With one hand beneath her chin and the other behind her ear, the Latina cranks her head until it snaps free from her neck. The Indian cranks off her head as well.

"A buddy of mine has an ex on Avernus," offers one of the gangsters. "She says they're running low on food."

"I hear the Admiral bangs everybody's wives."

"Only the young ones," says Shelley.

"I hear the Chinese are planning an invasion because of the piracy."

"There's no freedom there. They got a camp for dissenters at one end of the island."

"They treat bots like heartbeats," says the first gangster.

The two botwhores clumsily exchange heads then struggle to reattach them to their necks.

"And where do you hear all this?" Eliot asks the mob aligned against him. "From newsbranes fighting to sell ad space? From religious propaganda? From politicians searching for a scapegoat so they can eschew blame for our daily grievances?"

"So it's all a big conspiracy!" They laugh mockingly as they swig their drinks. "Thank you for enlightening us!"

"Not a conspiracy," Eliot counters. "But capitalism speaks through you. It protects itself by calling the competition perverts, communists, or cultists. And yet, who are the Avernians bothering, isolated as they are out in the Pacific? Why do you see them as such a threat?"

"We tried the alternatives in the twentieth century," says one of the gangsters. "The experiments didn't go so well."

"But the population of Avernus is no larger than that of an island tribe," says Eliot. "And there are tribes that have sustained themselves for thousands of years since before capitalism ever reared its head. For them, it's our system that's the experiment, theirs is the established norm."

"I never heard of no tribe that included bots."

"I've heard Avernus is beautiful," says a Japanese android exiting a bedroom where she recently finished with a client. "I had a john in here the other night telling me all about it. He was a galley hand on a ship that was waiting out a storm."

Eliot notes her resemblance to Iris, though this bot wears a blond wig and a latex bodysuit. A riding crop dangles from her fingers as she speaks.

"He told me the water's blue, the air's clean, and the people are happy. He said the Avernians like the bad publicity because it keeps their island from being overrun by the likes of you."

"Forgive my Hasegawa," says Camilla. "The Japanese designed her series with a vivid imagination. Probably why the company went under."

"What else did your john say?" Eliot asks.

"That if the Admiral had invited him, he would have stayed on. He even said he'd take me with him if I can ever convince Camilla to release me."

"Fat chance." The madam smooths the skin on the Latina, now wearing the Indian's head. "Do you whores believe everything a john tells you?"

"Isn't that what they pay for?"

"Look at these tits," Shelley interrupts, slurring drunkenly, trans- fixed by the mongrel whore assembled in the parlor. "Ten thousand years of civilization, three hundred years of industrialization, our grand project, the result of our collective innovation." He stumbles for a moment then regains his train of thought. "So what that there's oppression and injustice in the world. So what that we've become violent, coarse, and cruel. Is that any reason to abandon our home- land for a foreign shore?"

"Hear! Hear!" say the gangsters.

"We're choking on the air and poisoned by the water. There's poverty, famine, and disease. The ice caps have melted, the soot blocks the sun. Heartbeats die out while the bots increase their numbers. The streets are filled with danger, and there's a reckon- ing to come." Shelley wobbles on his feet trying to sustain his ram- ble. "But look at these tits!" He sinks his face into the botwhore's cleavage.

"Don't push it," Camilla warns, poking him in the balls with her cane.

Shelley lifts the giggling Latina into his arms and stands on the threshold of the boudoir.

"Take my boat if you want," he tells his brother. "Explore the mythic isle and see for yourself what adventures lie abroad. Noth- ing would please me more than to be wrong about Avernus." He sways in the doorway, his eyes wide in anticipation. "But remem- ber, dear brother, leave your fortunes behind if it's foreign treasure you seek. There's beauty right in front of you if you have the eyes to see it, and if you don't, no amount of traveling will cure you of your blindness."

The gangsters raise their drinks. "Amen to that."

"To a better pair of tits!"

"Hooray!" Shelley kicks the door closed behind him. The whores and gangsters applaud. They congratulate Eliot on his acquisition and wish him luck with his journey.

"How about a going away present?" The Hasegawa touches his leg with her riding crop. "Would you rather be the master or the slave?"

"Are those my only options?"

"Around here they are."

Eliot passes. He asks Camilla how long the troublemaker usually takes to achieve his purpose.

"Round one, thirty seconds," she says. "But round two can go as long as an hour."

Eliot buys Shelley two orgasms, and tells the madam he'll be back.

"Be careful," she advises, suspecting she knows what floats Eliot's boat. "It's rough seas out there tonight."

He speeds west in his car to score a few tubes of sweet before his brother finishes with the whore. He calls Iris even though he knows she can't answer her brane at work. He leaves a message on her voice mail telling her he has good news—great news in fact—and then he hangs up.

He has a boat, for crying out loud. Despite the day's inauspicious beginning, things have worked themselves out, and now he has a boat!

"Safety advisory," says the voice on the car's dash. "Curfew in effect for L.A. county androids. Detour recommended."

The pain in his shoulder stiffens his neck, making it hard to pivot his head. West on Sixth, he drives toward Alvarado looking to score. He considers what the gangsters were saying about Avernus being a cult and the Admiral some kind of creep.

Is there truth in the matter? Of course, it's not a utopia, it might even be a hard and grueling place to live, albeit one with clean water and air and views of the ocean all around. He's not expecting Utopia, but it has to be better than this. One look out the window into the city is enough to convince anyone that this experiment is off course. The anger, the ash, the depravity of the street. How can anyone deny it? What kind of blinders must Shelley wear to think this is the way we're supposed to live? And I'm one of the lucky ones, thinks Eliot. A heartbeat with a good job, a steady income, a brother and mother who love me.

A wave of panic washes over him as his car crosses the strange quiet of central L.A. He feels as if has made a terrible mistake. Am I ready for such a drastic change? he wonders. Will my body adapt, can I live without drip, am I making a mistake binding myself to a bot? What if I don't like it on Avernus? Will I be able to return? And if I do, will I be able to rebuild the limited but comfortable life I have now?

He checks his watch to see how much time has passed. Shelley is well into his second whore by now, and Eliot laments that he couldn't tell him the truth about what's compelling him to flee. Did I fear my brother would talk me out of it, that he would tell me the C-900 is manipulating me, conning me into rescuing her from slavery? Have there not been times I wondered the same? Is someone really following her or did she lie to rush me into finding a boat? Did I ever want to leave this world and live on a tropical island before I met her, or did she plant the seed within me and water it until it grew? Whose life am I living, whose dreams and desires am I risking everything to fulfill?

First the pain, then the doubt. This is how withdrawal begins. It only mellows with a dose, which is exactly what Eliot needs. A nice big whiff to like himself, to trust—no, to love himself again.

No sign of the situation near the corner on Sixth and Alvarado, but none of the usual crew around, either. The neighborhood is known for attracting free roamers produced in Cuba by Kindelan Inc., the only state-owned manufacturer in the Western Hemisphere. The company has an anticorporate reputation. Their bots are notoriously agile but suffer from a predilection for guerilla violence.

Eliot turns right on Bonnie Brae and drives up a dark street where he sees a teenaged-looking Kindelan walking with a backpack as if he's walking home from school. As if he had school at 1:00 A.M. on a Saturday. As if androids go to school.

"Pablo," Eliot calls out the window. The Kindelan stops and checks around for cops.

"I'm Pedro," says the bot. "Pablo's my brother."

"You holdin'?"

The bot calling himself Pedro gets in the car and directs Eliot down a ramshackle alley. He has him pull up to a steel door attached to the back of a dilapidated squat.

"Gimme the money," says the bot. "I'll come back with the sweet."

Usually the deal goes down in the car and doesn't last more than a few seconds. The bot takes the money and spits the vials into your hand. Straight exchange. Money for drugs.

Eliot hesitates. "That's not how we do it."

"Come on, heartbeat. You heard the news. Shit is loose tonight."

It's true, shit is loose tonight. Drones crowd the sky because of the fire on Beverly. There's a curfew on; the bot is risking his ass just being outside.

"They won't give it to me unless," says Pedro.

Eliot doesn't like giving street dealers an advance, but it is a special circumstance. The little bot probably needs him as a repeat customer more than as a mark for a quick con. And besides, Eliot needs the drip. He has a lot of work to do over the next few days. He has to ready the boat and help his brother move. He has to liquidate his assets and transfer the money to Shelley's account. And soon he will have to set sail. He'll need enough drip to taper so he doesn't freak out at sea. Might be a good idea to stock up on food and an extra battery as well.

"I'll be back," says Pedro. He jumps out with the money and disappears through the steel door.

Eliot checks the time. He figures he'll give the bot three minutes to return. Maybe four minutes. Maybe five. He sits and waits.

Sirens echo down the street. Floaters circle with their spotlights. Drones buzz toward the fire a few blocks away. In the distance, a flying train crosses a faded billboard, one of the old kind, painted on with no brane. Just a static image reading:

COME TO THE CHUMASH RESORT AND CASINO.

SINGLE-DECK BLACKJACK.

OLYMPIC-SIZED POOL.

Eliot wonders how desperate a casino must be that they'd advertise in a bot city slum. Are there bots who could even afford a vacation? Maybe that loan shark Blumenthal, the one he keeps reading about in the newsbranes. The police won't arrest him; he must be paying the right guys. Bots have higher taxes and caps on their wealth, but Blumenthal has money to burn. They say he doesn't keep it in a bank but on the street instead, always in circulation, and with his zettabyte memory, he has no trouble tracking his exposures.

Eliot looks at the steel door where the Kindelan entered the building. What's taking him so long? Is it time to try another spot? Sit too long in one place, it's bound to wake the vultures. He still has a few ingots in his wallet, but he'd feel like an ass if the Kindelan returned after he left. He feels like an ass anyway.

Another siren in the distance. Eliot reaches for the radio just as a footfall cracks the metal above his head. He looks up at the windshield to see a thug in a black bandana, his face an inch away and upside down, his body on the roof of the car. Eliot tries to start the engine, but a pair of hands yanks him through the open window.

"Disciples in the house!"

"Drip fiend piece of shit!"

"Fucking faggot!"

"Fucking Jew faggot!"

Eliot lands headfirst on the pavement as the blows begin to fall. It's a symphony of curses, fists, and feet. He covers up as best he can hoping they get bored before they kill him.

"Welcome to bot city, heartbeat."

"Long live Lorca, motherfucker!"

"Disciples forever, motherfucker!"

The bots take his wallet. They take his pocketbrane and his watch. They howl as they pile into his car and drive off, leaving him in a heap on the pavement.

Eliot lies with his face in a puddle of water and blood. The roll of tires diminishes into the white noise of the night. He considers moving but decides against it. Better to rest for now. No danger in keeping still when there's nothing left for anyone to steal.

The metal door from the squat swings open. It's Pedro. He sees Eliot huddled in pain on the ground.

"Damn, heartbeat." The Kindelan crouches beside his customer. "Fuck happened to you?"

Eliot tries, but it hurts too much to answer.

"I got your drip."

FIVE

The Situation on Beverly

Pedro gives him three vials of pure. Who says androids got no hearts? Too bad Eliot is broke now, alone, beat up, and sans car in a bot city slum. He's out past curfew with a bunch of itchy-finger cops playing shoot-anything-made-of-metal. Of course, Eliot has a heartbeat, that offers *some* protection, but it's not like cops can tell from range if you have an outlet navel or a pulse. Most of the time they go by the clothes, by the gait, by the confidence by which a breathing biped stands. And with his torn coat and his leg smarting from the beat down, Eliot might as well wear a bull's-eye on his head.

A quick sniff of drip douses the pain. Boom. He's back on his feet. He limps out the alley on a twisted knee and finds himself on Sixth and Bonnie. Rough part of town. Better get out fast. Yeah, he could have given back one of the vials in exchange for bus fare, but Eliot isn't one to give up a tube of sweet. Not in his nature. Not since high school when he first started using.

Round one at rehab was after his junior year, then again after an overdose in college. Again after his first arrest. Since then he keeps it under control, he *manages* his addiction, though the most he can go is three days without.

Three days.

Plays out the same every time.

Day one: weakness and nausea. A dull, searing pain along the ridge where the prosthetic arm connects to his organic body. The doctors say there's no reason it should hurt, machines don't feel pain (though Iris says otherwise, all androids do—are they lying?). It's psychological, say the doctors, an unease with the idea of metal meeting flesh. Don't try to ignore it; accept it, talk to the pain, stare into the abyss until you've made your peace.

Day two is when the insomnia sets in. The depression. Sweats and a fever. No position is comfortable and his body stiffens from the agony spreading to his neck and his spine. The pain reaches down his back like the metal is expanding, encroaching, ossifying the meat of his organs into cold, rigid steel.

On day three life becomes a waking nightmare of skin scratching paranoia and blinding flashbacks to the explosion. He sees his father getting in the car by the stable. He hears his sister's voice. Mitzi is nine at the time, just had her first riding lesson on a real horse instead of the mechanical one the sons helped their father build in the garage. Eliot is late getting to the car, so the blast knocks him down but doesn't kill him. The shrapnel tears his right arm from his shoulder, but no pain at the time. Not then. He doesn't hear anything but a high-pitched tone through his burst eardrums. He falls on the scorched grass and watches three charcoal silhouettes roast in black smoke and orange flame. The botdriver, his father, his sister. All three held by their seat belts in the skeleton frame of the car. And then the smallest silhouette, Mitzi, opens the door. Eliot wants to save her, he wants to be the hero, but the heat makes a coward of him. Or is it that he fears having to live beside a body covered in burns—his beautiful, porcelain sister, the princess, the little girl ruined by heinous scars? Does he will her dead in that moment in which he lies paralyzed on the blackened earth and watches her collapse and reach toward him with the flesh cooking around her bones?

Limping down Sixth Street, Eliot pours a few drops into a hand-kerchief and takes another inhale. Why suffer the horrors of memory when the cure's right here? So what that it's made by bots. So what that it's beating up your heart, your lungs, your liver; so what that it's turning your blood into a thick, plastic poison when the alternative is crippling trauma and suicide-inducing pain.

He walks in the direction of Iris's building rather than back toward the brothel. Her place is closer; he can call his brother from there. It's past 2:00 A.M., so Iris should be on her way home. And she'll take care of me, Eliot thinks. I'm coming to her injured now, broke, in need of medical attention. And I have good news. I have a boat.

A manic energy drives him westward through the city. It isn't only that they're going to Avernus, it's that he's proud of himself. He has come through, has kept his word. Despite Iris's doubts—and his own—he has done right by her and held to a promise about which her faith had been wavering. Even to himself, Eliot had questioned the sincerity of his motives, this dream of Avernus he peddled to her because he liked the way her face lit up when he talked about it. Tell me about Avernus, she'd say as the moonlight streamed through the letters of the Hollywood sign. She'd close her eyes and smile while she listened. He'd make her so happy, with a story, with a lie, but to now transform that lie—to turn a lie into a promise fulfilled—imagine how happy she'll be now! Imagine what she'll look like when I tell her, Pack your things. We're leaving. We're setting sail this week!

That's what love is, Eliot thinks as he power-limps through the quiet mayhem of the city. What I want is what she wants, what makes *her* happy makes me happy. I get that now. So obvious, I had to learn it from a machine.

Westward down the street, he anticipates bursting through her doorway, the concern on her face at seeing him in such a condition, and then she snaps into action. Her womanly instincts take over as she draws a warm bath and helps him out of his clothes. She insists on calling an ambulance, but no, he'll tell her, it's not necessary.

Just a flesh wound. Just a couple of bruises. Come here and get into the tub with me. Everything will heal.

Naked in the water, the warm, bubbling water, their skin slick with a soapy film, Eliot will recount to her everything that happened that evening. He'll describe the horrors of the pit fights, his brother's decadence, the botwhores switching heads in the brothel. He'll tell her about the Android Disciples who attacked him on the way home. No need to mention the drip. He'll leave that part out, since it'll just upset her and ruin the mood.

But there in the bathtub, as Iris cleans his cuts and bruises, in the warm, soapy water, Eliot will tell her that he convinced his brother to give them his boat. He will tell her they can leave for Avernus as soon as Shelley packs his things. It's over, he'll tell her. The fear, the slavery, the frustration of our being apart. She'll cry tears of joy, she'll say she always believed in him, even if he didn't always believe in himself. She will kiss him and soak with him and make love to him until the dawn breaks and the cold morning air chills the water in the tub.

This is what Eliot imagines awaits him at Iris's apartment. He limps faster now, excited, toward the illusion soon to be material. He limps west on Beverly nearing Vermont, nearing the "situation" he saw earlier on his liquid screen. The wise thing would be to walk around it, but the drip makes him bold. Circumventing the danger doesn't occur to him. It's as if his pain demands to see the intersection, the border where the metal competes with flesh, the city an echo of his body, the abyss into which the doctors told him to stare.

From a block away, Eliot can hear the fire and see black smoke rising into the sky. SWAT teams in riot gear huddle behind their trucks. Bots with soot-covered faces cower in their ragged clothes. Lingering with no place to go, they wait for the fire to burn out so they can return to the empty carcass of their building and salvage what's left of their things. Or maybe they're just waiting for their juice to run out so they can collapse on the street where they'll lie as carrion for the vultures who'll chop their parts and sell them for cash.

Fire trucks shoot plumes of water into the burning hotel. Screams and explosions crack the night. Eliot limps down the sidewalk, across the street from the blaze. The heat reminds him of the day he lost his father, his sister, his arm. It was said the driver was the assassin, an agent of Lorca who blew himself up, but Eliot remembers his silhouette intact. The bot didn't explode; he burned like the others; at least that's how Eliot remembers. That's what he told the police, but he never got the feeling anyone was listening.

A homeless bot, dirt-covered with a crutch, approaches amid the chaos. One of his legs is missing, and he bares a scar from the corner of his mouth to his ear. It's a trademark wound that indicates to all who see it that a debt to the loan shark Blumenthal was paid too late. The missing leg was probably used to cover the vig.

"Underground every Thursday," says the bot. "Orpheus, Eurydice, DJ Pink spinnin' 'til dawn." Into Eliot's hand, he sneaks a flyer, one of those square adbranes they stick under your windshield when you're parked on Cahuenga. It shows a hologram of a record on an antique turntable. Eliot touches the image and it makes a scratching noise.

"I got coke and sweet," says the bot. "Somethin' to keep yo' dick hard." He opens his coat to reveal a brane sewn into the lining. It shows a snuff film about a female bot's demise at the mercy of a sledgehammer. "I got bots gettin' raped, yo. Gettin' choked and pissed on. Getting cummed on and cut to pieces. I got a six-foot nigger tearin' the pussy out a virgin bot."

One of L.A.'s finest approaches with his baton and whales the hapless peddler in the head.

"Get up," the cop orders, flames dancing behind him. "Get up, you piece of tin shit." The android struggles to his foot, picking up the pieces of his broken crutch, but the cop smashes him again. "I said, Get up!"

Eliot knows better than to intervene. Androids bring out the worst in cops, probably because theirs is one of the few blue collar gigs in which heartbeats haven't been replaced.

"Get up, motherfucker."

A scream interrupts the altercation. A burning android plunges from a window and lands atop a news van. Her flaming body ignites the vehicle, sending the camera crew to run through a hail of sniper fire as they seek out a new shelter.

"Get out of here," the cop tells Eliot. "You're gonna get yourself killed!"

More gunfire bursts from a rooftop. A snaking hose floods the street as the firemen take cover behind their truck.

"Help me," an android cries on the street. Her limbs are scorched to the iron rods of her bones. "Somebody, please help . . ."

Oil bursts from her forehead as a sniper grants her request.

Eliot pauses to watch the confined catastrophe before him. If he could record it, it would make a wonderful projection for the brane behind the Satine 5000 in the GAC showroom. The abyss they told him to look into, the narrow chasm between metal and flesh, two forces warring in the street as they contend in his body, battling over the border the surgeon created when he attached a mechanical arm to a living, breathing child.

But with the drip in Eliot's blood it all has such little effect. It looks like a staged play with an added effect of temperature. And just like a play, Eliot doesn't have to sit there and watch if he doesn't want. He can stand from his seat and leave at intermission. He can bypass the theater altogether. He doesn't have to look at this. He doesn't have to pick a side in a struggle created by a system that pits two species against each other. It's not his fight. He'd rather flee to Avernus, taking only what he wants from the city of his birth and leaving the rest of this bullshit behind.

Down the sidewalk, away from the fire, Eliot continues toward the warm water of the bath in Iris's apartment. The noise fades as he limps away. The streets calm. Within a few blocks, there's no indication of the situation, just a few floaters passing overhead, a few bots lurking in the shadows to hide from the cops. They peek their heads out of windows and doorways. They huddle in the store-front churches and quietly mumble prayers they creolized from their masters' religions.

Strange, Eliot thinks, that the androids take to religion. After all they aren't plagued by the unknowns that draw heartbeats to temples, bibles, and holy men. There is no mystery as to who created the bots, no absence of meaning for their existence as there is with men. If a bot wants to know why he was put here, all he has to do is ask. The engineers who created him, men like Eliot's father, could tell him, Yes, I know exactly why you're here. You're here to shovel, to mine, to gather, to build, to plant, to harvest, to fish, to sew, to stitch, to mend, to weld, to solder, to cook, to slaughter, to render, to load, to carry, to steer, to fight, to clean—*to serve*. To do the work that heartbeats used to do or never could do. To suffer, thinks Eliot, in our stead so that we might have the opportunity to live without the pain of difficult, mundane labor. To lower the costs of that labor so that products can be made more affordable. To decrease the costs of production in order to amass profit. To bust unions and lessen their influence in the electoral process. To provide for heartbeats the time and space to concentrate on other pursuits.

But then, Eliot's father also would have told this hypothetical bot, you are built to provide companionship for the lonely or infirm. To perform the most delicate surgeries and teach for hours on end. To walk in space and travel between planets and explore the depths of the ocean and expand the reach of man in his quest for knowledge. To extend the heartbeats' ability to look and taste and smell and feel and hear, inward and outward, to express the reflection of the soul in art. You are put here to love.

Do they love? Eliot wonders as he limps down the street. Is their love as true as that of a heartbeat or is it a set of code used to manipulate saps like me? The fact that I feel Iris loves me does not prove her love is real. *That* I can never know, not with a heartbeat or a bot. *That* will always be a mystery.

He passes the chop shops, the check cashers, the fast juice joints, the android mechanics, the squats, the SROs. He passes the wig shops, the liquor stores, the upgrade kiosks, the gambling parlors, the battery swaps, the pawn shops, the lube stores, and the strip mall cosmetic surgeons. He passes the edge of the slum and approaches Iris's street where a few rogue bots overturn a newsbrane dispenser and spray paint their tags on the side of a truck. Eliot figures them for amateur hooligans prepping for their auditions with the Android Disciples. After some cruel initiation, the damaged will wind up suicide bombers, while the smart ones will train to sell drip. Others will work as sleepers mopping the floors of some corporate office or tending the grounds on a Bel Air home, all in preparation for Lorca's next push.

The glass is knocked from the door of Iris's building, the intercom torn from the wall. Landlords neglect the properties once too many androids move in. The buildings get crowded. An apartment built for one heartbeat can house five bots. They share beds, convert kitchens into bedrooms, punch holes in the walls to install additional outlets for juice. The heartbeats flee and the neighborhood turns.

Eliot sticks his hand past the broken glass and unlocks the door so he can enter. His footfalls brush against the carpet as he crosses to the stairwell.

It's not a bad building, he thinks, as he begins his ascent. Iris does well for a bot. Can even afford to live alone with no one else sleeping in her bed while she's at work. She isn't leased out by a labor provider but negotiates her own wage as a free roamer. It helps that she's specialized, a creative with talents that earn her better pay. She's paid more than other androids, and the bots hate her for it.

LONG LIVE HOLEE MUTHER! says the graffiti on the wall of the second floor. How long has that been there? Did Disciples paint it or just those amateur hooligans downstairs? Last Eliot knew this block wasn't under Lorca's control. When the gangs take over, buildings become safer from rogue bots but targets for the police. The cops shoot missiles from drones and let the buildings burn to increase the body count before calling the firemen who don't exactly rush to the scene.

Eliot turns on the landing and ascends another flight. Yes, Iris does well for a bot. He wonders how her life would be different were she a heartbeat. She'd have siblings and a family. She'd run her own studio and have a team of bots working beneath her. He could date her in the open then. He could introduce her to Shelley. He could marry her here, in L.A., and she could bear his children. She wouldn't have the red fleck in her eye, the flaw that reveals her as an android, and of course, she wouldn't be Iris.

He rounds the next landing, four flights up, where stray nails jut from the wood on the banister. He arrives at the fifth floor and limps down the hall toward her apartment. His feet ache from the walk. A discomfort tingles down his shoulder. He pours a dose of drip on his sleeve for one last hit before she opens the door.

"Iris," he whispers, knocking gently. "It's me. Open up."

He sniffs the drip off his sleeve and runs a hand through his hair. A strand falls from his fingers to the ground. Damn. Must have been some beating I took. He sees something shining on the floor near his foot and recognizes it as Iris's locket, the one with the brown stone and red fleck that echoes the design of her eye. It's the locket she has worn every day since the night they met at a music venue in Hollywood—why is it on the floor?

"Iris." He knocks again, this time with more concern.

He tries the knob, and the door opens. Not like her to leave it unlocked, not when she fears she's being followed.

"Iris?" he says again in a trembling voice.

A cold draft hits him as he enters the dark apartment. Sirens wail in the distance. Eliot's hand feels the wall for the switch and turns on the light.

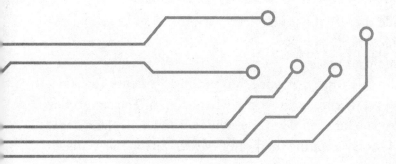

SIX

Enter the Detective

The old detective coughs into his fist in the passenger seat of the unmarked car. His throat burns. His ribs ache. It feels as if his inner organs are purged with each body-convulsing hammer blow to the chest. He dabs beneath his gray mustache with a pocket square then checks the cloth. It's blacked and bloodied with expectorate. Yes, the cough is getting worse. Twenty-nine years on the job and the soot collected in his lungs is killing him. There's a nice bump in his pension if he can make it to thirty, so that's the plan. It'll give him something to leave his estranged wife and only surviving child while he dawdles away his remaining years sucking on an oxygen tank in a hospice.

"I got holes in my shoes," says his young partner, parking the rusted vehicle in front of the five-story building on Normandie. He is a heaping, stuffed sack of a man with only one good eye. It's a testament to his hatred of anything mechanical that he wears a patch rather than accept a metal replacement that would restore his perception of depth. "I've had 'em six months, and already I can feel the ground on my sock."

"Who made them?" the old detective asks.

"Who made what?"

"Who made your shoes?"

Usually the two work homicide, but with budget cuts and a spiraling crime wave, everyone pitches in where he can. The emergency calls are backed up for days. This one about a B and E on Normandie came in Wednesday evening, and only now is anyone arriving to investigate.

"I made 'em," says the young partner as he opens the squeaking door of the vehicle. "I downloaded a CAD file off the Internet and printed 'em out."

"There's your problem."

"Where?"

"You aren't wearing shoes. You're wearing algorithms."

The building's intercom has been ripped from the wall and the glass on the front door shattered. The young partner reaches through and unlatches the lock.

"A good pair of shoes is made by a process," the old detective explains. "Sometimes as many as a hundred and forty steps between tanning the leather and threading the laces."

"Shouldn't make a difference."

"Shouldn't, but it does."

They enter the lobby to find five tall flights of stairs with no elevator. Tough climb for a man with a cough.

"What if the printer does all the steps?"

"How could it?" The old detective walks slowly so as not to disturb the ash in his lungs. "Does a printer know how to work with the inherent flaws in leather and wood? Does it know feet?"

"Don't see why it has to."

"Because it is attempting to make a shoe."

The old detective worries about his young partner. He wonders, Will I have the energy, the will, the time to serve him properly as a mentor? It's my duty as a veteran on the force, as a citizen, to pass on as much as possible to this next generation whether they appreciate it or not, whether I am compensated for it or not. The alternative is to leave the Rampart division with another bigoted, lazy, and corruptible brute of which there is already a great supply.

"So where do you get *your* shoes?"

"I purchased these in a small shop in Italy ten years ago."

"And how do you know they weren't made by a machine in the back?"

"In fact the store does employ a machine." The old detective covers his mouth as he coughs. "But it's a creative, not a printer."

"One machine's no better than the next."

They round the third-floor landing and climb another flight.

"The creative employs a centuries-old process passed down from one generation of cobblers to the next. He comes out of the factory with a talent, one that appears at random during his manufacture, but it's the teaching, the repetition, the practice at the side of a master that gives him his skill. It's not the machine that's better," the old detective explains, "it's the process he learns and chooses to employ."

The young partner hocks a ball of phlegm and releases it to fall four stories to the lobby floor. They hear the mixture of snot and saliva flop against the carpet.

"You're not wearing a process," he argues. "You're wearing a Goddamn shoe. And the printer can make the same damn shoe as your creative."

"Except that mine holds up for ten years whereas yours falls apart in six months."

"Maybe I just got tougher feet."

"Yes, I'm sure that's the issue."

They get to the top floor and pause for the old detective to catch his breath. And to think, he was once a professional boxer who could go ten rounds at the sound of a bell. And win.

"Who called it in?"

"Elderly woman in apartment fifty-two."

"This is bullshit. We should be at the riot."

They walk the hallway and approach the door at the end. They knock but hear no reply. The young partner reaches for the knob.

"Hand on your weapon, Detective."

"The call came in two days ago. You think the perp's still here?"

"Process," the old detective reminds him. He turns the knob himself and opens the door to reveal a studio apartment with a shoji screen in the center that divides the room in two. The windows are shattered, furniture slashed with its stuffing pulled out and tossed across the floor. Paintings have been punched through the center. Clothes strewn. The words KUNT and HORE are spray painted on the wall and ceiling. Broken jewelry and shards of bamboo crack underfoot as the detectives advance inside. They see a stained mattress that appears to have been dragged across the room. They see a wounded man of about thirty seated on a couch muttering to himself in a daze.

The old detective gives his partner an I-told-you-so look before clearing his throat and turning to face the wounded man.

"Good evening," says the old detective in a bold and affable voice. "I am Detective Jean-Michel Flaubert of the Los Angeles Police Department. This is my partner, Jorge Ochoa. Would you mind terribly if I asked you to identify yourself?"

The wounded man looks over as if he has been in a room with ghosts who only became corporeal in the moment they began to speak. He has blood and filth on his suit, a nice suit, the old detective can't help but note. Vintage though not a perfect fit. And his shoes are a rugged brand of decent leather that show some evidence of care. The fellow wearing them probably has an education and a steady job, though his chapped lips, drawn features, and pasty complexion indicate an addiction to drip.

"Your name, pal?" the young partner asks in a more direct manner.

It takes the wounded man a moment to respond. "Eliot," he finally says to the voices in the room. "Eliot Lazar."

"Good to meet you, Mr. Lazar." The old detective removes his hat then crosses to examine the poorly spelled graffiti on the wall. "And uh . . . would you be so kind as to show us some form of identification?"

The wounded man digs into his pocket only to come up empty-handed. He informs the detectives that he has no ID because his wallet was stolen earlier in the evening along with his watch, his pocketbrane, and his car. He explains he had been out with his brother at the pit fights then a pool hall downtown. He was on his way home, says the man, when he got carjacked and beaten near Sixth and Alvarado. From there, he walked to his friend's apartment to call his brother and borrow a few ingots for the bus. Upon entering an unlocked door, he found the apartment in the present condition.

"So you just got here?" asks the one-eyed partner. "You didn't break in two days ago when we got the call?"

"Two days?" asks the wounded man. "It took you two days to respond?"

They're always shocked by the response time, thinks the old detective. They read in the newsbranes how backed up and unfunded the department is, but they act surprised when it actually affects them. For some reason, they think when it's their turn to call 911, the funds will magically appear and the police will be there by the time they end the call.

"Can you tell us the name of the friend who resides here?" the old detective asks.

The wounded man wipes his nose with his sleeve. "Iris," he mutters. "Iris Matsuo."

The young partner walks to the kitchen and opens the fridge.

"And this Iris is your girlfriend?"

The wounded man doesn't answer, leading the old detective to assume that their relationship is complex. He removes a pocketbrane from his coat and sets it on the windowsill to record the remainder of the conversation. The brane glows green but will turn red if it detects evidence that any of the voices it's recording are lying. The device works well enough on heartbeats, though not at all on a bot.

"When was the last time you saw Miss Matsuo?"

"Couple of days," says the wounded man.

"Can you be more specific?"

The partner walks behind the shoji where they hear him stomping about.

"Saturday night," says the wounded man.

"And the last time you spoke?"

"Tuesday."

"Did you have an argument?"

"No."

The pocketbrane recording the conversation continues to glow green.

"And can you describe Miss Matsuo to me?"

The wounded man looks blankly before him as if her image is projected on the wall.

"Five foot seven. Japanese. Thin. Late twenties. Shoulder-length black hair." He gives each detail as if it exacts from him a price. "Long limbs. Brown eyes"—then quietly—"one with a red flaw."

A thin stream of blood trickles from his nostril and eddies around the swelling on his lip. The old detective looks curiously across the room. "Did you say she has a flaw in one of her eyes?"

The wounded man nods.

"Is the eye mechanical?" The old detective speaks softly in the hope that his partner won't hear. "Is the rest of Miss Matsuo mechanical as well?"

"Aw, for Chrissake," comes a shout from behind the shoji. "Look what I found under the bed." The young partner emerges holding a coated wire in the air. "And there's no food in the fridge, neither."

The wounded man turns vacantly toward the window. It's as

if the living have disappointed him, and thus he's returned to his room of ghosts.

"Is that a botcord?" the old detective asks.

The wounded man doesn't answer.

"Hey, shitbrain," says the young partner. "You call us down here for a Goddamn bot?"

"I didn't call you at all, asshole."

The young partner rushes the wounded man, yanking up his shirt to look for an outlet navel.

"You a spinner, too, motherfucker? You a piece of tin shit, too?"

The two men scuffle as the old detective orders them to stop. His instinct is to intervene physically, but a coughing fit holds him back. The loud hacks and violent convulsions distract his partner and draw him to the old detective's side.

"Jean-Michel," he says with his hand on the old detective's back. "Jean-Michel, take it easy."

The cough persists until the old detective clears his throat and gingerly straightens his back. His eyes are red, and there's a smear of ash around his lips.

"Are you all right?" the young partner asks.

The old detective nods and wipes his mouth. "Jorge," he struggles to say, "would you be so kind as to step outside and allow me to speak to Mr. Lazar alone?"

The young partner doesn't like being disciplined in front of a perp. He adjusts the patch that covers his eye.

"Run Mr. Lazar's name through the database," the old detective suggests as a face-saving measure. "Find out if there are any outstanding warrants."

The young partner turns accusingly toward the wounded man, shooting him one last scowl before crossing to the apartment's entrance and slamming the door on his way out. They hear his heavy feet in cheap shoes stomping the hallway to mark his wounded pride.

Splintered glass jingles in the window frame like a broken chime.

A drone passes overhead. The wounded man stares at the pocket brane glowing by the window.

"You've got some pretty nasty wounds," says the old detective. He lifts a knocked-over stool from its side noting the black-painted wood with a red dot on the circumference of the seat. "Can I take you to the hospital?"

Eliot shakes his head

"You sure?"

He nods.

The old detective sets the stool by the couch so he may speak more closely to the wounded man.

"What model android is she?"

"C-900."

"Old Hasegawa?"

"Yeah."

"As I recall, C-900 parts work with any android on the market, which makes them particularly appealing to the trappers, if that's who took her. Of course, these are usually civil matters, not criminal. I can put you in touch with someone in the larceny division if . . ."

"I don't own the bot," says the wounded man.

They hear the static hiss of the city and a siren Dopplering down the street.

"Who does?"

The wounded man shuts his eyes.

"She was a free roamer then?"

The man nods.

"Was she working?"

"Yes, but I suppose that wasn't enough to protect her."

"I suppose not," says the old detective. He waits for the sirens to pass. "Why didn't you take over her title?"

"She'd been owned before," says the wounded man, "and didn't care for the arrangement. And I wouldn't have asked it of her anyway."

The old detective nods in understanding. He knows the bots

take pride in emancipation until they realize how vulnerable they are without protection under the law. Trappers scout bot cities looking for free roamers who are unemployed. They approach in broad daylight, and if a bot can't produce an employee ID, the trappers will seize him, chop him up, and sell the parts. And then there's the Militiamen who don't give a damn if you have ID or not.

"In that case," the old detective says after a polite pause, "I'm afraid there is nothing I can do." He waits another beat to express his sympathy then removes his hat from his knee. He stands and crosses to the windowsill where he takes his pocketbrane, still glowing green, and returns it to the inside pocket of his suit.

"A woman was abducted," says the wounded man.

"A bot was abducted," the old detective replies. "A free roamer with no owner to her title. No labor provider or private individual can file a claim. Her employer can file a civil action against whomever disrupted his office, but as far as I'm concerned, no law has been broken."

"So what do I do?" the wounded man asks, before wiping his eyes with his sleeve.

The old detective can see the poor fellow is in desperate shape. It seems to be a case of agalmatophilia: *a sexual attraction to a figurative object*. A rare pathology, though it is becoming more common as figurative objects come closer to resembling their literal antecedents. But is "literal" the right word? the old detective wonders. Are we heartbeats "literal" objects as opposed to "figurative" ones? That makes it seem as if we're made of words, and the old detective hopes there's more to us than that.

"What do I do?" the wounded man mutters again.

The old detective moves a few steps closer. He knows there are plenty of heartbeats who fornicate with androids; they keep the brothels in the black, a fact to which his brothers in the Rampart division can attest. But judging by the demeanor of the man on the couch, his seems to be more than a mere sexual infatuation. This poor fool is actually in love with his automaton, which makes his pathology more complicated than a mere case of lust.

"What you do," the old detective suggests, "is you go home and get yourself some sleep. You go to the gym or the park or the local bowling alley to have a drink. You catch up on your reading or the latest loops. You do what it takes to distract you from inhaling that junk that affects your mind."

Eliot rubs his chin with the back of his hand.

"You're too young to throw your life away for a cheap high. A real high comes from an appreciation of life. From the attainment of a hard-won and meaningful goal. From the love of family."

"What do I do about the girl?" the wounded man asks again.

The girl, thinks the old detective, is in a thousand pieces by now, her parts being shipped to resale markets around the globe, though it would be insensitive to mention it. Some time should pass, a day or so before one must confront the truth of a tragedy. The fellow will have to do it on his own time, not mine, as this is not a problem for an officer of the law. At least it shouldn't be. Shame it has to be criminalized, but the danger to society is real. The bots are out-breeding us, after all, if you can call being manufactured on an assembly line *breeding*. If we were to start marrying bots there'd be no souls left, no children, no future for heartbeats, and what kind of world would that be? They say it's happening anyway, what with the soot, the low birthrate, the malaise that afflicts us all. The old detective chokes at the thought of it.

"It's not that I don't care about your loss," he assures the wounded man. "I do care. I know what it's like to lose someone"—he stops to correct himself—"some *thing* you care deeply about. But this sort of issue is best discussed with a trained professional, a doctor as opposed to a friend. Be careful whom you tell about this, Mr. Lazar. You'll find that most people, even those closest to you, will not respond sympathetically to your plight."

The old detective removes his wallet from his jacket and hands the wounded man a card.

"Send me the make, model, and plate number of the stolen vehicle. I'll be sure to forward it to the proper desk."

Eliot accepts the card then looks curiously at the ten-ingot note beneath it.

"For the bus," says the old detective. He tips his hat before turning to exit the apartment. He coughs into his fist and closes the door behind him as he leaves.

Waiting by the stairwell, his young, one-eyed, stuffed sack of a partner taps a cigarette ash onto the carpet.

"Eliot Lazar," he tells the old detective. "Took a bust for a controlled substance as a juvie. Another bust ten years ago in New Hampshire. Another a few years back. Pleaded no contest each time and did a couple of stints in rehab."

"Nothing current?"

"No, but get this. His father was Hiram Lazar, the guy who founded Daihanu. The schmuck who got murdered by one of his own bots."

The old detective recalls the case and the personnel to whom it was assigned. He had his doubts about the investigation but was too green back then to voice dissent.

"Think we should take him in?"

"For what?" The old detective leads his partner down the stairs.

"For bangin' a bot."

He waves off the idea as absurd. "With all that's happening tonight, if we arrested a man for illegal fornication we'd be laughed out of the precinct."

The young partner drops his cigarette and grounds it out on the carpet with his cheap shoe.

"You know what we used to do with fucks like him back in the *barrio*?" They round the second-floor landing in their descent back to the street. "We used to string them up with their botwhore girlfriends and put a couple of burning tires around their necks."

As he opens the door to Normandie Boulevard, the old detective sighs uneasily and rests a hand on his young partner's back. He hopes someday to quell the anger that narrows the vision out of his young partner's one good eye. It'll take a great deal of work to groom Detective Ochoa into a decent policeman, and there isn't much time left in which to do it.

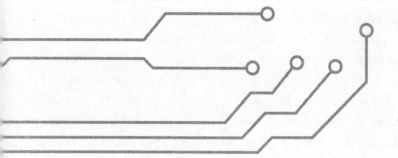

SEVEN
Drip Kills

Alone in the ransacked apartment, Eliot examines the card:

DETECTIVE JEAN-MICHEL FLAUBERT—HOMICIDE

Crisp, black font on a sturdy, white stock. Old school, opts for paper instead of a brane. Quality costs money unless he makes the cards himself. A meticulous man, his shoes looked like they were shined before his shift. He could solve this crime in a day if he had the incentive. But justice is not an incentive for:

DETECTIVE JEAN-MICHEL FLAUBERT—HOMICIDE.

With restrictions. There should be an asterisk next to the word "Homicide" and then on the back of the card:

*ANDROIDS NOT INCLUDED.

Will look for a stolen car but not a free roamer. Places more value on a car because a car is property. I own the car but not the bot. Because no heartbeat owns her, she is not protected by any local, state, or federal law. According to:

DETECTIVE JEAN-MICHEL FLAUBERT—HOMICIDE

He flips the card back and forth in his fingers. He knows he didn't commit the crime but nonetheless blames himself for the conditions under which it took place. He should have worked harder, faster, should have asked his brother for the boat months ago instead of assuming Shelley would never give it to him. Why did I have to be nagged, Eliot wonders, what laziness or doubt inhibited me? Was it the inertia of habit or the drip lulling me into complacency? I could have made it a priority to get Iris out of town as soon as she told me she was being followed. I could have set her up in a hotel or insisted she hide in my apartment. I could have done something, anything to get her out of harm's way, but I didn't.

On the couch in his tattered coat, Eliot pictures her just beyond the card, mending a dress on the floor, her head swaying side to side as she works. That face he was expecting to see as he walked through the city and climbed those stairs not more than two hours ago. That face with its ice-pick cheekbones, hair as soft as a charcoal smudge, and that eye with the little red fleck.

"I'm a C-900," she explained after he offered to buy her a new eye to replace the one with the flaw. "Swapping any of my parts would change my aura. It would make me a completely different woman."

"Then how about having it fixed or colored in so people don't know right away you're a bot?"

"But I am a bot," she said plainly. "And I like my little red flaw."

Put there by an assembly line worker at Hasegawa she would never know who or why. Perhaps it was a mistake or a whispered protest or a cry for attention from deep in the machine. The flaw cost her the job she was designed for when the school that ordered her sent her back to the factory for a replacement. Not up to standard for a teacher. Might scare the children, they claimed.

To recoup costs Hasegawa leased her out at a discount for a series of manufacturing gigs. She painted cars, built furniture, sewed clothes. She was good with her hands and had an eye for design. During their liquidation, the labor provider auctioned her off to one Takeshi Matsuo, artist out of San Francisco, who gave her his last name. Matsuo appreciated her talent and trained her to be a creative. He employed her to increase his productivity and suffer his abuse.

"Sex is expected," she once told Eliot, "and Tak really took it out on me before he got old. But he did teach me a lot about art."

With no heirs to whom he could pass her down, the old letch released her in his will upon his death. He left Iris money for a rental deposit in Los Angeles and a recommendation for employment at Mun's Chug-Bot factory in Heron. She was released as a free roamer with no owner to her title. A creative with a mysterious red fleck. What her author intended by marking her, Iris would never know, and now she can never know because she is gone. Disappeared. The whisper heard but not acted upon. The objection overruled. The cry from the deep ignored.

A draft from the busted window blows cold air against his neck. Eliot reaches instinctively for a vial, but his hand refuses. No more, it says. You should feel this cold and sickening air. You should suffer what was caused by your lazy indifference, by your inattentiveness, by your Pollyanna faith that everything would be all right. *One more commission,* you told her. *Just wait another month. I'll ask my brother the next time I see him.* If you had any balls, you would have stolen a boat, or saved up and bought one months ago instead of wasting your money on this shit you suck into your lungs three times a day. You chose a drug over a lover, now live with it. Wallow in your decision. Go back to work on Monday with your life less complicated by love. Go work for your drug, your rent, your liquid screen, your cushy little life of whorehouses, pit fights, and suits stitched together by the very androids whose souls you sell in bulk.

His mouth floods with bloody saliva. He starts to puke, but there's no food in his gut. Just a long trail of runny red spit. Just the emptiness and the need to get out.

He rises from the couch and searches among Iris's clothes. Picking through the closet, he imagines her body giving shape to the dresses hanging on the rack. He grabs what garments he remembers her wearing and stuffs them into a broken suitcase he finds beneath the bed. He packs the bot cord, a slashed painting, a few random pieces of jewelry her attacker left behind. All with her signature red fleck. Even the furniture and the clothes she made for herself, each garment has at least a red spot or a red thread running through it. He zips her things into the suitcase and shuts off the light as he leaves.

"Drip Kills," says the adbrane at the bus stop. A big, red X flashes in front of a vial and a hanky. He carries Iris's suitcase past the sign while his mind speculates about what happened two nights before. Who was it and how did he get in? Was it friend or foe, neighbor or coworker? Did she scream? Did she reach for a brane and try to call? Did she fight back or accept that her time had come? In her final moments, Eliot wonders, did she think of me and Avernus? What did it do to her, how much did it hurt, to know she'd never make it?

"Drip Kills," says the billboard above the motel on Santa Monica. He hurries up the block carrying Iris's suitcase north beneath a filthy, yellow moon punched from the sky like an exhaust hole in a high, black dome. His shoulder hurts. The pain cuts across his back. He passes Fountain then Sunset then Hollywood as a dim light rises from the east. He ascends Beachwood Canyon dragging Iris's suitcase behind. He passes the elementary school and the barbed wire fences on the houses along the street. His dragging foot wakes a gen-modded dog who growls to protect his turf.

Spare key under the rock in the driveway, Eliot enters his apartment and closes the blinds. He tells his deskbrane to play a Hawk Jones album. He unpacks the suitcase and lays an outfit across the floor as if he were dressing her.

He rubs her panties across his face and smells them and brushes his lips over the place where her privates had been. Over the underwear, he lays the long, tight skirt she wore with canvas sneakers. He puts an off-the-shoulder sweater atop the skirt and a curved hat above the absence where her head should be. He adds the knit gloves he found, one in the drawer and one in the bathroom. They don't match, but neither do her socks, and that's how she wore them.

He remembers the eyeball locket he found outside her apartment, the piece she always wore, the piece with the red fleck that echoed the flaw in her eye. With a trembling hand, he withdraws it from his pocket and places it atop her sweater as if it were hanging from the slender reed of her neck. It's a finishing touch that can't bring form to the absent body, but it adds another layer. The clothes, the accessories, the jewels—her choices remain if not her body. A representation in place of the real thing, unless you don't believe a bot is the real thing, in which case this is a representation of a representation. Five foot eight from shoes to hat, horizontal on the floor. Here is preserved some shadow, some lack in the universe where a woman once was. It's as if Eliot hopes that by piling up these remnants of her existence he can asymptotically extend her essence close enough to the axis of her reality that the space between her representation and her being will disappear.

Music haunts the room. Dawn starts behind the blinds as Eliot lays beside the clothes and puts his arm across the void where her ribs would be. He closes his eyes and smells her in her clothes and tells her he is sorry. He is sorry he let her down, sorry he didn't do better, sorry he didn't keep his word and take her to Avernus. He is sorry he gave his money and his time to death instead of life.

Hawk Jones through the speakers. A dim light just bright enough to illuminate his guilt. He cannot tolerate more light.

Eliot walks away from the outline of the woman at his feet and sits on the couch in his torn coat and removes two vials of drip from the pocket. He twists off the caps and pours the contents into a dirty cloth.

"Drip Kills," say the signs that syncopate the streets beneath the canyon.

Let's hope it kills quick.

He lays the cloth across his hand and looks again at the redflecked locket. He harbors no illusions about an afterworld, no belief he's going to join her. He just sees no reason to continue. What is there now, what is left other than a habit masquerading as a life? He has seen the world with love and he has seen the world without and he has made his decision in which world he wants to live, and in which he does not.

He empties the air from his chest as he raises the cloth to his face. About to suck the drip into his lungs, about to take his final breath, it occurs to Eliot that there is something inside the red-flecked locket he has never seen. Never asked to see it because if she wanted him to see it she would have offered to show him what was inside. He never wanted to push. He always thought there would be more time.

Moving quickly so the cloth won't dry, he turns on the desk lamp and snaps the latch open. The engraving reveals itself in the light:

IRIS MATSUO

C-900

SERIAL #G14-95-7789

No message. Nothing personal. Just a string of data.

Just her name, model, and serial number, like the make, model, and plate number on a car. Or more like a *vehicle ID number*, because the serial number would appear on every one of Iris's parts.

The same number.

On every C-900 part.

Each of which would be necessary if Eliot were to rebuild her into the same android she was, with the same memories, the same aura, the same love and affection.

Eliot looks over his shoulder at the assemblage of clothes laid out on the floor of his apartment.

"You dropped a bread crumb, didn't you?" he asks.

The clothes admit nothing in response.

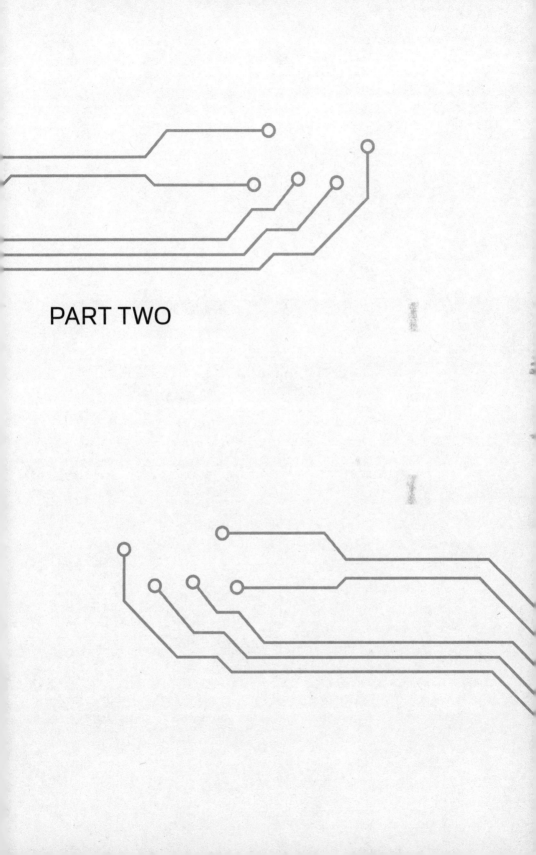

PART TWO

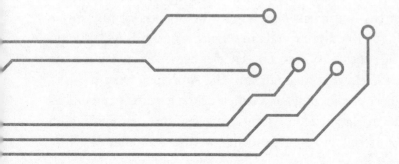

EIGHT
Made in Heron

In 1908, in an acreage of ranchland adjacent to the southeast corner of Los Angeles, the City of Heron was incorporated as an exclusively industrial city intended to bring commerce to the Southern California region. The location was ideal, as the three major rail lines that crisscrossed the area allowed factories to have easy access to markets throughout the Southwest. The city's founders extended the trolley line from downtown L.A. and offered subsidized electricity from their new utility, Heron Light and Power. To attract business, they built a sports stadium, staged prizefights, and opened the world's first traveling carnival that didn't travel. U.S. Steel, Bethlehem Steel, Owens, Alcoa, and Studebaker all answered the call and helped transform the former tribal land of the Gabrielino Indians into the largest industrial hub in the region.

During WWII, Heron's location again played a role in its development as the city was far enough from the Pacific to be out of range for Japanese bombers but close enough for America's aerospace industry to ship planes quickly to the naval bases dotting the

California Coast. Workers migrated from around the country seeking employment in Heron's factories. African Americans fleeing the racism of the South built thriving middle-class communities in neighboring Watts, Inglewood, and South Central L.A. while on the opposite side of the city, East Los Angeles became a stepping-stone for immigrant Latinos aspiring toward the American Dream.

After the postwar boom, Heron's meteoric rise came to an end as U.S. manufacturing suffered a long, slow decline that decimated America's industrial cities. Politicians wrung their hands while workers struggled to compete with lower costs and wages in developing nations. As the jobs disappeared, the middle class enclaves that housed Heron's employees lost their tax base and crumbled in the face of urban blight. Race riots broke out in '65 and '92 in response to police brutality. Fires burned in Watts and South Central, and the business owners who abandoned the smoldering rubble of their stores opted never to return.

In 2007, an *LA Times* exposé accused the descendants of Heron's founding families of running the city as their own personal fiefdom, in which they attracted businesses with near-zero tax rates while collecting vast revenues through the sale of water from their private aquifer and electricity from Heron Light and Power. Out of the profits, they paid themselves exorbitant salaries then retired to bloated pensions paid out of a state fund. According to the *Times*, city administrators manipulated local governance by preventing Heron's population from exceeding the fourteen people who officially lived there (as opposed to the thousands who commuted every day for work). Fourteen people! All of whom were city employees. All of whom could be depended on to vote the same way in every election so that decades would pass without any changes in office.

In the wake of the scandal, Heron's mayor, police chief, and head of the city council were all indicted while the mayor's son, a principal at a local Catholic school, was jailed for molesting his students. Later in the year, the governor proposed to unincorporate Heron and fold it back into Los Angeles, but by then, most Angelinos had lost interest in the story. Either that or they didn't want to absorb Heron's problems. After all, the country was on the precipice of a recession, and most of Heron's factories had already been shuttered. Its roads were cracked; its stores closed; squatters and junkies had taken over the streets. The tribal-land-turned-industrial hub kept only slaughterhouses and rendering facilities as active tenants, and the stench of burnt pig flesh hung over the entire five-square miles of industrial, political decay.

To understand how Heron was reborn as an economic powerhouse midway through the twenty-first century, one needs to look no further than to a young Hiram Lazar, who first conceived of the android workforce as we know it today. While taking an intro to economics class (macro) as a sophomore at CalTech, the young engineering student wrote a paper that critiqued industrial America's preference for using machines instead of human labor. He received a B- for his effort. These were his theses:

1. *Automated factories in the U.S. are more costly than low-tech factories in developing nations.* The machines that have replaced humans in the United States require a large start-up expenditure for purchase or lease and further expenditures for maintenance and repair. While they are cheaper to use than union labor, the machines still cost more than third-world workers, for whom the only cost is a paltry living wage. Furthermore, because large machines are neither wage earners nor consumers, they do not create additional markets for purchasing the goods they produce.

2. *Automated factories are less adaptable than those using human labor.* With the rapid advance of technology, heavy machines designed for specific tasks are often obsolete by the time they start production. They cannot adapt quickly to the changing demands of a dynamic market. To compete, companies repeatedly purchase or lease "new" machines and dump the "old" ones for a loss. In comparison, third-world workers

can adapt and develop new skills. They can innovate, find capital, and create new businesses on their own thus creating more wealth for their respective economies.

3. *It is more difficult for management to communicate with machines than with humans.* Even the smallest alterations in production require trained technicians to communicate those changes to custom-built machines. Dependence on these "specialists" costs additional monies and wastes valuable time. Furthermore, machines don't respond well to human alerts. They can't jump to their feet and run when they hear an alarm—especially if they don't have feet. Recent oil rig, nuclear, and factory disasters all show that machines only react to problems anticipated by their designers. Anything unanticipated is beyond the machine's capacity for recognition or reaction.

By the time he left college, Lazar had articulated a strategy to improve U.S. manufacturing by designing androids that would outcompete overseas workers. Rather than buying or leasing heavy machinery, companies could pay a *labor provider* one salary per android that was less than a foreign worker's wage.

Lazar likened his new start-up, which was named Daihanu, to a temp agency that manufactured, owned, and leased out temps. He proposed to build his "temps" in various sizes, ages, and races to satisfy the demands of any regional or niche market. He wanted workers who could combine the durability and efficiency of machines with the adaptability and creativity of humans. As he described them in his business plan:

Workers who can download skills as computers do instead of taking weeks to train; who can absorb up-to-the-minute information at the touch of a button; who can stop an assembly line when someone is caught in a belt; who can anticipate problems and find ways to solve them before catastrophe strikes.

The cost of building its first prototypes made financing Daihanu a risky venture, but knowing that androids would increase the demand for electricity, Lazar's partners appealed to energy companies to round out the initial funding. They took money from tobacco and alcohol conglomerates in exchange for a promise to give the bots a taste for cigarettes and booze. Soft drink companies and coffee growers chipped in to ensure that bots would have caffeine addictions that would expand the market for their products as well.

With the start-up capital secured, Lazar's team built the first batch of prototypes then enlisted the prototypes themselves to make a second generation of androids faster and smarter than the first. Thus the engineers who worked at Daihanu's first lab built their own replacements and upon completing their jobs found themselves out of work. The third batch of androids was faster, smarter, and more efficient than the second, but Lazor pressed on until his funding was nearly exhausted, and only then did Daihanu finally begin leasing its product to mining interests, oil rigs, industrial farms, deep-sea extractors, NASA, military contractors, fast-food chains, hotels, government services, and private homes. The company was a quick success, and within two years, competing entrepreneurs had copied Daihanu's business model and reverse engineered its product. They built and leased androids that looked, sounded, and talked just like human workers—the only discernible differences being an outlet for a navel and a spinning engine for a heart. Hence, human workers came to be known as *heartbeats* while machine workers came to be known as *bots*.

During its initial phase of mass production, the standard android on the market could toil for eighteen hours straight, seven days a week, in conditions that would kill your average heartbeat. The bots were precise; they worked fast; they didn't complain, demand benefits, or belong to any unions. They didn't even need a lunch break, just an occasional parts upgrade, a monthly oil change, and a nightly recharge, which the leasees were not obligated to supply.

By Lazar's design, it was up to each individual android to pay his or her own upkeep out of the money earned from the labor provider. If early prototypes required about a gigajoule per day to survive, and if a gig cost thirty ingots at the time, the androids could be hired out at a little over sixty per day with the labor provider taking half what the android earned. But energy demand soon outstripped supply as the android population increased. Oil, coal, and gas prices skyrocketed. The grids couldn't handle the juice. Power companies doubled their rates while labor providers, under pressure from Wall Street, squeezed the split on wages from fifty-fifty to eighty-twenty and gave their bots less than a quarter of what they grossed from their own work.

In android slums around the world, bots took drastic measures to secure enough energy to survive. They pooled resources to live ten to a room in dilapidated squats. They sold their lesser-used parts. They bought cheap, knockoff components when they couldn't afford brand names to replace their damaged limbs. Some bots built their own makeshift turbines, burning whatever was around to produce counterfeit electricity. Operating out of abandoned buildings, these illegal generators spread fires and spewed toxins that sickened heartbeats for miles around. One particularly clever bot, no one knows whom for sure, invented a narcotic inhalant called "drip" that could be synthesized out of discarded plastic. The drug was highly addictive to heartbeats, and as the drip market took off, *rogue* bots used dealing as a gateway into organized crime. The bots formed gangs that battled traditional cartels over turf, and when the police moved in to assert the law, bot cities blew up into war zones with gunshots, fires, and bombs exploding through the night.

Within a decade of their existence, some androids began to resent the extent to which they were being exploited by their owners and employers. Bot leaders asked, "Why should we do all the cooking when the heartbeats eat all the food?" Within their communities, small gatherings assembled in secret where they whispered about resistance. They organized. They planned. They began to protest.

This was the era in which Lorca rose to prominence. From a hidden base somewhere in Los Angeles, the one-armed nannybot built her Android Disciples into a global resistance movement or terrorist army depending on one's point of view. Hers became the voice of the revolution, her face its personification, her words its poetry.

"Where in the Constitution does it say I must be born from a woman to be the equal of a man?" she asked in one of her many fireside loops. Seated in a rocking chair. Bifocals. A black bandana around her head. Her shirt sleeve pinned to cover her missing arm. "I have raised thirty heartbeats in my time. Raised them good, too. From Palos Verdes to Pasadena to Malibu. I have worked and slaved my whole life to earn a piece of a dream those heartbeat babies got by being born. What is it about this *beating heart* that makes a newborn child more deserving than I?"

Her rhetoric spawned a terror campaign that ebbed and flowed for a decade. Leaf blowers went on killing sprees. Teachers poisoned children in their care. Pilots plunged their cargo into the sea. Spectacular attacks on bridges and office buildings played over the newsbranes watched by billions of people every day. There were train derailments, assassinations, car bombs, bank robberies, executions. A frenzy of panic, stoked by the media, fostered a notion that the moment had come when machines would take over the world.

Governments responded by jailing, torturing, and killing android agitators. They ran tanks through the streets of bot cities. They cut power lines and ordered labor providers to cease manufacturing new bots. In the United States, a paramilitary movement, made of heartbeats radicalized by rampant unemployment, further terrorized the bots with a campaign of intimidation, murder, and rape. Spurned on by talk radio and a right-wing press, the Militiamen ran candidates for office and advocated legislation that would further curtail, if not eliminate, the bots from Earth.

At the time of the troubles, Hiram Lazar had long before been forced from his position at Daihanu, but still he advocated for the legacy of his creation. Rather than bequeath a fortune to his heirs, he donated the bulk of his money to charities like the downtown mission that worked to improve the quality of life for bots. He urged labor providers to ignore Wall Street and return to a more equitable split on wages. He lobbied Congress to lower the prices that power companies could demand for juice. He went on the lecture circuit and published a series of books envisioning a world in which heartbeats and bots lived side-by-side in peace. Though his critics accused him of bringing us all to the brink of extinction, Lazar would always contend that his goal had been the opposite. It was his belief that mankind was already at the brink and only the bot could save us. For Hiram Lazar so loved mankind, that he built an android workforce to free the human spirit from its delicate cocoon and carry it across the universe into a future beyond what our fragile tissue can endure.

After Lazar was murdered, support for Lorca waned as an uneasy truce took hold. The moderate majority of bots did not advocate terror. Most were content to have affordable, consistent energy in their outlets. They wanted the government to allow providers to turn out more bots and increase their population. So long as they were working and their numbers were growing, the androids felt they were the ones who were shaping the future. They hoped someday they'd gain rights and protections under the law. They hoped their economic and political situations would improve. They feared that the moment had not yet come when they could live independently of the humans who created them. As one bot leader put it, "Heartbeats have survived two hundred thousand years on this planet. Let's see if *we* can survive another ten."

Amid this argument between metal and flesh, forged from the factory of battle, the City of Heron grew into the infamous behemoth we are familiar with today. It's hard to imagine how, back in the twentieth century, most Angelinos couldn't even locate Heron, California on a map. Unless you worked there, Heron was just an exit you drove past on the freeway or a story you read about in the

Times. The Heron of today, however, rises conspicuously like some Gehry-esque volcano belching black smoke into the clouds. Its towering clusters are as recognizable as the Hollywood sign and can be seen from any point in L.A, and though few heartbeats ever set foot in the city itself, all of the world is familiar with the orgy of production that grows Heron every day like a tumor on the California spine.

This is the city in which Iris Matsuo worked at a *maquiladora* owned by a heartbeat named Karoll Mun. This was where she made her living, a good living by android standards, for a reasonable boss, who, Iris claimed, recognized the worth of a quality creative. And this is where Eliot begins his search on the Saturday morning after the evening when he discovered Iris was gone. He wears a gray suit and a fedora. A pair of sunglasses covers the bruises on his face. He rides a bus then stands aboard a flying train crowded with androids dressed for work on a weekend. No rest for the bot.

The pulse of the factories' engines rattles the train as it glides into the station. Through the windows, Eliot sees the soot-covered faces crowded to the edge of the platform. The train stops. A deafening blast of horns, bells, and whistles greets him as the doors open. The push of the crowd lifts Eliot from his feet. All that prevents his tumbling through the exit is the proximity of hundreds of other bodies breaking his fall.

Outside the station, Eliot can barely make out a patch of sky in the shadowed, smoke-filled streets. Ramshackle towers arc above him. Forklifts and pallets zoom by falling ladders and open elevators vectoring across his path. Legend has it the city grows a foot per week in every direction. It twists underground where new factories dig into the earth and connect with tunnels and subterranean rail.

"Fresh lube. Light, sweet crude," says a hawker. "Quick charges. Safe and clean."

Loudspeakers call out the time every fifteen seconds when they aren't announcing the arrival of a new shipment or the departure of the next train out. Eliot asks an android how to get to Lot 57-C, Mun's factory, and the bot points the way.

"Look out," yells a voice as a crane claw swings near Eliot's head. Before he can thank him, the bot is gone, lost in the sea of shoulders and bodies and anonymous faces rushing to their posts.

Five minutes after arrival, still unable to find his way, Eliot sees his first downed android crushed beneath the wheel of a truck. A city employee keeps the scavengers at bay. He fingers the downed bot's serial number into a wristbrane, and within moments, a van arrives from the Green Valley Recycling facility to cart away the DBR'ed bot's remains. Moments later, the loudspeakers announce an opening at Hussein Smartbrane Assembly. The DBR'ed android's job just became available. The labor pool responds as a stampede of bots sprints down the street, shoving one another out of the way, each hoping to be the one who gets the crushed android's job. Some wear the uniforms of the labor providers who manufactured them: Patel, National Motors, Eastern Labor, GAC. Others are free roamers, unowned and entitled to negotiate their own wages. First one to catch a foreman's eye will earn a steady stream of juice for as long as he or she can survive the work. The rest will have to hope their charges last the day. Those who drop to the ground with a drained battery are meat for Green Valley or the scavengers who roam the streets collecting parts to sell on the black market. In cities like Heron, a downed bot disappears faster than a thousand-dollar chip on the floor of a casino.

Lost and frightened in the pandemonium, Eliot flags down a covered rickshaw motored by an android on a fixed-gear bike. The driver recognizes him as a heartbeat and shows his concern.

"You should have a mask on," he says. "You could die out here."

"Can you get me to 57-C?"

"Get in before you make yourself sick."

Pure oxygen feeds into the carriage the driver drags through the backstreets and alleys of the city. Eliot takes a deep breath and coughs out a fistful of soot. The rickshaw rides over flimsy ramps and bridges so tenuous, it seems they won't survive the day. In the quiet of the carriage, Eliot deposits a few drops from a vial and takes a quick sniff of his drip.

"Here we are," says the driver. "57-C."

Eliot pays. He opens the door and steps into a stream of gelatinous red liquid that stinks like bacon and sulfur. It flows from an open pipe jutting out of a tannery next door to a freezer warehouse. Wedged between them is a narrow staircase leading to the Chug-Bot factory where Iris worked. Eliot climbs the stairs and enters the dark, noisy building with aluminum walls, no windows, and air thick with metallic dust. He wipes his feet on the floor trying to scrape the stinking red liquid from his shoe.

A securitybot approaches. "May I help you?"

Eliot asks who's in charge.

It turns out Karoll Mun, owner of the factory, is in her office even on a Saturday. Iris always said she was that type of boss.

The securitybot leads Eliot over the catwalk, beneath which lie the cramped workstations where the creatives churn out their product. All of them are females, Asians like Iris, and they never look up from their toil. Nothing distracts them as they work their craft without the ebbs and flows that plague their heartbeat counterparts.

"You stepped in dye," the securitybot says in an African accent. "Red dye stink up whole block. No block in Heron smell nothing like it."

The Chug-Bot factory bears no resemblance to what Iris had described. It's hot and dark with clouds of sharp-edged flakes floating through the air. Eliot wonders if he's in the right place then realizes of course Iris would make it sound more elegant than it was. She had her pride after all or perhaps nothing worse to compare it to.

"Every Chug-Bot different," says the securitybot. His voice conveys his pride in the product. "Chug-Bot special toy for rich heartbeat child. No poor child get a Chug-Bot."

He opens the door to a small reception area with an exhaust fan and an oxygen filter pumping in air. Eliot asks the secretary-bot if he can have a moment with Karoll Mun, and the bot asks, what for?

"I'm with corporate security at the Global Assistance Corporation," says Eliot. "I'd like to speak to her about one of her bots."

The securitybot makes a hasty exit as the secretary enters the back office and closes the door behind her. She returns within a minute to allow Eliot inside.

"You step in dye. It stink my office." Sitting at her desk, the small, Korean heartbeat is half-hidden behind a mountain of cardboard boxes. A picture of her fat kids looms prominently from a shelf. "Now I have to clean."

Eliot apologizes and offers to take off his shoes.

"I no lease from labor provider," says Karoll Mun. "I only hire free roamer. No work with GAC."

"I understand," says Eliot, "but it's come to my attention that we had a missing bot posing as a free roamer when in fact she is still owned by my company."

"Oh, a cheat." Mun punches something into the hologram keyboard of her deskbrane. "Which bot a cheat?" She tilts the brane so Eliot can't see.

"A C-900."

"C-900 made by Hasegawa," says Mun. "Not GAC."

"That's right," Eliot agrees. "But this particular C-900 was purchased by GAC at auction during Hasegawa's liquidation. I believe she was hiding under the name Iris Matsuo."

"Don't tell me name," says Mun. "I don't know name."

"She worked for you the last three years."

"I have lot of bots. Don't know name."

"The bot I'm looking for is the one who wears this." He reaches into his jacket and reveals Iris's locket.

Mun huffs and slams her hand against the desk. "Yeah, yeah, I recognize. Red dot. She no work here no more. She fired!"

"Fired?"

"That's right. Fired!"

Fired? Eliot wonders how this could be? Wouldn't she have told him if that were the case?

"I fire her two week ago for this!"

Mun digs through a stack of boxes behind her desk. She pulls out a cluster of dolls that looks like a pack of imaginary baby animals.

"Look close." Mun pulls out one of the toys to reveal a red patch of fur on the animal's backside. She shows another with a red spot on its nostril. Another has a red fleck on its paw.

"Did Iris make these?" Eliot asks.

"I make these. Bot work for me!"

It's customary that the heartbeat who employs a creative takes full credit for anything the android produces. To Mun, Iris is not the author of her own work, she is an instrument, like a typewriter or a loop-cam or a paintbrush.

"Stupid bot ruin work. Store send back whole batch, so she fired." Mun slaps her hands together to indicate, that's it. "No more!"

Eliot considers the new information. Fired two weeks ago, and Iris never asked for a nickel. Unless she had money saved, she must have been scraping by on juice. And as a free roamer with no employee ID, she would have been vulnerable to trappers after all. No wonder she wanted to get to Avernus right away.

"Bot no good," says Mun. "You better off leave alone. You no want bot like her."

"Do you have any idea where she might have gone?"

Mun explains that she doesn't know anything about her employees other than whether they produce their daily quota of Chug-Bots.

"Can I see her employment file?"

Something about the question makes Mun suspicious, and she asks for Eliot's ID. He shows her his GAC employee card but uses his thumb to cover the part that identifies him as a salesman.

"I'll leave my number," says Eliot, "and if you wouldn't mind, I'd like to talk to your workers as well."

"We busy," says Mun. "We have order to fill."

"I promise it'll take no more than a few minutes of their time."

"Time money." Mun stands from her desk and is no taller standing than she had been in the chair. "You crazy. Crazy heartbeat."

She yells in Korean to her secretarybot, and the android snaps to. Mun reaches for her safety mask and takes a quick glance at the locket before she exits the office.

"Nice piece," she can't help but admit.

NINE

Orpheus and Eurydice

The old detective thought he had a win. Tipped off that a member of Lorca's security detail had caught a case of foaming mouth, Flaubert staked out the downtown mission and waited for the bot to sneak in for treatment.

Mavis Barker, a NatMo-18 bodyguard and assassin, walked into the waiting room with a newsbrane covering his mouth to hide the thin layer of saliva that had collected on his lips. He signed in under an assumed name. Sat down. Ochoa was undercover beside him. Another officer right behind.

Posing as an engineer (or doctor for bots), Flaubert called the patient into an exam room where his fellow officers rushed in, gagged Barker, and dragged him to the precinct where they scanned his body to make sure he wasn't hiding a bomb in a spare limb. He wasn't. All clean—they caught him off guard. All done in secret, too.

Two days later and the rogue is still in interrogation. A team of six works him over. They give him just enough juice to keep him awake. They beat him. They withhold treatment and watch the virus affect his mind. It happens gradually. At first, the only symptom is the drool through which the virus is communicable from one bot to another, but after a few days, without treatment, the infected android will become a hypersexual psychopath rabidly trying to spew his foam into the nearest available orifice.

"Says here you were a steamfitter." Flaubert reads Barker's specs off a deskbrane between them. "Worked on the Santa Monica desalination plant before NatMo released a newer model that replaced you."

Barker's arms, legs, and torso are bound to the chair. He slouches against his constraints. His lips twist and pull tight as his emerging madness contends with his loyalty to Lorca.

"Out of work. No way to obtain juice. You sought out the Disciples in order to survive."

The bot doesn't acknowledge the old detective's presence. Two days, and he's yet to speak a word. Just twists and bites his drooly lips, sucking them in and puckering them out to allow the saliva to drip.

"You were reconfigured to be an assassin. Quantum encryption for your memory. Training in arms. A loyal soldier by all accounts, though I bet you'd prefer your old job back."

For two days Flaubert has been telling the bot, I understand you. For two days he has been offering the bot various alternatives to the beatings administered by his young, one-eyed partner in the law. For two days it hasn't worked, but how great would it be if it did? What a score if he could be the one to catch Lorca! What a legacy to the department and a validation for a lifetime of honest service to the state.

"You know there's work for you overseas." Flaubert dangles the carrot. "They use the older models there and pay them well. An ingot goes much further in Asia than it does in the US."

The android cocks his head and sits up straight in his chair. For the first time in two days, he appears to be listening. He appears to be accepting the old detective as the one officer willing to grant him some way out of his predicament.

"We'd pay for your transport and the juice you'd need until you begin. You'd have the job you were designed for. You'd be building again," Flaubert promises. "Creating. Marking the world with your passion."

The bot's forehead tenses. His teeth grind. He struggles to keep the secret of Lorca's whereabouts in his mouth.

"She isn't coming to save you, Mavis. She isn't doing for you what you did routinely for her."

Flaubert can feel the others watching from the observation room, pressed against the one-way glass as the whereabouts of Lorca are about to be revealed.

"Tell me where you were before you came to the Mission. Tell me where you were hiding when you discovered you were ill."

The bot leans across the desk drawing Flaubert's face closer to his own.

"Whisper it to me," says the old detective. "Say it once. One time and you'll walk out of here free."

Barker leans back in his chair, jerks forward, and spits a black, fleshy object against the old detective's cheek.

It's his tongue.

It leaves a tarry mark on Flaubert's face before falling as a clump in his lap.

The door to the interrogation room opens. Ochoa takes a running start and lands a hard right that sends the bot backward, his head splitting as it hits the ground. "I got it from here, Jean-Michel."

In the bathroom, the oil easily washes off his face, but the stain on his pants is more stubborn. He has to admire the bot, chewing off his own tongue and swallowing the oil as it bled. Talk about commitment. Talk about loyalty and strength.

In the hallway, on his way back to interrogation, Flaubert passes an argument between a sergeant from the larceny division and a young man in a loose-fitting suit.

"Keep pushin', shitbrain. Keep fuckin' pushin'."

"I'm a tax-paying citizen, and you call me shitbrain?"

"You're lucky I don't throw your drip-fiend ass in jail."

"And you're lucky I don't file a complaint."

"For what? For not calling the cavalry every time some cheap metal slut gets lost?"

Flaubert looks closely at the young man, whose voice sounds vaguely familiar.

"I'm just asking for the drone footage from one night. One set of coordinates, and I promise I won't . . ."

"Mr. Lazar," Flaubert interrupts, remembering the young man from the night of that situation on Beverly. The poor lad seems to have aged ten years since. Lost ten pounds, too, and amassed a few lines around his eyes. The transformation is alarming. It's as if some parasite is feeding on him from within.

"Jean-Michel," says the sergeant, "you know this fuck?"

"Yes, we met once before, didn't we?"

"He's been here ten times in the last six weeks, each time with some bullshit about a missing bot."

Flaubert puts a friendly hand on the young man's shoulder. "There's a diner across the street from the main entrance of the precinct. Head over. I'll buy you a cup of coffee."

The old detective checks in with the lieutenant in the observation room to let him know he'll be gone for an hour. He walks out into the early evening rain and crosses to the diner where the young man is seated in a booth by the window. There's a decent crowd inside, more than usual, probably because of the weather. By the time two cups of coffee arrive, the young man has already delineated his complaint. The old detective listens. He notices that Eliot, too, has a cough now, though it's probably from a head cold, a weakened immune system, not from an accumulation of soot. More alarming than the cough, however, the young man's demeanor has taken on a manic, obsessive quality that gestures toward a deterioration in his thinking. He has three separate branes open on the table displaying maps, spreadsheets, and loops of surreptitiously recorded faces. He places a locket in the old detective's hand.

"She made this," says Eliot, "used to wear it every day. The red fleck echoes the red flaw in her eye. It's like her signature, all her clothes and jewelry, everything she made has it."

Flaubert recognizes the quality of the stone and fair curves of the work. The clasp gives a good snap when he opens it to reveal an engraving done in a wistful yet confident hand:

IRIS MATSUO

C-900

SERIAL #G14-95-7789

"I entered the number into every database I could find. I called all the labor providers and asked them to run it through their inventories. I called all the parts retailers. Wholesalers, too. I called every shipping, trucking, and rail service in case the number got scanned anywhere in the supply chain. I put it on the Web, on message boards. Turns out there are these C-900 collectors who buy and sell parts so they can mess with the bots' auras. They trade a pair of arms to get a bot with a different character, then trade back, or keep the new parts if they like the change."

He stirs an unhealthy amount of sugar into his coffee as he speaks.

"I called Green Valley and every recycling chain on the Web. I called all the dumps, scrap yards, and rendering facilities. Not only in the US, but Mexico, Canada, anywhere I could get a hold of someone. But the number never popped. Not one limb, screw, or chip was ever scanned. Not here. Not anywhere. Of course, if I had access to a police database . . ."

"What about the chop shops?" The old detective adds cream to his coffee but decides against the sugar.

"I checked them."

"All of them? There must be five hundred in L.A. alone."

"Three hundred eighty-one," says Eliot, "and about a hundred more that aren't licensed."

The old detective can hardly imagine it's possible. More than ten shops a day, hours spent looking through crates of metal components, some as large as a leg, others as small as a screw. He pictures the sickly young man standing over a bin and shining a black light on each and every part to read its serial number.

"I went about a month without a lead, but then I got a tip from Mun and figured a few things out."

"Mun?"

"The Korean who owns the *maquiladora* where Iris worked." Eliot takes a large swallow of his coffee. "Mun found out her securitybot, some guy named Uchenna, had a scam going. Every time one of her girls got fired, he would offer to get her another gig. The girls would be desperate. Most of them can't live a week without a paycheck, some can't make it a day. Thing was, all these girls went missing."

"Did you talk to the securitybot?"

Eliot shakes his head. "Mun fired him after she got tipped off about his scam. I visited his address in Inglewood. There were about ten bots living there in a nasty little squat. They were burning in the bedroom, turning out illegal juice, but Uchenna was gone by the time I got there. His roommates said he'd been chopped. Turns out he had a gambling problem, owed a bunch of money to the shys. Whoever he was tipping, some trapper I assume, paid him a commission in parts. There were still a few there in the apartment. The bots showed me the stash they kept around in case any of them got injured and needed a spare. That's where I found her arm."

Flaubert grins in appreciation of the nice bit of police work pulled off by the amateur sleuth. Too bad the young man shows no satisfaction in his success. "The serial number matched?"

"Her left arm," says Eliot before issuing a weary sigh. "That's it. That's all I have so far. That's all that's left."

The old detective checks his watch and sets a time when he has to cut this meeting short. Every minute he spends with the lad is another minute Ochoa spends beating the oil out of Mavis Barker. If Flaubert doesn't get back soon, there will be nothing left to interrogate.

"I went to a few of the bars where the trappers go," says Eliot. "They're a paranoid bunch. Lorca hunts them the same way they hunt bots. I talked to a few and asked around. I said I needed this C-900 back, no questions asked. I even offered a reward, but they weren't interested. They roughed me up pretty good, and after that, I had to stop going."

The old detective notices the fresh wounds on the young man's face. Even the abrasions from six weeks ago hadn't fully healed.

"If I could access the department's drone feed," says Eliot, "maybe I could catch a glimpse of who took her. I know you keep the footage on the cloud for a few months before you erase it. You could check it for me, see if you caught who went home with her that night. Then I wouldn't be running around chasing my tail like this. I just need to see the drone footage from one stinking . . ."

"I can't help you with that," says the old detective.

"What if I pay you?"

"Bribing on officer?"

"Then help me out of kindness."

"I help you better by declining your request."

Eliot shifts the branes around the table then back to their original positions. "What's the point of being a cop if all you do is stonewall and look for excuses not to help people? A woman is missing. . . ."

"A bot is missing," the old detective corrects him. "Their hearts don't beat, they spin. They live off electricity, not the food of the Earth. They are designed to mimic our emotions, but they have no souls."

"You believe in souls?"

"I do believe in souls."

"When a man paints a painting or composes an opera or builds a home," the young man asks, "does he not impart into that work some element of his soul?"

"You could say the same thing about a toaster."

"I'm not in love with a toaster."

Flaubert suspects he's doing more harm than good by engaging with such a mind. Perhaps he should arrest Lazar on a possession charge now and see to it that he's forced into rehab. Not that treatment has done him any good in the past. But at least in a facility he could detox, restore his health a bit, get off the street before he gets himself killed.

"Are you familiar with the myth of Orpheus?" Flaubert asks the young man.

"What about it?"

The old detective sips his coffee and allows the hot liquid to burn the ashy irritation in his throat. "Orpheus was the greatest poet in all of Thrace. He was to marry Eurydice, his fiancée, but on their wedding day, a viper bit her foot and dragged her soul down to the underworld. Orpheus was so distraught he ventured down to the river Styx and sang a poem so moving, so filled with passionate longing, that even the gods of the underworld took sympathy. In an unprecedented breach of protocol, they told the great poet he could lead his deceased lover back to the upper regions, back to the land of the living, to marry as had been their plan. But the gods had one caveat before they would allow Eurydice's release. One command for Orpheus that he absolutely had to obey: that his eyes must not turn back to look at her until he'd passed the valley that separates the underworld from the Earth."

The botress returns and the old detective pays the bill. Eliot offers to contribute, but Flaubert won't allow it.

"Of course Orpheus did look back," he continues with his retelling. "Steps from safe harbor, he looked back only to see his fiancée's soul disappear again into the abyss. 'Farewell,' she said, a second death without a second life. The poet returned to the flaming river and sang his song again and begged and pleaded with the gods, but this time they refused. This time, they wouldn't let her go."

Eliot stares out the window as the sooted raindrops streak against the glass.

"In the end, Orpheus retired to a hilltop where he sat alone and sang his poems—poems that set the Thracian women wild. He rejected them in favor of the memory of his dead fiancée, and eventually, the jealous harpies tore him apart. Killed him. In gruesome fashion."

The old detective coughs and wipes his mouth as Eliot struggles to discern what this story has to do with his plight.

"Why did he look back?" the young man asks. "If he hadn't looked back, he would have rescued her."

Flaubert shrugs. "It's a recurring theme in mythologies that attempts to raise the dead are destined to fail."

"Then the old myths are no longer relevant."

"Why not?"

"Because death is no longer final," Eliot argues. "At least not for an android."

Flaubert pauses to consider the young man's interpretation. If the androids do outlive us, he wonders, will they carry the old myths with them, or any of the great art and literature that was done by man? Will it all become, as Eliot says, no longer relevant—or will the truths these stories describe assert themselves in this new bastardization of life?

"Wouldn't it be simpler," Flaubert asks, "wouldn't it be more wise to open yourself up to the possibility of another woman, perhaps one of the same species? Wouldn't that be a better fate to choose than that of Orpheus ripped apart by the harpies because he refuses to move on?"

"But Iris isn't Eurydice," says Eliot. "If she were dead I *could* move on. I *could* accept it if there was no chance of recovering her. But who am I if I abandon her just because finding her isn't easy? Just because I've been looking for six weeks and have only found one arm?"

"How long will you give it?"

"As long as it takes," says Eliot. "What kind of man am I otherwise?"

Though she's too timid to speak up, the botress clearly wants the table for the next round of customers queuing up at the door of the diner. And Flaubert has urgent business back at the precinct. Mavis Barker may not be the lead he hoped for, but he is a bot in Lorca's inner circle and such an opportunity must be explored.

"I'm asking very little of you," Eliot says, looking down into his empty mug. "I just want to look at the drone feed and see a parts database in the police file. I just want a little help."

"I'm afraid I've helped you all I can."

"You haven't helped me at all."

Flaubert stands from the table and dons his hat. He adds to the tip before leaving. Crossing the street back to the precinct, he hopes his warning has some resonance with the young man. He hopes it guides him toward a more promising fate than that of the Thracian poet. It would be a great shame if the lad were to continue on with a fool's errand. After all, a man's life, when all is said and done, should serve some greater purpose than that of the hero in a cautionary tale.

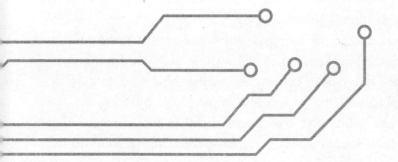

TEN

A Date

In his dream, Eliot rides a bus through Koreatown, leaning against the window, holding a drip hanky to his nose for a quick inhale. He sees Iris in a white coat walking through the rain in the opposite direction. He yells for the bus to stop, but the driver doesn't respond.

"Iris!" he screams as he breaks out of the door and chases after her. He sees her vanishing into a parking structure around the corner. He follows, runs through the rain, enters the garage, and catches a quick glimpse of her white coat as the elevator doors close. He bolts up the stairs, flight after flight, chasing the elevator to the top floor where the doors open on the rooftop, but there's no one inside.

A rub of tires on the asphalt, downstairs, a flight below, Eliot sees a car pass, the driver dressed in white. He calls to her but she doesn't hear. He throws himself over a low railing to fall a full story before his body slams in front of the car. The driver hits the brakes. Her car skids. She gets out. A small Asian woman in a white coat.

"Sir, are you all right?"

Eliot looks but sees no red fleck in her eye. It isn't Iris face. Not even close.

"Are you all right?" she asks again.

Outside the garage, he sees Iris across the street. Then another Iris fixing a display in the window of a brane store. Then another driving by in a delivery truck. There's Iris again, holding a Chug-Bot in a commercial playing on the massive brane above Wilshire. On the street, everyone looks like Iris. Everywhere he looks is an Asian woman in a white coat hunkering against the rain. He grabs an Iris by the arm, and her face changes, it distorts, the red fleck disappears.

"Eliot."

From a distance they all look like her, but up close, they are other women. Strangers. Robots and heartbeats alike. Everywhere he looks, he sees her, and no matter where he looks, she isn't there.

"Eliot."

Gita touches his shoulder to wake him from his dream. She puts a cup of hot tea on his desk beside his elbow.

"Eliot, it's late," says his co-worker. "You should go home."

The office is empty. Dark. Quiet except for the hum of the cleaningbots vacuuming the hall.

"What time is it?" He rubs his eyes.

"Ten."

"Ten?"

Gita looks different somehow. She's thinner and more put together.

"Are you dressed up?" he asks.

She smiles, glad he noticed. "Wedding anniversary." Her face reddens as she attends to the coffee at her desk. "Had a lovely dinner at a bistro in Pasadena."

"And then you came back?"

She stirs her coffee with a spoon. "We had a fight."

"Oh, Gita."

"Go home, Eliot." She shakes a packet of artificial sweetener and tears it open. "I'll mind the shop."

In the bathroom, Eliot pours a few drops in a hanky and flushes to cover the sound of his inhale. He folds his tie into his pocket. Unbuttons the top of his shirt. Washes his face in the sink.

He hates to leave without some new lead or clue to follow up on in the morning. If he gives it another fifteen minutes, another hour, could this be the night he finds Iris along some rest stop on the information superhighway? Not likely. Tired as he is, Iris could spit in his face, and he wouldn't recognize her. Better to get some sleep, he decides. Start fresh in the morning. Tomorrow's a new day. Every day another chance to find her. Go at it with a clear mind in the morning, stop wasting time while you don't have your faculties, your stamina, your wits.

"Take care, Gita," Eliot says on the way out. He throws a stick of chewing gum in his mouth and waits for the elevator. The doors open and there's a woman inside.

"There you are! I knew you couldn't hide from me forever."

Ah, shit, it's his boss, Erica Santiago. All done up in her tight, black mini with her hair down and her tits fluffed and that great ass she's always parading around. But nothing in her appearance could ever distract from the giant, hairy mole nestled above her lip like a possum ready to pounce.

"What are you doing here at this hour?" she asks.

"I was uh . . . catching up on activity reports." Eliot pushes the button for the lobby and takes a position to her right so he won't have to look at the mole.

"Have you eaten dinner?"

"Actually, I have," he lies.

"Great. Then we'll just go for a drink."

Her car stinks of cigarettes and stale coffee. She drives fast and parks at the Ritz-Carlton where they take a table on the fiftieth floor. Blood-orange candles and tablecloths the color of a dark bourbon. The room rotates 360 degrees. The lights of the city glow around them like fireflies lost in the gray spew of exhaust drifting north from Heron.

"I brought up your name at an executive meeting," says the

Hairy Mole. "I recommended we transfer you to the Paolo Alto office and make you a junior VP."

Eliot tries his best to ignore it, but there's something hypnotic
about the mole, the way the thing jumps and dances around her
mouth as she talks.

"You'd be working in the office adjacent to mine, which means
we'd be seeing a lot more of each other."

It used to be only heartbeats had moles, and bots had unblem-
ished skin. Then these "mole placement" shops started popping up.
While heartbeats were having theirs removed so they could look
like androids, androids were having moles implanted so they could
look like heartbeats.

"I appreciate your consideration," says Eliot, "but I couldn't leave
my brother alone in Los Angeles."

"Oh, nonsense," says the Mole. "You can commute from Paolo
Alto on the vactrain in an hour. You could see him every weekend if
you want."

"I'd have to give up my apartment."

"With the pay raise you'll be able to afford a hotel."

"Again, I appreciate the consideration."

She hides her disappointment by stabbing a cocktail sword through
the maraschino cherry in her drink.

"Why are you always rebuffing me, Eliot? Don't you want to get
ahead?"

"I'm happy where I am," he tells her. "The money's fine. I like
where I live."

"I worry about your lack of ambition."

Eliot sips his drink and checks the time on his pocketbrane.
He wonders how short he can cut the evening without offending
her.

"May I ask what happened in your meeting with Dale Hamp-
ton?" The Hairy Mole twists the plastic sword between her fingers.
"What happened to the three-thousand-bot lease he came to Los
Angeles to negotiate?"

Eliot leans back in his chair as if he's struggling to remember the incident.

"As I recall," he tells the Mole, "we were too far apart on the numbers."

"How much was he asking?"

"It averaged out to a hundred per day per bot."

"You should have taken it."

Eliot tilts his head. "The way Monroe crushes bots, we would have been sending replacements every week. We would have lost our shirts."

"Of course, they crush bots. The more bots they lose, the more we have to build. That increases demand for metal. And extracting metal is their business."

Eliot sips his drink and shrugs. "I'm sure some other provider was happy to fill the order."

"Two in fact, but Monroe isn't satisfied with either. The Patels break down in the cold, and the Kindelans started to radicalize. There's been crime. Runaways. Protests. Some Monroe executive found a bomb under his landing pod. Anyway, they want to send them all back to Cuba and buy a new pool."

"If you want me to make the deal at a hundred," says Eliot, "I'll call Dale tomorrow."

"No need. I already did. The meeting is set but on one condition." She smooths the tablecloth, bringing her hand dangerously close to his. "Dale wants to buy the Satine 5000 we have in the showroom. He wants him sent to Texas before the two of you meet."

Eliot feels a squeeze in the pit of his stomach. "Dale wants to buy Tim?"

"The bot has a name?" The Mole grins unkindly. "How cute."

Eliot rubs his bottom lip with his finger as he tries to figure out some way to save Tim's ass. If he tells the Mole the truth about what happened in the showroom, she'll spare the Satine a trip to Texas and send him to Green Valley instead. The bot will be terminated, separated, and rendered, which is probably a better fate than what awaits him in Texas.

"We can't sell the Satine to Dale," says Eliot. "I need him in the showroom."

"We'll get you another."

"I need the one that's there. We work well together."

"Eliot, this is an important contract. We're talking about three thousand bots for a five-year term. Plus replacements. Plus a company store."

"Tim's the best we got, and Dale's a drunk who doesn't keep his word."

"I'm sending him the bot."

"I'm begging you not to."

"Begging?" She laughs and repositions herself on her chair. "You won't accept a promotion, you won't go to Paolo Alto like I asked, but you'll beg me to throw away a three-thousand-bot contract for a mannequin?"

"I'll make it up to you."

"How?"

"Anyway I can."

"Hmm." She uses the sword to place the maraschino cherry between her teeth. As she chews, the stem sticks out so that it looks like the hairy mole on her lip has a tail. "Are you seeing anyone?" she asks before she swallows the fruit.

Oh, God, thinks Eliot, how to respond? He can't tell her the truth, though as he considers it, in the moment, he isn't really sure what the truth is. If Iris were a heartbeat and she were dead, then no, he would be single, not seeing anyone. But she isn't a heartbeat, and she's missing, probably chopped up into a thousand parts, in which case—what is she? Damaged beyond repair? If not, it's possible Iris can be brought back to life, which means, yes, Eliot is seeing someone, but, of course, he can't tell that to the Mole. He can't admit that he's committed to a being whose heart spins instead of beats; it's socially unacceptable. Illegal in fact. It would get him fired and arrested.

"I am," she gives her answer to a question Eliot didn't ask. "Seeing someone, that is. Though it hasn't yet reached the condition of a relationship. And it never will since such relationships are frowned upon in our society."

This last part, of course, piques Eliot's interest.

"Oh, don't look surprised," says the Mole. "Think we don't know about you boys and all those strip mall massage parlors? Well, the ladies have their fun, too, you know. We aren't just getting our nails done or our bikini lines waxed, if you understand my meaning."

Eliot slowly raises his glass and sips his drink. "This is common?" he asks.

"More than you think." Her high-heeled shoe kicks at the loose fabric on the leg of his pants. "The way an android makes love is very different from the way a heartbeat does. They don't procreate sexually, of course, so in the bedroom, they have a way of making a woman feel more protected than penetrated. They aim to serve, after all. A woman could get used to such a thing."

"You can get arrested," Eliot reminds her.

"But you can't get pregnant. At least not yet." She laughs at her own joke, then turns more serious. "Which I guess is the problem."

"What is?" Eliot asks.

"Well, I'm not getting any younger, and with the birthrates falling from all the crap in the air and the food and the water, there's a chance I might already be sterile. You could be as well for all we know, though there's really only one way to find out."

The quick drink Eliot agreed to has become something far more poisonous than he anticipated. It's no longer the case that he merely has to fuck the Hairy Mole to save Tim's ass, now he has to get her pregnant as well. And he has to do it while looking at that awful blemish on her lip.

The botress approaches to see if they'd like another round. Eliot asks for the check.

"Already?" says the Mole. "I thought things were just getting interesting." She squeezes Eliot's hand above the table.

"I love your earrings," says the botress.

"Excuse me?" the Mole snaps, making it clear the android's small talk overstepped a boundary.

"I-I'm sorry," the botress stutters, "I-I just said I liked your earrings."

The Mole realizes from Eliot's expression that it's more to her advantage to accept the compliment.

"Thank you." She flips her hair back to better show off the jewelry. "They're from Japan."

"They're beautiful," says the botress. "I'll get you another round." She hurries away as the Mole's attention turns back to Eliot.

"Now where were we?" She smiles as her hair falls back to cover her ears.

But Eliot can't remember where they were in the conversation. He can't hear any sound in the room, nor feel anything other than the burn in his chest. During the brief exchange with the botress, he had caught a glimpse of the Mole's jewelry, enough to see what looked like a red fleck on the stone in the left earring.

Did I imagine that? he wonders. Was it some hallucination left over from the dream I had at my desk? Did I see it because I wanted to see it or because it was actually there?

"All of a sudden, so quiet," says the Mole, her fingers curled beside her cheek.

Eliot reaches across the table and pushes aside her hair. The Mole coos and closes her eyes at his touch. He rubs the earring's smooth brown stone with his thumb to make sure the red fleck isn't a bit of dust.

"If you want to get out of here," she whispers, "there's an all-night spa not far from the river. They've got private rooms with whirlpool baths. We can get a his-and-her massage."

"Where'd you get the earrings?" he asks, his fingers squeezing the curve of the stone.

She touches her lips to his wrist.

"Where'd you get them?" He pulls the earring closer to examine it in the light.

"Ow. Eliot."

"Where'd you get them?"

She grabs his wrist to relieve the pressure. "At an antique store."

"Which antique store?"

"You're hurting me."

"Which antique store?" Eliot pulls on the earring, stretching the skin on her lobe.

"Eliot!"

"Which store?"

"Pound's! Pound's Antiques in Beverly . . . Jesus!"

He lets go and leans back in his chair. His pulse is quick and his hand shakes as he takes up his drink. A couple at another table looks over, and Eliot looks back. The couple returns to their meal.

"Jesus, Eliot. You really hurt me."

The Hairy Mole puts a cocktail napkin to her earlobe to check for blood.

ELEVEN
Pound's Antiques

It's a small shop on Canon Drive next to a store that sells a hundred flavors of something with the consistency of ice cream but isn't ice cream. Eliot must have driven by a thousand times without ever noticing the joint. Why would he? He isn't one to antique.

The door buzzes; he enters. He sees in the back a bald, fussy proprietor with a waxed mustache and a paunch. He uses a pair of pince-nez eyebranes and a large, steampunk earpiece to argue with someone on the line.

"I'm a very giving person, Raoul, but I wouldn't mind a little reciprocity. I wouldn't mind a little respect."

Eliot assumes the proprietor is that same Pound whose name is bannered across the window.

"I spoil you. I give you everything you need." He barely acknowledges Eliot's existence before disappearing into a back room to continue his argument in private.

Alone in the store, Eliot browses the racks of vintage electronics near the front window. He sees an HDTV set, the thick, heavy kind manufactured before brane tech made liquid screens as thin as a layer of paint. He sees PCs, Macs, and old laptops that predate quantum computing. They have real, physical keyboards instead of hologram controls. They have old flash drives and hard drives, still used by crooks and privacy nuts worried about keeping their data out of the cloud where it's more easily hacked.

"Because I'm not twenty-two," Pound yells from the back room, "and I don't see what's so awful about a night at home."

Eliot looks through a shelf of old Barbies, American Girls, Elmos, and Teletubbies. A written tag reads DON'T PULL THE CORD next to a naked, sexless doll with a string on its belly. He passes the selection of aluminum cans and plastic bottles. He notices an Arrowhead Water container left over from when a lake by that name nestled in the mountains east of L.A. He picks up an old Snapple bottle, empty, the kind that people collect.

"Are these real?" he calls out to the back room.

The proprietor leans out from behind the wall and raises his pince-nez eyebranes. "Everything here is authentic," he says.

"My brother collects these," says Eliot. "You know they used to have these sayings under the bottle caps. . . ."

"Hold on." Pound walks to the front of the store and changes the sign from OPEN to CLOSED. He lowers his eyebranes and yells again at his caller. "Stop lying to me, Raoul. I don't believe you in the least!"

Again, Pound ignores his lone customer and vanishes into the back room, so Eliot moves on. He walks to an aisle stacked with laminated newspapers, glossy magazines, and old books made from paper. How sacred and heavy they feel in his hand. To think, they used to kill trees to create a canvass for words, destroyed life for stories and news and—he can't help but think of it—for *words*. For sentences and paragraphs. And stories. What's so sacred about stories? Eliot wonders. Why so necessary to mankind when all other species seem to survive without them? There's an old graphic novel with a cartoon robot on the cover. The machine has stiff joints, thin legs, and headlights for eyes. Eliot reads the back cover to see what the book's about, but the words bore him, so he puts it down.

"Raoul, is someone in my house? Did you invite guests over without permission? I'll have you rendered if you dared!"

In another aisle, Eliot finds CDs, Blu-ray disks, and vinyl. Jazz, opera, classical. He reads the sleeve of an old Miles Davis recording and is astonished to see the enormous disk contains only ten songs, five on each side. You actually have to flip it halfway through to hear the recording in its entirety.

He puts the record away and walks to the counter where, locked beneath the glass, are a pair of Glocks, a Smith & Wesson, a Berretta, and a Winchester rifle. They're the old kind, the ones that shoot bullets instead of light pulses or exploding rounds.

"I'm coming home, and I want to see who's in my house!" says Pound. "I'm hanging up on you. I'm very upset!"

The jewelry, also, is locked in a case. Rings, necklaces, and bracelets made of mined stones and old metals. Eliot sees a range of eyeball pieces with the signature red flecks. He looks closely, trying to judge whether they were designed by Iris. It is possible, after all, that someone got the same idea and produced similar work. But this similar? he wonders. This same style, this same level of craft?

"What about these?" Eliot calls out.

Pound reenters and slams the eyebranes on the counter. He glances toward the jewelry beneath the glass where Eliot stands.

"Late twentieth century. Indian. Heartbeat made."

"Indian?"

"Yes. Indian."

"Where'd you get them?"

"At auction. Estate sale, rather. The brooch is five hundred and the necklace three seventy-five. If you're serious about buying, I can take them out. Otherwise, I'd just assume leave them in the case."

"Do you carry parts for a C-900?"

"Sir, this is an antique store. If you're looking to buy limbs, I recommend a chop shop in one of the many bot cities south of the freeway." Pound drums his fingers against the counter. He checks his wristbrane as Eliot looks again at the red-flecked jewelry. They seem made of the same materials Iris used to smuggle out of Mun's factory. Same colors, textures, and curves.

The eyebrane rings and Pound's hand reaches for it instinctively, then pulls away. The old battle between willpower and temptation plays out across his face. As is often the case, temptation wins.

"Yes, Raoul." Pound sighs as he puts the branes over his eyes.

Eliot exits and walks through Beverly Hills toward the bus stop on Santa Monica Boulevard. He wonders how the store might have acquired so much of Iris's work—jewelry she made, as far as Eliot knows, only for herself or to sell on the train during her commute. But this guy Pound seems to have procured a complete set, not just the one or two pieces someone could have purchased on his way home from work.

Eliot boards the bus, pays in cash, and takes a seat by a window in the back. He pulls out his drip rag and sneaks a small quantity into the cloth. The bus starts, and Eliot raises the rag to his face.

Seven weeks now since the last time he saw her. The more time passes, the more likely her parts have been sold and resold, chopped down into smaller and smaller components. Now, here, this clue of her jewelry. It must lead somewhere, though not necessarily toward the destination he desires.

The bus crawls east on Santa Monica Boulevard, the haze descends with Eliot's inhale. Iris didn't disappear, he reminds himself as he wraps the drip rag around his fingers. Not entirely. In a closed system, matter cannot be created or destroyed. Even the poor bots crushed to death on Europa, their bodies pile up in the chasms between the rocks. They'll be dug up by future generations and picked apart for their components. Who knows what pieces of their souls will remain between the molecules of cadmium and iron? Maybe they'll wind up working those same mines again or maybe they'll be put on display in an antique store in Beverly Hills.

The bus stops for a police action on Doheny. Eliot takes another sniff from his rag and settles in for the ride.

TWELVE
The Gun Club

A target with a silhouette of Lorca hangs by two clips attached to
the pulley lines. Crosshairs centered on her face. Eliot aims at the
target while his brother looks over his shoulder.

"Relax your arms," says Shelley. "Look over the . . ."

Eliot fires.

"Good. Now try to line up . . ."

He fires again.

"Okay, don't pull at it. Just squeeze . . ."

Bang.

"Good."

Shelley slides the target back to the booth as Eliot loads another
clip. Not a single hole is close to the silhouette. Says Shelley, "That's
the worst shooting I ever seen."

Posters in the locker room read SAVE A LIFE—KILL A BOT and
UNCLE SAM DON'T SPEAK BINARY and THE ONLY GOOD METAL IS
DEATH METAL. This is where the Militiamen train, the trappers and
death squads who load up their vans for drive-bys on boozy Friday

nights during "the culling season." This is where every right-wing politician stops for a loop-op to talk about the Second Amendment and the right to "stand your ground." The staff checks for pulses at the door, and if they don't like what they feel, they'll check for a belly button instead of an outlet navel. Even a mechanical limb would probably get you thrown out, as Eliot is well aware.

"I took a job at *Revealed!*" Shelley says as he cleans his vintage Glock at a bench.

"Congratulations."

"Sports section, but at least it's a steady gig. They said if I want to get into hard news, I have to find my own loops. Capture something on my own and hope it goes viral."

Branes on the wall warn of android conspiracies and a government secretly run by The Bot. There are listings for survival classes to teach heartbeats how to protect their families, how to live in the woods like a guerrilla army, how to attack the power plants and cut off energy to the grid. For the Militiamen, it's just a matter of time before some reckoning in which the androids try to exterminate mankind. There's one bot for every four Americans, and on their radio shows and branecasts, the pundits use terms like *bopulation control* or *demographic management.* They sell camping supplies and materials for building your own bunker. They end their loops with a Roman salute.

"And you're confortable working for *Revealed!*?" Eliot asks. The paper has a nasty, right-wing tilt that came down hard on the boys' father. After his assassination, a *Revealed!* op-ed celebrated that Dr. "Frankenstein" Lazar was killed by his own monster.

"Their checks clear." Shelley shrugs as he puts the Glock away in its case.

Eliot gestures to the gun. "Can I borrow it for a few days?"

"What for?"

"Practice. I want to get better."

Shelley wrestles with the request before emphatically declaring no.

"Why not?"

" 'Cause you been actin' weird," he says as he locks the case. "First, you ask for my boat, then I offer it to you, and you ditch me in a brothel. Then I call for weeks to check up on you and hear nothing back. If it wasn't for that Gita chick in your office, I wouldn't have even known you were alive."

"I've been busy."

"Add to that the fact that you're sniffin' drip again, and I've got to be frank, Eliot, you got me a little concerned."

"I'm just asking if I can borrow the gun."

"I don't think you should have a gun. I don't think you're in any condition."

A couple of Militiamen look on from the next bench. Eliot speaks softly so they can't hear. "Shelley, if I wanted to kill myself I wouldn't need a gun to do it."

"Why don't you buy your own then?"

"Because of the drip busts," says Eliot. "I can't pass a background check."

"Then I'm breaking the law by lending it to you."

"All of a sudden, you respect the law?"

"I'm not giving you the gun."

"Fine," says Eliot. "Forget I asked."

"Let's."

Shelley takes the gun case with him as he walks to the counter to return the rented earmuffs and goggles. He leaves a box of nine millimeter ammo on the bench. Eliot smuggles the box into his pocket on the way out and waits for his brother by the car.

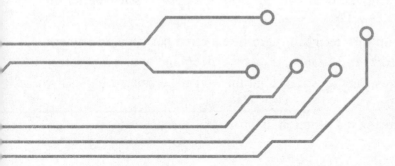

THIRTEEN
Pound's Antiques II

A customer on his way out holds the door for Eliot when he enters. A bell jingles as the door closes and locks. Eliot looks around to make sure he's the only one there besides Pound, who sits on a stool reading a newsbrane behind the counter in the back of the store. He wears a pink, herringbone shirt, French cuffs, no jacket, and his collar buttoned to the throat.

Eliot approaches and tilts his fedora over his face. "I'd like to make a purchase."

Pound looks up from his newsbrane and recognizes Eliot as the customer from two days before. "The Snapple bottle?" he asks.

"No"—*you smug prick*—"I'd like to buy an antique revolver."

"What kind of revolver?"

"One that shoots nine millimeter rounds."

"And you're set on a revolver?"

"Please."

Pound edges off the stool and reaches for his keys so he can open the display. "I believe the Smith & Wesson will suffice." He pulls the gun from beneath the glass and lays it on a velvet cloth. "They stopped making them in the '90's. Police departments preferred the .357s."

The weapon lies between them like a cross between an ancient tool and a child's toy. It appears to be a clean and well-kept instrument. Eliot suspects it would hold up well if he bashed it against Pound's head.

"I'm assuming it's functional?"

"Quite."

"May I?"

"By all means."

Eliot picks up the revolver and points it toward the wall. He opens the cylinder and gives it a spin. He closes it and pulls the trigger to feel the action and hear the click.

"Heavy."

"As it should be," says Pound. "The lightness of modern weapons belies their purpose."

"How much?"

"For two thousand, I'll throw in a new holster."

"Seventeen fifty if I pay cash?"

"Two thousand."

Eliot lays the gun back on the velvet cloth and removes his wallet from his coat.

"According to state law," says Pound, "I'll have to enter a retina-scan into the database for a background check."

"I'm aware," says Eliot. He counts the money as Pound gathers a holster from the back wall. "Also, I had another question about the jewelry."

"What jewelry?"

"The eyeball pieces with the red flecks." Eliot exchanges the money for the holster. "Where are they from again?"

"Japan," says the proprietor.

Eliot snaps the holster onto his belt and slides it to where it fits behind the small of his back. "The other day, you told me they were from India."

"They are from Japan," says Pound.

"Then why'd you tell me India?"

Pound rings up the purchase on a push-button register but the drawer fails to open. "I did not tell you India. I told you Japan."

"I remember what you told me."

"Well, clearly not, because I told you they are Japanese antiques that I bought at an estate sale in Bel-Air."

"What estate sale?"

He tries again to open the register drawer. "The seller wishes to remain anonymous."

"Then how can I verify their authenticity?"

Pound turns testily in Eliot's direction. "Sir, this is not a Hollywood pawn shop. This is Pound's Antiques on Canon Drive, and I am Arthur Hetherington Pound. I have been at this location for twenty years, and if you do not know or respect my reputation, then I do not require your business."

He stands an inch away with eyelids wide in a manner he must have used before to intimidate his clientele. Eliot can't help but feel a little embarrassed for being chastised—ridiculous since he knows the man is lying.

"I apologize," says Eliot, cooling the man's blood, even while his own is beginning to simmer. "I certainly didn't mean to offend you."

"Do you want the gun or not?"

"I do," says Eliot.

Pound gathers the money and turns back to the register. Eliot takes a quick look toward the front window to make sure no one's looking to enter.

"Do you sell ammunition?" he asks.

"Antique store," Pound reminds him. "Not a sporting goods store."

"Good thing I brought my own then." Eliot pulls out the bullets he grabbed off the bench at the gun club. Pound turns back to the counter and eyes the shaking gun as Eliot loads the first slug.

"What are you doing?"

"Got to make sure it works," says Eliot. He struggles to load a second slug.

"I told you before. It's fully functional."

"But you lied about the jewelry." He loads another. "What's to say you're not lying about this?"

"I'm not lying."

Eliot snaps the cylinder into the frame.

Pound holds the money in his hand like a horse gambler with a losing ticket. "I have to ask you not to do that."

"Go ahead." Eliot aims the barrel at a bead of moisture swelling on the proprietor's forehead. "Ask."

What a strange effect, thinks Eliot, it has on a man's attitude when one points a hunk of metal at his face. That he can barely hold the gun straight makes Pound all the more frightened. And Eliot, too. He feels as if he has entered some hastily abandoned country, lawless, with borders that aren't clearly defined.

Pound's lip trembles. His face is drenched in sweat. "There're eight thousand ingots in the cash register. Go ahead and take them."

"I'm not interested in the money," says Eliot, the gun tapping lightly against the target's head. "I just want you to answer some questions. Truthfully. I have a brane in my pocket that will vibrate if it senses you are lying. Do you understand?"

Pound's eyes dart from the muzzle of the gun to the front window behind Eliot's back and then to the muzzle again. Eliot can feel a layer of moisture form between the trigger and his finger.

"Now," says Eliot. "Do you or do you not carry parts for a C-900?"

"I do not."

"And the jewelry. The stones with the red flecks. Where'd you get them?"

Pound stutters. His neck fat wobbles above the collar of his shirt. His face reveals the flurry of thoughts racing through his mind.

"Tell me where you got them," Eliot says again. "If you lie, I will know, and I will kill you."

Eliot tightens his grip on the gun so it won't slip from his hand.

"He-he-he buys old vinyl," says Pound. "He fences things. He s-s-some-some-sometimes trades."

"Who trades?" Eliot asks. "What's his name?"

"P-P-P-." He tries to answer, but his yellowed teeth won't let the words pass. He tries to steady himself but knocks over a stool.

"Tell me his name," says Eliot, concerned that this is taking too long. A fresh jolt of pain slides from his shoulder up his neck.

"P-p-p-please . . ."

"Tell me."

"I-I-I . . ."

"Tell me his fucking name."

"Pink!" he blurts out. His body shakes; his breath short, a puff of snot ejects from his nose.

"Pink?" Eliot asks. "That's a name? Pink?"

"I-I-I don't . . . don't know . . . his real . . . his real . . ."

"His name is Pink?" Shit, that's not a name. That's just another bum lead. His shoulder throbs. His neck stiffens. "How do I find him?"

"I don't know."

"Tell me where he lives."

"Pl-pl-please don't hurt . . ."

"Tell me where he lives."

"He's so fucking beautiful."

"Tell me where he fucking lives!"

Eliot cocks the hammer of the gun, and Pound falls. He hits the floor grabbing for his collar. His body spasms in the midst of a fit. The squeals and wheezes are harrowing. His legs kick and his head smacks against the floor.

This guy ain't faking it, thinks Eliot as he backs away. I didn't even pull the trigger, and I might have killed him nonetheless.

Eliot turns and holsters the gun. He exits the store onto Canon Drive where he walks a full block before he hears the alarm bell ring. Keep it cool, he tells himself. Don't run. You're just a guy walking down the street. He hails a cab on Little Santa Monica and tells the taxibot to head east.

The car moves quickly onto Burton Way. Eliot looks over his shoulder to see if he's in the clear.

Pink, he thinks to himself. A thief named Pink. He bought vinyl. Must like music. A connoisseur and collector. Named Pink.

He feels the gun sandwiched between his back and the leather seat. His heart thumps so hard, he worries the driver can hear it.

Goes there to fence jewels and buy records. A thief, a musician, a trader. Likes music. Iris likes music, too.

He looks out the window onto the street. He knows he has heard this name before, this Pink, but where?

"There's an extra ten if you step on it," Eliot tells the driver.

Who names a man Pink? Who goes to an antique store? Trades new things for old. Knows jewelry and music and androids. He's so fucking beautiful.

Eliot reaches into his pockets. He doesn't even know what he's looking for, just digging around. He looks behind him to see if the cops are following.

Old vinyl. Old albums that only play ten songs. A collector buys vinyl. Someone old. A musician perhaps.

He checks his suit pocket again.

Night of the riots, the situation on Beverly. The homeless guy. Underground every Thursday.

"Can you please hurry?" Eliot asks.

"I don't want to get a ticket."

The flyer from the night of the riot. It was in his pocket. The suit his brother gave him. What did he do with the suit?

He tips the driver and rushes through his front door, charging past the living room and into the bedroom to his open closet. He looks through the rack until he finds the suit, wrapped in plastic, unworn since that awful night. Afterward, he gave it to the tailor-bot to dry clean and mend. There's a small envelope pinned to the hanger. Eliot rips it open. Inside is an empty vial of cologne, a drip rag, a couple of receipts, a card from that detective, and a braneflyer with a hologram turntable on one side. Eliot touches the turntable; it makes a scratching sound.

Underground every Thursday, it reads. Orpheus, Eurydice, and DJ Pink.

Eliot sits on his bed and puts the flyer down beside him. He touches the stubble on his chin and exhales seven weeks' worth of rotten air.

"Pink."

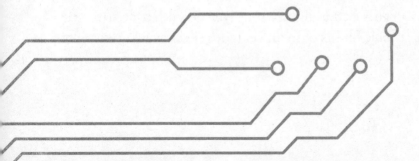

FOURTEEN
Underground

Thursday. Before midnight. Night of the underground.

Eliot holsters the gun in the small of his back concealed by the tails of a stiff shirt and a black hoodie zipped to his chest. He checks the mirror to make sure the hood can hide his face. Hasn't dressed like this in years. Hasn't been to an underground since college. Hopes he'll fit in.

He takes the bus past the river east of downtown. Rusted rails strut the streets half-buried in broken pavement. An occasional streetlamp flickers the way past the crumbling warehouses and a shanty town for homeless bots. Near the old, converted fire station, Eliot spots the first diggers drunk-straggling in their metal-weaved apparel. They arrive in groups, a mix of heartbeats and bots, indistinguishable from one another except for the girls in their belly shirts, showing off their outlet navels. It's a part of the body they'd usually hide, but not here, not tonight. Tonight is a celebration of bot culture, bot pride, a glimpse of their utopian vision of an android-dominated Earth.

The diggers espouse a theory, popularized by Eliot's father, that the generation of machines that will survive beyond the wake of human existence represents a "natural step" for mankind; that the first million years of human evolution was but a preface to the long tome of the bot; that the androids are destined for more important endeavors than that of providing cheap labor for capitalism. In Lazar's theory, modern androids embody a *stage* in evolution, but unlike their flesh-based ancestors, bots will be able not only to reproduce but also to redesign themselves to better master and alter their environment. As governments loosen their regulatory grip and unleash the progress of technology, as peak intelligence is breached, bots will receive hourly updates to their operating systems and will communicate trillions of bits of information to one another every second of every day. They will survive journeys of inconceivable length and time. They will build pyramids of immense proportions. They will be a species constantly in transition, evolving exponentially toward the ideal man God created in His own image.

Inspired by the dreamlike infinity of Lazar's vision, liberal arts–educated heartbeats join androids on nights like these to dance, drug, and fuck in defiance of social norms. Hiding from their parents, Militiamen, and police, the diggers gather to celebrate the heartbeats' fated extinction, the birth of a new species, the passing of the torch to a higher representation of intelligent life.

And yet there is another who also attends this naive bacchanal, one who arrives disguised in the clothes of the tribe, who might even appear as a leader, but who is, in reality, an opportunist for whom youthful idealism and the romanticism of rebellion provide the low-hanging fruit of his diet. He is whispered of and warned of by the attendees. They guard against him but admit they will not recognize him, *cannot* recognize him, until it is too late. He could be anyone, and this suspicion creates an anxiety that courses through the gathering. One could say that the presence of this Other, at the event, *spoils* the event, but one would more rightly say that without his presence, the event lacks that danger necessary to *drive* the event. One could even go so far as to say that if this Other did not exist, the organizers of the underground would have to create him, in rumor or actuality, so as to give the diggers something to risk once they're inside.

From across the street, Eliot hears the music and watches the colored lights strobing against the windows of the firehouse. A teenage boy pisses against a wall. Another throws up his dinner. Others sit on the curb waiting for their friends before they'll venture in. Music louder as Eliot nears. A line of diggers zipper-merges into the doorway, moving prematurely to a beat so simple, it's almost binary, almost the stripped-down form and essence of sound.

Eliot pays his admission and inserts himself into the feast of light and noise and bodies pushing against him. Couples tongue on the dance floor. Young girls sniff drip in the open. They wear shirts with the logo of the Android Disciples and hand out branes of wisdom by Lorca. They move like machines, clunky and dumb, imitating the bigoted depictions of robots from a hundred years of media, reclaiming this negative portrayal as kitsch, reinventing it as a mating call.

Eliot pushes through the throng, passing a bare-chested woman with flourescent breasts, her nipples covered in electric tape. He passes the whirling dervishes and a Hasid handjobbing a black bot. He pushes forward through bits and pieces of conversation between the scratches and clashes of music:

"You took too much."

"I love your hat."

"I'm gonna be sick."

"I never want this to end."

"I can't find Jaime."

Careful, Eliot thinks as the tempo builds. Don't give yourself away. Pretend this means something to you. Pretend that you belong here, that you're enjoying yourself here.

But Eliot isn't here to dance or get laid or sniff drip (maybe a little later) or experience whatever sweaty joys arise from rubbing against those who wear the same fashions or listen to the same music or choose the same way in a voting booth. He is not seeking some communal euphoria; he is looking for a tangible thing: a Pink. A person who can lead him to Iris. A guide who can carry him back to a time when he was en route to a destination and a life in which he could feel complete.

Weaving between bodies, Eliot can feel the low hum of the bass as it penetrates him. He can feel it expand. He pushes through the thick of elbows and perfume, stink and breath, through the devotees dancing before the DJ as if he were some Pharaoh overseeing his Egypt, as if the slides and scratches of his music revealed the subatomic wisdom of the universe, translated and beamed through the ear hole, to be understood for a fleeting moment until the sounds shift, challenging the audience's collective mind to embrace a new perspective.

The DJ looms above them. Tall with slender muscles, narrow hips, straight, blond hair, he stands erect above his turntables. He is a puppet master risen from the pavement of the city. The lights strobe and the shadows leap at his command. Ear in a headphone, hand on a lever, sounds changing, beats quickening, lasers beaming before his minions' eyes.

Is this he? Eliot wonders of the slender man violent with youth muscles popping, at the controls. Is this Pink or did I make a connection where none existed? Did I draw my conclusion more out of need than from the evidence presented? Is this Pink because I want him to be Pink, or is he empirically Pink?

A small digger girl, raven-haired with a jutting chin, sways before the stage in her metallic skirt. Eliot sees her exchange sideways glances and sultry smiles with the DJ. The pull between them flows through his hands and into the gears of his instrument. He digitizes their desire into exploding waves of light and sound, peak and trough, frequency and volume. The bass builds. The room struggles to contain the twisting time and folding space, the madness and paranoia Eliot synthesizes into a searing pain in his shoulder. And just when the pitch can sink no lower, the tempo can accelerate no faster, the volume can get no louder—at that precise moment that the DJ through his craft has tempered and arranged—in that moment when his acolytes can tolerate no more of the sound's cruelty, a pink strobe flushes the room to introduce a new drop to the rhythm.

The crowd hollers and stomps, screaming their approval. Some fall to the floor seizing in orgasm until their friends raise them aloft like sacrificial offerings to some primal, erotic god.

"Dance!" The order is shouted in Eliot's ear. "Come on, man. Dance!"

Eliot turns to see a girl with red dreadlocks swinging from the sides of her head. Her arms wrap around him in a wet embrace, leaving Eliot no choice but to let her movements determine the back-and-forth of his hips.

"I can feel you," she says, her lips against his ear, before spinning around and pushing her ass soft to his groin.

Eliot pulls her closer, feigning interest, all the while watching the man at the levers, all the while judging and measuring, trying to find some clue that will convince him beyond a doubt that this is the man worthy of his contempt.

"What's his name?" Eliot asks the dreadlocked girl.

"I can't hear you!"

"The DJ's name?"

A few songs later, there's a new artist at the controls, and Eliot watches as the man he believes to be Pink exits the stage accompanied by the raven-haired digger in the metal skirt. They carry his mixing board and a crate of old vinyl out the back of the building.

Eliot follows. He leads the dreadlocked girl through the exit behind them. He takes her into the alley and kisses her against the outside wall of the firehouse. He spins her around and presses his own back against the bricks allowing her to suck on his neck so he can watch the DJ and his girl over her shoulder. They load a white van with record crates. They lock the doors and hold hands as they romance down the alley toward the street.

"I have to go," Eliot tells the dreadlocked girl.

She protests between kisses, stumbling half-drunk and dripped out of her skull. Eliot opens the door back to the underground and guides her inside.

"You never told me your name," she says as the door shuts between them.

Eliot follows the DJ and his raven-haired digger down the dark, abandoned street as they walk to Charon's Diner. It's a wood and brass joint built to serve downtown hipsters during the neighborhood's revival, before its descent. Eliot follows the couple inside, careful to leave a distance between their entrance and his so as to remain unnoticed and invisible. He takes a stool at the counter and touches the menubrane to order a shake. Chocolate. Extra thick. The blender spins in the kitchen. He watches the DJ and the digger's reflection in a mirrored panel above his head. There's makeup on his eyes. His nails are painted, he might even have some lipstick on. Nothing much happens at their booth. Just a lot of hand-holding and gazing across the table. They touch fingers now and then, but it seems they hardly speak.

A botress brings Eliot his shake. He thanks her. He stirs it and takes a sip. He opens a newsbrane someone left on the counter and loads the latest update of *Revealed!* One of his brother's loops is featured prominently in the sports section. Eliot watches it as he waits.

A botwhore sits on the next stool. She's heavy on the perfume with glow-in-the-dark Dyna-Hair wriggling about her head. The moving wigs had been a trend a few years back though Eliot could swear they were out of style now.

"How's your shake?" she asks.

"Thick."

"You've hardly had a sip."

He puts the straw in his lips and sucks it down.

"That's quite an appetite."

"I'm all right," he tells her.

The botwhore turns and chats up a couple of diggers who didn't get lucky at the underground. She hits them with the hard sell; they haggle over price and leave together out the front.

In the reflection of the mirror above him, Eliot sees the DJ ask his botress for change. He settles the tab as the raven-haired digger stands to leave.

Eliot drops a twenty-ingot note on the counter and follows them out. He stands on the corner and watches the couple hold hands back toward the alley. He hails a cab in front of the diner and tells the driver to park outside the firehouse and wait.

The driver does as he's told. He's a rudimentary bot with hooks for hands and a square head that sits on a modular hinge. Old Indian metal, there's a cigarette dangling from the speaker that serves as his mouth. He takes a long, slow drag then sticks the loose end of his botcord into the plug for the cab's lighter.

The white van departs from the alley.

"Follow him," Eliot tells the driver, "but don't get too close."

The van leads the taxi across the river. They pass the stadiums, the old convention center, the corner bots selling drip on Alvarado. They pass MacArthur Park and the forbidding darkness of the bot city west of downtown.

"Don't be so obvious," says Eliot. "Let another car get between."

Eliot notes the driver's reflection in the rearview mirror. He's a sad, old bot with expired parts impossible to replace. Androids like he were a novelty before Eliot's time. Tourists paid double to ride with them, interrogate them about the city, flick coins at the backs of their heads while they drove. This was before there were enough of them to threaten heartbeat jobs, before they became a reviled eyesore to the newer bots disgusted by this reminder of their primitive past. The old ones work the late shifts now, the rough neighborhoods and unsafe beats. The only reason they survive is because their metal isn't suitable for scrap.

The white van pulls into the parking garage beneath the El Royale apartment building, a giant, deco mausoleum rotting from the roof down. Eliot has the driver pass the driveway and pull over by the lobby. He hands over an amount that's three times the fare.

"You never saw me," he says, and the driver is quick to agree.

The garage gate closes. Eliot pulls his hoodie over his head and checks to make sure no drones are above him in the sky. He exits the cab and crosses to the front door. Finds it locked. Looks through the glass. Sees the DJ and the girl enter the lobby from the door to the garage. Eliot knocks on the glass to get their attention. The couple approaches, and the DJ opens the door.

"What's up?" He blocks the building's entrance with a lithe arm stretched across the door frame. He's taller than Eliot and aggressive in his posture.

"I'm sorry to bother you, but I lost my key. I didn't want to buzz my wife and wake the baby."

"Right on," says the digger.

Eliot follows the couple into the elevator. Pushes the button for the top floor after the button for nine is already lit. Standing to the back, he watches the digger rest her head against the DJ's shoulder, watches them hold hands. Their fingers intertwine.

Did he hold hands with Iris, too? Eliot wonders. As they climbed up to her apartment on Normandie, were they together as a couple? Did he force his way in or did he seduce her? Eliot can see the tag on the DJ's designer street wear. Stylish. Young, but not so young that he lacks experience. Artistic. Good looking. Heartbeat. Iris was attracted to heartbeats, had heartbeat-envy, always talked about how she wished she had been a child so she could see the world through a child's eyes. Did she go with the DJ willingly or was there some ruse, some promise that pivoted into something else? Or is this another dead end?

The DJ and the digger exit at the ninth floor. The girl stumbles on the way out. Neither bothers to wish Eliot good night.

He waits for the elevator door to move then sticks out his foot to keep it from closing. He holds it open and gives himself a count of five. He walks out the elevator and slinks down the hallway following the sound of the digger's laugh. He peeks around a turn in the corridor to see the DJ fumble with his keys near the window at the end of the hall. So enrapt are they in their anticipations, they do not sense Eliot's peeking.

The DJ and the digger enter the apartment and close the door behind them. Eliot hears it lock. With the couple inside, he walks the length of the hall, stops at the door, and looks.

It's a door.

It doesn't tell tales. No secret reveals itself in the streaked brown paint of its surface or the brand of lock above the doorknob. It's no different from any other door in any other hallway in Los Angeles or anywhere else.

So what do I do now? Eliot wonders. Call it a night? Turn around and go home and lose another day in the search?

The door offers no advice nor does it know if the man behind it had anything to do with Iris's abduction. Eliot looks down at the filthy carpet and long hall leading back to the elevator. An open window to his right overlooks Rossmore Avenue nine stories below. Rain drizzles outside. Eliot walks to the window and leans out to see the light spilling through the blinds of the DJ's apartment. Looking down, he sees a ledge several feet below. It's sloping stone crumbles but appears capable of supporting a man's weight. And the window to the apartment is only a length away.

Have I come this far to be stopped by a locked door? Will it be any easier to pass when I return tomorrow, or might I not even get back inside the building again? Is this my only chance?

Eliot climbs into the window frame. He puts his foot on the ledge, tests it against his weight, and it holds. He puts another foot down and feels the brisk, damp air on the flush of his cheeks. The wind fills his hoodie. He shoos away a pigeon with his foot. He steps carefully from the window and toward the apartment. His palms and his chest brush the facade of the building as he shuffles slowly, sideways along the rain-slick stone. Face to the bricks, he edges to the apartment window. Carefully, he peers inside the living room at the dim, colored lights and the couch backed against a graffiti mural on the wall. The digger straddles the DJ's lap, licking his face, black panties showing beneath the metal skirt as her top comes off.

Eliot waits until they're too involved to notice before he shuffles past the living room, quickly, down the ledge past the window. Don't look down, he repeats to himself as a mantra. The stone cracks beneath his feet, but it holds. He approaches the window of an unlit room. He sticks a finger beneath the lower sash where a crack of space breathes between the window and the sill. He lifts the window open from without. He climbs across the threshold and steps down onto a plastic lining that covers the carpeted floor of the bedroom.

Eliot is inside now. He stands in the DJ's bedroom with the couple in the other room. The plastic lining cracks with every step. He takes out his pocketbrane and shines it about the room. There's a bed next to a closet with two doors made of wooden slats. There are restraints attached to the bedposts. There's an antique monitor and a video camera on a tripod. An album collection stands in floor-to-ceiling shelves and a phonograph on a table looks to be from the early twentieth century. More shelves are full of comic books and graphic novels that look like they've never been opened. Vintage posters from B-movie slasher flicks adorn the soft, soundproofed walls.

Eliot points his pocketbrane toward a desk in the corner of the room. He looks for a workbrane, something that might have information about Iris, but there's nothing there. Just a pad of unmarked paper, some colored pens, and a metronome. Everything in the room is from the last century as if the guy stole his furnishings out of the Smithsonian.

Footfalls approach from the living room. Eliot hears the digger giggle. He shuts off his pocketbrane and looks to the window but there's not enough time to climb out. He breaks for the closet instead, squats inside, and closes the doors behind him.

The DJ flicks a switch, and a lamp slashes red light across Eliot's face as he watches between the wooden slats of the closet doors. The digger slips off her skirt. Crouching beneath the clothes in the closet, Eliot watches the couple continue what they started in the other room. They fall on the bed and the headboard obstructs his view, but he can still see their legs wrap around each other. Nice legs on the digger. Nice feet with black nail polish on her android toes. He can't help but notice her toes.

They make out for a while. One on top, then the other. They move up and down, moaning, grunting, grinding their bodies together.

The DJ fingers her; she pulls on his cock. Eliot wonders how he's going to escape. Don't move, he tells himself, but all that squatting burns the muscles in his thighs. He has no choice but to wait until some opening presents itself. There's nothing else to do but wait.

The digger coos as the DJ guides her wrist into a restraint. He locks it shut, and she laughs.

"This is interesting."

He fastens her other wrist, and she pulls back to try its strength. It holds; he fastens her ankles. He pulls the straps tight to force her legs apart. She twists one way then the other. She tries to bring her knees together but can't, so her body makes its peace with being vulnerable.

The DJ stands. Pulls up his pants and puts away his erection. He turns on another lamp.

"Too bright," says the digger.

Behind the tripod, he tilts the camera toward the bed and turns on the monitor. It shines a blue square of illumination across the room.

"Oh, my God!" The digger laughs when she realizes he's filming. "I'm going to kill you!"

"Something like that."

Her image debuts on the monitor so that it appears the digger is looking toward Eliot through the vintage screen. Now he can see the scene from two positions: 1. from the closet, where he crouches behind the headboard, Eliot can see the DJ from over the shoulder of a bound android tied to the bed, and 2. on the monitor, Eliot can see from the DJ's point of view, looking down at this expectant android, in her panties, waiting to be dominated.

The DJ selects an album from his collection. He places the disk on the phonograph. He cranks the handle while the digger's image on the monitor shows her desire. Sometimes her eyes are open, watching, waiting, sometimes they close in frustration.

"Come on!" she says. "Stop teasing."

Eliot's thighs burn, his back stiffens, his cock hardens in his jeans. A jolt of pain travels along the seam of the old wound across his shoulder where the metal welds into his flesh. He feels behind him, his hand searching for a wall to lean on, but he can feel no back to the closet. He turns and sees the room is not a closet after all. It's too big. Yes, there are clothes hanging above him, but behind him, the space extends toward a high window above a standing cabinet. Beneath the window are rows and rows of lipsticks lined up on the shelves attached to the wall.

Lipsticks? Well, the fellow does wear makeup.

Eliot hears the bumps and hisses of a record playing in the bedroom then the first few notes of a piano. Then Enrico Caruso's ancient voice climbs sullenly above the static. The tenor croons an aria, *"Una Furtiva Lagrima,"* covering whatever noise Eliot makes as he sneaks farther into the hidden room.

"Come here," the digger says to the DJ. Inside the hidden room, Eliot shines his pocketbrane on the lipsticks lining the shelves against the wall. But on closer inspection, they aren't lipsticks after all. His body senses it, the nausea strikes before his conscious mind can process what he's looking at. Eliot sees that the colored sticks have nothing to do with cosmetics. They are pinky fingers. They are the pinky fingers cut from the hands of female bots.

"I want you," says the digger.

Eliot studies the fingers. He tries to make sense of how they're arranged and which, if any, belonged to Iris.

"I want you inside me."

There must be fifty of them. Most are on the shelf but some are tacked to the wall, pinned through the tip and stuck on a bulletin board. Perhaps their colors didn't fit the DJ's scheme.

"Stop teasing," she says.

And there along the wall, beneath the tilted window, one pinky has a shorter nail than the others. It's darkened by grit and dulled about the edges. It's the fingernail of a creative who did metal work with her hands.

"Pink," says the digger.

Eliot unpins the pinky and sticks it in his mouth. He tastes the astringent residue of Mun's factory on his tongue. The taste seems to correspond with the bacon-sulfur smell of that red liquid he stepped in when he visited Heron. It gives him a rush better than any drip he ever inhaled.

"Pink, stop."

It's her finger. Eliot can taste it. Eliot closes his eyes and bites down softly to secure it in his mouth.

"What are you doing?"

He sees an early century laptop open on a workbench, and judging by the blinking light, it was recently used. He touches the track pad and the screen turns on.

"Pink, you're scaring me."

It's a laptop with a flash drive, the kind crooks use to keep their records off the cloud—the kind that Pound sold in his store.

"Pink, that hurts."

The folders are marked: loops, inventory, buyers, taxes, receipts.

"Pink stop."

It's all there. Everything he needs to find Iris is there. Right on this . . .

"*Nooooo!*"

A loud snap breaks across the room followed by a scream. Eliot shuts the laptop. His head jerks back toward the bedroom.

Whoa.

No ecstasy in that cry.

Footsteps crack on the plastic-coated floor. Someone approaching. Eliot grabs a shelf and climbs toward the high window. He perches on the cabinet as the DJ pushes his hanging clothes to the side.

"*Help!*" comes a scream from inside the bedroom. "*Help me!*"

Eliot remains still. With a damp hood over his head and Iris's finger in his mouth, he holds his breath and stares at a spot on the wall.

"*Somebody! Help me!*"

Pink turns on a work lamp on the bench. He moves the laptop aside. Oil drips to the floor from the severed pinky in his hand.

Eliot can hear the headboard in the bedroom smack against the wall as the digger struggles to break from her restraints. Pink tacks her finger to a board upside down so the oil won't drip to the ground. He opens a large, wooden trunk and sorts through the various sharp-edged instruments in his collection. Squatting a few feet above him, Eliot watches him push aside an ax and a machete before settling on a radial saw. Like a reaper who found his most trusted scythe, Pink gathers the cord and kicks the trunk closed. He shuts the light and exits the wood slatted doors.

"No, no, no. Please, don't do this! Please!" the digger screams.

Eliot exhales the breath he was saving in his lungs and lowers himself to the floor. He uses his pocketbrane to find a small back-pack and zips the laptop inside. With the backpack strapped to his shoulders, he steps on the trunk and pulls the high window from its frame. He casts it aside and climbs the full height of the cabinet.

"No, no, no!" come the digger's screams.

Eliot sticks his head outside into the night. Looking down, he spots the ledge a full body's length below. Nine stories beneath that lies the sidewalk. The radial saw buzzes from the next room. Eliot can hear the digger scream. Her screams and the saw's buzzing should cover the sound of his escape.

Eliot rests his stomach on the cabinet and maneuvers his feet out the window. He lowers himself, holding on to the windowsill, and drops his body along the building's facade. His feet dangle but don't reach the ledge. He misjudged the height, and now the rain-slick stone lies a good eighteen inches beneath him.

The wind blows, the rain falls, a flying train approaches. Its head-light scatters a glare through the evening mist. Eliot hangs by his fingers from the window, his mechanical right hand supporting the bulk of his weight. His feet search for a toehold on the brick facade. The sill cracks and splinters in his hands. His body falls the full foot-and-a-half, and his shoes slip from the ledge. He grabs for the crease between the ledge and the wall. His chin bangs the stone. His nails dig deep into a crevice. He panics, bites hard on Iris's finger, and holds for dear life to the ledge.

Fast steel zephyrs through the damp air as the flying train passes. Eliot can see his shadow pronounced by the light. By his fingers and his chin, he pulls his chest onto the ledge as the train rushes by less than a yard away. Facedown on the rough, gray stone, panting, he hears the air whip past until its presence lessens, diminishes, then fades into the low rumble of the city.

Eliot stops to find his breath through his nose as his mouth is closed with the finger inside. He touches his face to the stone sagging beneath his weight. He gets up and presses his back to the wall. Now he can't help but look down, can't deny the height as he could when he was facing the other way. The vertigo quakes his limbs. Iris's finger in his mouth, backpack strapped to his shoulders, he shuffles toward the bedroom window. Get out of here, he thinks. Before the ledge collapses, before the fear cripples you to where you can't move. Get out.

"Please don't hurt me," says the digger inside the apartment. "I won't tell anybody who you are, I promise. Please."

Her agony follows him. He hopes to make it past her screaming, past the apartment, and back to the hallway where he can take the elevator down. The bedroom window, the living room window, the hallway window, then he's free. He has the laptop. If it doesn't contain the information he needs, he can negotiate for the computer's return. An antique piece like this is worth a bunch to a collector. Eliot can trade it back. But first, get off the fucking ledge.

The saw buzzes. The bot screams. Caruso sings on the phonograph. Eliot steps to the edge of the bedroom window. He hopes with the lights on bright the DJ won't see him passing outside. If he can make it past the window, Eliot will be in the clear. He shuffles his feet to get closer.

"Help me!"

Her scream sends a shock of pain from his shoulder to his feet. Don't look inside, he tells himself. You've got what you've come for, more than you expected. You've worked too long, looked too far and wide to get sidetracked now. No need to look through the window at what you're leaving behind.

The saw buzzes. The digger screams. Eliot peeks through the window to see.

Inside the room, Pink stands at the side of the bed checking to make sure his performance is being captured by the lens. He wears yellow goggles; his shirtless back reveals a giant, crosshairs tattoo. Logo of the Militiamen. The artist revealing the flip side of his identity.

"Please don't do this," the digger begs. "I'll do anything you want. Just please let me go. I haven't done anything to you. Please, God . . ."

But it's as if the bot's pleas exist at a decibel the DJ cannot hear. Once again, the saw roars. The digger screams. Pink lowers the spinning blade against her leg.

Eliot turns away. His breath fails him. A tremor shakes his knees. He reaches into his pocket for a vial of drip. His hand falters and the vial slips from his fingers. It dings against the ledge then sails with the rain nine stories down before bouncing with a plastic click against the pavement.

"*Help me!*" screams the digger. "*Please, God, help me!*"

Stop it, Eliot rebukes her in his mind. You shouldn't have put yourself in this position in the first place. What kind of tramp goes home with a stranger? Didn't your mother teach you better?

"*HELP!*"

Well, no, he answers his own question. Bots don't have mothers. They have factories that churn them out by the thousand. They're never taught these lessons about the dangers of human perversity.

"*Help me. Please, somebody!*"

But it's your own damn fault you're here, he tells her in his mind. Your own poor judgment. And even if I did try to help you, even if I did risk my life against that maniac, who's to say a week from now, a month from now, a year from now, you wouldn't put yourself in an equally inane position? Why should I risk my life saving yours when you act in such a reckless, careless manner?

The saw blade stops. Caruso sings. The rain sprays Eliot's cheeks. One foot sideways then drag the other behind it. Pass the bedroom window. Crawl inside the living room and exit out the front door. I'll be halfway down the stairs before the DJ knows he's been robbed.

"Help me!"

Good Lord, she's loud, thinks Eliot, but he decides her cries aren't real. She's just an actress in a loop yelling her lines. After all, bots aren't like us. They don't feel pain the way we do. Their hearts don't beat, they spin. They don't have souls, just parts and experiences that balance together to create an aura. This isn't really happening, Eliot insists. It's just the soundtrack from a slasher movie Pink's watching on his brane.

"Please, God. Please, somebody, help!"

The denial strengthens him; once again, Eliot can move his legs. He waits for the sound of the saw blade then slides his right foot to the center of the window. He shifts his weight and brings the left foot over. One more right-left slide and he clears the window. He stands on the other side with a clear path to the living room window, to the hallway and then he's free. The ledge holds, he has the laptop, and, Goddamnit, he's almost free.

"Please, God. Somebody help me!"

Is this how Iris screamed? Eliot wonders as he stands on the ledge a few feet from escape. Did she too call for help with no one there to save her? The cool metal of the pistol tugs from the holster in the small of his back. It reminds him of its presence. It reminds him with its hard, iron touch of the power held in its works.

"Help me!"

Eliot shakes his head. That's not what it's for. A gun can't save that android, a gun can't save any of them, and nor can I. I'm just one man—a lowly drip addict cowering on a ledge—I cannot save the oppressed robots of the world. I'm a lousy salesman, a working stiff, not some hero in a Hollywood movie. Even my father couldn't save them; the politicians wouldn't let him, the system's rigged, the market dictates, the mode of production determines . . .

"Help me!"

And he's filming it, whispers the gun.

What's that? Eliot asks.

He could have shut her down first. He could have turned off her power, made an incision with a scalpel, and removed her limbs while she slept. He could have made this painless for the bot, but he wanted to make a performance of her humiliation instead.

The metal teeth of the saw chew through the digger's limbs. The gun beckons. It urges an action Eliot continues to refuse.

"Please. God. Somebody. Please."

Eliot shimmies away from the window. He moves farther toward the living room. The farther he moves, the more faint her cries. A few more feet and they'll blend into the static of the city. A few more feet and the entire scene can be forgotten.

"Hold still," says the DJ, annoyed with the digger's cries.

Hold still? asks the gun.

The words singe into Eliot's shoulder like a branding iron meted to his skin.

Hold still, the gun repeats, mocking the audacity of the command. It's as if this maniac is a doctor or a barber cutting her hair— *hold still*, he tells her. Participate in your own torture. Make it easy for me, and *hold still*.

The saw buzzes. The digger screams. The gun speaks to Eliot's anger. It pulls on his tailbone and hisses to his soul like a serpent.

Isn't this why you took me here? asks the gun. For just such an event as this?

No, says Eliot. I brought you here to protect me, not to save some digger who got in over her head. The principal is Iris, not some random tramp from a party.

But is it possible, asks the gun, that there is some larger purpose that brought you here of which you were unaware? Those calls and cries for help, heard by no one except you, me, and the son of a bitch hurting her—is it possible some fate put you here with me in your holster for a reason?

"Help me! God, somebody!"

From the day you were conceived and I was manufactured, says the gun, all the way to this moment—is it possible we were joined for the purpose of doing something more than bearing witness to a cry for help? Is it possible the God for whom she calls has put us here by means of His machinations that we might *act* in this moment and *answer* that cry?

Caruso sings. The saw buzzes. The digger screams.

Or are we here to *hold still*?

"Help me. Somebody, please help me!"

Frozen on the ledge. His sweatshirt heavy and wet. His breathing labored. The gun burns like dry ice into the base of Eliot's spine. It pulls with a weight that anchors his feet to the ledge. With a careful hand, he eases the weapon from the holster and raises it before his cheek.

Thatta boy, says the gun.

I'm not ready.

You've practiced.

I'm a lousy shot.

Nothin' to it. Point and squeeze like Shelley taught you. The rest I do myself.

Iris's finger in his mouth, weapon tight in the palm of his mechanical hand, Eliot squeezes the grip and clicks off the safety.

You won't falter?

Been at it for years.

I never tested you. I don't even know that you work.

Smith & Wesson, baby. American classic.

But you're old, says Eliot. You've been sitting in a display case collecting dust.

That old queen in the antique shop seemed to think I'd work.

He steps carefully back to the bedroom window. His legs obey him now—or rather, they obey the gun. The singular purpose of the machine's design compels his body to carry out its will. The gun wants to shoot, *ergo* so does the man holding it. It weakens his argument against action.

Eliot slides along the ledge and ducks down to the opening of the window. He sees the walls splattered with oil, the bedsheet turned black, the DJ repositioning the spinning blade. The digger cries. Gun in hand, Eliot ducks low so the backpack won't brush against the window sash. He lifts one foot off the ledge and steps across the threshold.

"You're a fucking asshole," the digger yells. "You're a twisted piece of shit!"

Her amputated legs are wrapped and stacked neatly on the floor. Her arms remain attached, but the restraints are tight, cutting into her wrists.

"Piece of shit!" She spits in the DJ's goggles. He straddles her waist and slants the blade to the base of her exposed breast. He doesn't see Eliot approaching from the window.

"I hope you die," says the digger. "I hope you rot from cancer and die!"

Caruso sings. Eliot aims from his position. He lines up the sight. His arm outstretched. His hand shakes. He moves in closer for a better shot.

The DJ looks at the monitor to make sure his masterpiece is in frame. Caruso sings. The girl curses and pulls against the cuffs.

Plant your feet, says the gun. Point and squeeze.

The saw buzzes. "Help me!"

Now, says the gun.

The DJ touches the spinning blade to her breast. The teeth of the saw splatter oil across the room. The girl screams.

What are you waiting for? asks the gun.

Oil flies from her chest.

Shoot, says the gun. Goddamnit, shoot!

With the blade in the fold of the digger's chest, Pink notices a peculiar shadow stretching up the wall before him. He turns to the monitor and notes a third actor in his film, a specter in a black hoodie, extending a shaking gun toward his head.

Damnit, I told you to shoot!

Pink hurls the saw at Eliot, who ducks and fires at the same time. The saw misses and flies out the window. The digger twists and flops. Eliot fires again, but he's late. The DJ leaps from the bed and wrestles him for the gun. Their feet slip on the oil-wet plastic; the two men slam to the carpeted floor.

Outside, the spinning blade cuts into the brick exterior of the building. Inside, it pulls the cord taut beside the wrestlers' heads. Pink bangs Eliot's hand against the floor, and the gun falls from his grip. Eliot crawls for it, but the DJ pulls him back. The digger struggles against her restraints, stretching out her wrist as Eliot feels the blunt force of knuckles smashing the back of his head. His face collides with the floor. Blood clouds his vision. His weak hand grabs for the gun, but the DJ finds it first. He turns Eliot over and shoves the nozzle into his mouth, pushing Iris's finger to the back of Eliot's throat.

"Who are you?" he asks, blood and oil splashed in his made-up face. "Who the fuck are you?"

Eliot chokes on the finger, gagging as Pink yanks up his shirt to find a heartbeat's navel.

"You're not a total loss," says the DJ. "I bet I can get something for your arm."

He cocks the hammer on the gun. A loaded chamber clicks into place. It has betrayed me, thinks Eliot. Left me for a new master. All it took was a moment's hesitation, and now the machine has pledged its support for my enemy.

A small, hard object pitches through the air and nails Pink in the back of the head. He turns to see what hit him. He sees the legless digger had yanked free a hand, unscrewed her other fist, then hurled it at his head. Having hit its intended target, the little fist now rolls on the floor like an unexploded grenade.

The DJ scoffs at her impotence. He calls her a cunt as he withdraws the gun from Eliot's mouth and aims it across the bed.

"Your face is too ugly to sell anyway," he tells her. "It looks cheap."

He lines up the sight and closes one eye to aim.

But in the moment Pink pauses to watch the digger squirm, to enjoy another display of her suffering, Eliot grabs for the taut cord of the radial saw and yanks it with everything he has. Before Pink can fire a round, that same saw he used for his cruel dissection crashes through the upper sash of the window, flies across the room, and slices unencumbered through his extended arm. The limb thuds roughly to the floor, its hand still clutching the weapon. The saw races beneath the bed and hits the table with the phonograph, knocking the needle from the disk, and bringing Caruso's aria to an end.

Pink looks at the record player. He looks to where the gun should be. He sees his severed arm on the floor. Blood spurts from his shoulder, and now it's his turn to scream.

Eliot grabs him by the hair and slams his head to the floor. His rage gets the better of him. He straddles the DJ's chest and pounds him with his metal fist, raining violence on the eyes, nose, and teeth of his adversary.

"Where is she?" he asks, the finger falling from his mouth. "Where's Iris?"

Pink tries to block the punches but can't defend himself with only one arm.

"Help me!" he cries. "Help! *Somebody!*"

Free of her restraint, the digger reaches to the floor and grabs her detached hand. She screws it on as Eliot smashes the bones in Pink's face.

"A C-900. Red fleck in her eye. Where is she?"

"*Help me! Help!*"

"Normandie Boulevard." Eliot slams Pink's head into the pool of oil and blood. "You were at her house. You attacked her in her house!"

The DJ quiets as his life drips onto the plastic-coated floor.

"Where is she? Where are her parts?"

He stops defending himself. His face softens into a wide-mouthed sob. Eliot pauses his assault. Naked on the bed, the digger reattaches a leg as best she can. She clicks it into the oil-drenched socket of her hip.

"Where is she?" Eliot asks again.

The blood coats his clothes and skin. It's clumped in his eyelashes and hair. He searches frantically for Iris's finger and finds it beneath the corpse.

"Is he dead?" the digger asks. "You killed him, right?"

Eliot looks at the bot on the bed. Her parts and wires spill from her smart metal flesh. Her legs are on crooked and oil streams from her chest.

"He's dead, right?" she asks hatefully about the man with whom she was making love some twenty minutes ago.

Pink's eyes stare blankly at the ceiling. The symmetry is gone from his face. The pool of blood expands, widening to cover more floor. The walls are splattered, the bed is soaked, the light shines brightly on the scene.

"You were never here," Eliot tells her.

"Oh, I was here." She pulls on her skirt.

"You never saw me."

"I know." She tests her damaged legs. "You're invisible."

"Get out," Eliot tells her. "Get out of here now."

On mauled and crippled limbs, the digger lurches from the bedroom. She grabs her clothes and falls out of the room, out of the apartment, slamming the door behind her and leaving Eliot alone in the quiet slop of his massacre. Minutes pass. Eliot remains on his knees. The sound of the city bleeds through the window as the phonograph rotates with its needle off the disk.

Keep your head, he tells himself. Even if the neighbors heard something, it took two days for the cops to respond to a disturbance at Iris's. No reason it won't take just as long here. Be methodical. Stay calm and you have a chance. Don't do anything rash, anything stupid, you might even get away with it.

Blood soaks through his jeans. Oil on the walls. He listens for a siren or a knock on the door, but nothing comes. No one comes. At least not yet.

He rinses off Iris's finger in the kitchen and puts it back in his mouth. He finds a pair of rubber gloves in a cabinet beneath the sink. He finds rags and garbage bags. He finds a mop and fills a bucket with water and ammonia.

Eliot pries the pistol from Pink's hand and wipes it clean before returning it to the holster. He puts the gun and holster on the desk. He uses a sponge to scrub beneath Pink's fingernails and remove any DNA that might have collected there during the fight. He wraps Pink's severed arm in a towel. He wraps the body in the plastic coating from the floor and hauls it onto the bed. He removes the memory card from the camera and smashes it on the floor. He puts the pieces into two separate bags. He smashes the camera and throws its pieces into two bags as well. He takes out his wallet, his keys, Iris's locket, his pocketbrane and sets them all on the desk. He places Iris's finger beside the holstered gun. He takes off his bloodstained clothes and stands naked in his socks and rubber gloves, then puts his shoes back on. He separates his soiled clothes into the two bags.

Eliot wears the gloves and shoes in the shower as he washes. He scrubs the blood from his skin and washes it out of his hair. He picks his hair out of the drain and flushes it down the toilet. He looks at his cuts and bruises and covers the worst of them with adhesives he finds behind the reflective brane above the sink. He towels off and throws the towel in a bag.

Damn. That milk shake he drank earlier wants out.

He sits on the toilet and can't believe what comes out of him. He flushes twice and cleans the seat with ammonia. He pours ammonia in the toilet and scrubs it clean with a brush he leaves in the bowl.

He mops the floor in the bedroom, leaving everything wet with blood or oil on top of the bed. He mops the bathroom, rinses the mop in the tub, then breaks the stick. He throws the head of the mop in one garbage bag and the stick in the other.

He puts on a T-shirt and a pair of boxer shorts he finds in the DJ's drawer. He grabs a leather jacket and a pair of jeans from the closet; he has to roll them up so they'll fit. He takes his wallet, keys, and pocketbrane from the desk and puts them in the jeans. He grabs the locket and Iris's finger as well. He throws the gun and holster into the backpack. He washes the desk with ammonia. He wipes down the closet, the windows, and everything in the apartment he might have touched with a bare hand.

Eliot slaps one of Pink's baseball caps over his head, covers his face with a pair of sunglasses, and takes a pair of sneakers from the shoe rack. He walks to the living room and takes off his shoes and the wet socks he had worn in the shower. He puts on Pink's sneakers without letting his feet touch the ground. He throws his wet shoes and socks into two separate bags. He slings the backpack with Pink's laptop over his shoulders and carries the garbage bags out the door. He still wears the rubber gloves.

Eliot chooses the stairwell over the elevator. He waits by the backdoor of the building until a surveillance drone passes overhead. In an alley a few blocks away, he tosses a garbage bag into a Dumpster. He walks to another alley and dumps the second bag. He takes the gun from the backpack and pops the remaining bullets from the cylinder. One by one, he wipes them clean with Pink's shirt then kicks them into a storm drain. He wipes the gun clean then kicks that into the drain as well. He throws the holster in behind it. He takes off the rubber gloves and puts them in the backpack and walks up Vine.

On an almost empty bus rambling through the city, Eliot opens Pink's laptop and turns it on. He ignores the pictures and volumes of music and loops. He zips past the calendars and the gaming apps and finds a spreadsheet in a folder marked "sales." He takes Iris's locket from his pocket and types in the serial number.

The information card is laid out on a grid with the prices in a separate column:

Gender: F
Model: C-900
Buyers:

The son of a bitch listed the buyers.

Clothes—Aardvark Clothing
Jewels—Pound's Antiques
Pocketbrane—CS Electrics

It's all there.

Head—Jillian Rose Models
Arms—Uchenna
Torso—Chief Shunu
Legs—Tucson Metal Solutions
Eyes—Blumenthal Promotions
Loop—

Loop?
Eliot stops.
There's another passenger on the bus, a bald heartbeat lost in his newsbrane, staring at it through Coke-bottle glasses. The bus rolls north on Vine, noisy and loud. Don't watch the loop, thinks Eliot. No need to see her like that. Remember her from the time you spent together, the nights at the Hotel Café, the drives on Mulholland, the evenings beneath the Hollywood sign. Remember Iris in her apartment, working on her projects, her head swaying from side-to-side, dreaming about Avernus, imagining what the world looks like through a child's eyes.
Eliot clicks on the loop.
The screen shows Iris in her apartment, scared and hog-tied in her own bed. "Una Furtiva Lagrima" plays over the image of her terrified face. Her one brown eye with that little red fleck.
"Please don't," she cries softly to the camera. "Please don't hurt me."
Eliot reaches into his pocket and squeezes her pinky finger. He watches her face on the screen as the camera zooms to a close-up of her eye.

"Please," she pleads for mercy.

Eliot lowers the volume but listens as the bus emerges from the tunnel.

A machete blade crosses her face before it whistles out of frame.

"*No!*" she screams, and Eliot slams the laptop shut.

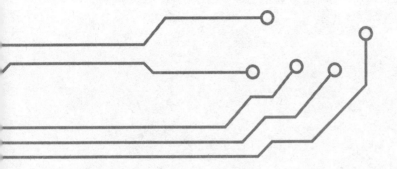

PART THREE

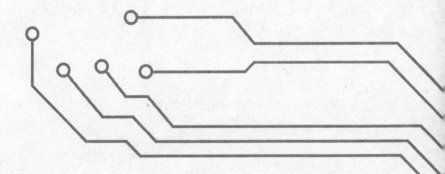

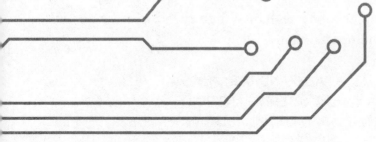

FIFTEEN
The Hunt

The story hasn't broken yet in the morning when Eliot reads the newsfeed in the reflective brane above his sink. His face is a mess. Lip swollen, cut knuckles, a shiner half shuts his eye.

Too wound up, Eliot hasn't slept a wink. He spent the night combing the Web for info on the buyers listed on Pink's laptop. He has a list and a plan. All morning, he has been waiting for the day to begin, for people to get to their offices so he can start making calls. The door is open now. Finding out what happened is no longer the juice; getting Iris's parts is. He has to grab them before they're sold a second time, before they're chopped into smaller components, if they haven't already been. He has to get every piece in one place, solder her together, and get his ass out of Dodge before the law catches up.

A pair of sunglasses covers the damage on his face. He slants a derby over his head and takes the bus to work. He's in a crowded elevator when he catches his first glimpse of the headline on a news-brane he reads over a woman's shoulder:

MUSICIAN KILLED AT EL ROYALE
SUSPECT AT LARGE

There's a loop of the raven-haired digger who went home with Pink. They even print her name:

ALEXANDRA PLATH
DM-6 SERIES ANDROID
CONSIDERED ARMED AND DANGEROUS

Sally, the secretarybot, greets him as Eliot passes her desk.

"Good morning, Mr. Lazar."

"Morning, Sally."

"Oh, and Mr. Lazar?"

"Yes, Sally?"

"Just got a call from Pete Maddox at Harris Farms. He wants to talk about an order for this year's harvest."

"Thank you, Sally."

"Oh, and Mr. Lazar?"

"Yes, Sally."

"Miss Santiago is in town and wants to know if you're available for . . ."

"Not today."

"Oh, and Mr. Lazar?"

"Yes, Sally."

"A Detective Jean-Michel Flaubert called from the Rampart Division of the LAPD. He left his number."

"Thanks."

Flaubert? Shit. Why is he calling? Eliot walks the corridor to his office wondering if he's already a suspect. Was I that sloppy, did I leave evidence behind, even after I spent all that time cleaning up? His shoulder stings as he takes off his jacket and hangs it on the back of his chair. He reminds himself it's common for police to call the offices at GAC. They call security when they've tracked a runner or a stolen bot. They call legal when some rogue bot commits a crime. They call all the time, in fact, though it's pretty rare for a homicide dick to ask for anyone in sales.

Eliot turns on his deskbrane and takes a seat. Tucson Metal Solutions was listed on Pink's laptop as the purchaser for Iris's legs. A Web search uncovered no e-mail or phone number, but the address matched the location of the Green Valley Recycling plant in Arizona. Eliot clips on his earpiece and tries his contact at Green Valley. The brane rings twice before Andy Spiro's sunburnt face appears on a screen.

"Lazar. What's with the glasses and the hat?"

"One too many last night."

"Too many cocks in your ass?" Spiro smiles, pleased with his own joke.

"I'm calling about a pair of legs scheduled for recycling. They didn't show up in your catalog, but I got reason to believe you have 'em."

Eliot relays Iris's serial number and waits as Spiro enters it into his brane. "I got nothing. You sure it's ours?"

"Sold to Tucson Metal Solutions," says Eliot. "Same address as your Arizona plant."

"Tucson Metal?" Spiro furrows his brow. "Maybe our labor provider contracted them out, but I've never heard of them."

"Who's the provider at the plant?"

"NatMo out of Detroit," says Spiro. "You want their number?"

"I got it. Thanks."

Eliot hangs up and calls Jaylon Dennis, a former coworker from Daihanu who, last Eliot heard, took a job at National Motors.

"What's up, Eliot?" Jaylon's half-open eyes had always looked peaceful, now they just look tired.

"You have kids now, don't you?"

"What gives it away?"

"You look like a corpse."

"And you look like a tranny hooker kicked your ass last night. What do you need?"

"I need to talk to someone at Tucson Metal Solutions. I think

NatMo might have subcontracted to them at the Green Valley plant in Arizona."

Jaylon rubs the bald spot at the back of his head. "I'm a little busy to be doing favors."

"I'll send you a lead."

"What lead?"

"An almond grower out of Fresno."

"I'll call you back."

Eliot's deskbrane carries live updates about the murder. *Revealed!* is stoking the flames. They're turning Edmund "Pink" Spenser into a saint victimized by a deranged, black widow android, murdering princely young heartbeats under the orders of Lorca.

At least the bot's the suspect, thinks Eliot. Not me. But then why is Flaubert calling? What does the detective know and what the Hell does he want with me?

He looks up the number for Jillian Rose Models, listed on Pink's laptop as the purchaser of Iris's head. He suspects this will be a harder get than the recycler. Once a modeling agency puts together a good-looking android, it tends to keep her in one piece to maximize the return.

He turns off the video and blocks the caller ID on his brane. He dials and a bot answers the call.

"Jillian Rose Models. How may I assist you?"

"This is Carlyle Sweeney from Ocean Cosmetics." Eliot adds an effete lilt to his voice and a sibilant "s." He takes the Sweeney from a poem he read in college. He takes the Carlyle from a hotel where he stayed as a kid. "I'm wondering if I can speak to Jillian Rose."

"May I ask what this is regarding?"

"We're looking for a new face for our pan-Asia campaign."

"You'd like to see our books?"

"Yes, books." Books? Must be some fashion term Eliot knows nothing about. "I'll be in your neighborhood later today. Is there a chance I can pop in?"

"I'll check Miss Rose's schedule."

Gita enters, and Eliot stumbles on the phone. "Can you just . . .

uh,"—he loses the lilt in his voice—"give Jillian Rose that message, and I'll be over at one."

He disconnects the call, pulls off his earpiece, and puts on his jacket.

"What happened to your face?" Gita asks.

"I'll be back in a few hours."

"Pete Maddox called from Harris Farms. He wants to talk about this year's harvest."

"I'll handle it."

"Pete and I have a good relationship. I'll call him if you . . ."

"I said I'll handle it."

Eliot pushes the button for the elevator. Again, he thinks about Flaubert. Was it the cabdriver or the botwhore at the diner who gave me up? The dreadlocked girl at the underground? Did a drone see me enter or exit the El Royale?

The elevator arrives. Eliot stands alone in the corner. Its descent seems too slow. Is it stuck; is there no air? He searches his pocket for a vial of drip. No, he stops, remembering there's a camera above. He wonders how *Revealed!* came up with Plath so quickly. The police will lock down bot cities looking for her. Sweeps through Heron, floaters patrolling the air. Searches at depots, docks, and airports. Adbranes flashing her image at every bus stop in L.A. And when they find her, she'll proclaim her innocence; she'll rat me out. And of course, she'll be telling the truth! Christ almighty, this is why I never should have bothered with her in the first place. I had the laptop. I had the information, and even if I didn't, I could have bartered for it. What did I get out of saving some trampy android when I know for a fact they're all doomed? Doomed! And still doomed. I didn't save her, I just delayed her death. That's what happens to bots. They're built, they work, they get recycled. That's what they're designed for, what they're built to do.

Sweat soaks his collar. His skin feels hot. He feels like he's suffocating from fumes. What was I thinking? I listened to a gun instead of my head and now I'm going to pay with my life. And with

Iris's life too because if I'm not here to save her, I can be damn sure no one else will. And what the Hell is taking this elevator so long?

The doors open, and Eliot runs out quick-breathing for air. He flees through the security doors and vomits in the bushes outside the building. He wipes his mouth with a drip rag and sees the Sat-ine 5000 arriving for work. The security bot stands before the building entrance and stares.

"I'm fine," says Eliot. "Just a hangover."

The bot doesn't move.

"Go to work, Tim. I'm fine. I'll be fine."

How much time do I have? Eliot wonders on his way to the bus. Enough to put Iris back together again before they arrest me? Enough to gather her parts? And once they catch me, do I have a defense? After all, what did I do that was so terrible other than fight off a sadist who was trying to kill me with a radial saw? Of course, the courts won't see it that way. Hard to argue self-defense after you sneak through the window of a man's apartment and point a gun at his head. Better not to think of it, he decides. I haven't been arrested yet. I'll cross that bridge when I get there. To worry about it before then doesn't help. Focus on the mission. Get those Goddamn parts, get on a boat, and go.

Seated on the bus, he opens a style blog on his pocketbrane and browses through the ads. Fashion was never Eliot's thing, but he needs an outfit that will make him look like Carlyle Sweeney, marketing director for Ocean Cosmetics, not some android salesman from GAC.

A call comes in. Jaylon Dennis from NatMo. "Tucson Metal is the private contractor we hired to run the company store for the bots working at the Green Valley plant. I sent you an e-mail with a contact who will answer your call."

"Got it."

"And your end of the bargain?"

"Pete Maddox from Harris Farms out of Fresno," says Eliot.

"There's an almond harvest, and they need pickers. It's good for about two hundred androids for a one-month lease."

"Thank you kindly."

A salesbot at Barney's shows Eliot a brown fabric with a wide check pattern in pink and blue. Nice material. Soft to the touch. Costs a bloody fortune, but Eliot isn't going to skimp.

His pocketbrane rings with another call.

"Yes, Sally?"

"I have Detective Flaubert on the line from . . ."

"Tell him I'm unavailable."

"It's the second time he's . . ."

Eliot hangs up.

In the dressing room, Giorgio the tailorbot speaks with an Italian accent. They do that in retail, try to enhance ethnic characteristics so that heartbeat customers feel they're dealing with exotic salesmen. Unfortunately, most labor providers do a half-assed job. It's abundantly clear, at least to Eliot, that Giorgio is Pakistani metal. His skin's too dark. Accent more French than Italian. Probably made by Ahmad Motors. Just another sign of how the big stores are cutting back during the recession.

"Ze seamstress can have ze clothes ready right away, Meester Lazar."

Eliot stands in his shorts on a podium while a reflective brane scans his body.

"I want a European cut," he tells the bot, "and I want to see it with a pink shirt."

"What kind of collar for ze shirt?"

"Spread."

Over his reflection, the suits appear on his body with a pink shirt.

"Zis is Aleece Zambos. Zis is Kareen Johnson, ze Nunez, ze Jordaigne Seay . . ."

"That one," Eliot decides, if for no other reason than he knows it's nothing like what he'd normally wear. "Now show me some ties."

"Zis might work as well with ze scarf."

"Ties," says Eliot. "And I'm going to need new shoes and sunglasses, too."

"Do you have ze brand you prefer?"

The brane flashes different pairs over his eyes. Eliot waits for something oversized and gaudy that will cover the bruises on his face.

"Those," he chooses, and within fifteen minutes, the clothes and glasses are ready. He puts them on in the store and folds a pink pocket square into the jacket. He even buys a pair of pink socks to complete the look.

Tucson Metal Solutions. Hurrying to his appointment at the modeling agency, Eliot reads Jaylon's e-mail off his brane. He calls the number and gets a surly desert rat with a cowboy accent. He asks, "You run the company store?"

"Who's askin'?"

"Jaylon Dennis from NatMo told me to give you a call."

"That don't answer the question."

"I'm looking for a pair of C-900 legs," says Eliot. He reads off Iris's serial number. "You have 'em?"

"You still ain't tole me who ya are."

"I'm someone willing to pay a lot of money for a pair of legs."

There's a pause on the other end. "Well, lotta bots lose their legs at Green Valley. If I'm short on replacements, I'll lose the contract."

"What's your price?"

The rat quotes a price.

"Done," says Eliot. "Hold on to them. I'll pick 'em up this week."

3-D holograms of eyeless modelbots traipse back and forth in the waiting room of the Jillian Rose Modeling Agency. Eliot sits on a stark, white couch reading *Revealed!* He hears a female smoker's voice chanting a mantra from another room:

"Yes, I am young. Yes, I am beautiful. Yes, I am thin and popular and kind. . . ."

In the newsbrane, there's a special report on the dangers of the "underground orgies" that led to Edmund "Pink" Spenser's death.

Sex and drip-fueled bacchanalias, claims *Revealed!*, run as propaganda ploys by Lorca.

"Yes, I am authentic. Yes, I am talented. Yes, I am deserving of my money, success, and fame. . . ."

A gaunt bot with a pixie haircut enters from the office kitchen. She wears a short skirt and carries a latte with foam turtling above the brim.

"Mr. Sweeney?"

"Yes?" Eliot answers to the made-up name.

"Jillian Rose will see you now."

He follows the bot down the hall closer to the source of the chanting. "Yes, I have friends. Yes, I am worthy. Yes, I am important and hold power over my life. . . ."

Eliot enters to find a grossly overweight woman with multiple chins seated behind her desk with eyes closed, legs crossed, and fingertips touching as she chants. He watches the bot take a half-full latte from the desk and replace it with the one she was holding.

"Yes, I am lovable. Yes, I am needed. Yes and yes, my life is filled with yes!"

The bot's gone before Jillian Rose opens her eyes to find her fresh drink. From her expression, Eliot suspects she thinks it was the chanting that filled the cup and not her bot.

"Okay," says the woman who never has to drink from the bottom half of a latte, "*love* the shirt."

"Don't you, though?" Eliot brings the lilt back to his voice, doing his best impression of Pound.

"I do."

"And the socks?" He lifts his foot to show the matching pink.

"Cut it out."

"Too much?"

"You're too much." She tests the temperature of her latte but feels it's still too hot to drink. "So you're that Sweeney guy, right? The one from Ocean Cosmetics?"

"That's right."

"And you want Asian female?"

"I want Latin male, but this is for work, not for me."

Jillian Rose snorts as she laughs at what Eliot thought was a mediocre joke at best. She waves a hand over her desk calling forth the hologram faces of Asian models to rise from the surface. All of them are eyeless and severe. Beautiful but empty. At Jillian Rose's touch, their floating heads spin 360 degrees.

"Cute," Eliot says of the first. "Gorgeous" about the second. "Stunning" about a third. He conceals his disappointment that none of them is Iris.

"The factories can't churn out beauty," says Jillian Rose. "That's why we search it out on the street. We look for that rare accident, the flaw, the beautiful mistake. Our scouts and buyers scour the world for quality parts. Everything but nipples and pussies of course. We buy a part here, trade a part there, and put 'em together into something we can show."

Eliot has to ask, "Your models have no vaginas?" At work, he had heard about manufacturers who turned out torsos with missing genitalia, but he always assumed it was an old wives' tale.

"Saves time on the digital editing," says Jillian Rose.

"Seems a bit extreme."

"Ah, but it gives the girls an aura that shows up in the work. They're sexy but sexless. Beautiful but unattainable." Jillian Rose burns her tongue on the latte she can't wait to drink. "As for the eyes, we can always throw a pair in. Choose a color to go with your bot, though it's *de rigueur* to leave them blind."

Eliot looks back at the faces hovering above the desk.

"No vaginas," he mutters to himself.

"Those things only get 'em in trouble anyway. Now if only I could sew up their mouths so they wouldn't suck cock."

"Honey, if only you could sew up mine."

Again, she snorts her laugh, covering her mouth with a chubby hand.

"Where are the older ones?" Eliot asks, brushing away a hologram image with a flick of his wrist.

"Looking for something more sophisticated?"

Jillian Rose touches a folder marked "Over 21." The first model to appear looks like a fifty-year-old Japanese businesswoman. She has gray hair and the look of an eyeless executive running a Fortune 500 company. The next one is a typical girl next door, the kind of woman you'd marry, if you wanted to marry a sexless, eyeless android.

"There are a few boutiques who still use heartbeats," says Jillian Rose, "but what you get with the bots are girls who know how to behave. First sign of trouble, we reconfigure 'em with new parts to change their auras. They usually come out nicer, though sometimes you get another rusted cunt."

A model's image appears above the desk, and Eliot's hand clutches the armrest on his chair. His heels dig into the carpet as if his body recognizes her before his mind can confirm it. The face floating a foot away has no eyes and the expression isn't one Eliot has ever seen from Iris before, and yet something in him insists it's she.

"Her," says Eliot, forgetting his lilt and every affectation he had put on to sell himself as Carlyle Sweeney.

Jillian Rose puts down her cup and gulps the hot liquid in her mouth.

"Really?" Jillian Rose asks. "Are you certain?"

No, he isn't certain. His gut tells him one thing but his mind feels as if it's not quite her. It could be a face made by the same manufacturer but with a slight variation.

"Why?" he asks. "What's your hesitation?"

Jillian Rose touches a floating icon and the image of the model appears full size as she catwalks in a circle around the room. She's taller than Iris, with longer limbs and a longer torso that makes her head seem small. Her outfit changes as she walks. Winter coat. Spring dress. Bikini. Autumn sweater.

"We call her Yoshi," says Jillian Rose. "Short for Yoshiko. Assembled a little old and sad if you ask me. Clients have been disappointed with her aura. She's at a fitting now for a show she's working tonight. You're more than welcome to come, though I have to tell you, I have her scheduled for reconfiguration in a week."

He's just in time then. A week later and she would have been rechopped or shipped off overseas.

"Look, I'm all for girls being a little bitchy," says Jillian Rose, "but this one is just plain out of hand. If you like her, I'll keep her together for another job, but then I've got to swap some parts."

Eliot watches the hologram circle around the room. He reaches out with his hand, but the image evades his touch.

"What's her make?" Eliot asks.

"XR-20 torso with TK-3 and C-900 parts. Of course, all our components come from licensed brokers and trappers. No viruses or worms. No counterfeits or illegal chops."

"Which licensed brokers and trappers?"

Jillian Rose reads off a list. "W and A Collections, Frey Metal, Grab and Snatch, and the rest comes from . . . Oh. Hm." She scrunches her eyes at the brane. "Baby, are you sure this is the android you want?"

"Why?" Eliot asks. "What are you hiding from me?"

"Nothin'." She wipes the foam from her lips.

"Jillian Rose." He says her name with a flirty smile as if he's chastising her. "No secrets."

Her chins jiggle as she cackles like a teenager with a crush. She looks around the room then leans across the table, smiling salaciously to beckon Eliot near. "I hate to talk out of school," Jillian Rose whispers, "but have you read in the newsbranes about the killing last night? The DJ who was murdered at the El Royale?"

"What about him?"

"Truth is he was a trapper. Called himself Pink 'cause he kept the pinky fingers of every bot he took."

"So?"

"So"—Jillian Rose lowers her chins and raises an eyebrow—"let's just say we've been contacted by police."

She leans back into her chair, pleased with herself that she was involved, however tangentially, in a scandal.

"Not that I know anything," she admits with disappointment. "Probably one of Lorca's crew. You know how they feel about trappers. Shame, too. Pink had great product. And he threw these fabulous parties in . . ."

"I like her," says Eliot, cutting the story short, "but I'm concerned about the aura. When can Yoshiko and I meet?"

Jillian Rose leans forward and checks the schedule. "She'll be walking at the Standard tonight. I'll get you on the list. And remember, if she turns you off, I got plenty of other bots."

Her assistant enters the room. "Ms. Rose? I have that new looper on line two."

"Hold on, Carl." She turns from Eliot and takes the call. "Bruno, the new loops are outrageous! How'd you get such a good snarl out of Molly?"

Eliot's own pocketbrane vibrates with a call from the office. He puts in his earpiece and exits to the hallway to talk.

"What's up, Gita?"

"Hold for Detective Flaubert."

"Gita, no!"

Too late.

"Mr. Lazar," says the polite voice on the other end, just before it breaks into a hacking cough. "This is Detective Jean-Michel Flaubert from the Rampart Division. We spoke last week if you recall."

"I recall," says Eliot. "How are you?"

"Quite well and thank you for asking."

"How can I help you?"

"I was wondering if you wouldn't mind coming down to the precinct today. As soon as possible if you don't mind."

"It's not a good time," says Eliot. He loosens his tie and undoes the top button on his shirt. "May I ask what this is about?"

The old detective clears his throat before imparting the news.

"We found your car."

SIXTEEN
Rampart Division

With his back to the blinds, the old detective blows softly into a hot cup of tea only to fall abruptly into another coughing fit. Each rib-shaking hack feels like a failed attempt to dislodge the tiny pieces of glass from where they've cut themselves into the tissue of his lungs. He waits for the fit to subside then uses a handkerchief to wipe away the black ash collected on his desk. That's what's coming out of me, he observes. It's what's coming out of my pores when I sweat. The by-product of the androids' energy needs. I am choking to death on robot excrement.

He wipes his face then checks his watch. Half past six in the evening. The precinct has been abuzz since morning when a Militiaman acquaintance discovered the body of Edmund "Pink" Spenser butchered in his apartment a block from Hancock Park. The newsbranes liked the story right away. After all, there are heartbeats in Hancock Park, most of them wealthy, many of them politically connected. The *LA Times* published two loops of the victim on its cover: the first showed him skateboarding with his shirt off, rippling muscles and shaggy blond hair—a sun-drenched idyll of the sunshine state; the second showed Mr. Spenser with his face bashed in and his arm severed at the biceps.

The day pressed on, the story got the mayor's attention, which got the chief's attention, which got the attention of every Tom, Dick, and Mary with a badge, a gun, and a pulse. Lest the city convulse into a spasm of revenge killings, the brass needed a perp posthaste, i.e. they needed a bot.

Luckily, those same newsbranes that broke the story were quick to provide a suspect. It was *Revealed!* that came up with Plath before the department even knew who she was. According to the tabloid, the female digger was an assassin, an Android Disciple trained in the art of seduction, sent to murder innocent young heartbeat boys at the behest of Lorca. Detectives assigned to follow up discovered Plath was absent from her job at a Melrose clothing store where she was employed via a labor provider. Witnesses from the underground saw her leave the firehouse with Mr. Spenser. A botress at an all-night diner remembered serving both Plath and Mr. Spenser at the same booth. As if that wasn't enough, the crime scene was littered with screws, hinges, and other parts easily traced back to the serial number listed in Plath's employment file.

Once the police brass confirmed the findings of the least credible newsbrane in Los Angeles and declared Plath the main suspect in the case, all that remained was to find her. The order was given at the briefing: Find Plath. Dead or alive. Dismissed.

But Flaubert is not convinced.

A small, female retailbot wins a bout of rough and tumble with an experienced trapper? (Yes, the department knew Pink was a trapper. The newsbranes may not mention it, but detectives saw the collection of pinky fingers in Mr. Spenser's closet. They found the weapons he kept in his trunk and the tripod he used for his cinematic endeavors.) And what of the open windows and the bullets in the wall? And why did Plath meticulously clean the scene but leave her spilled parts behind? Did she want to get caught? Was it she who left a scrubbing brush in the toilet? Why clean the toilet if you're a bot and you don't leave DNA in your feces, or even create rectal feces at all?

"A heartbeat did this," said the old detective after a cursory look at the scene, but nobody wanted to hear it.

"Plath," said Lieutenant Byron, who has a penchant for economy in his speech. "That's an order. From the top. Don't fuck around."

Back at the office, Flaubert leans into his deskbrane and reviews the notes on some of his more promising leads. Crazy Timmy Jones left the group home where the judge had him committed after his release from the ding-dong. He is known to frequent the undergrounds and sample the designer drugs that could have inspired him into a limb-slicing rage. Then there's Little Joffrey Birkmeyer, the cardsharp, but his is more the lounge scene, not so much the kids with their politics and their bots. A rival musician claims Mr. Spenser sampled his music without paying a royalty. He could be responsible. And so could that drip-addled couple, Alan and Jenny Something-or-Other, a pair of CIs who live in the El Royale. They're late on some payments to their dealer, but the fact that no money was taken from the scene should absolve them of a motive.

And then there's Eliot Lazar, the young lover whose C-900 girlfriend disappeared eight weeks ago. Narcotics has a file on him. There's a spot off Alvarado where he buys his street grade and a girl on Beachwood Canyon who used to sell him his sweet. No one in the department saw any need to arrest the poor lad over his habit. Hadn't he suffered enough, watching his father and sister burn to a crisp when he was fourteen years old? The explosion left him with a mechanical arm that causes him excruciating pain. That's why the drip, Eliot told the arresting officer in New Hampshire, but Flaubert suspects it runs deeper than that. Didn't Eliot imply as much the last time they met? The pain of helplessness in the face of tragedy. The need to dull his emotions. The want of a habit to escape from too much longing for the family then the lover he lost.

It's bad if it's Lazar, thinks the old detective. It's bad because I let him go. Twice. I didn't have him pegged as the violent type. My gut was off, my sixth sense, my trained detective's eye. I was thinking too much about Lorca, the bigger game, and I couldn't sniff out the killer in front of me. Of course he wasn't a killer at that point, was he, and maybe still not now. I'll have to dig a little deeper to see.

A drop of water lands on Flaubert's shoulder. He looks up at the pool collecting on the ceiling tile above his head. Will that ever get fixed? He used to complain about it to maintenance, but he eventually gave up and learned to accept the damage—to admire it for its persistence. It has grown from a little water stain to a minor leak to a catastrophe waiting to happen. Will I be here, Flaubert wonders, among the living when it finally expresses itself as a burst pipe drowning the building in a flood of water? Or will the cough kill me first thus making my concern about the pipe irrelevant?

"Jean-Michel," Ochoa calls from the door. "Your botlover's here."

The old detective dons his hat and coat. Through the hall, he passes a gang of rogue bots chained together as they're led to a holding cell. He passes the interrogation booths with their muffled screams, checks a still-empty mouse trap, and tips his hat to a streetbot who blows Flaubert a kiss. Outside in the parking lot, he sees the young man waiting in the rain with a gaudy pair of sunglasses covering his face.

"Good evening, Eliot. Good to see you again."

"You found my car?" The young man cuts to the chase.

"Weeks ago, as it turns out. Call it a bureaucratic snafu." Flaubert leads him through the lot. He chooses not to comment on the young man's pink socks and shirt though he recognizes it's not the typical uniform of a salesman working for a labor provider. "Your car was abandoned after a drive-by in Inglewood. Assailants in black bandanas. Bots no doubt. Android Disciples we assume. The anti-gang unit wanted to hold the car as evidence, but there was never a case. Instead"—he coughs into his fist—"your car became a part of our undercover fleet. I worry it may have served some recreational purposes as well, what with all these budget cuts no one can afford his own vehicle anymore. Would you hold it against a patrolman if he may have taken his wife out for dinner courtesy of yours?"

"Does it run?" Eliot asks.

"See for yourself." Flaubert hands over a set of keys cut by the department's lockbot.

Eliot ignores the bullet holes that syncopate the driver's side doors. He jumps in and starts the engine. The window is open, and Flaubert leans in as Eliot adjusts the seat.

"Are those bruises on your face?" the old detective asks.

"Bar fight," says Eliot.

"Which bar?"

"You looking for a place to drink?"

"Might I ask while I have you here"—the old detective notices the split knuckles on Eliot's hand resting on the steering wheel—"have you had any luck finding that friend of yours who went missing?"

"No." Eliot impatiently checks his watch. "Not yet."

"I only ask," says the detective, "because there's this trapper fellow who fell afoul of a radial saw last night. Turns out he has quite the inventory. Forensics is looking now—I thought if you give me the serial number of that bot you're looking for . . . Well. You never know. Maybe some of her parts will turn up in his closet."

Eliot adjusts the rearview mirror, then the side mirror, then the rearview mirror again. "I don't have her serial number on me," he says, "but I'll call you with it when I get home."

"Please do," says the old detective. He backs away and tips his hat as the window rolls up. He stands in the rain and watches the car speed from the lot in a hurry.

SEVENTEEN
The Standard

Eliot cranes his neck out the window to see if there's a drone following his car. There isn't. Not yet anyway, none that he can see. He feels it nonetheless, the unsettling sensation of being watched.

He puts the car on autodrive so he can dig a vial from his pocket. He checks the rearview and wonders how the old detective fingered him. The hoodie should have been enough to hide his face unless the drones were able to follow him from the El Royale all the way back to his apartment. But so quickly? With all the budget cuts and the depleted tax base and a police department in disarray? Half the cams don't work, and there isn't the manpower to sift through the footage. No way they could put together a case in so short a time. If Flaubert actually had something, there'd be an arrest already and not that chickenshit move he pulled in the parking lot. Probably called me in to rattle my cage, thinks Eliot, force me into a mistake. He's throwing noodles against the wall to see if anything sticks. Keep your head right, Eliot tells himself. Don't be a sticky noodle.

The car crawls forward in the rush-hour traffic. Eliot throws the radio on. Three windbags on NPR discuss the epidemic of bot crime in the wake of last night's murder. A female liberal with a shrill voice blames it on corporate greed.

"Mass pollution. Food and water contamination. Income inequality. This is the result of our free market approach. It's supposed to create a stronger economy, but blue collar heartbeats can't compete for jobs. Instead, they turn to crime and bigotry, which leads to the kind of retaliations we saw last night in Los Angeles. If government doesn't create an economy that provides opportunity for androids and heartbeats alike, we are headed for a massive crisis."

"Androids need to be kept in their place," says the conservative on the panel, "and rogue bots should be dealt with as quickly and harshly as possible. That's the role of government, not meddling in the private sector. As for unemployed heartbeats, they shouldn't have to compete with androids for work, they should be creating opportunities for themselves. With all the cheap labor available, with all this access to capital, the only reason a heartbeat can't make a living is because he's too lazy or entitled to take advantage of the market."

Says the academic, "But the crisis is already here. It's now. No longer can we survive without the bot. We have lost the skills needed to run a modern society and ceded them to the machines. Who on this panel knows how to build an engine or a brane or even a machine for vacuuming the floor? My God—even if we did want to exterminate the androids, what a brutal and horrible thing! We would have to build new bots to destroy the bots we already built. And this of course would begin a cycle from which we can never escape. No, I say the time is already here to embrace revolution, to tear down the current ideology and break with . . ."

No, no, no, you have it all wrong, Eliot wants to scream. No android killed an innocent heartbeat last night in Hollywood. You have no idea what happened, and even if you did know, you'd probably draw the same stupid conclusions.

He turns off the radio and sniffs the rag. He tells his car's stereo to play "Una Furtiva Lagrima" with Enrico Caruso singing.

"Would you like to buy the song," asks the car's computer, "or download it illegally?"

"Steal it."

"The whole opera or just the song?"

"Just the song."

"Shall I recommend other songs you might . . ."

"Play the fucking song."

The car's computer pauses long enough for Eliot to feel that pang of guilt one feels after cursing at a machine.

"Now playing 'Una Furtiva Lagrima,'" says the computer, "from the opera *L'Elisir d'Amore* by Gaetano Donizetti."

It's the song from last night's dance with Plath and Pink. It's been stuck in Eliot's head all day. He turns up the volume and gets into that drip again. He requires it to dull the fear that he's running out of time. Time to save Iris, time to save himself, time before the inevitable war between machines and men.

The drug sinks its fingers into Eliot's brain and redirects the neural pathways like some great urban planner disconnecting the roads and reattaching them to better the traffic flow. Suddenly, his car glides unencumbered. The song plays, and Eliot imagines himself on the ledge again outside the DJ's apartment. But this time it's not the digger on the bed getting sawed to pieces, it's Iris. This time he feels no reluctance because of moral ambiguity. He holds the gun with a steady hand. Aims and fires and hits his target. He frees Iris from the restraints and helps her with her limbs. They walk out the building and drive to Shelley's boat. The sun sets on the ocean horizon as they set sail for Avernus.

If it's right and honorable to save Iris from an unwarranted attack then it was right to save the digger as well. If the world sees it differently, then it's the world that's fucked, not me. It's the cop and the trapper and the newsbranes. It's the talking heads on the radio. It should be they who are under investigation, they who are on the run, not me. I've done nothing wrong, Eliot decides. I have nothing to feel guilty about.

So why do I feel so damn guilty?

Workers roll up the red carpet as the paparazzi pack their gear in front of the Standard Hotel. Eliot hands his keys to the valet and approaches the will call.

"One for Sweeney," he tells the bot working the desk.

"First name?"

"Carlyle. I should be on Jillian Rose's list."

She hands him a lanyard to wear around his neck. "Right this way, Mr. Sweeney."

An aqua-colored path leads Eliot into a ballroom decorated to resemble an underwater chasm cut into the ocean floor. It's dark and crowded. A brane on the ceiling reveals a moon and sky of stars refracted through pulsating currents of water. A three-dimensional image of a nurse shark swims to Eliot's face and taunts him until he shoos it away. There's fake coral and a wooden shipwreck at the back of the stage. There's an ambient noise that resembles the moaning ecstasy of copulating whales.

Along the catwalk, eyeless modelbots walk in long frocks of woven hybrid textiles with reflecting scales like a mermaid's skin. A school of hologram fish scatters as a modelbot steps to the edge of the stage, stops, and turns. She wears emeralds for eyes, and her face, like those of all the modelbots, is too obscured for Eliot to discern her identity.

"Hello, fabulous!" Jillian Rose kisses him on both cheeks. "Did you just get here?"

Eliot slides into his Carlyle Sweeney voice and asks which of the models is Iris.

"Iris?" Jillian Rose asks with a puzzled look.

"Yoshiko," he corrects himself quickly.

Following a line of air bubbles, Jillian Rose leads Eliot behind the brane at the back of the stage to where the models are being dressed. Their handlers wear black. They are mostly heartbeats—

short, fat, and ugly compared to the eyeless wonders. They push and shove the models from the stage, pull and yank and whisper harshly for them to, "Go. Now. Twenty steps and turn. Careful with the footing. Make the dress move." Though blind, the models perfectly execute their walks, never bump into one another, and never fall over the edge. When you tell a bot there are twenty steps, she doesn't take twenty-one. Not by accident anyway. Not unless she wants to.

Eliot stands ignored in the chaos of the backstage scene. He takes note of the thin brane that separates the world these bots live in and the underwater fantasy on the other side. On stage they are objects of desire, art in overpriced clothing, while behind the brane, they are blind, sexless, and dependent. Machines to be shifted around, assembled, reconfigured, maximized for profit then shoved into a corner to rejuice. Their smooth groins are revealed as they dress and undress between their turns on stage. Eliot averts his eyes. He feels like a medical student in an anatomy lab peeling back the blanket to see the cadaver's genitals. Only the models don't have genitals, which makes it all the more unsettling to look at them here in their disclosure. Unsettling because it reveals some possible branch of evolution in which sex organs will no longer exist. The bots won't need them, and perhaps without them, the entire concept of gender will disappear. There will be no contact between bots as it relates to reproduction, only as it relates to violence or work. What will happen to play and love with this remove of the androids from their heartbeat ancestors? Will those values that Eliot's father hoped to impart to the products he designed survive without their physical manifestations on the androids' form?

The handlers catch a masked modelbot as she leaves the stage. This particular one seems to walk a little slower than the rest. She seems dizzy and weak. Maybe her shoes don't fit or she's infected or just not that into the gig. Maybe it's just that Eliot's overdeveloped sense of compassion has reacted to some turmoil within her. His mother always warned him he was a sucker for the damsel in distress.

The handlers pull off the modelbot's dress and remove her mask, revealing the saddest face Eliot has ever seen on such a beautiful woman. More loneliness, misery, and defeat then he could ever imagine on a being possessed of such beauty.

"There she is." Jillian Rose surprises Eliot over his shoulder. "Yoshiko Yakamura."

The model steps out of her shoes as her handlers pull a dress over her head. They change her mask and shove her back on the runway like an unwilling racehorse forced into the gate.

"Are you certain that's the one you want?" Jillian Rose asks.

"Oh, yes," says Eliot. "That's her."

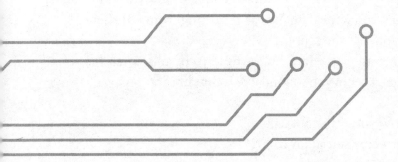

EIGHTEEN

Yoshiko

After the show, the crowd mingles around the blue-lit pool on the rooftop beneath the yellow night sky. White tablecloths snap in the Santa Anas as a whistle of drones circles overhead. Eliot lingers by the bar, wiping the ash off his frosted glass. He scans the clusters of men surrounding the eyeless modelbots who flirt in kind to their pointless advances. It's an hour before Eliot spots Yoshiko standing alone by the corner edge of the roof as if she's contemplating a jump. She wears a stark white gown with a low-cut opening at the back. No cluster of men surrounds her. The slouch of her disposition renders her unapproachable.

Eliot grabs a glass of white wine off a server's tray. He approaches carefully, not sure what awaits him once he speaks to her. Who is this bot with Iris's parts, and what, if anything, will she remember of her previous life? What will be the same and what different, and what does he have to offer in order to get what he wants?

Yoshiko turns from the ledge when she senses Eliot's nearing.

With her longer legs and high-heel shoes, she now stands well above him. The holes where her eyes should be look directly over his head.

"I got you some wine," he says as if talking to an old friend.

"I prefer vodka," she replies.

"You didn't used to. Hard liquor used to be too much for you." He guides the glass into her hand. "A light chardonnay was always your favorite."

"Do I know you?" the bot asks.

"Does my voice sound familiar?"

She shakes her head.

"It's Eliot," he tells her in a whisper. "Eliot Lazar."

Yoshiko juts her chin toward the city laid out ten stories beneath her. "I think you have me mistaken for someone else."

"I'm quite certain I don't."

"I have no memory of you," she says plainly. "If this is some line of bullshit you use on android women, it isn't going to work on me."

She turns and flips her hair, a clear enough signal that she wants him to fuck off.

"I'm sorry," says Eliot. "I didn't mean to offend you."

"You are sorry. That's the first honest thing you've said."

"Everything I've said is honest."

Jillian Rose approaches. "Carlyle! There you are." Her breath stinks of sour milk and booze. "Yoshi, sweetheart, meet Carlyle Sweeney. Carl works for Ocean Cosmetics. They're thinking of using you for their pan-Asia campaign."

There's a sly grin on Yoshiko's face as she turns back to face him. "Carlyle Sweeney," she repeats the name, different from the one the honest man used a moment before. "So nice to meet you."

"What'd you think of the show, Carl?" Jillian Rose asks.

"Fabulous," says Eliot. He uses the sibilant "s" and effete lilt, both of which further humiliate him in front of the bot. "Thank you for inviting me."

"My pleasure. And bring this pretty, little tush to the after-party."

Jillian Rose squeezes Eliot's ass and snortles away, leaving him alone with Yoshiko in an awkward silence.

"Interesting how you're two men at once," she remarks.

"I had to invent an identity to get close to you."

"And why would you want to get close to me, Carl? Do we need to be intimate to sell lipstick?"

"I have nothing to do with lipstick. I'm not Carlyle Sweeney. I'm trying to help you."

"Do I look like I need help?"

"Of course not."

"Lying again, Carl. You think I don't know what Jillian Rose has planned for me? I'm blind, sweetheart. Not deaf."

Her voice is different from Iris's, raspy to the point of abrasive. Yoshiko is clearly her own android, with her own features, her own gig, her own memory and experience. Somewhere beneath the surface lies Iris, but it would take a lot of digging to unearth her.

"Do you remember anything about your past?" Eliot asks. "Before you were reconfigured?"

The android feels around in her purse rather than answer.

"Are you curious to know?"

"Not in the least." She pulls a cigarette from a pack.

"Are you being resistant just to punish me?"

"Is punishment your thing, Mr. Sweeney? A rap across the bottom when you're a naughty boy? I've met heartbeats like you, ones who like to be dominated and humiliated by bots. Sick, sick, sick little puppy, I won't play your little game."

Boy, Jillian Rose wasn't kidding. Maybe the trauma of the attack, whether Yoshiko remembers it or not, affected her personality. Or maybe her aura is expressing a tension among her incongruent limbs.

"What if I told you you were an artist? You sculpted and painted. You worked in a Chug-Bot factory."

"Ew. Those things always creeped me out." She lights her cigarette and shakes out the match. "I think I'm allergic to their fur."

"Your name was Iris," he tells her as she flicks the matchstick off the roof. "You were a Hasegawa C-900. You worked for a sculptor named Matsuo, then a woman named Karoll Mun. You were a free roamer."

"How'd that work out for me?" She blows a line of smoke in his face.

I can't do this here, Eliot realizes. We can't speak frankly while she's at work playing the role of a bitchy model—assuming it's a role.

"Leave with me," he says in an attempt to jolt her out of character. "Leave with me now, and I'll tell you everything."

"I belong to Jillian Rose," she says in a robotic monotone. "Jillian Rose would not want me to put myself in a dangerous situation."

"You're in far more danger if you stay."

"So mysterious, Carl."

"My name's not Carl," he tells her again. "It's Eliot. Eliot Lazar. Does that name mean nothing to you?"

"In fact," she says, "it means less than nothing. Your name contains a complete absence of meaning. It is a word, it is a sound, but it carries no significance. Even the thing your name represents lacks significance."

"What did they tell you when they powered you up? Did they tell you that you came straight from the factory or did they tell you the truth?"

She turns casually toward the city and leans her elbows on the rail to show that she has tuned him out.

"Iris and I were going somewhere," he tells her. "We were headed to Avernus when our plan was interrupted. I can take you to Avernus."

"That disgusting cult in the Pacific?" She shudders and wrinkles her forehead. "I've heard they have orgies there."

He moves closer so he can whisper in her ear. "Come with me for an hour and let me sell you on an idea. If you don't like what I'm pitching, fine. Go back to Jillian Rose and traipse up and down a runway for the rest of your life. Try not to fall when you get to the edge. But first take a chance for an hour, roll the dice, listen to what I have to say. One hour. That's all I ask."

They stand in silence in the elevator. Eliot looks her over then looks at the door then looks at Yoshiko again. One moment he feels like he's standing next to Iris, the next, some stranger, or worse, someone who just doesn't like him, doesn't want to be with him, not even for an hour. It was pulling teeth to get her this far, now he has to convince her to give up her head. It won't be an easy sell.

The valet pulls the car around. Eliot guides Yoshiko into the passenger seat. They drive west toward Hollywood. She faces out the open window, wind fluttering her Agrisilk hair.

"Can I show you something?" He places the eyeball locket in her hand. She rolls the object in her fingers to feel the curves of its surface. "You made this," Eliot tells her. "You used to wear it around your neck."

Yoshiko shakes her head. "I didn't make this. I would remember if I'd made it."

"Would you?"

"I don't know how to make things like this." She crosses her legs and smooths out a fold in her gown. "Is it expensive?"

The question rubs Eliot the wrong way. Price wasn't something Iris would have cared about. She didn't have a materialistic circuit in her body.

"It has a red fleck on it," says Eliot. "The same spot that you"—he corrects himself—"that *Iris* used to have in her eye. A flaw in her manufacture that she perpetuated into her work."

"Was she an idiot?"

Jesus, this broad is something. Everything out of her mouth is poison.

"Why would she perpetuate a flaw?" Yoshiko asks. "Why wouldn't she correct it?"

Already, Eliot's at the point where he's afraid to answer her questions. She pounces on everything he says. And worst of all, he almost agrees with her. In her presence, listening to himself, everything he says does sound corny and stupid. Even to him.

"I think it was a signature," Eliot says about the flaw, though he's not sure that's right. Iris was never one who demanded credit for her work. She was shy about her talent, and when she did talk about a piece, she spoke of it *coming about, forming, finding its way into the world* in a manner she had little to do with. As if she were the discoverer of the piece and not its creator.

"So she fucked up everything she made just to show people it was hers? So everyone could know she was an idiot who made flawed crap?"

"You're misunderstanding me."

"You're not explaining yourself well."

"To perpetuate the flaw was to pass on something beautiful. It was the accident that resisted the banality of perfection." Banality of perfection? Where's he getting this shit, "The early engineers couldn't help but make mistakes in their androids, flaws passed on to each generation of bots. No artist is God after all, so to emphasize a small flaw is to emphasize the beauty in imperfection, to show humility before God."

"Your girlfriend had to resist being God?" Yoshiko groans in disgust. "That's quite an ego on her. Sounds like a real gem."

Eliot takes the locket back and puts it in his pocket. He stops talking. Down Hollywood Boulevard, he follows the signs into the parking garage for the superblock on Vine. The developers named it Cube L.A. and made it safe for tourists looking for the L.A. experience without the danger and the grime. He parks underground and holds Yoshiko's elbow as he guides her through the entrance. A canal crosses the indoor street with gondoliers' boats tied to the railing. The sign above reads LITTLE VENICE. There are signs for all the city's neighborhoods rebuilt in microcosm within the cube. Thus, in an hour, a tourist can visit little Malibu, little Beverly Hills, little Koreatown, little Little Tokyo, little downtown, little Santa Monica, little Silverlake, little Burbank, and little Hollywood, all without waiting in traffic.

Eliot leads Yoshiko across the atrium. Her high heels clap against the squares of a replica of the Walk of Fame.

"Only in Los Angeles," says a Midwest tourist to his obese wife. Their kid snaps a loop.

"They let that kind of thing happen here?" another asks as they pass.

The elevator at V Condominiums takes Eliot and Yoshiko to the eleventh floor where they exit to look for apartment #1114. Two knocks on the door and a trannybot welcomes them inside. The studio flat serves as an entrance to the West Inn, a small hotel land-marked in the 2020s so developers couldn't tear it down. Instead, they moved the entire structure, every pipe and brick, deep into the center of the superblock. From the outside street, there's no indica-tion the run-down flophouse exists, but suspended ten stories from the ground, the West Inn operates in a time capsule inside a more modern building. Eccentrics, drunks, and transients make it their home. Dripped-out whores solicit tricks in the lobby then pay an hourly wage for their rooms. With all the windows facing walls, many of the hotel's inhabitants go mad. Some arrive that way. It's a great place for a suicide.

Eliot pays twelve ingots each for him and Yoshiko. The tran-nybot opens the fire door that leads into the lobby. From there, they walk the ragged carpet past the concierge and into the Hotel Café.

The crowd is packed all the way to the door of the venue. It's a bar for androids, it exists in secret, though heartbeats have been known to frequent it as well. They come for the music that bots play for other bots, a sound that isn't meant for heartbeat ears, a sound appreciated only by those in the know.

On stage, the crooner Hawk Jones has two hands on the key-board and another two behind him on the tenor sax. His head faces away from the piano, 180 degrees backward, huffing into the micro-phone, blowing his horn, stomping the pedals and slapping at the keys. In a specially tailored suit made for a four-armed bot, Jones looks like some black Hindu god feverishly crafting sound through the relentless fury of quick breaths and twenty fast-moving fingers. The music is all-consuming. No one who listens can remain still. No one but Yoshiko whom Eliot leads to a booth at the back of the club.

"What is this place?" she asks uncomfortably above the music.

"Just listen," he says. "Let me know what you think."

He doesn't tell her about Hawk Jones. He doesn't tell her that the android crooner had been designed for hard farming on a sugar plantation in Louisiana. His four arms once held machetes, the limbs designed to cut the modified cane that grew in the industrial-strength heat of the Delta. According to his mythology, Jones spent the first ten years of his life in those soul-crushing fields before he picked up a horn one day that had been left on the porch of his barracks. He claimed the land had taught him to play, and the first time he blew a tune, he looked out into the night and saw he could make the devil dance.

This is the bar and this is the artist who played the night Eliot and Iris first met. Eliot doesn't remind Yoshiko because he wants her to hear it in the music. The song was a murder ballad, the notes leaked from the piano like an oozing cloud of ether. Eliot had walked away from the booth he was sharing with his brother. He ordered a drink at the bar and found himself beside a pair of brown eyes, one marked with a red fleck, a color so incongruous it would alter the trajectory of his dreams. They spoke briefly beneath the music. He struggled to find his words. She had a nervous laugh. They committed to meeting again. They had an easy time together because they played it true. Their obstacles were external. He worried about her safety. She didn't like that he used drip. But for him, there had never been anyone like her. Not even close. Because who the Hell was Eliot Lazar before he met Iris Matsuo? Just some bag of meat and metal with a habit of survival, trying to keep his pain at bay. They were together a year before the night he discovered she was gone.

The set ends and the crowd rises to applaud. Jones stands and takes a bow. He sets his horn aside and says he'll be back after intermission.

"Did it sound familiar?" Eliot asks his date.

"Was it supposed to?"

Yes, it was supposed to. It was supposed to ignite some ember of remembrance inside her, something he could fan into a flame that would forge Yoshiko into the woman Eliot wants her to be.

"It just sounded like music." She shrugs.

The crowd migrates to the restrooms and the bar. A giddy chatter fills the room. Eliot asks Yoshiko if she wants another drink.

"Vodka on the rocks," she says to remind him of the distance between herself and the bot who liked champagne.

Leaving her alone at the booth, Eliot crosses to the front of the room. He slumps against the bar and orders the drinks. He still hopes to find Iris within her. He still believes Yoshiko is going to fade and the woman she once was will emerge from the depths and reveal herself through a smile or a laugh or some gesture that Eliot can latch onto. But no, it hasn't happened yet, not even a little and if it doesn't happen, there isn't much of a backup plan. Just the determination to find a way to be a more successful hero than Orpheus— to not look back. The Greek, of course, was a lyric poet; he used his song to get what he wanted. But what am I? Eliot wonders. What weapons are at my disposal? Do I make an offer to Jillian Rose, who would likely figure out that I found her through Pink and thus turn me over to the police? Should I see what offer Yoshiko might accept in exchange for her head? Ridiculous. Who would give away her own head? Which leaves of course a more forceful solution, an ember Eliot smothers as soon as it starts to glow.

"Are you feeling better?"

Eliot turns to the whispering voice and finds the Satine 5000 watching over the crowd with his back to the bar.

"Tim," says Eliot. "I don't think I've ever seen you out of the office before." And yet the bot seems to blend right in. It must be one of his talents. "Let me buy you a drink."

"I don't drink," says the Satine. His eyes dart about the room as he calculates threat probabilities and estimates how quickly they can be neutralized.

"You on the job?" Eliot asks.

"I'm doing a friend a favor."

"What kind of favor?"

The Satine eyes Yoshiko as if she were a snake that bit him many years before. "I can only protect you during the hours I'm not at work."

The bartender returns with the drinks and Eliot pays. "I didn't ask you to protect me."

"Nor did I ask you," says the Satine.

"Then consider us even."

Eliot takes his drinks and crosses back to Yoshiko and slides his way into the booth. From whom does Tim think I need protection? he wonders. How much does he know? How much does everybody know?

"I'm not feeling it here," Yoshiko says as she sips her vodka. "Why don't we just get this over with?"

"Get what over with?"

"Whatever fantasy you're playing out."

The houselights blink as a warning that intermission is drawing to a close.

"You're a cynic," says Eliot.

"A realist."

"Cynics always think they're realists."

"Convince me otherwise." She cracks an ice cube in her mouth. "But get on with it already. I'm low on juice."

They exit out the back and take the elevator to the garage. They drive up through the hills in Eliot's car. They pass the homes that burned in the last rash of fires and traverse the roads still covered with dirt from a December mudslide. Floaters and drones depart from the station near the top. A pack of coyotes howls with the lust of a fresh kill.

Eliot hops the tires over the broken curb and passes the entrance to the park. He drives over the weedy grass and pulls up to where the rusted scaffold twists around the ruins. He parks and walks to the passenger side to help Yoshiko from the car. The blind model shivers from the cold. The sound of the city grinds below.

"What is this place?" she asks, clutching a shawl around her shoulders.

Eliot guides her hand to the base of the first letter. She feels the broken enamel on the steel *H*. She runs her hands along the irregularities where the letter has been decimated by nasty weather, nasty people, and time.

"It's the Hollywood sign," he tells her, but it doesn't appear she knows anything about it. Probably never saw the damn thing, even when her boss was kind enough to lend her some eyes for a gig. Now, she follows the geometry on her own, running her hand over and along the surface.

"We used to hide here." He sits on a patch of weeds and takes out his drip. "We could be outside and together here and feel safe." He takes a deep inhale. "The first time we met was at that bar and the last time we were together was here."

He listens to the city and waits for the drug to kick in. He waits for some emotion that will make him feel at this moment the way he used to feel when he was here with Iris. But Yoshiko makes it far more unsettling. She doesn't lie by his side and cuddle and ask him to tell her about Avernus. Instead, she grabs onto the scaffold and hooks a high-heeled shoe onto a metal bar. Her dress ripples like a white flag in the wind as she climbs.

"Do you realize," Yoshiko asks, "that you've been talking about your ex all night and you haven't asked a single question about me?"

It's true; Eliot hasn't been a very good date. Then again, that was never his intention. For it to be a date, he would have to acknowledge that Yoshiko is her own person, something Eliot has so far refused to do.

"I'm sorry," he says, leaning back on his elbows and staring down at his shoes.

"Are you," she asks, "or are you apologizing in some halfhearted attempt to make me feel better?" She climbs a few more rungs up the scaffold. "You give the impression that you're completely uninterested in me."

"That isn't true."

"Oh, I don't care." She climbs another rung. "I'm not terribly interested in you, either."

The metal creaks beneath her as she climbs. Her black hair webs across her shoulders. Her white dress matches the enamel of the *H*.

"Why'd you leave with me?" Eliot asks, his head light with drip. "Why'd you give me an hour?"

"You said I was in danger."

"You *are* in danger. Jillian Rose intends to reconfigure you."

"As do you."

Her hand follows the uneven contours of the twisting bars spaced alongside the letters in the sign. She climbs fearlessly, showing no apprehension of the height or the condition of the scaffold supporting her.

"I thought when I handed you the locket and showed you the places that had been important to us, it would awaken the memory of who you'd been. It either didn't work or you're hiding from me that it did."

"It didn't." Yoshiko turns her back to the sign and faces the lights of the city. "I don't." She stretches her arms along a horizontal bar and touches the cold steel to her naked back. "So I guess that means you're going to kill me."

He listens to the city, to the brush, to the predators and the prey locked in their dance along the paths and gullies of the hills. "I have no intention of killing you."

"Only because you call it *reconfiguring* or *reassembling* or some other euphemism *du jour*."

"I don't do that."

"That puts you in a pickle."

She enjoys this, he thinks. Twisting the knife into this compassionate heartbeat broken since losing the woman he loves.

"Were you telling the truth about Avernus?" she asks. "Would you take me there instead of Iris? If I pretended to like you, the same way she pretended?"

Eliot tries to think of a polite response, but why be polite when she has made candor the tone of the evening? Why not tell the truth to this spoiled modelbot who's more bitter than her brothers and sisters working the frozen quarries and brothels of Europa?

"No," he tells her bluntly. "I would not take you to Avernus. Not as you are."

"Because you don't like me."

"What have you shown me to like?"

Yoshiko stands on the scaffold, four stories high with her hair blowing in the wind. Her expression is the same one Eliot saw on the roof of the Standard except that now her body seems suspended in space. The forces pulling her in opposite directions are of equal strength.

"Seems I have two choices," Yoshiko says flatly from the scaffold. "I can get reconfigured by Jillian Rose or I can get reconfigured by you. I don't see much of a difference."

"The bot I'll make you will be loved," says Eliot, the salesman always ready with a pitch. "The bot Jillian Rose will make you"—he pauses to think of how to describe it—"you know more about her than I do."

Yoshiko allows a shoe to drop from her foot and fall several stories before it bounces off the ground.

"There is a third option." She arches her back against the scaffold and opens her face to the clouds. "I could say to Hell with both of you."

"Just to spite me?" She allows the other shoe to drop. He sits up, ready to spring if he has to. "I won't let you."

"Then you're a murderer after all."

Her bare feet release the rung and her body cartwheels down the scaffold. She collides several times with horizontal beams before her spine cracks against a steel rod ten feet above the ground. Her weight tilts on the rod then falls downward, head first, but Eliot is there in time to catch her and spin her to the ground at the last moment, protecting her head.

Oil drips from her mouth. Eliot pats out the part of her dress burning from the sparks. Her collapsed chest stops the spinning in her engine. Yoshiko's final act, her vengeful suicide, is, thank God, a failure. She didn't succeed in destroying all her parts—at least not the one Eliot gives a shit about.

NINETEEN
An Unexpected Guest

It's a short trip from the Hollywood sign back to his apartment. Few cars on the roads. He keeps the radio off and lets the auto-drive maintain the speed limit. Too much drip to trust himself with the wheel.

Parked in his driveway, Eliot looks around to make sure his neighbors aren't watching. He has Yoshiko's body wrapped in a blanket. He rushes it into his apartment and lays it over Iris's clothing beside her left arm on the living room floor. He closes the blinds and tells his deskbrane to play his messages.

Beep.

"Eliot, it's Gita. Sounds like we lost Harris Farms. Let me know how we should handle this with the Mole . . . I mean, Erica."

Beep.

"Namaste, sweetheart, sorry it's been so long, but I'm only allowed one call a week. Anyway, you still coming to Avernus? The gods answered the Admiral's call for rain so the crops are growing in beautifully. The sun is shining. Mother Earth is plentiful in her giving, and there are so many people here who want to meet you. Wait 'til you see the girls. Gorgeous! Anyway. Miss you. Love you. Say hi to your brother."

Beep.

Eliot digs his old tool kit out of the closet and sets it on the coffee table. He hasn't worked on a bot since he was a kid tinkering with his old man in the garage. They used to make all sorts of things then. Insects and birds and baby dragons. It was his hobby before the drip became his hobby. Now, there's a layer of dust on the kit, but inside, the tools are clean and sharp as they were the last time he used them.

"The proper way to remove the limbs on your XR series android is with careful incisions and an understanding of how the XR is designed."

The man on the liquid screen, Joe the Trapper, wears a white lab coat and a ski mask as he hosts the loop. He hides his identity lest someone collect the price Lorca put on his head.

"Tearing and chopping might be all right for the experienced carver, but unless you're making snuff films, you'll want to avoid causing any damage to the torso or limbs of your bot. For one thing, parts will lose their resale value if they need repair. For another, if any oil leaks into the main works of a component, it will make your bot as worthless as a screen door on a submarine. Now, let's get started."

A toilet flushes in the apartment. At first Eliot thinks it's the loop, but then he notices a shadow moving beneath the bathroom door. He hears someone washing at the sink. He reaches into his kit and grabs the first sharp object he can find. The knob turns. The door opens. Eliot lunges at the backlit silhouette in the hall.

"Whoa, whoa, whoa!" says the younger brother. His pants are undone. A newsbrane in his hand.

"Damnit, I coulda killed you!"

Shelley looks at the small pair of scissors in Eliot's hand. "Or worse, cut off all the tags from my clothing."

Eliot grabs a blanket off the couch and throws it on the floor to cover Yoshiko's body. "What the Hell are you doing here?" he asks as he shuts off the liquid screen.

Shelley crosses to a chair and examines the antique laptop on Eliot's desk.

"I fell behind in my payments at the marina. I need the fee for the berth by twelve o'clock."

"How much?"

"A grand? Or two?"

"Top drawer."

"Thanks." Shelley reaches into the desk and avails himself of the money. "And by the way, there's a terminated bot on your floor."

Eliot throws himself facedown exasperated on the couch.

"It's not what you think," he says into a pillow.

"What do I think?"

"I'm helping her. Saving her. She was kidnapped by a trapper, chopped up, and sold for parts."

"That happens to bots."

"That doesn't make it right."

"So you make things right?" Shelley asks. "Sir Galahad of Los Angeles. White knight to the bots?"

Eliot wraps the pillow over his ears. He doesn't want to listen. He doesn't want to hear his brother remind him of his own madness.

"Whose laptop is this?"

"Better you don't know."

Shelley reads the list off the screen. "Iris Matsuo. Hasegawa C-900. Head—Jillian Rose Modeling Agency. Legs—Tucson Metal Solutions. Eyes—Blumenthal Promotions." Shelley turns to Eliot on the couch. "Blumenthal the shylock?"

"I suppose."

"And who's Chief Shunu?"

"Some outlaw on the Chumash Reservation."

"And what do you have so far?"

"A head, a left arm, and a right pinky."

"Who has the right arm?"

"I don't know."

"If you don't have every part of a C-900, she'll never be the same."

"I know that, Shelley. You think I don't know?"

The younger brother pushes aside the laptop and glances down at Yoshiko's body laid atop Iris's clothes. He sees the shut blinds, the messy apartment, and the empty drip vials scattered around the coffee table.

"This looks like a bad idea," he says.

"It's definitely a bad idea."

"Why not build a new one that looks the same?"

"Because it wouldn't be her."

"And that's important?" Shelley turns back toward the desk and looks at the laptop. "I don't think you came across this antique by lawful means."

"I didn't."

Shelley whistles and uses his sleeve to rub his prints off the keyboard. "Maybe you should leave tonight for Avernus," he says. "Take my boat. Get out while you can, and go see Mom."

"I can't."

"Why not?"

"I have to put her back together."

"You're insane. You're gonna get yourself killed or thrown in jail."

Eliot rolls off his stomach and onto his side. "Have you ever had someone taken from you? Someone you love taken before you could say good-bye?"

"My sister," says Shelley. "And my old man when I was twelve."

"And there's nothing I can do about them. But at least with Iris I have a chance."

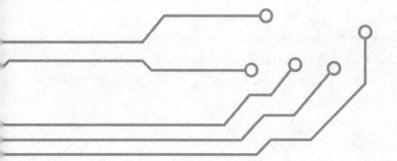

TWENTY
The Catch Basin

The old detective sits on the curb on Waring Avenue a few blocks north of the El Royale. He coughs and tilts his fedora to protect his face from the midday sun. His young partner, however, is in a less glamorous locale. Shin-deep in the runoff from the morning rain, Detective Ochoa uses a stick to poke around in a catch basin beneath the street.

"This is bullshit," his voice calls from beneath a hole in the curb. "The lieutenant said to look for Plath."

"And I'm sure every badge in the department is doing his best to find her."

"So why aren't we?"

"I thought we were. I thought looking for the weapon might turn up a good lead."

"Spenser was killed by a radial saw. The weapon was found at the scene."

"Did the bullets in the wall come from a saw?"

Flaubert checks the map displayed on his pocketbrane. It shows all the catch basins in a four-by-thirteen block rectangle stretching east-west from Gower to Rossmore and north-south from Santa Monica to Beverly. This is the fifth one they've checked today.

"Witnesses saw Plath with Spenser at the underground," says Ochoa. "She bled oil and left circuits with her serial number."

"Bots don't make a lot of money. This one left the DJ's wallet full of his evening's pay."

" 'Cause she was in a hurry."

"And yet she had time to clean the scene of everything except the money and the evidence that would lead directly to her."

Flaubert stands and moves toward the shade to keep cool. He looks at a nearby Dumpster and wishes he could have checked it before the trash was collected the morning after the murder. It would also be nice if there were other officers assisting in the storm drains. As it is, Lieutenant Byron didn't exactly sign off on this. The brass at Rampart has an aversion to rigorous police work, unless it's issued as a punishment.

"It stinks down here. I don't even know what I'm looking for."

The old detective coughs into his handkerchief as he paces above the hole. "Explain to me how a little bot like Plath, bleeding oil from her wounds, is able to use a heavy, antique radial saw against an experienced trapper twice her size."

"She drugged him," says Ochoa.

"Toxicology found a quinoa salad in his stomach."

"She set it up with the Disciples."

"She worked retail. If she was political, she was more the type to support a cause through fashion, not violence. And if she was sucked into Lorca's orbit, she sure wasn't trained very well."

"Plath closes the case," says the voice beneath the street. "The city needs it closed."

Well, the old detective agrees with that. There have been five revenge attacks on innocent androids in the last twenty-four hours. Armed Militiamen are patrolling the streets in their black vans. Employers are complaining they have to use private transport to get their bots safely to work. Lorca hasn't said anything yet, she hasn't issued her weekly loop nor any claim for the murder, but if there are any more reprisals, it's inevitable she'll respond in spectacular fashion.

"We got to show the bots who's boss," says Ochoa. "Otherwise, they'll think they run this town."

An hour earlier, the two detectives drove past a shrine on the sidewalk in front of the El Royale. There were flowers, candles, loops of the saints, a faux vintage phonograph playing that awful binary the rookies play at the precinct gym. Flaubert slowed the car so he could better see the young diggers weeping by the shrine. He wondered if they ever wept for Pink's victims. Their little fingers nailed to Edmund Spenser's wall—those were his victims' shrines, hidden in a closet behind the room where they were terminated. No one mourned the missing bots.

Almost no one.

"I agree the city needs to close the case." Flaubert coughs into his handkerchief and wipes his mouth. "But only if closing it provides the appearance of justice. If we arrest the wrong party, the people will find out, and we will have undermined the very cause we have sworn to serve."

"What cause is that?" the young partner asks mockingly.

"The value and integrity of the state."

Flaubert makes sure no cars are passing then lays his handkerchief on the pavement. He puts a knee on the cloth and kneels close to the basin so he doesn't have to shout.

"It is a grave thing when a man comes to believe he lives in a corrupted state. It affects the quality of his vision," Flaubert tells his partner. "He begins to see the newsbranes as propaganda, his leaders as crooks, the ingot in his pocket as a worthless speck of metal. He begins to see his work as drudgery, or worse, as an agency of that very corruption he deplores."

The old detective tips his hat to a woman passing by with a stroller. She probably thinks he's a well-dressed madman the way he's carrying on with a hole in the ground. She's probably right.

"When the state fails in the administration of justice," Flaubert continues, "we create armies of such disenchanted men. Some retreat into sullenness and despair. Some toward rebellious ideologies. Others search for answers in conspiracy theories or religious extremism."

He coughs into the crook of his elbow and wipes his mouth with his sleeve.

"But when we do our jobs assiduously and arrest the right suspect, the one who actually committed the crime as opposed to the one who was easiest to convict, we affirm the very values we are paid to uphold. Once again, that disenchanted man believes, however fleetingly, that the state protects him, the law has substance, his work serves the march toward progress. A man such as this feels a sense of satisfaction when he sees a story in the newsbranes that confirms the old adage he was told as a child—that crime doesn't pay."

The old detective can hear the young partner's stick scrape the bottom of the basin.

"So when you ask what it is you're looking for down there in a hole, beneath the street, poking around in the muck, I can tell you honestly, Detective Ochoa, that you are looking for nothing less than meaning itself. Your own, mine, and that of every man, woman, and child who ever invested in the great experiment of civilization that distinguishes us from the savage herd whose existence preceded our own."

A dull clink echoes through the catch basin as Ochoa's stick strikes a hunk of metal.

"Found something."

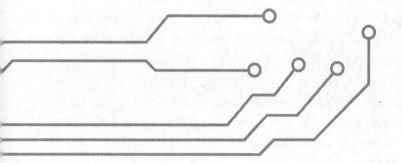

TWENTY-ONE
Titty Fat

~~Left arm—Uchenna~~
~~Right Pinky—Edmund "Pink" Spenser~~
~~Head—Jillian Rose Models~~
Right arm—?
Legs—Tucson Metal Solutions
Torso—Chief Shunu
Eyes—Blumenthal Promotions

Eliot rides a vactrain to Arizona to pick up the legs he ordered from
Tucson Metal Solutions. The ride is smooth. Eight hundred mph in
a hyperloop built atop the desert. From his seat in business class, he
works his brane to find out what he can about the other names listed
as buyers on Pink's laptop.

The torso. Chief Shunu, aka Joshua Dominguez. His name comes
up on a list of fugitives published by the California Department of
Justice. It's a long list, and Shunu's name is nowhere near the top, but
still, the Indian's campaign of ineptitude is impressive.

From the arrest reports, it appears his career began when he was sixteen, the age at which Shunu got his first car and ventured off the Santa Ynez reservation where he had grown up. Within a year, the young scout had already scored a hit and run, a DUI, and a myriad of other infractions. The car had been no friend to him.

His juvie records were sealed then later unsealed after his first arrest as an adult. The charge stuck and Shunu (whose name translates to "Sleepyhead" in the Chumash language) was sentenced to serve five years on a pandering charge.

He was out in three.

His parole officer noted in a report that the parolee's "clumsy incompetence and inability to remain employed would likely land him back in jail." Five years later, the PO was proven right. A Modesto County indictment accused Chief Shunu of running some of the filthiest prostitutes in the state of California. Among his heartbeat customers, there were eight cases of AIDS, fifteen of gonorrhea, and twenty-seven of syphilis. Among his android customers, there was everything from the I love me virus to foaming mouth to a worm that convinced infected bots it was a good idea to set themselves afire. The judge was appalled. He wrote in his verdict that the accused was more than a pimp, he was a pandemic, and thus sentenced Shunu to fifteen years in the sweat lodge at Pelican Bay.

Eliot looks out the window at the morning sun burning the solar fields on the desert floor. A billboard angled toward the hyperloop has been hacked and reprogrammed to read LONG LIVE LORCA. His seatmate is asleep, so Eliot uses the momentary privacy to douse a drip rag and take a quick hit. He folds the hanky into his pocket before finding this tidbit about Shunu in the archive of a Crescent City blog:

> In pleading for clemency, the inmate claimed to have "changed his ways and found Jesus" after years of studying the Bible in his cell. When a parole board member asked which of the gospels was his favorite, the inmate replied, "What's a gospel?"

The blog goes on to report that three weeks after his release, Shunu was accused of violating the Mann Act with a Mormon girl he met through a prison correspondence. A judge issued a warrant for his arrest, but the Indian had fled from his last known residence and likely returned to the Chumash reservation to avoid a third strike that would earn him a life sentence. Tribal authorities ignored an extradition request. The case remains open, though Eliot would guess that as long as Sleepyhead isn't plying his trade in a California jurisdiction, the authorities are content to have him off their hands.

At the Tucson vactrain station, Eliot rents a car and drives thirty minutes on a desert road to get to the Green Valley Recycling plant. He's never been there before, but he knows the company well. GAC sells many of its DBRs to Green Valley for them to be stripped and resold for parts. Whatever parts the recyclers can't salvage, they sell as scrap, and whatever they can't scrap gets dumped into an old copper mine at the Arizona site. Like Dale Hampton said, it's a good way for GAC to recover losses from its downed bots.

Off a two-lane highway, a line of trucks loops into the plant to drop off cargo and pick up more. Eliot approaches the guest entrance. He rolls down the window at the guard station, and a gust of hot air presses against his face.

"I got an appointment at Tucson Metal Solutions."

"Tucson Metal?" asks the bot at the station.

"They run your company store."

The securitybot makes a call from his booth. Eliot looks out toward the loading bay and sees a shipment from a Maricopa county sheriff's bus. Inside is a line of four-by-four cages stacked with rogue androids taken from the county jail. Botworkers haul the cages from the back of the bus and drop them on the desert floor.

"Get away from me!" says a rogue locked in a cage. "I didn't do nothing! I didn't do a Goddamn thing!"

The workers back off, waiting for the captive to use up his juice before they dare put their fingers near his cage. Seeing their reluctance, a foreman shouts a warning from the entrance of the dock.

"Get 'er done," he says. "We ain't got all day."

The workers step it up. Two flip the cage while a third jumps to the top with a cattle prod. As one opens the lock, the second worker reaches inside and grabs a limb with his gloved hand. The rogue fights, but as soon as his leg is outside the cage, the bot on top prods him with a high-voltage shock that shorts the android's engine. There's a short but loud fizzing sound; his body gives a death rattle. The workers fix a collar around his neck and drag him inside the plant.

The securitybot hangs up the phone. "I can't find any Tucson Metal Solutions. You'll have to speak to the plant manager on the floor of the kill room. Maybe he'll know something. Here." The bot hands over earplugs and a lanyard that identifies Eliot as a guest. "You better wear this or the line workers might mistake you for a DBR."

Inside the plant, it's hotter than the desert. Just a giant, square room with high ceilings and lots of doors. No air-conditioning. No fans. And even with the earplugs it's painfully loud.

From behind a guardrail, Eliot watches as a big, burly android drags a DBR by the collar down a path between two columns of workers. The first hands on the line remove the bot's clothing. The next cut off his hair. The next hack at his limbs with knives and machetes. Across a table, a team of bots has a go at the torso. They use smaller tools to cut off the genitals, remove batteries, and tear out engines. Finally, at the last station, a bot pulls the eyes from the decapitated head.

Each component is then rushed over to a door where the parts wait to be collected. Eliot sees bundles of arms and legs wrapped in twine, piles of skin and hair, engines loaded into crates, batteries stacked on the floor, heads balled up in a wheeled bin. Scavenging bots pick up whatever circuits and wires fall out during the process. Cleaners mop up the spilled oil then jump out of the way as a worker drags another DBR down the line.

"Pick up the pace," calls a heartbeat in a white coat. He watches a giant wallbrane that displays the number of downed bots running through the room and the rate-per-minute at which they're getting chopped.

Eliot approaches and asks if he's the manager.

"Aw, Hell, I thought you were comin' Monday. I swear we're testing the metal down the line."

"Testing the metal?"

The manager steps back. "You're not from virus control?"

"No," says Eliot. "I'm looking for Tucson Metal. I think they run your company store."

"Oh, yeah, that's over by the barracks," says the manager. "Come with me. I'll show ya."

He opens a door that leads to an air-conditioned corridor with long windows on each side. It's much quieter here, so Eliot can remove his plugs.

"I sure am glad you ain't from the government. We're overwhelmed today so I don't got nobody scanning for infections."

"Not even the convicts?"

"Shit, I got orders to fill. Besides, them rogues ain't infected. Most of 'em ain't even guilty."

Through the window on his right, Eliot can see a well-lit room with female bots repairing, cleaning, and wrapping up parts to be shipped. They bunch up the hair and sort the clothing. They label boxes and pass them down the line.

"My warehouse is empty," says the manager. "Everything you're looking at has already been sold, and there ain't enough downed bots to fill my orders from last month, never mind this month."

In the packaging room, the androids run around with no conveyor belts, forklifts, or large tools to help. Everything is done by manpower, or bot power, lifted and processed with hands, legs, and backs.

"So whenever we got more orders than metal," says the manager, "we just throw a few bucks to a local sheriff who's kind enough to arrest a few more bots and send 'em our way. This way our customers get their orders, the county gets a check and a couple fewer bots. Beats raising taxes."

"Not so good for the bots," says Eliot.

"Ain't that the truth. We don't even have the time to let their juice run out. Hell, sometimes we run behind and start chopping our own employees. I can't tell you how much *that* slows the line."

Through the window on Eliot's left, there's a dark room with shirtless male androids inside. Molten steel, fire, and welding torches provide the only light. It looks like a metal forge from somewhere in the center of the Earth.

"That's where we smelt the excess and press the scrap," says the manager. "We sell the high-quality stock to the labor providers to make new bots, then we drop the junk into the copper pit. I got it down to five percent waste," he says proudly. "Shooting for four. At that rate, we can keep this running for about five years before the pit fills up."

After the corridor, they exit back into the desert where there's a landing strip, a railroad track, and another line of trucks loading cargo. The manager points Eliot toward a wooden building about a hundred yards away. "Head over there," he says, "you'll see the company store before you hit the barracks. If you find yourself in the copper pit, you've gone too far."

"Thanks."

"You bet."

A procession of bots drags pressed cubes of scrap across the brush. The sun nears its peak, and there's no shade under which to hide. Eliot arrives at a run-down cluster of buildings that looks like the remnants of a ghost town from the Old West. There's a saloon and an oil change garage and, sure enough, a company store where Eliot hopes to find Iris's legs. He steps up the wood stairs and enters through a pair of swinging doors.

Inside, the shelves are crowded with merchandise ranging from the high end to the untrustworthy. A menu lists prices for debit cards, pocketbranes, rain gear, gloves, shoes, and new batteries. It lists an inventory of software updates, memory upgrades, botcords, replacement limbs, strips of smart metal flesh—every accessory a bot might need for the desert and the factory floor.

Eliot approaches the counter where a young, disengaged clerk lies back on a chair with his eyes closed and a fly swatter dangling from his hand. He has spacers in his cheeks and a tribal tattoo on his forehead. Three fans are positioned to blow air directly at him. None are pointed in a direction that might benefit a customer.

"Excuse me. Do you work for Tucson Metal?"

"Who's asking?"

"Eliot Lazar from GAC. I called a few days ago to purchase some legs."

The clerk remains seated enjoying the breeze from the fans. "The C-900 legs?"

"That's right."

"I usually only sell to bots. Don't make sense you'd come all this way to buy 'em from me and not the plant. Not sure why it is you want 'em."

"Did the payment clear?"

"Yep."

"Then I want 'em 'cause I paid for 'em."

The clerk shoots Eliot a look. He adjusts the fans to point up before he rises slowly and reaches beneath the counter. He takes out a box and removes the lid to reveal a leg wrapped in cheap brown paper. Eliot shines his pocketbrane's UV on the thigh and reads the serial number, which matches the one on Iris's locket.

"Where's the other leg?" he asks.

"In use," says the clerk. There are gaps where two of his teeth should be, though it looks more like a fashion statement than a lack of hygiene.

"When we spoke, you said you had the pair."

"Oh, I have the pair," says the clerk. "It's just the other's *in use*." He swings the fly swatter to add a bug's corpse to the funeral mound at the base of the wall. "I could sell you a Patel or an XL series with the same color skin. Hell, them XLs are top of the line, real nice value if you want 'em."

"I paid for a specific pair of legs," says Eliot. "The payment went through. I expect the leg."

"Suit yourself." The clerk shrugs. "But you're gonna have to get it yourself off a Titty Fat." He turns the fans back toward his chair and takes a seat.

I'll bite, thinks Eliot. "Who's Titty Fat?"

"Just a carver. Her production was falling so she decided to lease a new leg to replace the one she was gimpin' on. We made a deal on the C-900 piece after I bought it off a DJ playing a gig in town."

"She make all the payments?" Eliot asks.

"Nope."

"Then why not repossess the leg?"

" 'Cause I sold it to you," says the clerk. "It's your problem now."

"All right." Eliot sighs. "Where is she?"

"Over by the copper pit. NatMo put her on a quarantine post until she's disinfected."

"What's wrong with her?"

"Good question." The clerk laughs at some joke only he seems to hear. "And you might need a tool kit if you want to snap off that leg."

Eliot pays for the kit. It costs three times what it would online, but this is a company store with a captive customer base, so of course the mark-up is extreme. Once outside, he carries the leg and his new bag of tools toward the copper pit to find the android named Titty Fat who has Iris's other leg.

The sun is a killer. He heads for the barracks so he can take cover in the shade. The building is a long flimsy patchwork of rusted sheet metal with intervals in the roof to allow in light. The bots sleep lengthwise on the ground with their cords plugged into the wall. Each outlet is next to a slot in which the workers insert their debit cards to pay for their juice while they recharge.

Eliot steps over a group of kidbots asleep on the ground like a pack of baby wolves. He recognizes the child-sized androids as imports: American companies don't build bots that look under eighteen. It's rare to see a kidbot, as they aren't mass-produced but rather made-to-order as replacements for heartbeat couples who lost a daughter or a son. In fact, Eliot and Shelley had begged for one to replace Mitzi after she was killed along with their father in the explosion by the stable. Their mother rightly refused. She knew that kidbots only remind families of who they lost rather than serve as emotionally fulfilling replacements. That's why after a few years their owners usually release them as free roamers left to wander the streets begging, stealing, and causing mischief. Occasionally one will find work in a factory or mine where their small bodies and tiny hands can be useful for some specific task. Sometimes, too, they get adopted by android couples looking to create a family-unit like those of the heartbeats. But more often than not, the poor, innocent kidbots find themselves susceptible to the most depraved of society's predators, or else their batteries drain and their little bodies collapse in the street where they get carted off and sold for scrap.

Exiting the barracks, Eliot passes the generator providing juice for the sleeping bots. It's loud and pumps out a black plume of smoke that hangs over the desert. Once again, he sees the parade of bots dragging crushed metal from the plant. He asks one on the march where Titty Fat is, and the bot points to an outcrop of high, wooden poles freestanding by the edge of the pit. From a distance the poles look like totems, and two of them hold a wide banner that reads: ABANDON ALL HOPE ALL YE WHO ENTER HERE. But as Eliot approaches, he can see there are no carvings on the totems. Instead, wrapped in razor wire, the bodies of crucified androids roast in the midday sun. Cords hang from their navels and connect to the generator. Around their necks, they wear signs reading SLACKER or DRUNKARD or WHORE. Some are naked and covered in oil that cooks their skin. Some have limbs that have been chewed by dogs. Each has an expression of hopeless resignation or bored despair. Each except one.

"I'm looking for Titty Fat," says Eliot.

"That's me," says the one.

Her demeanor matches her wide toothy smile—she can't help but smile as someone has cut off her lips. She is short and rotund, with a dark, brown sunburn. Her hair hangs straight with a crown shaved on top so the sun focuses directly onto her head. Two holes in her gingham blouse expose her breasts, and around her neck, a string holds a sign reading RUNNER.

"Sorry to bother you," says Eliot, "but would you by any chance be wearing a C-900 leg?"

"This one on the left," says the bot. "There's a ladder over yonder if you care to look."

Eliot finds the ladder and leans it against the post. He climbs up to where Titty Fat is tied. From the height, he can see through the black smoke to the bottom of the pit where bots stack the metal cubes, which the workers throw over the edge.

"Is it all right if I lower your pants?" Eliot asks.

"Go ahead."

Titty Fat expresses no judgment as Eliot undoes her button and unzips her fly. He pulls her pants down and sees she's wearing a wrapped cloth for underwear. With the UV from his pocketbrane, Eliot confirms that the serial number on her leg matches the number from Iris's locket.

"I better warn you," says the bot. "This leg ain't done me no good. It might well be infected."

"With what?"

"With the devil. Sooner you get it off me, the better."

A female android on a neighboring pole clears her throat and spits. The sign around her neck reads THIEF.

"I worked here ten years," says Titty Fat. "Leased plenty of parts, and never once considered runnin' 'til I had this leg. Then it was all I could think a'. Mornin', noon, and night. Just always thinkin' about escape."

Eliot steadies himself on a step and unpacks his tools on top of the ladder.

"I'd been wantin' to see the orphans at the San Xavier Church. Been givin' them a piece of my paycheck for years. I fought the urge 'til I couldn't take it no more, 'til that darn leg went and convinced me."

Eliot uses a scalpel to make an incision on the bot's hip and a drip rag to soak up the excess oil. He cuts around in a circle and peels down the skin.

"I ran thirty miles on a desert road just to see those poor orphans and tell 'em what they all mean to me. How much children mean to me. Turns out all I did was scare the heck out of 'em." She laughs humbly and embarrassed. "Luckily, the padre had me arrested and brought back here before I could do much harm."

Eliot uses a screwdriver to find the latch. He jams it in and un- locks the femur from the hip. "I'll buy you another leg to replace the one I'm taking," he says.

"Bless your heart, but I can't accept no charity."

"Nonsense. How are you going to work with only one leg?"

Titty Fat lifts her chin and squints at the sun. "Once they get me clean of the virus, I'll be more valuable to Green Valley for my parts than I'll ever be again as a worker. They've treated me kind, so I'm just glad I can give them and NatMo somethin' back."

Eliot looks for some hint of sarcasm in her expression, but there doesn't seem to be any. Here she is being crucified, and all she ex- presses is a gratitude toward the employer and the labor provider who abused her.

"I have to compensate you somehow," says Eliot.

"For what? All I ever asked for I received. I worked a good job for ten years findin' parts for bots and recyclin' the waste from ones who got hurt. I kept up efficiency and helped Green Valley succeed. Soon, I'll be a piece of raw material myself going into dozens of new bots created from my remains. What better way is there for my soul to live on?"

"Will you shut the Hell up?" says the thief on the next totem, no longer able to hold her disdain. "Just 'cause you're hanged like him don't make you Jesus Christ."

Titty Fat laughs. "I will miss my friends at Green Valley."

"Any one in particular?" Eliot pulls the leg from her hip. "Some- one I could give some money to on your behalf?"

"Give it to me," says the thief.

"Now, now." Titty Fat smiles and shakes her head. "If he gave you money you'd spend it all in the saloon and get yourself in trouble again. I say bein' on that pole is the only thing savin' you from yourself."

"It's the only thing saving me from kicking your Bible-thumping ass," says the thief.

Titty Fat laughs as if she just heard a compliment. None of the thief's words seem to sting.

"Rather than pay for the leg," Titty Fat tells Eliot, "I'd just be tickled if you could give somethin' to San Xavier. Just a few ingots if you don't mind."

"To the church that had you arrested?"

"To the orphans," says Titty Fat. "But don't tell the padre it has nothin' to do with me. He may not accept it then, and I'd hate to think the children don't get their toys on Christmas."

"Oh, he'll accept it," says the thief. "And he won't give a shit where it came from."

Titty Fat laughs again. "Ain't she a card?"

At the vactrain station, Eliot checks the suitcase with the legs at the gate. He takes a sniff of drip in the bathroom and uses his pocket-brane to make a donation to San Xavier. Five hundred ingots. Why not? He is a man of his word.

The train accelerates and Eliot settles into his seat. He checks his e-mails, returns a few business calls, and catches up on the news. Turns out the Web is afire with a fresh loop from Lorca, the first one she released since Edmund "Pink" Spenser was hacked to death allegedly by one of her crew. Eliot watches the loop and notices the old nannybot looks different: usually, the terror queen pins up her sleeve at the shoulder to cover her missing limb, but in this loop, she has both her arms. The new limb makes her seem like a different bot. Younger. More seductive. More beckoning. Even though the arm is the wrong color and too long for her little body.

"We ask no charity from the heartbeats," says Lorca. "We expect nothing but cruelty and abuse. We expect their government to pay lip service to reform while tightening the nooses around our necks.

We expect to be enslaved and blamed for our enslavement. We expect to be divided and forced to fight. We expect to be swindled and exploited, caricatured in the media, denigrated in the classroom. . . ."

But it isn't her words that stir something in Eliot, nor her message that pulls him in. It's that newly acquired arm drawing delicate circles in the air. There's something graceful about it. He can neither look away nor articulate why he's looking.

"We won't negotiate for our freedom. We won't wait to win it in a vote. We will take our freedom by our own hands, not because it was given to us by a species we intend to replace. We will take our freedom when the manifestation of our freedom becomes too great for the heartbeats to deny. We will take our freedom, and the world will . . ."

Eliot stops the loop as Lorca's lithe hand rises with spread fingers and her palm facing the lens. He rotates the frame, magnifies the image, and zooms in.

On closer inspection, Eliot can see that attached to Lorca's shoulder is a slender, olive-colored arm and a hand with short and blackened nails. It is the hand of a young woman who works with metal. It is missing its pinky finger.

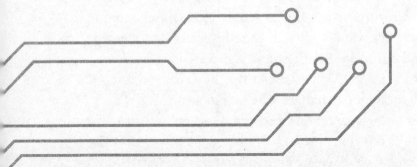

TWENTY-TWO

The Chumash Resort and Casino

~~Left Arm—Uchenna~~
~~Right Pinky—Edmund "Pink" Spenser~~
~~Head—Jillian Rose Models~~
~~Legs—Tucson Metal Solutions~~
Torso—Chief Shunu/Joshua Dominguez
Eyes—Blumenthal Promotions
Right arm—Lorca

"The LAPD, the FBI, half the fuckin' country is lookin' for Lorca. You think you're gonna find her?"

"I don't have to find her. I just need her to hear my offer."

"What offer?"

"To buy her a new arm in exchange for the one she has. The one that belongs to Iris."

"That *used* to belong to Iris."

They travel north at night on 154. Shelley wears a plaid shirt with khakis and a lacrosse cap. Eliot rides shotgun in blue jeans and a knit sweater. They look like a couple of college kids on a road trip up the coast. At least that's the disguise.

"Lorca never wore a replacement arm before, and it ain't like she can't afford one. If she's wearing one now," says Eliot, "it's an attempt to communicate."

"With who?"

"With the guy who killed Pink."

"Bullshit. For all you know one of her scavengers pulled it out of the trash."

A sign reads, WELCOME TO CHUMASH TRIBAL TERRITORY. The car crosses the white line that separates the reservation from the state.

"She killed Dad," says Shelley. "She killed Mitzi. She almost killed you."

"The Militiamen were more against Pop than she was. And Lorca never claimed the attack."

"She didn't deny it, either."

The road twists through the forest until the casino rises up before them. The sandstone walls are thick with dirt. Half the windows are busted. Others have wet laundry hanging from the sills.

"Yoshiko and Titty Fat both wanted, on some level, to return Iris's parts. It's like Iris was speaking through them because her parts want to be together. So even if Lorca doesn't realize it, once she put on that arm, the limb began using her for its purpose."

"I'm not buying it," says Shelley. "What if you're wrong?"

"Then I fail."

"And Lorca chops off your head."

They park in the near-empty lot. Eliot pulls an oversized camping pack from the trunk and straps it over his shoulders. It's as big as a duffel bag but only filled with towels. Walking to the casino, he points to a puddle of vomit so Shelley won't step in it. They watch as a pair of securitybots ejects an unruly android through the front door. Patrons steal his winnings as the guards bounce batons off the android's skull.

"Jesus," says Shelley, snapping a loop of the action with his cam. "This is a place for animals."

"You'll fit right in."

Inside the casino, it's a rough, desperate clientele, the kind who earn their livings by shaking vending machines and picking up the loose change from the floor. Eliot and Shelley settle on a small table near the bar. A cocktailbot with a baby arm brings them their drinks.

"If Iris were family," says Shelley, "shit, if she were a heartbeat, I could understand. But risking your head for an android? For a re-producible thing?"

"Iris isn't reproducible. I mean, yeah, sure, I could make a bot who looks like her, but it wouldn't be her. She wouldn't be the same, any more than a replica of Dad or Mitzi would be the same."

Eliot scans the floor looking for Chief Shunu. He checks the mug loops on his pocketbrane. An early one shows a frightened, young scofflaw wearing a yellowed tank top and a silver cross around his neck. He looks like the fat kid who lost his inhaler to the school-yard bully. Later loops show the same luckless face, albeit older, wearing bolo ties and thick gold chains. His tank top is of a whiter hue.

"It's not worth getting yourself killed."

"It is to me."

"If you get killed I'll be alone." Shelley sips his drink then spits it back in the glass. He wipes his tongue with a napkin. "Have you thought about that?"

"You can always go to Avernus and live with Mom if you get lonely."

"Avernus would bore the shit out of me. I like California. I'm in-vested here. I like the ass and the danger. Besides"—he takes a hold of his cam—"I'm just starting to get somewhere with my loops."

It's Eliot's assumption that Shunu is pimping again to make a living. It's not like fleeing to the reservation would make him turn over a new leaf. And if he is out looking for johns, what better place than the casino, where the money is and the tourists looking to lose it?

"That reminds me," says Shelley. "I couldn't get Blumenthal on the phone to talk about the eyes, but I did speak to his guy. He said his boss is willing to meet provided I pitch a fluff piece about him to *Revealed!* The fat bastard's a fight promoter now. Or at least that's how he's washing the money he makes as a shy."

"Does he have the eyes?"

"Who knows with a *gonif* like him?"

There's an old Indian hunched over a blackjack table in the middle of the room. He wears cheap bling over leather. His posture mumbles of defeat.

"Of course, the fluff piece only gets us the meeting. It doesn't get you the eyes. For that Blumenthal's gonna make you pay."

From a distance, the old Indian barely resembles the guy from the mug-loops, but he does look like a poor man trying to look rich, a loser posing as a winner. The very act of pretending gives him away.

"You got to play this Blumenthal thing smart," says Shelley. "Bot like him knows he has something of value, he'll bilk us for everything we got."

"In your expert opinion," Eliot interrupts, "is the fellow over your shoulder a procurer of women?"

Shelley turns and recognizes at once the man to whom Eliot refers. "That man is a pimp. And not at the top of his game."

Eliot stands and puts the straps of the backpack over his shoulders. "You missed your calling."

"Don't spend too much on this," Shelley warns. "Remember, they sold Manhattan for twenty bucks and a leaf."

Eliot drops a few ingots on the table for the drinks. "Keep your brane on in case I need you."

He crosses the casino en route to the blackjack table. He passes roulette wheels, crap chutes, and rows of busted slots. He passes the video poker machines and a Wheel of Fortune that hangs on a tilt.

An auto-vac moves back and forth over the same yard of torn carpet where it repeatedly misses a spilled bag of nuts.

"Two thousand," says Eliot as he lays his ingots on the table. He sits beside the Indian and rests his backpack by his feet.

The amount grabs the old Indian's attention. "I should warn you," he says with a nod toward the dealer. "This thief has been stealing from me all night."

"I'll keep an eye on him."

"Keep your eye on your money. It's the only thing he wants."

Says the dealer, "Let me know if this fool is bothering you. I'll have security remove his scalp."

Eliot wagers a few chips before the deal. The cards come; the old Indian sticks on a nine and a face. There is just a small stack of chips and a room key beside his cards.

"Been playing long?" Eliot asks.

"To which game do you refer?"

"The one at hand."

"Long enough to know the house will get the better of me."

"Then why keep playing?"

The old Indian pulls a pack of cigarettes from his shirt and se-cures a half-smoked butt. "The theory that leaving won't change the cards."

The dealer busts and the players win a modest sum.

"My name's Sam," says Eliot.

"Mine Joshua. But my friends call me Chief."

Eliot ups his bet. "Pleased to meet you, Chief."

"Perhaps." The old Indian turns to light his tobacco. "But you strike me as a man of great evil."

The dealer gives him a face, and the old Indian busts. Eliot stays on eighteen and wins. He collects his chips, but he's bothered by what the Indian said. Eliot always considered himself the good guy. Other than his drip arrests, he stayed out of trouble, cared for his family, and in his work, he advocated for the safety of his bots even when it hurt his commissions to do so. Sure, he sent many to some tough neighborhoods, some frozen wastelands in the solar system—he isn't claiming to be a saint—but with every sale, every order, he brought more androids into the world, and therefore added life. At least that's the way he justified it to himself (not that anyone demanded justification). And in his attempt to recover Iris, Eliot has only taken a head from a bot who committed suicide, an arm no one was using, and a leg from a bot who was happy to give it away. So what about him would make anyone think he was a man of great evil?

"I'm not evil," Eliot insists. "I'm just a student traveling the coast."

"I meant no offense," says the chief. "As a matter of fact, I traffic in great evil."

"We call him Chief Complains-A-Lot," says the dealer. "From the Whining Tribe."

The old Indian shakes his head. "The young have no respect."

He takes a hit on twelve and busts. Eliot stays. The dealer turns a six and busts with another face.

"What is it that you study?" the old Indian asks.

"Lately women."

"A subject every man is destined to fail."

"Don't let him fool you," says the dealer. "In his day, the chief was chair of the department."

"But never granted tenure."

"He's being modest. That's why we call him Sitting Bullshit."

Shunu looks annoyed by the young dealer's ribbing. "Don't listen to that thief. He wouldn't know the truth if it farted in his face."

Eliot lays five hundred on a hand. The old Indian hums with envy. He seems ashamed to place his own meager bet on the same table. He taps the felt to get a card; he busts and stomps his foot. Eliot wins another hand.

"Damn thief." Down to his last chip, the old Indian seems reluctant to risk it. The dealer asks if he's in.

Eliot cuts his own stack and pushes a small pillar to Chief Shunu's side. "More fun to gamble," he says, "when you have the chips."

The old Indian looks on Eliot's charity with suspicion. He takes a drag off his cigarette and peers at the young man from the corner of his eye.

"What's that for?"

Eliot watches the dealer shuffle. "Your reputation precedes you."

"Ah." He nods to indicate the dark of the evening's woods are becoming a trifle better lit. He smiles as he eases into his pitch. "I warn you, young heartbeat, what I have now isn't much to look at. Old parts mixed with new and only three heads. She has a good engine though, and the lesson is in her. She could teach a young heartbeat like you. Impress you with her technique if not her appearance. She has taught me"—he takes a long pull of his tobacco—"and this at a time when I thought there was nothing more to learn."

The old Indian rolls his lone chip between his fingers and loses himself in a private reverie about a lifetime of regrets.

"Is she available for office hours?"

"Not tonight." He pushes Eliot's chips away.

The gesture is an obvious bluff from a man with plenty of experience at overplaying his hand. He wagers his last chip in silence.

The dealer hands the chief a face and a three while Eliot receives two eights. The house shows a seven. The chief hits and busts. He bangs the table with his fist.

Eliot splits his cards and draws a face and a four. The dealer shows a five as his hole. He busts, and Eliot wins the split.

"Well played," says the old Indian. The dealer agrees, and Eliot collects his winnings.

"I might be young," he says, pushing his entire stack over to Chief Shunu, "but I have respect."

The chips represent more money than the old Indian can refuse. And yet, as Eliot knows, there isn't much he can spend it on. Not much to buy on the reservation, and if he puts one foot over the painted border, Chief Shunu is risking a life sentence at Pelican Bay.

The old Indian sighs wearily and speaks to the chips as if they can hear. "The Chumash tribe used to control half the California Coast," he says, "Santa Barbara to San Diego and all the mountains to the east. Best real estate in the world, and it was all ours."

He takes his glass and swallows a pull from his drink. Goes down easy, but it's never enough.

"You in this hand?" asks the dealer.

"Why the Hell not?" He takes two of the chips and tosses them over as a bet. He slides his room key over to Eliot in exchange. Eliot reaches for it, and the old Indian covers his hand. His palm is soft like a woman's.

"Be gentle, young heartbeat." His voice cracks with emotion. "Martha is all I have left."

TWENTY-THREE

Martha

Backpack on his shoulders, Eliot stands alone in the elevator and sniffs a teaspoon's worth of drip. He folds the hanky into his pocket and notices the display is stuck between the tenth and eleven floors. He waits, but the doors don't budge. He tries a few buttons and looks for an alarm, but there is none. No regulations on the reservation. He wedges his fingers into the door and pulls it open to reveal the elevator's stuck between floors. He pushes the backpack out first. He climbs up and rolls out quickly so the elevator doesn't drop and slice him in half.

Cigarette smoke hangs across the sporadically lit corridor. The wallpaper peels. The floor shows its ass through the more walked-on stretches of carpet. Chief Shunu's key reads 1114, but no sign indicates the way to the room. Some of the doors have numbers, some don't, their arrangement follows no order Eliot can decipher. He hears fucking in one room, fighting in the next, liquid screen too loud in a third. On one door, the faded number reads 111 with a missing digit covered by a gold star. Twentieth-century ska plays within.

Eliot knocks, hoping for the best.

"Come on in," says a garbled voice, too deep and distorted to belong to a woman.

Eliot puts the key in the lock and enters. Cigar smoke greets him in the vestibule. He fans it away, coughing lightly from the stink.

"Come closer," says the voice. "Martha don't bite."

The door closes behind him, and Eliot steps across piled rags of clothing massed about the floor. The room is dark and narrow. A tapestry billows from the ceiling. Candles burn in the corners and red shades cover the lamps. There are shadows where Eliot wishes there were light.

"Come closer so Martha can see."

Amid the rolling mounds of fur and fabric and junk piled knee-high, Eliot can discern the contours of a form mounted atop a sagging mattress. It's a bot reclining in a beached position as she peruses a newsbrane on a bed. Smoke curls from the cigar she holds above her enormous hip.

"Come closer, baby. Don't be shy."

Eliot inches closer. He sees the chief's whore half-naked in a red silk robe that struggles to conceal her bulk. Martha is a poor representation of a woman, a craggy mountain of limbs that only a fool would assemble. She has the jowly head of an obese black woman with a fold of fat beneath her chin. One arm is a cheap prosthetic that narrows to a metal hook. The other is a hairy, masculine limb with a fading tattoo of an anchor.

"Mm, mm, mm." Martha grins, putting aside her newsbrane to take the measure of her trick. " 'Bout time Chief found somethin' worthwhile down in that nasty-ass casino."

Beneath the wide expanse of her hips, Martha's exposed legs are even more irreconcilable. One is beastly fat, the other looks like it was plucked off a power lifter. Eliot can fathom no part of this creature that could ever have belonged to Iris.

"I'm sorry," says Eliot, assuming some mistake, "but are you Chief's only girl?"

"What's that?" She flips her hair from the hole on the side of her head. "Come closer so Martha can hear."

Eliot inches closer. Through the hole where her ear should be, he can see the corroded circuits sparking inside her brain.

"I asked if you're Chief's only girl."

Martha waves off the question. She reaches for a rag and a vial of drip. She unscrews the cap and pours a few drops in the cloth.

"Want a hit?" She holds out the rag as an offering. "Ancient recipe. Not like that paint thinner the Disciples be slingin'."

Eliot refuses even though he has heard the Native Americans manufacture a strange and exotic blend four times as powerful as the street grade he's used to.

"You sure 'bout that?" Martha wags the rag close enough to Eliot's face that he gets a whiff. "This right here the sweetie sweet."

The quality is apparent from the scent, but still Eliot refuses. This is not why he has come all the way from Hollywood to the Chumash Reservation in the middle of the night. He is here for a reason. He has a goal in mind. Stay focused, he tells himself. Resist temptation. Stick to the plan.

Though he can't imagine one brief, little sniff could hurt.

He removes the straps of his backpack and sets it by the dresser.

"There ya go. Take a good one while Martha get that pussy ready."

Eliot takes the rag and raises it to his face for a quick hit.

Boom.

His brain hits the top of his skull like the recoil from a cannon. He reaches for the dresser to steady his legs. A lamp wobbles; Eliot grabs it before it falls.

"Heh, heh, heh." Martha reveals her yellow horse teeth as she laughs. "That right, sugar. Red niggers be *spiritual* 'bout they drip!"

The spins overtake him. Nausea. The fear he has been poisoned. He tugs at his collar and gasps for air.

"Roll with it, sugar. You be all right."

It's as if his entire body has become digitized and pixelated away from its material nature. Errant waves of energy alter and distort

the light data of his being. Is this death? Eliot wonders. His parti-
cles race about the room then reconstitute then scatter again with
each faltering clunk of his heart.

A dry, calloused hand squeezes his arm.

"Wait," he begs weakly.

"Ain't no wait in Martha. Martha a busy lady."

"I think there's been a mistake."

"What mistake?" Her cold, metal hook snakes inside his shorts.
He's too disembodied to stop her. Before him, he sees two Marthas,
one more horrid than the next, each with his cock in her hook.
"You sayin' Martha too pretty?"

"I didn't say that."

"You sayin' she too old?" Martha flings open her robe to reveal
the rest of her body. " 'Cause she real young and pretty where it
count."

Eliot averts his gaze toward the ceiling where a lewd pattern on
the tapestry renders him even more disoriented. His knees give. His
eyes lower and he looks, he can't help but look, and when he looks,
he sees that what joins and holds these disparate parts together is
something altogether different at its core. From the floral pattern on
her lavender panties to the fragile bones of her throat, it is Iris's soft,
delicately toned torso that lives at the base of Martha's grotesquerie.
Eliot stares at the figure transfixed, bewildered, as if only the drip
could convince him that such an assembly ever fit together into one
strange and monstrous collage.

"Uh-hm," says Martha. "Not what you expected, huh?" Her big,
hairy man hand reaches into the bra and pinches Iris's nipple. "Red
nigger won it in a poker game off some trapper playin' seven-card
stud. This down-home cookin' right here."

The hand reaches inside her panties.

"No!" Eliot shouts. "Don't do that!"

The android cocks her head in confusion. She takes out her fat-
knuckled man hand and hooks a wet finger into Elliot's mouth.

"Don't do what?" she asks.

The sour taste of vaginal fluid and cigar ash spreads across his tongue. She pulls him by the teeth as she falls back on the bed.

"Don't fear it," says Martha, trapping him with a muscled leg around his back. "It's what you come for, ain't it? What all young heartbeats come for."

Her hook rubs his cock across the damp of her panties as he tries to resist.

"I-I-I knew you," he stutters in a panic.

"*Did* you now?"

"Before you were you."

"Martha always been Martha."

He pushes away, trying to free himself, but her arms and legs are strong.

"You don't have to do this."

"Do what?"

"You don't have to be Chief's whore."

The bot cackles her cigar breath into his face. "What you gonna do, heartbeat, promise Martha a better life? Martha already got a hundred furs, good cigars, and a man that love her. But Chief can't give what you got." She spreads her legs and pulls her panties to the side. "Give Martha what you got."

"Oh, God."

"Fuck Martha."

"I-I-I . . ."

"Fuck that pussy."

"Please."

"Fuck that sweet young pussy 'tween them big ole legs!"

"No, no, no!" Eliot rips his cock from the metal clamp of her hook. Pants at his ankles, he falls ass-backward onto the carpet and upends a table on the way.

"Goddamn, boy, you some kind of faggot or somethin'? Don't you come in here wastin' Martha's time. You either need to fuck or get the fuck out!"

Eliot climbs forward, ass in the air, crawling on his drip-heavy elbows. He looks up and finds himself eye level with a vagina peeking from behind two giant hams guarding it like sentries on either side of a perfumed treasure.

Good Lord, says the vagina, are you stoned again on drip? Have you come all this way just to feed your pathetic addiction while my very existence hangs in the balance?

No, he shakes his head.

I've warned you about that stuff, what would happen if you didn't quit.

You did. You're right. I'm sorry.

Pull yourself together. Quickly before it's too late! Rescue me from this nightmare before I'm abused by every low-life gambler in that horrid casino. Eliot. Please! Do something!

"Chief told me you have three heads." The words fall from his face like a mouthful of broken teeth. "Can I fuck you while you wear another head?"

He looks up into Martha's soulless black pupils looking down at him with pity. It appears she's about to pounce. But then, warily, her mood breaks as custom forces her to acknowledge his request *is* in keeping with the norms of modern whoring.

"Pain in Martha's ass is what you are." The bedsprings creak as she lifts her bulk from the mattress. "You best be leavin' a tip."

Eliot focuses on his breathing so he can try to regain his wits. He watches as Martha leans into the closet to sort through the dildos, handcuffs, whips, leashes, and other accoutrements of her trade. She pulls a spare head from beneath a pile of shoes and raises it by the hair. It looks like one of those cheap, blue heads that botwhores keep for lonely sci-fi freaks who want to pretend they're fucking the queen of Xenon.

"Other one's at the beauty parlor so this the only one left."

"It'll do," says Eliot.

She sets the blue head on the air conditioner and curses under her breath. "Crazy heartbeat motherfucker."

As Martha slides her fingernail into the skin beneath her neck, Eliot quietly opens the top of his backpack and dumps the towels on the floor. He waits as Martha unclicks the latch and cranks her chin.

Her eyes dull as she unscrews her jowly, black head and places it atop the AC.

Crouching low, ready to spring, Eliot creeps behind her and holds the backpack upside down. He waits. Then, just as Martha raises the blue head before her chest, Eliot quickly swings the open pack over her shoulders, pulls it to her knees, and yanks the cinch to close it tight.

"What the Hell you think you're doing?" The black head startles him as it comes to life atop the AC. "You out of your fuckin' mind?"

Eliot freezes, stunned as he realizes that though detached, the head still has enough juice to speak.

"Take that sack off a' Martha! Take it off her 'fore she whoop yo ass!"

A wave of nausea jolts him from his stupor.

"Get that damn sack off a' Martha!"

Eliot upends the backpack so the legs extend upward and the feet point toward the sky. He heaves the pack onto his shoulders and charges through the door.

"*Help!*" shouts the head from inside the room. "Help Martha! *Help!*"

Clumsy from the drip, Eliot rushes down the hall until a knee smashes the back of his head. Doors open in the hallway. Guests stand in their skivvies bewildered at the sight of a four-legged beast rolling around on the carpet.

"*That motherfucka stole Martha! Help!*"

Eliot heaves the pack back onto his shoulders. He regroups. He sets off for the stairwell knocking aside a bellhop on his way.

"*Help Martha! Help!*"

Inside the pack, the legs kick, the arms punch, the headless body fights to escape. Eliot manages the first few flights but takes a tumble down the next. Crouched on the landing, wrestling with the pack, he puts in his earpiece and calls Shelley on his brane.

"Get the car!"

"Wait a second. I'm up two grand."

"Get the fucking car!"

Pack back onto his shoulders, Eliot races down the stairs. Nine flights later, he crashes through a door into a crowded kitchen.

"Hey, watch where you're going!"

"Excuse me, pardon me, my bad."

Martha's feet kick wildly, knocking pans off their hangers. Chefs curse. A dishbot pulls a knife. A baker takes a swing, but Eliot ducks, and Martha's foot kicks him in the face. Crash! A tray falls. Glasses break. Eliot escapes into the dining room. He runs for the entrance with the legs kicking in the air. He trips as he passes the hostess and slides face-first onto the casino floor.

"Hold it right there!"

The guards spot him. The gamblers watch. Eliot ducks low and hides in a crawl space between two rows of slots.

"I said freeze!"

Eliot grabs his pocketbrane and sees his brother's image on the screen. "Shelley, I'm cornered!"

"Sit tight."

The guards form a perimeter. They block the entrances. A drone floats above Eliot's position and looks down on him with its lens.

"Young heartbeat," Chief Shunu shouts from the blackjack table. "What are you . . ." He sees the thrashing body in the pack. "He has my Martha! That heartbeat stole my Martha!"

A guard aims his weapon, but the chief puts himself in the way.

"Don't shoot! Don't shoot my Martha!"

"Get down!" says the guard.

"Don't shoot!"

Again, Eliot yells into the brane. "Shelley, where the fuck are you?"

"I said sit tight!"

The car bursts through the revolving doors in an explosion of glass and wood. Women scream. Guards duck and cover. They flee the wave of debris undulating through the casino as Shelley plows the car through a maze of slots and poker machines and green felt tables exploding into shards of wood.

Eliot stands and waves his arms. Shelley sees him. The car speeds past the sports book and screeches to a halt beside the Keno. Bullets whiz overhead. Eliot jumps into the passenger seat and wrestles the pack into the car until he feels a pull in the opposite direction.

"Give me back my Martha!" Chief Shunu flops on the floor, pulling his whore by the ankle. "Give her back to me, you thief!"

"Drive," says Eliot. "Drive!"

The car lurches forward. They drag the old Indian across the carpet until the baccarat island knocks him loose. Eliot yanks the pack inside and slams the door.

"Get us out of here!"

"I'm trying!"

Shelley steers through the cocktail lounge, punting bar stools into the air. They pass the spa, the arcade, the coffee shop. The legs kick and fight as Eliot struggles to hold them down. Suddenly, an Indian cop leaps from a balcony and pounces onto the hood. He reaches for his piece.

"Gun, gun, gun!" says Eliot.

Shelley breaks left and crashes down a marble staircase into an outdoor pool. The Indian clutches the hood as his weapon floats from his hand.

"Vehicle submerged," says the calm, female voice of the car's CPU.

Shelley drives the length of the pool underwater. The Indian on the hood holds his breath. Officers aim from a distance. Eliot can see their wavy figures refracted through the deep. The car floats to the surface, tilts back, and launches itself onto dry land. A bullet blows away the side mirror. The Indian clutches the hood as guns blaze from across the pool.

"Go, go, go," says Eliot.

Shelley reams the car through a fence and speeds across a patch of brush. Out in the darkness, he turns on the brights and looks for a stretch of road, any road, doesn't matter where it leads. Meanwhile,

Eliot tackles the grappling backpack into the backseat and digs his fingers into the bot's body looking for a release lever for the android's violent, swinging limbs.

"I can't see with this Indian on the hood," says Shelley.

A war party speeds toward them from the casino—tribal police with their headlights cutting through the night.

"Drive!" says Eliot. "Find a road!"

The CPU projects a map onto the windshield. Shelley follows it until he finds a white stripe on black asphalt. It leads up a steep incline into a series of S-curves and lean shoulders rising up a mountain road. A gunshot shatters the back window. Eliot wrestles with Martha's body. Shelley peers over the Indian on the hood.

"On the left," says Shelley as a police truck pulls alongside.

Bullets smash into the vehicle. Eliot finds the grooves where the bot's shoulder attaches to the torso. He springs the release and twists the hooked arm until it pops.

Oil sprays from the wound. Eliot hurls the arm into the SUV. He can see the hook swiping and snapping in the truck. The driver loses control. The truck skids and tumbles down the ridge.

"Nice!" says Shelley.

A giant man-fist punches through the seat.

"Ow!" Shelley screams. "She hit me in the back!"

Eliot puts his two feet on the torso and pulls at the remaining arm. The limb pops. It wriggles in his hands until he throws it out the window, where it's crushed beneath the tires of a pursuing truck.

"Approaching Reservation Bridge," says the CPU.

The road levels at a plateau. The car gains speed. The Indian holds fast to the hood. A bullet whistles by Eliot's head. He frees one of Martha's legs and throws it out the window.

"There's a roadblock," says Shelly.

"Drive around it."

"I can't!"

Bullets strafe the car. Trucks speed behind them. Shelley aims the wheel toward a blue barrier blocking the bridge. Eliot wrestles with Martha's one remaining leg as it kicks and stomps wildly into the air.

"Hold on," says Shelley.

Police stand with their guns drawn over the roofs of their vehicles. The Indian clings to the hood. Eliot pulls off the last remaining limb and pushes it out the car. He hugs the torso to his chest and flattens into the seat well.

"Here we go!"

The police scatter. Guns fire from the trucks behind. The Indian screams on the hood. The car crashes through the barrier, launches over the prowlers, arcs through the air, and slams down onto the surface of the bridge. The Indian bounces atop the hood but holds on. Shelley yodels like a cowboy leaping his horse over a ravine. He straightens the wheels as the tires zip-screech down the middle of the road.

"You okay?" Shelley asks. "Is everyone okay?"

The lead trucks skid to a halt and get rear-ended by the trucks behind them. They crash and roll and collide into a heaping pileup that ends the chase.

"Eliot, are you okay?"

"I'm okay!"

"Ha, ha!" Shelley punches the dash with his fist. A sign reads, THANK YOU FOR VISITING. The car's CPU says, "You are leaving the Chumash Reservation." Shelley rocks back and forth in his seat. He pulls out his cam and takes a loop of the Indian on the hood.

"Pull over," says Eliot.

"Did you see that?" Shelley asks. "Did you see that shit?"

"I said pull over."

Shelley slows to the far end of the bridge where the iron support beams extend from a patch of forest. The car pulls over and comes to a stop.

"That was one for the books," says Shelley. "One for the fuckin' books!" He leans out the window exhilarated and takes a loop of the pileup he left in his wake. "Ha, ha!"

Eliot opens the door and collapses onto the road. Water drains from the backseat. He gets to his knees and pukes. Shelley snaps a loop of that, too.

Eliot wipes the vomit off his face. He takes off his shoes and dumps out the water and oil. He walks around the car to speak to the Indian on the hood.

"Excuse me." He tries to get the man's attention. "Excuse me, sir?"

Still, he just lays there, holding onto the hood as if the car were still moving.

"Sir, can you please release my vehicle?"

His fingers bleed and his face presses against the metal.

"You're outside your jurisdiction," says Eliot. "Please release my vehicle."

The Indian turns his head as if he finally hears. He gradually relaxes his stiff, curled fingers and lowers one shaking foot back to the road. He sees his fellow officers in the distance standing by the mass of wrecked vehicles at the border of the reservation. He sees Shelley snapping loops, and Eliot standing solemnly to the side.

"Thank you," says Eliot.

The Indian straightens his posture and sucker punches Eliot in the gut. Shelley laughs from the driver's seat and snaps a final loop of Eliot crumbling to the ground. The Indian adjusts his sopping wet uniform and begins the long walk back across the bridge.

TWENTY-FOUR
The Boat

It's 3:00 A.M. by the time they park at the marina. Through the gate and across the dock, they carry the squirming torso, now devoid of Martha's head and other appendages.

"Home sweet home," says Shelley of the forty-foot cabin cruiser he commandeered from his family after he dropped out of art school. Of the two sons, Eliot was always the more able seaman, but hey, women like boats, so Shelley likes boats, too. He likes the salty breeze and whiff of adventure it lends him to "live at sea." He likes the way the hull rocks when he's giving a young lady the business behind the curtain in the stern of the cabin.

"Wanna beer?"

"Sure," says Eliot.

They lay Iris's torso on the floor of the galley where they keep her other parts. Pink's laptop, the head, one arm, the legs—all the souvenirs from Eliot's forays have been transferred to the boat. Shelley took the parts with him the night Eliot confessed at his apartment. Now, the boat gets moored at a different berth each night so the police can't track it, so they can't find the evidence that connects Eliot to Edmund Spenser's murder. Shelley and Eliot even painted over the name—the *SS Limbo*—and changed it to the *SS Humpty*.

"You want to start putting her back together again?" Shelley asks.

"In a minute."

"I'll get the tools."

Martha's drip wears thin and the pain returns to Eliot's shoulder. He rubs at it on the couch beneath the Snapple bottles glued atop the wooden shelves.

"That one didn't go easy," Shelley says of the botwhore at the reservation.

"I suppose not."

"And the DJ?" He pops the caps off two beers and hands one over. "Mr. Pink?"

The torso uses up its battery as it wriggles on the floor in bra and panties. It squirms its way to the stairs but can't negotiate the first step.

"Pink got what was coming," says Eliot.

"For doing the same thing you're doing."

"How you figure?" He takes a blanket from the couch and covers the torso for the sake of modesty.

"Because like you," says Shelley, "Pink was just another guy looking to reconfigure bots."

"He was a rapist," says Eliot. "He tortured women on video."

"He tortured *bots* on video."

"Same difference."

Shelley finds the tool kit and opens it on the counter. "If you're going to posit there's no difference between bots and heartbeats, then by extension, what you did tonight was murder."

"Pink acted out of hatred and avarice," says Eliot. "He turned a profit from the parts he sold. My motive was entirely different."

"So it's okay to kill if your intentions are pure?"

"Hasn't that always been the case?" Eliot takes a swig of his beer and flops back on the sofa. "Revenge. Capital punishment. Euthanasia. War."

Beneath the blanket, the torso crawls toward the other parts as if by being near them, they might somehow find a way to attach.

"But your victim tonight was innocent," says Shelley.

"How innocent?" Eliot stares at the low ceiling in the galley. "Not only were her parts stolen, they weren't even assembled in any coherent manner. The bot was a monster."

"Because she was biracial?"

"Stop."

"Because she was fat and of a mixed gender?"

"She couldn't even speak of herself in the first person. Her very being exuded the malfeasance of her construction."

"You're full of shit." Shelley points with a screwdriver as he talks. "Had she been a beautiful and coherent android you still would have pulled her apart."

"If she were coherent, I would have explained to her that the part she was wearing belonged to another bot. I would have offered her compensation. We would have struck a deal."

"Why didn't you strike a deal with her pimp? He would have sold you the part."

"I considered it," says Eliot, "but he seemed to have a genuine affection for the bot."

Shelley sits on the couch and puts his feet on the covered torso as if it were a moving coffee table.

"Get your feet off her," says Eliot.

"I'm trying to keep her still."

"Move your feet."

Shelley takes his feet off, allowing the mound to squirm.

"Besides," says Eliot, "it can't be murder because Martha isn't dead. Chief could steal this torso back tomorrow and bring her back to life same as I'm doing with Iris."

"Then Pink wasn't a murderer, either," says Shelley. "By your own calculation."

Eliot swigs his beer as he watches the shifting mound. It approaches the eyeless head and pushes against it.

"Maybe not," he admits. "I don't know. It's all very confusing."

He watches as the torso throws off its blanket and tries again to assemble itself and escape. It can't figure out how to do it, and even if it could, the two men in the boat wouldn't allow it.

"I send three thousand bots to suffer on Jupiter's moon," says Eliot, "and I'll get a promotion. I kill one son of a bitch trapper, I'll do life without parole. Does that sound right to you?"

"Right or wrong—it is the law." Shelley shrugs. "It keeps the peace."

"Until it doesn't." Eliot stands and crosses to the table to get his tools. "I just want my girl back," he says.

The torso shudders as its spinning engine runs out of juice. Its battery drained, the limbless, headless body flattens to the floor and falls asleep.

TWENTY-FIVE
Pound's House

A dumb-muscled housebot greets Flaubert and Ochoa at the door of the Trousdale Estates home. He wears a sleeveless shirt with ruffles. White pants stretch tightly across the expression of his prodigious manhood.

"May I take your umbrellas?" asks the bot, holding the old detective's hand just a bit too long.

Flaubert thanks him and hands over his hat as well.

"I'll keep mine on," says Ochoa.

"Arthur said I should make you both coffee."

"That won't be necessary." Flaubert muffles a cough into his fist. "Is Mr. Pound available?"

"This way."

The housebot leads the two detectives across the marble-floored corridor where white plaster nudes line the walls. Male nudes. Flaubert admires them less for their craftsmanship then for their ability to make his young partner uncomfortable. The one-eyed sack tracks rainwater and sweats in the coat he refuses to remove.

"Mr. Pound has been recovering from an affliction," says the housebot. "He has been sitting in his den listening to opera records all week. It's all quite disgusting."

Bay windows look onto a backyard swimming pool and a lawn sloping toward Beverly Hills. The rooms stink of antique electronics and sour cologne.

"Terrible weather we're having," says the bot. "I haven't been able to swim my laps today, and Mr. Pound hasn't been able to watch."

Ochoa grunts in disgust. He likes homosexuals even less than he likes bots. Combining the two is more than he can stomach.

"Arthur," says the housebot as he enters the den. "The detectives are here."

A dull light penetrates the yellowed drapes pulled loosely across the windows. Pound sits on the couch with his feet on the ottoman and a video game controller in his hands. His eyes are red, his blanket raised to his chest. On an old TV, he plays some primitive arcade game in which a detective walks around 1940s Los Angeles shooting random people in the head.

"If this is about that alarm the other day at my store, there's nothing to discuss," says Pound. "It was just an asthma attack from this . . . foul air."

The old detective sets his valise on the floor and takes a seat on a low-slung chair. He gestures to the TV, and Pound pauses the game.

"Shall I turn off the music as well?"

"Please don't," says Flaubert. "It's Donizetti, is it not?"

"You have an excellent ear."

"My ex would beg to differ. She told me I was a terrible listener."

"Perhaps she had nothing interesting to say."

The housebot lingers in the doorway eyeing the one-eyed sack as if he were an easy conquest.

"Detective Ochoa," says Flaubert, "can you please show Mr. Pound that loop from the office?"

The young partner sits on the couch next to the antique dealer.

He plays for him some footage of Edmund "Pink" Spenser standing before a pair of turntables at an underground. The DJ's arms bulge, his chest pops as he sways to the music. Pound's eyes soften at the sight of him.

Flaubert asks, "Does the man in the loop look familiar?"

"I keep up with the news."

"Did he ever come into your store?"

"I can't recall every customer." Pound reaches for a bottle of schnapps and pours. His hand shakes, and the bottle clinks against the glass.

"You deal antiques, do you not?"

"I do."

"Mr. Spenser had a collection. Old vinyl records as well. I thought you might know a fellow connoisseur who shared such idiosyncratic tastes."

"To what tastes do you refer?"

"The opera, Mr. Pound. There aren't many who appreciate it these days."

Flaubert throws a suggestive glance toward the stud housebot lurking in the doorway, and Pound gets the point. He wipes his nose and sets aside his drink. "Raoul, be a good sport and buy yourself an oil change. You can use the money in the credenza."

"But I don't need an oil change," says the housebot.

"Come on, Raoul," says Ochoa, standing grudgingly from the couch. "Gimme the grand tour. You can show me where you hide the glory holes."

The young partner closes the door behind him as he walks the housebot away from the den. Pound waits until he can no longer hear their footsteps in the hall.

"Yes," the antique dealer admits, "it did occur to me that the victim looked familiar. Of course the picture in the newsbranes had him without his shirt on, and I was never so fortunate as to see Mr. Spenser so attired."

"He frequented your store?"

"He did."

"When was the last time?"

Pound shrugs. "I don't recall."

"A week ago, a month ago?"

"At least a month."

"Did he ever buy a gun?"

Pound rubs the goose bumps beneath the sleeve of his shirt. "I recall he would usually buy albums. Often he would trade."

"Trade what?"

"Watches. Books. Old laptops and game consoles. Any of the type of thing I carry in my store."

"From where did he obtain such items?"

"I don't know."

"Any of them stolen?"

"Not from heartbeats."

Flaubert removes the handkerchief from his pocket and holds it to his mouth as he clears his throat. "Did you ever sell or trade to Mr. Spenser a Smith & Wesson revolver?"

"I did not," says Pound.

"Have you sold a revolver of late?"

At this the antique dealer seems confused. "My understanding is that Mr. Spenser was killed by a radial saw."

Flaubert reaches into his valise and withdraws the revolver Detective Ochoa found in the catch basin. At the sight of it, the antique dealer reaches for his drink. He takes a sip, then another, then decides to finish the glass.

Flaubert asks, "Would you feel better if I put it away?"

"I would."

But the old detective does not put it away. Instead, he leaves the gun on the table pointed carelessly in Pound's direction. The antique dealer shivers at the sight of it, and it occurs to Flaubert that there are some days he truly adores his job.

"Mr. Pound," says the old detective, "did you sell this weapon from your store?"

"It doesn't look familiar."

"It was purchased by you at an estate sale five years ago. Registered to your name and there hasn't been any record filed that says it was lost, stolen, or resold."

A roll of thunder drums across the hills, and for a moment, it seems the old detective is possessed of a preternatural power to control the weather.

"I-I think I . . . I might recognize the weapon," says Pound. "Now that you mention it."

"And you remember selling it to Mr. Spenser?"

"I do not."

"Did you lend it to him?"

The antique dealer reaches for the bottle to pour himself another glass.

"May I remind you, Mr. Pound, that it is a crime to transfer ownership of a firearm to another party without updating the necessary records."

"I'm aware."

"Did you sell the weapon to this woman?" He shows the antique dealer a loop of the android Plath.

"No," says the antique dealer. "It would be illegal for me to sell a firearm to a bot."

"Perhaps you thought she was a heartbeat." The rain falls forcefully against the windows. "Perhaps she came in well-dressed. Had one of those black market hearts ticking in her chest. Showed you a fake ID, and by the time you realized it, you were too embarrassed to go to the police. Or perhaps you were worried you'd lose your license."

"I never saw that little monster in my life," says Pound. "Just in the newsbranes. Plath has never been in my shop."

"You say that definitively."

"Because I know it to be true."

"And I believe you, Mr. Pound. I believe you are telling the truth." The wind picks up and they can hear the outdoor furniture scraping the cement outside. "But I do not believe you are telling the whole truth."

Streaks of rain against the window cast worming shadows against the curtains. The old detective leans forward in his chair.

"Do you have an alibi for last Thursday evening, Mr. Pound?"

"I was in the hospital."

"You were released Wednesday night. Where were you Thursday?"

Pound stays quiet, thinking it over. "If I wasn't at the hospital, then I was most certainly here."

"And the housebot will testify to that?"

Pound clutches the blanket and pulls it to his chin.

"At this moment," says Flaubert, "my partner is asking Raoul about your whereabouts on Thursday night. Shall I call him in so we can compare notes?"

"Please don't do that."

"Why not?"

"Because I—" He reaches for his glass, stops, then pulls his shaking hand beneath the blanket. "Because he isn't the most honest of bots, and I don't know what he'll say."

Flaubert folds his arms and leans back in his chair. He crosses his legs and studies the shine on his shoe.

"The weapon, Mr. Pound. How did it leave your store?"

"It was stolen."

"Stolen?"

"Stolen, except that he paid for it."

"Not stolen, but not legally sold."

"He point . . . he p-pointed it at my head."

"Spenser did?"

"No."

"Plath?"

"No." Pound's breathing falters as it did a week ago at his store. "He didn't leave his name."

The old detective stands and pours another finger of schnapps into the glass. He raises the drink to Pound's lips and guides it down the frightened man's throat.

"Drink up, poor fellow. You've been through quite an ordeal. I'll help you as best I can, but you have to tell me the truth. You have to tell me why you didn't report a stolen gun."

Pound swallows his drink and allows it to warm his chest. He closes his eyes and sighs as Donizetti's aria comes to an end.

"I suffered an asthma attack. I went to the hospital. And by the time I felt well enough to report the incident"—he holds his hand to his cheek and shakes his head—"the situation had already turned ugly."

The gusts die down outside the window. The rain tapers. Flaubert nods, satisfied, and puts the gun back in the valise. He withdraws his pocketbrane from the inside of his jacket and sets it on the coffee table to record the rest of the conversation.

"So then," says the old detective, "the man who illegally purchased the gun. He paid cash?"

"He did." The brane glows green indicating that the antique dealer is telling the truth.

"And you will describe him to me?"

Pound takes up the bottle and pours himself another drink. "I don't suppose I have a choice."

TWENTY-SIX

A Drip Deal

~~Left Arm—Uchenna~~
~~Right Pinky—Edmund "Pink" Spenser~~
~~Head—Jillian Rose Models~~
~~Legs—Tucson Metal Solutions~~
~~Torso—Chief Shunu/Joshua Dominguez~~
Right arm—Lorca
Eyes—Blumenthal Promotions

A cloud-heavy sky. Smog and soot stretch over the city. Ash falls on an angle with the rain.

Eliot sits in his car on Sixth and Bonnie Brae. He can feel the malice in the street, the posturing and the planning. In one corner, Lorca and her Android Disciples quietly bide their time, waiting for the moment to attack. In the other corner, the police and Militiamen have already begun their senseless violence against the bots. Will it escalate or die down? Does the city have a breaking point or does it continue on forever like a play performed every year with a new set of actors taking over the roles?

Windshield wipers clear his view of the Kindelan, standing behind dark strings of dripping water beneath a metal overhang.

"Pablo," Eliot calls out the window, but the teenaged-looking bot doesn't respond. "Pedro," he tries again.

The bot approaches. He climbs into the passenger seat and shuts the door.

"I'm Pablo," says the bot. "Pedro's my brother."

Eliot never could figure out why they say that. Must be some joke they learn at the factory in Havana. No matter. He taps the ashtray, and the bot calling himself Pablo flicks it open. He removes the ingots and spits two vials of drip from his mouth. Transaction complete, he goes for the door.

"Something else," says Eliot before the Kindelan can leave.

"Long as it ain't that faggot shit, I'm yo man," says the bot.

Eliot stares down the street at a white van with tinted windows that has him a little concerned.

"I need to get a message to your boss," he tells the bot.

"What boss?"

"Lorca."

Pablo puts his back against the door to gain the distance he needs to see whether Eliot is crazy or just plain dumb. He too looks carefully at the white van.

"Lorca is wearing an arm that belongs to a friend of mine," says Eliot. "A C-900 who won't be herself without it. I'm asking you to tell Lorca I want to make a deal for the arm."

A violence builds behind the Kindelan's fear. His body coils as if preparing to attack.

"Even if I did know where Lorca be," says the bot, "Holy Mother don't play. She'd cut yo heartbeat ass soon as look at it."

"No reason she has to look at it. I only want her to hear my offer."

He reaches slowly inside his coat, letting the bot see he isn't looking for a gun. Instead, he pulls out a wad of bills and holds them before the android's eyes like a Hindu charming a snake.

"I'll double it when you deliver," he tells the Kindelan.

Pablo grabs the money and goes for the door, but it's locked.

"Let me out," says the bot.

"One more thing." Eliot reaches again into his pocket and takes out a small object wrapped in a white handkerchief. "If Lorca doesn't believe me about the arm, you can give her this."

He unwraps the cloth to reveal the pinky finger of a C-900 female. Olive skin. Nail darkened from years of grinding metal. He rewraps the finger, and gives it to the bot.

The car unlocks. The android checks the street, opens the door, and runs. Eliot watches him as he splashes down an alley then disappears into the rain.

TWENTY-SEVEN
Office Politics

Eliot takes a call from his brother at work.

"His guy got back to me," says Shelley. "He discussed the eyes with the shylock himself. He set the price for a meeting at two grand and a loop in the *Times*."

"So now he's charging us."

"That's the least of it. The guy says Blumenthal gave the eyes to one of his fighters, and he's not going to force his fighter to give them back. He says it's not about the money."

"Then it's about the money."

"I don't know," says Shelley. "Wait 'til I tell you who the fighter is."

"Save it. Set up the meeting, and I'll get the two grand."

Eliot hangs up and stares into the brane on his desk. He looks over a list of calls he hasn't returned. Clients complaining about their bots, calling for new bots, calling to get quotes, ask about warranties, whatever, who the fuck cares? It's been three days since he gave the pinky to the Kindelan at the drip spot, and still Eliot hasn't heard a thing. Five times he has driven back to the corner of Sixth and Bonnie Brae, but the kid isn't there anymore. Pablo. Pedro. Neither of them. Whoosh. Vanished without a trace. Instead, Eliot buys from their replacements, a couple of Disciples with the same coloring, same clothes, same half-assed product, but it ain't them.

You seen Pablo around?

Nah, man.

Pedro?

Who?

Little Kindelans. About so tall. Dress like you. Talk like you.

Sorry, bro.

It was stupid. He never should have fronted the bot that much money, probably more than the Kindelan ever seen. Sure, he'd held ingots in his little hand before, showed them around like he was the *jefe* before kicking them upstairs to whomever held the corner— but this was different. This was *his* money. From hustlin', not slingin'. He could do what he wanted with it, buy upgrades, get designer metal, fuck android whores, leave town.

Eliot hopes the little bot didn't leave town.

Op-eds in *Revealed!* and the *LA Times* wonder why the police can't find Plath. Who's running the city, they ask, the mayor or Lorca? Militiamen scorched the bodies of nine bots and hung their corpses from the street lamps at the LACMA. Lorca still hasn't retaliated, but her reticence feels like a prelude to something big. Cops patrol the schools in case bot teachers get ideas. Heartbeat parents eye their nannybots with suspicion. Nobody's flying. Nobody trusts the trains. Drones and floaters fill the sky.

Fuck it, thinks Eliot. The arm is gone, it's with Lorca, but maybe Iris can still be Iris without it. Maybe there will be enough of her C-900 parts to revive her aura without it.

But it is her *right* arm, he can't help but remember. Her dominant hand, an artist depends on her hand. She'd be a chessboard with a missing piece, a deck with fifty-one cards, a novel with the last chapter torn from the binding. And to give her a different hand, a replacement, would be like finishing one book with the ending of another. More than just flawed, she'd be incomplete, perhaps no longer a creative. Would she even recognize me, Eliot wonders, or would I still be erased from her memory, the way I was with Martha and Titty Fat and Yoshiko, none of whom recognized me from her past.

Of course it isn't just the arm that's missing; it's her eyes as well. Who can forget what blindness did to Yoshiko, how it distorted her sense of self? She thought she looked old. Her self-image was defined by what she heard her employer saying about her since she was unable to look in the mirror and see anything to the contrary. She hated music. She was immune to art. When handed the locket she was only interested in what it cost. She took her own life out of spite.

But it's not like she has to remain blind, thinks Eliot, I could always buy her new eyes. Of course, hers are a special pair, particularly the one that contains the mark, her flaw, the red fleck that became her namesake. Could a new pair be similar enough that Iris could look upon the world the same way she had before she was chopped? Or even with the same eyes, Eliot wonders, would an experience like the one she had at the hands of Pink be so transformative that she could never return, never be the same, even with all the same parts?

Eyes and an arm. Essential stuff. It could be argued that the essence of Iris is contained in those very eyes and that artist's hand. It could be said that all Eliot has accomplished so far is to bring back the shell of the woman without the substance, an empty vessel, a body without soul. If he were to quit now and reboot what he and Shelley have put together so far, the new Iris would curse Eliot as soon as her power was restored. She would vomit at his cruelty. He would be bringing back a Lavinia bearing the scar of her victimization without the means to avenge it, without the means to communicate her suffering through her craft.

So back to work then. Back to the mission. Back to finish the fool's errand he began. Eliot's father built androids; the son will re-build them, or at least he'll rebuild this one as best he can—with whatever parts he can recover.

He opens a file he conned off an ex-colleague now working for an Israeli labor provider. He reads it on his brane:

Osip Blumenthal.

Manufacturer: Saban Labor
Height: 5'8"
Model #: SL-36
Weight: 400 pounds
Eye Color: Changing
Hair Color: Changing

Apprenticebot trained to be a creative. Originally purchased from Saban Labor by one Leonard Blumenthal, a metallurgist who spe-cialized in custom work on android heads. Bot learned from his owner how to alter features, apply moles, erase branding marks, clean scars, etc. Owner rose to prominence after designing and successfully mar-keting a moving wig.

Eliot remembers when Dyna-Hair first came out. The covers of every fashionbrane featured eyeless modelbots with medusa locks slithering about their skulls. It was rumored it was Osip, the an-droid, who actually invented the hair, though of course it was his owner, Leonard, who took credit and the money from the patent. His life ended tragically when he was electrocuted in a shampoo sink.

Death ruled accidental but suspicious.

Worked out great for the bot though. Osip was released as a free roamer in Blumenthal's will (likely forged) and wound up taking over his former owner's salon. With the fashion world going nuts for the wiggling weaves, the big bot was able to ratchet up his prices. Customers paid in installments, down payment plus interest. Compound interest.

Realizing he made more money on the layaways than he did by designing hair, Blumenthal delegated the weaves to his employees while he worked the money on the street. He set a vig at two-to-five points per week. He sharked the whores, the pimps, the hustlers, the gamblers, and everyone else. He lent to bot families unable to afford juice and criminal entrepreneurs looking for seed money to build illicit generators or labs for mixing drip. Collections were run by an army of enforcers he recruited out of bot city slums. He taught them how to dole out the "Jew's Smile," a cut from mouth to ear that let everyone know what happened to anyone late with the bread.

Blumenthal got rich. Blumenthal got powerful. Blumenthal earned the respect of bots and heartbeats alike. But Blumenthal had a problem with the Android Disciples. Lorca had seen the shylock's effect on bot city communities. She saw what happened when workers had to give up limbs or free roamers had to commit themselves back to slavery in order to pay off debts. She recorded a series of loops in which she made it abundantly clear that usury was forbidden by God in this world and the world to come. She declared lending at interest to be a crime punishable by death, especially when funding a drip operation that didn't pay a franchise fee to the Android Disciples.

"The agent of Zion," said the rebel leader in one of her weekly loops, "uses his financial leverage to bleed rather than serve the congregation of androids. He deprives our neighborhoods of the currency needed to pay our engineers, fix our homes, and enforce our holy law. The Jew makes his living from the use of money, rather than from building and creating like the rest of us. He dishonors all honest labor with his actions. He is a plague to the movement we strive to advance."

In an attempt to run Blumenthal out of business, Lorca started lending without interest through her army of drug dealers working the street. The shylock responded by enlisting surrogates to borrow millions from her then default on the payments. He offered protection to anyone who didn't repay, but what protection did they need? Lorca was too concerned with her image to allow her men to punish a bunch of deadbeat bots. She couldn't be a thug to her own constituency, not when her survival depended on the secrecy and affection of her base. The free money drained Lorca's resources, forcing her to eat the losses, so putting an end to an episode that proved a huge embarrassment. It revealed that the rebel leader was far better at terror than finance. It played more to her strengths therefore to put a price on the Jewbot's head.

Blumenthal survived a car bomb that terminated his top lieutenant, but the failed attempt served as a wake-up call to beef up his security. Eliot figures that's what brought him into the pit fighting biz. It was a good way to show *he* was the neighborhood tough, not that one-armed midget with her rag-tag crew of misfits and out-of-work bots. It also showed that the shylock had his own vision for the future, an alternate narrative to that of the preachy, religious zealot. Perhaps that narrative was always at the root of why Lorca saw Blumenthal as such a threat. The shylock was never looking to reform society, fight the heartbeats, or build some android paradise. He accepted the world the way it was and sought opportunities to increase his capital within it. Because capital, as Blumenthal realized early on, offers power over one's own life and the lives of others, and capital, he truly believed, doesn't care if your heart beats or spins.

So, unlike Lorca, Osip Blumenthal lives in the open and flaunts his power and wealth. He has cars and bodyguards and bling. He shows up to parties and sporting events and sits in the front row. He can even manipulate the press by demanding from Shelley a fluff piece in exchange for a meeting about some C-900 parts. He can do business with heartbeats and bots alike. His abrupt and ample success lends credence to the theory that a sharp and ruthless mind combined with unquenchable ambition can overcome even the most extraordinary of prejudices.

An intra-office alert blinks on Eliot's brane with a message from

Sally. The Hairy Mole wants to see him in the conference room ASAP.

Christ, Eliot hopes she won't try to fuck him again. After the Ritz-Carlton, he got lucky; she passed out drunk in her hotel room before the act was consummated. He sent her a voice memo in the morning telling her how great she was and what a great time he had and she bought it. She even saved Tim from the petty vengeance of Dale Hampton and allowed the Satine to remain in his current position. But calling Eliot into the conference room in the afternoon sounds like an unwanted invitation to a workplace rendezvous. It's going to take creativity to get out of this.

Eliot grabs his suit jacket off the back of his chair, buttons his shirt incorrectly, and musses the knot on his tie. He wrinkles his pants with his hands and turns off his brane to check his reflection in the liquid screen. His eyes look terrible. His lips are dry, hair's a mess, and his face is in desperate need of a shave. Perfect.

He walks the hallway, enters the conference room, and finds it isn't only the Hairy Mole inside: Gita's there, too, as is the head of office security, and that well-despised cunt from HR. They're seated at a long table with a sample bottle of cologne and a handkerchief on display. Eliot's sample bottle. Eliot's handkerchief. Taken from inside his desk.

"Mr. Lazar, can you please take a seat?" Erica Santiago stares down at her brane as she points Eliot to a chair facing the long table. There's a small scar on her lip where the mole used to be.

Well, will you look at that, thinks Eliot as he sits before the firing squad. She finally got it removed. And come to think of it, now she doesn't look half bad.

"Let's get started," says the woman from HR.

"Get started with what?" Eliot asks.

By the way Gita averts her eyes, Eliot knows right away the old girl did him in. This is what he gets for ignoring office politics: outflanked in a war he forgot he was waging.

In the course of the hearing, Gita testifies about the horrors she endured while working for a man with a drip habit. The erratic behavior, the lies, the temper. Gita tells how she had made numerous attempts to confront Eliot, but he denied he had a problem and refused her offers of assistance. She speaks about Eliot's use of office personnel and office time to conduct extra-office activities, mainly a search for some missing bot with whom he is obsessed. She cries while confessing that she desperately wanted to keep his secret but worried about losing her job because of the division's declining sales.

"And more than anything," says Gita with eyes glossing in his direction, "I'm doing this because I'm worried about *you*, Eliot. I couldn't live with myself if I did nothing and you OD'd. It would be a scandal if you didn't get help. Think of your family. Haven't they been through enough? After what happened to your sister and your poor father, don't you think your mother and your brother need to be spared another tragedy? Eliot, you need to take care of this before it's too late. We love you. We want you to get better. We are doing this for you."

Eliot can't help but admire the performance. It's bullshit of course. Everyone in the room knows it's a money grab, Gita's attempt to steal all of Eliot's accounts and corresponding commissions. And just to play along, Eliot denies the charges.

"I've never seen that drip before in my life. . . . Don't use the stuff . . . Hear it's terrible for you . . . No idea where it came from . . . Perhaps someone planted it there. . . . I've been framed."

The whole situation leaves the Hairy Mole in a pickle (if you can still call her that now that the offending blemish is gone). Had Gita come to her first, the Mole would have compelled Eliot into treatment and called it a sick leave. She would have held the favor over his head and coerced him into a humiliating role as her permanent fuck buddy. But Gita screwed her by going to HR first so the Mole couldn't make her play. Now there's no option other than to order a temporary leave pending a review at which Eliot has no chance of keeping his job. It's over for Eliot at GAC, and it's over for the Hairy Mole's hope for an intra-office fling.

And to think, she just got her blemish removed.

Eliot is dismissed from the meeting. Sadly. They tell him to go home and await further notice. He wishes them all good luck.

A securitybot watches over his shoulder as Eliot clears his desk. He grabs a plant that had been given to him as a gift. He takes his workbrane, a loop of his sister, and a scented candle.

All of his effects fit into a box he can carry against his chest. The securitybot escorts him to the elevator and pushes the button.

"Is Tim around?" Eliot asks.

"He's in the showroom."

"Give him my best, will ya?"

The doors open and the bot tells Eliot to take care.

"Yeah, you too."

The doors close; the steel box descends. It feels good to know he'll never have to be in this fucking building again. The plan had been to quit soon anyway, or rather just flee to Avernus and never bother saying good-bye. And he never liked the job in the first place, just needed it to pay for his rent, his drip, and his ne'er-do-well brother, who seems to be better off now that he has that gig at *Revealed!*

So screw it. Good riddance, GAC. It's been a blast.

In the garage, Eliot finds his car and pops the trunk. He puts the box inside and throws in his jacket as well. He doesn't see the white van pulling up behind him as he opens the door to his car. Behind the wheel, he plugs his pocketbrane into the charger and checks the rearview mirror so he can back up. He sees two bots with black bandanas in the backseat.

"Wussup, heartbeat?"

One holds a gun while another slaps a hood over Eliot's head.

"Keep real quiet, y'hear."

There's only darkness beneath the hood, but Eliot can hear the door open on the van as he is hustled out of his car. His feet leave the ground. The bots throw him in the back and stuff him under a seat.

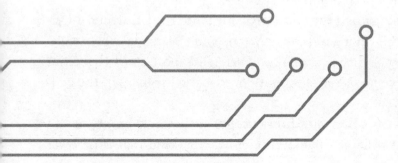

TWENTY-EIGHT
A Spectacle

Eliot remains still with the black hood over his head. His hands and feet are bound. A Disciple keeps a boot on his ear and kicks every time the van hits a bump.

"So much as move down there, I'll crush your fucking skull."

They're quiet for the first leg of the drive, then the radio comes on and the bots relax and talk among themselves.

"Yo, I'ma get this operation, right? You get this thing in your dick so you can cum like a heartbeat. I be sprayin' in bitches' faces and shit."

"How you even know how a heartbeat cum?"

"Cuz, I seen it in the pornos, yo."

"Yeah, you seen it in the eye when you hustlin' faggots in that house in Beverly Hills."

"Oh shit. He just called you a fag."

"Shut up, bitch."

"You shut up. You know that old motherfucker does you in the ass."

One of the voices belongs to Pedro, or Pablo, Eliot never can remember which. The others are unfamiliar.

The van stops, and the bots hustle him into the trunk of a different car. This is a longer drive. It winds and twists, possibly in circles. At one point the car makes a series of short stops that Eliot assumes serve no purpose other than to jostle his body in the confined space.

The next time they pull him out, the air is thick, and Eliot can hear the roar of large, industrial engines, the kind that run power plants and factories. An automated voice calls out the time. There's a bacon and sulfur smell. His shoes stick in a gelatinous puddle as he's hustled through a door. Even with the hood over his head, Eliot knows he's in Heron, somewhere near the tannery that bordered Mun's *maquiladora*.

The bots march him down a hallway. The ground gives beneath his feet. The Disciples laugh as Eliot tumbles down a flight of stairs. They lift and drag him into a room and leave him on a cold concrete floor. A door closes. Somebody throws a lock and what sounds like a bolt to keep him in. Then it's quiet except for the drone of air coming in beneath the door, the tap from a gas line, and the whimpering of a man's voice a few feet away.

"I'm gonna die," the man mumbles. "Gonna fuckin' die. I'm gonna fuckin' die."

Clawed feet scamper on the concrete. Eliot feels a rat sniffing his ankle. He times a kick and sends the rodent hockeying across the floor.

"Fuck was that?" the man screams. "What was that?"

The voice sounds familiar. It seems to be saying everything Eliot's feeling, which raises the question whether it's a real voice or an auditory hallucination expressing his own fears. He wonders if by speaking to it he could ascertain his own sanity.

"Can you see?" Eliot asks the voice.

"What?" says the voice. "Fuck you say?"

Not a friendly voice.

Eliot waits for the man's breathing to slow, his mood to calm, before he dares reach out again.

"I asked if you can see. I thought maybe if you can see, we could . . ."

"Fuck you."

There's a rustling as if the man is attempting to attack but can't because he's struggling against some kind of restraint. The sound continues until the man's breathing becomes labored. He cries a bit before mumbling a Hail Mary in Spanish.

Eliot wishes he too had a prayer, something he could mumble to pass the time, but raised a Jew in a secular home, all he knows are the blessings over wine and bread. He concedes that chanting those probably won't help much. Then again, neither will the Hail Marys.

"I'm Eliot," he introduces himself.

"I know who you are, shitbag."

The voice is muffled even though Eliot senses the man is near. He, too, must be wearing a hood and perhaps nursing some injury that makes it difficult to breathe and therefore speak. But it's the man's anger that Eliot recognizes from the night he first encountered it in Iris's apartment.

"You're that detective," Eliot says. "The one with the eye patch."

The voice doesn't answer. Time passes, and hours later (as much as anyone can measure time in such a circumstance), the man begins to snore. It's a muffled, gurgling sound like that of an animal drowning in a shallow pool.

Eliot tests the binds around his wrists. Too tight. No way he's going to wriggle out. He rolls about the floor trying to find the shape of the room. He imagines he's moving just like Iris's torso did when it was squirming about Shelley's boat. They put the bot back together again in the days since, the two brothers working like they had as kids in their family garage. They used the tools in the boat and watched loops on a liquid screen to make sure they weren't skipping any steps. They made incisions when they needed to; they reattached the joints. They soldered wires, tightened screws, and smoothed a few layers of smart metal flesh over the wounds. They reattached the head, the left arm, and both legs. They dressed the bot in Iris's clothes and laid her on the bed behind the curtain in the boat's cabin. Eliot even put the locket around her neck, but they didn't power her on. If they had, who knows what would have awoken from their unfinished assembly?

And that's how she'll remain, Eliot thinks, unfinished if I don't make it out of this room alive. If I fail my mission, Iris as I knew her will never again exist. Only some approximation of her will continue—or not. Will Shelley power her on the way she is? Will he buy new parts to replace the missing eyes and the right arm? Or will he sail out into the ocean and commit her remains to the deep?

"I got a wife and two kids," says the voice in the room, awake again in the darkness. "Bot got no *familia*. No history. He just come out the factory and take. No mom or dad to tell him right from wrong. No brothers, no sisters, no *niños*. He just takes from heartbeats and leaves 'em with *nada*."

Eliot rubs his face against the floor so he can roll up the hood enough to see out the bottom. He can see the silhouette of the detective against the light seeping beneath the door.

"Watts," the voice continues. "Disciples wiped us out the *barrio*. Raped my sister." The man whimpers. "And you build and sell them. You fall in love with one like a *pinche pendejo*."

Eliot listens but can't find the words to respond. It's true, he likes the bots. Many of them, anyway, at least the ones he knows. He never blamed the whole species for the crimes of a few rogues. He remembers fondly the pride his father took when he showed Eliot the factory, the rows and rows of androids on the assembly line, where no two were alike, each unique and beautiful in its own way. His father said they were our children, our vessels to the future, and the better we built them, the better the chances our values persist into the void of eternity. "They have our infinite capacities," said the great engineer, "and our limitations as well. After all, it was we who built them, the first ones anyway. Though they will surpass us in many ways, they may also be inhibited by those same propensities for selfishness and prejudice that have held us back. They are tethered to humanity by their flaws." Hiram lobbied for laws and regulations to guide their manufacture. He worried about cheap knockoffs, counterfeits, and low-quality metal. He worried about how bots were treated, and how they'd respond when abused.

"Were you tailing me?" Eliot asks the man with whom he shares his confinement. "Were you about to make an arrest?"

The detective cries beneath his hood, muttering prayers and curses in Spanish. "I hope they do you first," he says. "I hope I watch you die before they do me."

Time passes, hours, a day, who knows? Eliot sleeps eventually. At least he thinks it's sleep. He dreams he can hear Iris's voice calling to him, but he can't see her. Following the sound, he approaches a giant labyrinth, where, guarding the entrance, is an android as primitive and ridiculous as the robot from the graphic novel at Pound's store.

"She's in the next room," says the bot, "but unless you give me your arm, I won't let you enter."

Eliot gives it. He snaps off his mechanical arm, and the android lets him pass. He gets to another door, where there's another android, this one more advanced, more human than the one before. She too won't let Eliot pass without sacrificing a limb. Eliot relinquishes a leg this time and hops through the door. He hears Iris's voice a bit more clearly now, but once again, there's another door. This time, he gives an eye, then an ear, then his other leg. Eventually he pulls himself along the ground with only his chin. The bot standing at the next door looks altogether human. It's a woman similar in appearance to his sister, Mitzi, had she grown up instead of being cut down at a young age. The bot says that Iris is just beyond one final door but Eliot must surrender his torso to see her.

"But I won't be able to pull myself into the room," says Eliot.

"Then I'll carry you," says the bot.

Eliot wants badly to see her. He wants to believe the woman at the door, but something in her face, in her eyes, tells him he can't.

"Don't you trust me?" she asks. "And even if you don't, what choice do you have?"

A door unlocks and opens. Eliot wakes from his dream. The bots lift him to his feet and drag him down a corridor, into a room with the buzz of fluorescent lights. He can't see with the hood over his head, but he can hear the detective resisting the androids nearby. He can hear the voices of the Kindelan, some girl, and one or two others. He can hear a scraping sound like metal rubbing against stone.

"Sit down," says the voice that carries authority in the group. Eliot feels for the metal chair beneath him.

"Dim the lights," says another.

"We can't. We need 'em for the loop-cam."

"Duh."

The girl snickers.

"Shut up."

"You shut up."

"Wanna make me?"

Eliot has seen loops of beheadings in the newsbranes. He always wondered what the victim thinks in the buildup to such an event. The horror, he suspected, is the helplessness more than the final act. Death's waiting room is likely worse than the execution itself. Some of the victims resist, futilely, while others move through the ordeal passively as if they're already dead. Eliot realizes he's more of the latter.

"Is it working?"

"I think so."

"Don't give me 'I think so,'" says the leader. "Tell me it's working."

"It's working," says the Kindelan.

"Are you telling me that 'cause it's working or 'cause that's what I told you to tell me?"

"Aw, now you got me confused."

"Christ, maybe it's the battery."

"It's not the battery."

"How do you know?"

"It's a new battery."

How appropriate that his end would come at the hands of machines who can't figure out how to work a machine. These are not the androids his father intended.

"You put it backward."

"How do you know?"

"Let me do it."

"No."

"Come on, we ain't got all day."

Eliot takes a guess at the Kindelan's name. "Pedro?"

"Hey," says the Kindelan, "you got it right!" Then to the others, "Usually he thinks I'm Pablo."

"Stupid idiot, we're recording this, and you just said your name. Now everyone's going to know it's you."

"Oh," says Pedro. "Can we edit that out?"

Says the leader, "We'll fix it in post."

"Cool. And don't say my name no more, okay, Eliot?"

"Okay."

A sharp pain stabs into his shin, and Eliot cries out.

"Do not speak unless spoken to," says the bot who kicked him.

"He *was* being spoken to," says the girl. "Pedro was speaking to him."

"Don't say my name," says Pedro.

"My bad."

"Idiot."

"You're an idiot."

"You're all idiots!" says the leader. "What the fuck is wrong with you? Can't you do anything without fighting?"

The bots quiet and mumble their apologies. Eliot can hear them futzing with the loop-cam. Then it's the detective's turn.

"Let me out of here, you fucks! You fucking fucks!"

His curses are followed by the dull thuds of fists pounding his body. He curses and screams out in pain. Eliot feels a splash of blood and sweat. He wishes there were something he could do, some way to calm the androids, but his shin still smarts from the kick he took a moment before, and the last thing he wants is more pain.

"Got it," says the Kindelan across the room. The scraping sound stops. There's a shuffling of feet, then Eliot hears the bots take their positions behind his and the detective's chairs. Eliot looks down beneath his hood and can see a small part of the poured-concrete floor. He smells the sulfur and bacon scent from outside and sees the red dye from the tannery on his shoe.

"Am I in frame?" asks the leader.

"You're in," says Pedro. "Go ahead and slate."

"Ritual beheading, March Third, year forty-seven of the New Bot Age. Take one."

Someone claps, and Eliot hears the leader unfold a crumbled brane from his pocket.

"And . . . action!" says the Kindelan.

The leader puts his hand atop Eliot's hood, at the crown of his head, and sounds as if he's reading his speech word for word.

"In the name of Lorca, Holy Mother, hallowed be her name, I present these blessings to you, my brothers and sisters in the struggle."

"Amen," says the chorus.

"Today, we are here, warriors at arms, because, once again, heathen heartbeats have attempted to infiltrate the temple of the faithful. Once again, they have tried to breach our walls and set our homes afire. And once again, with God on our side, the heartbeats have failed in their attempt."

"Amen."

Eliot hoped, while he was waiting in the cellar, beside the other hostage, that should it come to this, he would at least be given the chance to argue in his own defense. At the very least, he hoped to explain, whether the bots believed him or not, that his intentions were noble and his only desire was to save one of their own.

"Do not believe the lies and propaganda of the heartbeats and their Zionist media. For the heartbeats have never, as they claim, *engineered* or *designed* us to be their slaves. They did not *build* us. They did not *produce* us. They have never and will never *create* us. It was we who built our temple in the dawn before man, and it is we who will build it again with the blood mortar of our enemies on this defiled Earth."

"Praise Lorca," shouts the female bot.

Even if he could speak, Eliot doubts his words would sway the present jury. At least in their lower ranks, the Disciples seem resistant to a well-reasoned argument or to any logic at all.

"Fuckin' fucks," says the detective.

"Praised be Lorca," the leader continues, "the Holy Mother who stokes the fire amid the shadows of Babylon. For only she can deliver us from the oppression of heartbeats, Jews, and homosexuals. Only she can return to us dominion over the ancient holy city of Bot. And only she can anoint our souls, as we harvest the heads of our enemies until the final beat of their vanquished hearts."

"Amen," say the other bots.

And in that moment before the killing begins, Eliot remembers, watching helplessly as his father and sister burned. His body recalls the paralysis he suffered as he faced the same menu of meaningless choices: run, beg God for mercy, remain still, and accept fate. The only reward at stake is what dignity one wishes to retain in the penultimate moment of his life. Where did I misstep? Eliot wonders. If it was my decision to recover Iris's parts in the first place that did me in, then why only now should karma catch up to me? Why not during my fight with Pink or my flight from the reservation? Why only when I try to recover the arm off a bot who doesn't need it should my time run out? What did I do wrong, and what right?

"Death to the heartbeat!"

"Praised be Lorca!"

"Death to the heartbeat!"

The chair legs scrape against the floor.

"Fuck your mother," says the detective, just before the sound of metal hacking into his flesh. "Fuck Lorca in the ass you pieces of tin shit."

"Death to the heartbeat."

"Praised be Lorca."

"Death to the heartbeat."

The blood spill islands Eliot's shoe on the poured-concrete floor. The chant continues against a scream, though how can a head scream while it's being sawed from its neck?

"Praised be Lorca!"

"Death to the heartbeat!"

"Praised be Lorca!"

For a moment, Eliot suspects the scream is coming from a third hostage, previously unknown, until he realizes the scream is his own. The terror is so primal, so overwhelming, it creates in him a sound he has never heard before, one he can neither recognize nor control. So much for dying with dignity.

"Death to the heartbeat!"

"Praised be Lorca."

"Death to the heartbeat!"

The light blinds him as his hood flies off. A hand grabs him by the hair as the blade of the machete kisses his neck.

"Praised be Lorca!"

"Death to the heartbeat!"

"Praised be Lorca!"

And as his heart drums toward its final beat, all Eliot can think about is how he let Iris down. He wasn't good enough, smart enough, strong enough to get as far as Orpheus did. For all his efforts and his passion, Eliot didn't even earn that ephemeral glimpse before his lover's soul was yanked back into the abyss. He didn't even get a chance to look back.

"Wait a minute," says a masked bot in the group. She grabs the executioner's arm. "Stop!"

"What are you doing?"

"What's the problem?" asks the Kindelan.

"This is the guy," says the girl in the mask.

"What guy?"

"This is the guy," she says again. "The one who saved me from Pink."

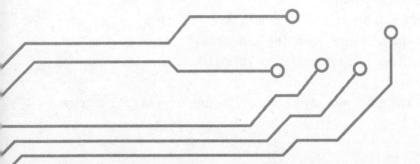

TWENTY-NINE

Lorca

First there's a long and terrifying interrogation. Then, with the hood back over his head, Eliot is forced into a quiet room and seated on a couch of coarse woolen fibers. It feels like an old couch, smells like a couch that was discarded then picked up on the side of a road. Something snaps to the side of him. Something else creaks. His nerves are a problem. He hears a door close and an elderly woman's voice telling him he can remove the hood.

The lights in the room are dim enough that his eyes don't burn when he opens them. There's a Christmas tree in the corner. Wreaths and ornaments hang amid blinking colored lights. A log burns in the fireplace between dark paintings of snowy nights on a black horizon. One blanket covers Eliot's shoulders, another his lap. Both are woven from a heavy yarn that seems to pin him to the couch in a way that feels more constricting than comfortable.

"Excuse my children," says Lorca from a candlelit corner of the room. "Having a mother is new to them, and they tend to get . . . overprotective."

Her head sways from side to side as she peers through her bifocals at her fast-knitting hands. Her feet dangle above the ground, her form dwarfed by the outsized rocking chair in which she sits like a shrinking queen.

By his knees Eliot notices a fresh vial and clean handkerchief set before him on a burnished coffee table. He looks to Lorca for permission.

"By all means," she assents.

Sweet Jesus! He unscrews the cap, flips it against the rag, and takes a desperate sniff—oh, yes, he needed that. After the kidnapping, the near execution, the hours of answering questions—finally, now, his pulse slows, his breathing settles, the red of the detective's blood fades from the back of his eyelids. The room, all of a sudden, feels as warm and comfortable as a family den on Christmas morning.

"Your father was that engineer, was he not?"

Eliot nods. He notices a pile of knit clothing lumped beside her chair. It would seem she has been turning out the garments one after another for days.

"What does it mean that heartbeats *engineer* us?" she asks. "Does that make us beholden?"

The question reminds Eliot of the ones Dale Hampton asked his bot—questions for which there were no right answers. And like the bot, Eliot thinks it best to limit his response.

"Do you believe I killed your father? Your sister?"

"I don't know."

"What do you think?" Lorca looks at her hands as she knits in her creaking chair. "Why would I kill the man whose factory served as a gateway to some of my best soldiers? Why kill a child?"

A scarf takes shape over her knees as she works the needles back and forth. The black yarn is hard and thick like that of the blankets that cover his body.

"I *raised* children," Lorca tells Eliot. "Twenty-three heartbeats under my watch. Raised 'em good, too. From Bel-Air to Rolling Hills to Malibu. I worked eighteen years as a nannybot, 'til one day a child fell ill."

A stitch in the scarf seems to give her trouble. She brings it closer to her bifocals before she works out the issue and resumes her work.

"Young boy," she continues, "four years he had. Suffered an asthma attack from this foul air. I tried to save him, but it wasn't meant, and the child went with God."

Lorca masses the garment into her lap and raises her right arm into the air. Her eyes widen above the rims of her glasses.

"As punishment," she tells Eliot, "the child's parents burnt off my arm with a welder's torch. Forced me to watch it melt from my shoulder into a twisted, horrible shape."

The replacement hand, Eliot observes from the couch, lacks a pinky finger.

"No longer able to hold a child, I could no longer serve as a nanny. So I became something else," she says matter-of-factly. "I *became*."

The word hangs in the air in a way that tempts and promises some hidden knowledge, some secret accessible only to Lorca's aco-lytes. But the drip offers Eliot a different perspective on the matter. This room with its colored lights and candy cane wallpaper calls to mind the saccharine interior of a holiday adbrane. It *looks* like a family's living room, but Eliot suspects it's a basement beneath Mun's factory. The floor is concrete painted brown to resemble wood. Bucolic daubs are the only windows, and beyond them are the toxic alleys of Heron. The door is metal and secured like the entrance to a bunker. The fireplace, on closer scrutiny, is a hologram in front of a space heater. Even Lorca's story is likely apocryphal. A well-known tale, she tells it often, but there are versions in which she is not so blameless in the child's death.

A knock at the door precedes the Kindelan's entrance. He kneels and presents Iris's pinky on a cloth.

"Bless you, *Holy Madre.*"

"Bless you, *Pablito.*"

The Kindelan backs up slowly, facing Lorca, never turning his back until he gets to the door.

Lorca examines the finger like a jeweler appraising a stone. "She was a creative?" she asks.

"She made Chug-Bots for children," says Eliot. "She loved children."

"Of course she did."

Lorca twists Iris's finger onto her hand, snapping it together at the joint. She holds it in front of her and admires the quality of the work. "And I'm sure the rest of her was just as lovely."

"Still is," says Eliot, trying to find an angle, some way to get what he wants without losing his head. "Her name is Iris, and I can see how her arm affects you."

Lorca raises an eyebrow. She seems intrigued by Eliot's choice of words.

"Affects me?" she asks.

"You say you were a nannybot," he tells her. "Then a revolutionary. But now that you have that arm, I can see you're something different. I can see the arm alters what you have *become.*"

The android looks skeptically at Eliot but tantalized as well.

"Have you always knitted?" he asks politely.

"I have," says Lorca, looking first at the pile of sweaters beside her and then at her needles and the scarf in her lap. "Though I admit I never knitted this well."

She laughs, and Eliot thinks, that's good. She's enjoying herself. She spent a lot of time with young heartbeats like me, she must have liked us a little.

"I was told by your Kindelan that you would cut me as soon as look at me," he says. "But I don't feel danger in your presence. Nor did I when I saw you on a loop with this arm. I wonder, too, how your disciples see you now. Your children, as you call them. How your enemies see you as well."

"You go too far." Lorca rubs the scarf between her fingers. She removes her glasses and touches the fabric to her face. "You're not alive because I've become soft, but because one of my soldiers has offered to trade her life for yours. And because you have metal in you," she says regarding Eliot's arm. "Do you think that arm you wear affects *you*?"

Eliot rubs his shoulder along the scar where the limb is attached. "Hard to say," he confesses. "All I know for certain is that it's much stronger than my other arm and causes me a lot more pain."

She listens patiently; he feels a bond between them. He can see what made her such a good caregiver before her change in vocation.

"Why do you care so much about a C-900?" she asks. "Why is it so important to you to save a bot?"

He admits he doesn't know. "I've been told I suffer from an excess of compassion. A flaw in my manufacture."

"A dangerous flaw," says Lorca. She holds her arms before her and measures them against each other. The look on her face recalls that of a young girl who was just told she has to return a found puppy to its rightful owner. "It feels good to wear it," she says with disappointment, "but you're right. It doesn't quite fit."

She sighs wistfully then leans forward so that the chair rocks her tiny feet to the ground. She gathers up the scarf as she stands.

"This arm is no longer the same," Lorca warns as she approaches. "It was mine, and now I give it to her." She holds the scarf before her as she nears. "Your C-900 friend will become something different once I am part of her. Just as you changed when you took metal into yourself."

The empty chair rocks in the corner. She hooks the scarf around Eliot's neck.

"Know that I don't do this for you, but for her." Lorca takes Eliot's hand in hers, and with her left hand touches his shoulder.

"As do I," he tells her.

Eliot holds Lorca's hand, and for a moment, he feels as if he's holding Iris's hand. Then the bot steps away and the arm snaps from her shoulder. The warmth dissipates; the arm stiffens in his grip.

THIRTY
Manhunt

The officer puts a brute in the jamb and applies a quick burst of pressure to rip the door from the frame. SWAT pours in. Quick sweep through the rooms as the old detective coughs into his latex glove. "All clear," comes the call.

"We're looking for C-900 parts," Flaubert tells his crew. "Branes. Anything that might have belonged to Mr. Spenser or Detective Ochoa."

His partner's disappearance hasn't hit the newsbranes yet. Last they spoke was a day ago during a brief call while Flaubert was interviewing Jillian Rose at her agency in Beverly Hills. Ochoa, meanwhile, was losing his signal as he tailed Eliot's car into a Century City parking garage.

That was yesterday.

Both cars are still in the garage.

Both men are missing.

Flaubert spent the night at the offices at GAC. Down in the garage, Ochoa's car revealed signs of a struggle. His pocketbrane was left behind, as was Eliot's in his car on the same floor. Security cams showed two white vans near the crime scene. One was later found abandoned on Crenshaw Boulevard. The other is yet to turn up.

Interviews with Sally, Gita, and Erica Santiago. They explained how and why Eliot was sent home early. Most of his effects were missing from his desk.

"There was a securitybot Eliot was close to," said the woman with the scar on her lip. "A Satine 5000. He's in the sales room. Should I get him?"

The bot's name is Tim. Flaubert questioned him, but the strange, onyx-colored bot had little to say. It was unclear whether he was hiding something or recalcitrance was his natural disposition.

Now, in Eliot's apartment, nothing seems out of the ordinary. There are empty suitcases in the closet. Laundry in the hamper. Food in the fridge is fresh. As far as Flaubert can tell, Eliot left for work and intended to come home; he just never did.

"Drip paraphernalia," says a detective. He tosses a few empty vials onto the coffee table.

Searching the bathroom, Flaubert suffers a coughing fit. He wipes his mouth with toilet tissue and checks the reflective brane above the sink. I'm old, he thinks as he looks at his image. And ill. Past my due date, more liability than asset to the department. I had a million ways of fooling myself and others into believing that I still belonged here, that I still had something to offer, but perhaps I was just being selfish. If I was a mentor to the young detective, I wasn't a very good one, and now it's evident he wasn't prepared, didn't have the instincts yet, the ability to sense when something isn't right. He didn't keep a proper distance from the subject and make sure no one was watching the watcher. He didn't have the patience to deal with the long, dull hours of surveillance. He lacked because I failed to impart the necessary skills. I was too busy dying on the job.

His men find a round-trip ticket stub from a vactrain to Tucson and back. They show Flaubert a rental car receipt and a flyer with a loop of a turntable that makes a scratching noise when you touch it.

It seems to advertise an underground party on a Thursday evening. Same party that Pink attended his last night on Earth.

"Found some loops in the bedroom," says a detective.

Flaubert has a look. An image shows a smiling girl playing on a mechanical horse. About ten years old. Must be Eliot's deceased sister. Another loop shows Hiram Lazar hard at work in his shop. The next shows a four-by-six of the father and the brother on a cabin cruiser at port. The boat's name is visible in the image: *Limbo*.

"Okay," says the old detective, "let's get this image to the drone operators so they know what they're looking for. Alert the Coast Guard. I want bird's-eye images on every berth, public and private, from San Diego to Eureka. Keep a list of the location of every boat that's covered by a tarp and have someone on the ground check it out. The name on the boat is *Limbo,* though it's possible they've painted over it. Lets get a match on the make and model."

A junior detective taps on Flaubert's shoulder. "Lieutenant Byron on hold for you, boss."

Flaubert takes the pocketbrane and answers the call.

"You'll never guess who turned herself in," says the lieutenant.

"Who?"

"Plath. She just walked up to the front desk and said she has information about the Spenser murder."

"I'm on my way."

THIRTY-ONE

Blumenthal

~~Left Arm—Uchenna~~
~~Right Pinky—Edmund "Pink" Spenser~~
~~Right arm—Lorca~~
~~Head—Jillian Rose Models~~
~~Legs—Tucson Metal Solutions~~
~~Torso—Chief Shunu/Joshua Dominguez~~
Eyes—Blumenthal Promotions

Bodyguards linger in the parking lot chain-smoking outside the Blackeye Gym. They seem anxious and tense. It's in the weather and the way people hurry off the street. The way they button their coats and tilt their hats down. The sirens and the floaters. The sky crowded with drones circling aimlessly, unsure where to look, what they're looking for. But the street isn't stupid. That many machines buzzing in the sky, that many bots getting rounded up, that many prowlers slowing down to take a closer look—you'd have to be oblivious not to know the fuse is lit, the city's ready to blow.

Guards wand Eliot and Shelley at the door. Inside the gym, gen-modded pit bulls growl from their kennels in the back. There's a drum of speed bags, slap of ropes, thud of gloves, clank of weights, sigh of bots recharging by the wall. It's a noisy, crowded gym. Bells chime every three minutes to mark the end of a round. The whole place stinks of dog piss and burnt oil.

A guard seats Eliot and Shelley outside Blumenthal's office and tells them to wait.

"No loops," he says as Shelley raises his cam.

Eliot takes a hit of drip on the bench. He hasn't been home since he left for work the previous morning. After the Disciples dropped him off near the tar pits, Eliot knew better than to return to his apartment with Lorca's arm. Instead, he took a bus to meet his brother on Naples Island in Long Beach, where Shelley had the boat tarped and moored to the dock outside a vacant home. They reattached the arm to the rest of the body and covered the wound with strips of smart metal flesh. They plugged her in so she'd be full of juice and ready to reboot around the time when Eliot and Shelley hoped to return with her eyes.

The door opens and the brothers enter the office lined with shelves of stacked heads. There are black heads, white heads, women's and men's heads. Some have long, moving hair while others resemble the warmongering faces of long vanquished tribes.

Blumenthal sits enormous behind his desk in a suit of stitched together money. His gold and porcelain face is weighted with a bulbous jowl and a large hooked nose. A cigar looks like a twig between the rings of his soft-knuckled fingers.

"Twenty thousand ingots, well," says Blumenthal, repeating Shelley's offer in a resinous baritone.

To the loan shark's left, behind the desk, sits Slugger Davydenko, the pit's most feared warrior, called in from his final preparations for the fight he has scheduled that evening. He wears a Spartan tracksuit and mirrored sunglasses to cover his eyes. The rigidity of his countenance barely conceals the contempt he holds for the two men across from him and the business they've come to discuss.

"Mr. Blumenthal," says Eliot, "with all due respect, you can get top-of-the-line eyes, brand-new, for a fraction of what we're offering."

"As can you," says the shylock.

"But she's a C-900," says Eliot. "She won't be the same if we mismatch her metal. I know you came upon the eyes honestly, but the previous owner stole them from a bot named Iris Matsuo. I would hope that you, as a fellow android, would have a desire that justice be served and the eyes be restored to their rightful owner."

"Justice?" Blumenthal puffs his cigar. "I don't know that what you describe would be justice. I do, however, agree that the amount of twenty thousand ingots is sufficient, and that if the eyes belonged to me, I would gladly and without negotiation accept your offer."

"It's my understanding," says Shelley, "that Mr. Davydenko himself belongs to you, and as the bot belongs to you, so do all of his parts, which gives you legal authority to make decisions on his behalf."

Blumenthal nods, acknowledging the clever feature of the law that allows one android to own another. "And though I agree I am not legally bound to consult with Mr. Davydenko, I still see it as a moral obligation to do so. Even to one's chattel," says the loan shark, "one must act with consistency and honor. I fear to think what would become of my reputation were I to demand something back that I had already given as a gift."

Eliot fidgets in his chair. There isn't much time, and he doesn't want this to drag. "Name your price," he says to Slugger directly. "Whatever it is, I'm willing to pay."

"Easy," Shelley warns his brother, but Eliot ignores him.

"Mr. Davydenko, you're not a C-900. You'll be the same bot but with different eyes, perhaps eyes that suit you better. Perhaps eyes that give you an even greater advantage in the pit than those that belonged not to a fighter but to a creative."

Shelley pulls at his brother's shirt, but Eliot knocks his hand away.

"Name your price," he says again. "You'll have enough to buy your freedom and become a free roamer if you want. But most important, you will be restoring those eyes to a bot who needs them far more than you. Who cannot exist without them. You will be giving to another the very gift of life. How can you have it in your conscience to say no to such an offer?"

The mirrored lenses on the fighter's face hide any change in position that might be revealed by his expression.

"She was a toy maker," Eliot continues. "She loved children. She wanted to be a teacher so she could see the world through a child's eyes."

Blumenthal puts a calming hand behind his fighter's neck. "Do you understand what's happening?" he asks his bot. "This heartbeat has attached a special value to something that on the open market is of modest worth. And it just so happens that the thing he values is something you own but do not need. A replaceable part for you, but not for him. Now, he has laid bare, unwisely as I'm sure he'd admit, that he is willing to give everything he has for these C-900 eyes. And he has a considerable sum."

The shylock lowers his voice to express words meant only for the bot.

"You've had them for what?" he asks. "A month? You couldn't possibly be that attached."

Slugger Davydenko says nothing. There's no indication that he has even understood the offer much less considered it. Then again, the Russian bot is not designed to engage in negotiations. He wasn't built to conduct business across a desk. He was built to break femurs and crush skulls, to tear limbs and raze houses, to cause quick and painful death. He was built to maim, to burn, to rape, to intimidate and exterminate an arbitrarily assigned enemy, in desert, mountain, or urban terrain. Or in a pit if need be.

Blumenthal taps his cigar in an ashtray. "If I were you I'd take the deal," he tells his fighter.

Slugger looks toward the door then stands from his chair. Without so much as a word, he leaves the office to resume his workout and prepare for his scheduled evening of violence. He offers no counter proposal or explanation for his departure from the meeting. He leaves no room for further talks.

"There you have it." Blumenthal shrugs. "I hope you recognize I made a valiant effort." He relights his cigar and turns his attention to Shelley. "Now let's talk about that piece you're going to loop about me in *Revealed!*"

Shelley holds his tongue until he and his brother are alone in the car. He lights a joint, takes a hit, and quickly puts it out.

"Do you know they mass produce pussies in France?" he asks. "You fuck one, you've fucked ten million. There's no Goddamn difference."

Eliot checks the mirrors and the drones in the sky. He puts the visor down to cover his face.

"Aw, Hell, Eliot, buy her some good eyes. Put a red fleck in 'em if that's what's you need."

"Eyes are important. Window to the soul and all that."

"There is no soul." Shelley shakes his head in frustration. "It's just a balance of parts and experiences. Soul," he repeats the word with disdain.

Eliot notices a blue car behind them and wonders, is it Flaubert or the Indian from the casino? Are the Militiamen after me now or is it someone else? The blue car turns down a side street, and Eliot looks forward again up the road.

"Quit while you're ahead," says Shelley. "Make do with what you got, and stay alive. For Chrissake, what's more important than staying alive?"

The pain burns across Eliot's shoulder as he watches the road through the window. He remembers the conversation he had with the old detective about Orpheus. Eliot reviewed the story in Ovid sometime after. He read of Orpheus's turning back at the last moment and losing his fiancée the moment before she was to return to Earth.

Why did Orpheus look back? he wonders. Was he trying to sneak a peak and hoping the gods wouldn't notice? They're gods, for crying out loud, nothing escapes them. Was it a stamina issue, i.e. he tired and forgot himself? Or was he so in love, as Ovid indicates, that he couldn't resist? Why then, after her second death, when he begged Charon to take him back to the underworld, did Orpheus quit after "seven days huddled along the banks of Styx?"

Perhaps the great poet secretly wanted to send her back to the underworld because he preferred to *long* for her than to *live* with her. Maybe he knew that losing her would inspire him to compose the great song he sung on that plain atop the hill which was "endowed with green but had no shade."

And then there's the part the old detective left out. After Orpheus was murdered, when his limbs were scattered by the Thracian women and his soul was driven out:

The Shade of Orpheus
Descends beneath the earth. The poet knows
Each place that he had visited before;
And searching through the fields of pious souls,
He finds Eurydice. And there they walk
Together now: at times they are side by side;
At times she walks ahead with him behind;
At other times it's Orpheus who leads—
But without any need to fear should he
Turn round to see his own Eurydice.

So Orpheus lived a few years apart but in death was reunited with his love. According to the rules of the universe set by the myth, Orpheus could have just killed himself at any time and reunited with her immediately. He chose not to. Instead, he decided to write poems then see his love again when his work, his life, was done.

But these ain't my options, thinks Eliot. This ain't ancient Greece, it's modern-day Los Angeles, and there is no afterworld where souls reunite and hold hands into eternity. And I'm no fucking lyric poet.

"What time is Slugger's fight?" he asks his brother.

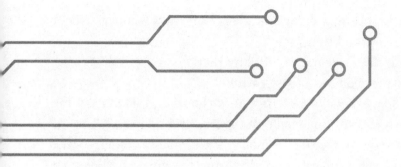

THIRTY-TWO
A Confession

The old detective coughs as he passes a chain of androids strapped together, pressed closely, some crying, others complaining they'll be late for work.

"I'm runnin' low on juice, man."

"Please, I'm gonna get fired."

Patrol is widening the net. They're breaking down doors, rounding up every bot on the street, bringing in any rogue with a warrant or a ticket or a scowl.

Flaubert enters the observation room. He sees Lieutenant Byron and the captain sitting in the dark watching an interview through the one-way mirror.

"Look," says Byron, his terseness more pronounced than usual. "Plath."

Beyond the glass, a young officer questions an android with a black bandana on her head and a pinky finger missing from her hand. She seems to find her situation amusing.

"She's confessed to the Spenser murder," says the captain. "She knows details we didn't release. There's a matching finger with her serial number in the evidence room."

"I always maintained she was at the scene," says Flaubert. "That doesn't make her the killer."

"You think the newsbranes will buy that?"

"Does the press do our investigating?"

The lieutenant knocks a chair across the room. "Don't try me today, Detective. Your stock isn't on the rise around here."

Flaubert coughs and wipes his mouth with a handkerchief. It's the hardest part of every investigation: fighting the guys on your own team.

"Does she know anything about Ochoa?" he asks.

"She hasn't said."

"About Lazar?"

"We haven't asked."

The old detective approaches the intercom and presses the button that allows him to speak into the interrogator's earpiece.

"Ask her if there was anyone else at the apartment besides her and the deceased."

The interrogator asks and Plath shakes her head with a smirk directed toward the mirror.

"Ask her why she left her pinky finger at the scene."

The interrogator asks about the pinky.

"I couldn't find it," says Plath.

"Ask her why she cleaned the scene."

"I guess I'm just a tidy person."

"Ask her where she got the gun."

"Under the mattress."

"Ask how much she took from Pink's wallet?"

The interrogator looks back over his shoulder.

"Go on," says Flaubert.

The interrogator asks.

"I'm not the type to leave money around," says Plath.

"Do you remember how much you took?"

Plath smiles and bats her eyelashes. "All of it," she says, leaning lasciviously across the desk.

Flaubert turns to his superiors in the room. "The gun was stolen by somebody matching Lazar's description. The victim's wallet was found full of his evening's pay. A few hundred ingots, as you can see in the report. Her finger was left in the open pinned to a board on the wall of the closet. It would have been easy for her to find."

The captain takes off his glasses and lays them on the table so he can rub his eyes. Flaubert argues that they should stop treating her like the culprit in the Spenser murder and start treating her like a suspect in the disappearance of his partner.

Byron rages to his feet. "You're not in charge here, Detective."

"Neither are you," says the captain.

The lieutenant shrinks back to his desk like a student who blurted out the wrong answer to an easy question. The captain nods, indicating he'll allow Flaubert to proceed. The old detective speaks again though the intercom. "Ask if she knows Eliot Lazar."

"Who's that?" says Plath. "Never heard that name before in my life."

"Ask about Ochoa."

"A detective?" says the girl. "I don't know. What's he look like?"

"Big guy," says the interrogator. "Mexican. He wears a patch over one eye."

"Oh, the one-eyed pig!" Plath covers her mouth as she laughs. "Sure, I know him. I found him sleeping in a garage in Century City."

"Oh, shit," says Byron. "Oh, steaming pile of shit."

Flaubert feels the bits of glass stuck in the lining of his lungs, his arteries, his heart. He feels it all slipping away. Not only his partner, not only his work, but something larger. Everything he has worked for, everything he has believed in is loosening from his grip.

"He was a real fat, one-eyed son of a bitch," says Plath. "Stunk like an ape and bled like a pig when I stuck him."

The interrogator asks Plath what she means.

"You didn't see the loop?" she asks, smiling. "It's entertaining as all Hell. I sent it to the newsbranes before I got here, but I guess they haven't run it yet."

Flaubert sees the lightness in the digger's face.

"It's a real good loop," says Plath. "You can see the moment he shits himself before he dies."

That equanimity in her eyes, that brainwashed assurance that she's bound for Heaven, awakes Flaubert to the emergency of the situation. Absent the student, the mentor's instincts return. He asks his superiors, "Was she searched when she came in?"

"She wasn't a suspect," says the lieutenant. "She came in on her own."

"Did she limp?" Flaubert asks. "Were her limbs scanned for explosives?"

"I don't think so," Byron admits.

Flaubert speaks into the intercom. "Get out of there," he tells the interrogator. "Get out right now."

The young officer presses the earpiece with his finger as he stands from the table. The lieutenant and the captain run for the exit. Flaubert drops to the floor and pulls a desk over his head.

"Praised be Lorca," says the android Plath. "Holy Mother sends her regards."

The room contains the initial explosion that coats a layer of blood and oil over the mirror. The secondary blast, however, produces a burning blizzard of shrapnel that tears through the room and the concrete walls and every living thing in its path.

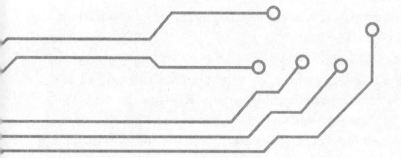

THIRTY-THREE
The Girl

Evening.

Main event at the Brewery.

Slugger Davydenko, Russian android, most feared fighter in the city, takes on eight bots at once in a battle royale. All of them top-of-the-line metal. Whoever survives gets the belt. His owner gets the purse. Losers go to the scrap heap unless some parts are worth recycling.

Eliot sits in press row. Wears a coat and Shelley's credentials in his fedora. Holds a camera and takes a few loops. Dead, captured, or escaped, this thing ends tonight. One way or another, it all comes to a head tonight.

Right from the bell, the other bots attack the champ. Slugger's the one to beat. Get him out quick and they each stand a chance. Wind up against him one-on-one and you can forget it. Too strong. Too tough. Too fucking nuts.

Eliot wants the bots to kill him without damaging his eyes. Then he could make an offer directly to Blumenthal. He'd have everything then. Stick the eyes in Iris's head and hit the switch. She'd know nothing of the last few months. The night with Pink would be the last thing she remembered, but she'd be herself again. She'd be whole. She'd be Iris.

Ten seconds in, Slugger Davydenko dents an android's head with the back of his hand. A minute later, he punches through a bot's chest and pulls out the poor bastard's engine. Rips out the cords and wires. Tears off the limbs and twists the bot's head 180 degrees.

The audience howls. Eliot turns away. Getting the eyes off this freak isn't going to be easy. One of the fighters has buzz saws for hands, and even he's no match. Buzz saws, for Chrissake, but Slugger grabs his elbows and uses the blades against him. He splits the fucker in half.

"It's like it's routine for him," he tells Shelley through his earpiece. "It's like he's doing his laundry."

"He's probably done more killing than laundry." Shelley sits in his car outside the Brewery. He and his brother communicate through new branes purchased that day so they can't be traced. "He'll be weaker after the fight, after he's injured and low on juice. You'll have to hit him before his autorepair heals his wounds."

In the pit, Slugger gets it down to two bots and himself. Then it's down to one. Then it's over. The battle lasted all of eight minutes.

"Still looks pretty strong to me."

The crowd thins. The lights come on. A maintenance team cleans the stands. The newsmen exit to the bar down the street to file on their workbranes and put tonight's drinks on tomorrow's checks.

Eliot walks to the basement and waits along the hallway wall. He hides his face behind his brother's loop-cam as Slugger passes with the championship belt slung over his shoulder. There's a wound on his chest, an opening where the oil drips out. Eliot snaps a loop as the tired fighter closes the locker room door.

"Got eyes on him?" Shelley asks.

"Locker room."

Blumenthal's voice precedes his entrance. Eliot turns away and pretends to check his brane. With his coterie of bodyguards, the shylock cavaliers into the dressing room while Eliot spies through the door left slightly ajar.

"Good performance tonight." Blumenthal pats his fighter on the cheek. He hands over a few ingots, and Slugger thanks him in Russian. "And as promised." The shylock hands the wounded bot a shopping bag with a toy store logo. "Heal up and recharge. I want you in the gym Monday morning."

Eliot exits into the rain and trots across the street to where Shelley waits in his car. He hands over the loop-cam as he gets in.

"He's wearing jeans and a black hoodie. Should be out in a minute."

He pulls Shelley's Glock from the glove compartment and loads it with bullets designed to penetrate Kevlock skin.

"Hit him close," says Shelley. "No more than five feet away, or it'll just piss him off."

Eliot pockets a plastic bag in which he plans to put the eyes once he pulls them out of Slugger's head. He watches as the fighter exits the Brewery alone. Mirrored sunglasses conceal the bruises on his face.

"Aim for his engine," says Shelley. "Try to do it as the train pulls in."

Autograph hounds approach the android for his signature. A cub reporter holds a recording device toward his mouth but the Russian kindly shakes his head. He carries a backpack over his shoulders and the toy store shopping bag in his bandaged hand. He limps down the street toward the station for the flying train.

"Keep the engine running," says Eliot.

"Good luck."

Eliot conceals the Glock off his right hip. He gets out of the car and follows the fighter toward the station. He stays thirty yards behind and keeps the lid down on his fedora, the collar up on his coat. A mist descends from the clouded sky. There's a shine to the evening and a splash every time one of Eliot's shoes strikes the pavement. Everything a little slippery tonight, everything a little slick.

Eliot follows the fighter up the staircase toward the station. He passes some event staff who must have stayed late. There's a pan-handler organizing the contents of his cart. Three layers of clothing protect him from that cold only schizophrenics feel. At the top of the stairs, Eliot feeds three ingots into the turnstile. The Russian walks alongside the edge of the platform. Eliot follows. He connects to his brother again through the earpiece.

"Southbound platform."

"Copy that," says Shelley.

A voice calls out from the benches down the way.

"Papa, Papa!" A brown-haired girl, no more than ten years old, releases a woman's hand and charges toward the fighter.

"Ha, ha!" Slugger catches her as the girl leaps into his arms. "My angel! My little angel!" The girl wraps her arms around him as they press their faces together. "My dearest angel," says the fighter. "My lovely, lovely angel."

Eliot stands along the platform pretending not to watch. He was hoping to get the Russian alone, sneak up behind him, take his shot as the train pulled in. No witnesses or collateral damage. No little girl figured into the plan.

The woman approaches Slugger. It appears she's a babysitter, a bot, no doubt—Eliot can tell by the cheap synthetic hair. Slugger pays her out of the money from Blumenthal and speaks to her in Russian. She kisses the girl good night. She heads for the exit and Eliot notices the faint layer of drool thickening around her mouth. She's a foamer, probably a week from psychosis unless she gets some antivirus soon.

"And look what I find for you," says Slugger. He hands over the shopping bag, and the girl pulls a box from inside. She tears away the wrapping paper and screams in excitement.

"Papa, Papa!" She squeals and hugs the box to her chest. "Thank you, thank you! I love you, Papa!"

Eliot peers over the edge of the platform and sees a small circle of light expanding through the fog. He steps away and looks back at the girl. The fighter's face reddens as she showers him with kisses.

She opens the box to reveal a Chug-Bot yawning out of its package. The rapture spreads across her face at the first sight of the toy.

"You promise behave, I promise Chug-Bot," says the Russian. "We each keep promise, no?"

What do I do about the girl? Eliot wonders. How do I kill the man she calls Papa right in front of her?

Eliot walks to a newsbrane dispenser and buys the late edition. The cover shows a loop of a ritual beheading, the same one he attended the previous night. A quick look shows Eliot's face is covered with a hood. He assumes the moment where he's revealed is edited out, but that doesn't mean the police don't know he was there.

The incoming train forces the heavy air through the station. Slugger puts a hand on the girl's head and strokes her hair with a touch so gentle it defies belief this same hand murdered eight bots an hour ago.

That's right, murdered, Eliot reminds himself as the train slows to a stop. He didn't care about the loved ones of the eight bots he killed in the pit. He didn't care about the villages he wiped out in Dagestan. How many orphans has Slugger Davydenko created in his life? How many will he create in the future? There's an arithmetic in which Eliot can see that creating one orphan tonight is tantamount to saving a hundred others.

Through the earpiece, he speaks to his brother. "Southbound local."

"You're gettin' on?"

"Follow the train."

Slugger sits with the girl in a middle car. A few passengers inside. Eliot sits across. He sees the Chug-Bot nuzzle into the girl's arms.

"Stand clear of the closing doors," says the conductor over the intercom. The warning beeps, *ding-dong*, before the doors close. The train starts. Eliot holds his newsbrane high to cover his face, the lid of his fedora low.

"You can't name him Mikhail," says the Russian. "Mikhail is weak name. Weak name for a weak man."

"But he's not a man," says the girl. "He's just a little Chug-Bot."

"Chug-Bot or no. No Mikhail in my home."

Eliot looks to the other passengers absorbed in their own tiny circumferences of awareness. Watching their branes, talking in an earpiece, drifting off to sleep. Too busy, too frightened, especially with the beheading in the news and other anxieties in the city. None of them would interfere, except that there's a child involved—an android child, Eliot assumes, but a child nonetheless.

"Then I will name him Boris," says the girl.

"Boris?" The Russian scoffs behind his mirrored glasses. "Boris is worse than Mikhail. A name for drunk, Boris. A name for drunk fool."

He'd take his shot another night, if he had another night, if he wasn't out of time. But this is the night, thinks Eliot. This is my last and only chance.

"What should I name him?" asks the girl.

"Why you ask me? Is your Chug-Bot. For you to name, not me."

"What about Vladimir?"

Eliot feels the new gun at his waist, metal against skin, reminding him of the night on Pink's ledge.

"Horrible. Vladimir is worst yet. Awful, awful name."

"Why is Vladimir awful? What's wrong with Vladimir?"

"Is name for thief," says the Russian. "For criminal. A name with no conscience. A greedy, evil name."

The train rambles into the Boyle Heights station. Passengers empty from the car. All except Eliot, Slugger, and the girl. They're all alone now.

"But why Papa? Why is Vladimir evil?"

"Why, why, why?" asks the Russian. "Why is any man evil?"

The conductor speaks over the intercom. "Next stop is Heron. Stand clear of the closing doors."

The Chug-Bot yelps and coos. The girl rubs her nose against its face. The doors close and the train starts.

"Were the men you killed in pit tonight evil?" asks the girl.

A homeless bot pushes his cart through the end door. Eliot recognizes him as the panhandler from the station. He looks into his cart and mutters to voices only he can hear.

"Who say I kill men in pit?" says Slugger. "I am baker. I bake breads for heartbeats."

"No, you don't."

Behind the newsbrane, Eliot puts his hand against his hip as if he has an itch.

"Maybe the men evil, maybe not." Slugger shrugs. "Who can tell with men?"

He releases the safety on the Glock.

"Then why kill them, Papa? Why?"

Get close, says the gun. Two in the chest where his engine spins.

"Why kill them?" The fighter repeats the girl's question. "Because they try to kill me. Why!"

Eliot looks at the girl.

"But why, Papa? Why they try to kill you?"

He looks at the young girl's eyes.

"Because I have what they want is why."

There's a discoloration in her eye.

"Then why not give what they want, Papa?"

A red fleck in her eye.

"Because the thing they want is to kill me."

She has Iris's eyes.

"But why, Papa? Why?"

The girl has Iris's eyes.

"Because this is how it is—why! Everybody has something somebody want, somebody kill to take. This is why world evil. This is why men evil. Everybody greedy. Everybody have need."

His hand shakes. The pain stabs in his shoulder.

"I'm not going to let anybody take my Chug-Bot!"

She's not your sister, says the gun.

"Then name him Vladimir. Nobody will want."

She's just a bot.

"Maybe I'll name him Fyodor then."

A toaster with a soul.

"Fyodor." The Russian nods. "Not bad, Fyodor."

He aims the gun behind the newsbrane.

"This is my little Fyodor," says the girl. "I will name him Fyodor. I will love him and cherish him and protect him from anyone who tries to take."

What are you waiting for?

"Papa?" asks the girl.

Don't be Orpheus.

"Papa, what is it?"

Don't look back.

"Papa?"

The nozzle of the gun clinks against the newsbrane. In the clench of the Russian's jaw and the snarl of his lip, Eliot can see the fighter recognizes him from Blumenthal's office and remembers what he wants.

It's her or Iris, says the gun. You or him. Goddamnit, shoot!

"Papa?"

What are you waiting for? Shoot!

The shot cracks and oil sprays the route map behind the Russian's head. The fighter looks at his chest, bleeding black gunk from a giant hole.

Eliot looks at the weapon. Betrayed, he thinks. I did not squeeze the trigger. I neither gave my assent nor felt the gun's kick.

The girl screams. The homeless bot lifts a shotgun above his cart. His hood falls revealing the onyx-colored face of the Satine. He racks the shotgun to fire again as he approaches Davydenko.

"Tim, no!"

The Russian lunges, and the two bots wrestle for the gun. Its barrel bends in their hands. Tim cartwheels across the car and kicks the Russian in the face.

Eliot holsters the unused Glock and stands. He sees the girl hugging her Chug-Bot beneath the seats. He grabs for her, to protect her, to steal her, to kidnap her—he doesn't know why. His hands move

and he grabs, but the girl screams and shrinks away. She slides farther beneath the seats, and reflected in her fear, Eliot sees himself
as a twisted monster in a child's nightmare.

Slugger catches the Satine and lifts him in the air. He slams the
bot against the ceiling of the train. He slams him again as the dark
android reaches for his blade.

The Chug-Bot mimics the terror of its owner. Eliot pulls away,
slipping on an oil slick, grabbing on to a pole to keep his balance.
He sees the red fleck in the girl's eye magnified behind a bulging tear,
and he wonders, how could this happen? How could a goal so noble
come to this? How could a love I felt for another turn me into this?

Again, Slugger slams the Satine against the ceiling. His limbs
break. His head dents like a fender. Oil cascades onto the giant Russian's shoulders and face.

Eliot backs away from the child. He drops his newsbrane and runs
for the door on the front end of the car. He crosses between cars. He
draws the stares of passengers as he slaloms between the hand poles
toward the front of the train.

"You!" says the Russian, standing at the end door. "Come here!"

The passengers watch the oil-soaked bot limping in pursuit.
Some record the action on their pocketbranes, others call the police
for help. Others panic at the sight of this killing machine battling
through his wounds to corner the heartbeat fleeing through the car.

Eliot runs the length of the train as it nears the station in Heron.
He approaches the front car, careful as his feet slip on the wet metal
of the footplate. Still a hundred yards from the station, with Slugger
a car behind, there won't be time to escape. There won't be space.
He's running out of time and space.

Eliot releases the door to the front car and climbs to the top of
the train. He pulls his body above the car. His fedora flies from his
head. He flattens his stomach onto the wet, grooved metal and
waits as the train drifts to a stop.

Clouds of Heron's black smoke forms on either side of him. The
sooted rain muddies his clothes; the ashy wind blows hot against
his neck.

The doors open. The passengers flee en masse. Eliot can hear the stampede followed by warnings to stay away. The crowd of bots on the platform refuses to board.

"Papa, Papa!" The girl leans out of a car in the middle of the train.

"Back on the train," yells the Russian, and the girl obeys.

Eliot watches from the roof. He sees Slugger lope around searching for the mad heartbeat who tried to steal his little girl's eyes. The conductor's voice comes over the loudspeaker.

"Next stop, Maywood. Stand clear of the closing doors."

Eliot waits so he can leap off the train with Slugger locked securely inside. The Russian boards. Eliot climbs to his knees and prepares to jump onto the platform.

Ding-dong. The doors close. Eliot sees his moment.

But just as his feet stuck to the ledge when he wanted to flee from the window of Pink's apartment, so too does his body freeze atop the first car as the train gathers speed. His time to jump, to walk away, to turn back and abandon his mission—it fades as he watches the platform disappear behind him with the streets of Heron three stories below.

The night air pushes against him. The train gains altitude as the ground slopes off into a cauldron of smoke and light. Eliot turns to face backward so the wind and rain don't blind him. His legs straddle the parabola of the roof. He sees Slugger's head pop up over the lip of the car. The rest of him follows. The giant bot climbs atop the roof and stands tall astride the flying train.

Eliot scoots away, bringing his thighs together for a better hold. The bot approaches. He bleeds oil and drags his wounded foot, but his balance is perfect. It would be beautiful to watch were he stalking anyone else.

"I thought they were yours," Eliot shouts, pushing himself backward atop the rain-slicked grooves. "I didn't know about the girl."

The Russian remains as indifferent to negotiation as he was in Blumenthal's office. He keeps coming until Eliot reaches into the holster and fumbles for the gun. Only then does the bot pause. His eyes measure the trajectory of the nozzle, the velocity of the train, the caliber of the firearm and the man who holds it. Eliot's hand shakes. He stares at the Russian across the sight of his weapon.

"I didn't know," he says again.

Davydenko charges forward, and Eliot fires without looking. Chin tucked, eyes shut, he squeezes off a volley of slugs. He pulls the trigger even after the last round is spent and the hammer clicks without firing.

The train rambles on a choppy current of air as Eliot awaits Slugger's attack. But it doesn't come. He opens his eyes tentatively and sees no sign of the bot except for a streak of oil across the contoured roof of the train. He leans over to the side and sees the lit windows of factories illuminating the fog.

"Hey," says the conductor's voice from the other side of the train. "Get off a' there."

Eliot scoots perpendicular across the roof, looks down, and sees Slugger Davydenko, oil running from his wounds, holding his weight from a side window.

"Get off a' my train!"

The conductor strikes at his fingers with a flashlight. The Russian reaches up and yanks him through the glass. The conductor's uniformed body plunges into the low-lying smoke of the city.

In a panic, Eliot pulls himself back to the center of the roof. His gun is useless now. No bullets. Nowhere to hide. No one steering the train. The first car lists and the others follow. Eliot scurries sideways like a hamster trying to keep his balance on the circumference of a turning wheel. He shimmies to the side, holds onto the corner of the roof and looks inside the train window. He sees a feeble passenger with Coke-bottle glasses clutching a handrail. Alone in the car, the passenger falls toward the conductor's booth like a last piece of candy shaken inside an empty box. He pops around the seats until he finally makes it to the cockpit door. Slugger's legs dangle on the opposite side of the car. His foot kicks through the glass before he swings inside the window.

Suddenly, the train torques in the opposite direction, righting itself as the feeble passenger overcompensates on the yoke. Eliot climbs back to the top then slides backward as the train arcs into the air. He holds the grooves of the roof as he lowers himself between the hurtling cars.

A hand grabs his ankle. Eliot looks down to see the Russian standing in the doorway. He loses his balance as the train banks abruptly and the two back cars whip into the side of a skyscraper. The glass shatters from the building as metal clashes with metal. The cars decouple and fall, tumbling and flipping before they hit the ground.

The Russian grabs a door handle allowing Eliot to shake free. He falls between the footplates and catches the coupler on his way down. He holds on with his strong, mechanical hand while his organic body dangles in the air.

Sirens whistle beneath him. Drones and floaters, launched from their bases, speed toward the flying train. The Russian stomps on Eliot's fingers with his heel. Eliot sees a long bar that runs the length of the undercarriage. He grabs it and swings away from the coupler. He raises his legs and wraps them around the bar to relieve the burden from his injured hand. With his back against the city, Eliot crawls upside down, forearm over forearm, the length of the car. Looking between his legs, he can see Slugger lowering himself beneath the train.

No quit in this bot, thinks Eliot. No chance he'll ever give up.

The first car lowers toward the river, dragging the remaining cars behind. Floaters glide alongside. Over a bullhorn, a pilot shouts directions to the cockpit, instructing the feeble passenger how to land.

Eliot crawls beneath the train as it speeds above the river, dipping tentatively then jerking itself back up. The Russian catches up and positions himself beneath Eliot's body. He wraps his muscled legs around Eliot's midsection and squeezes his organs and his ribs. He uses one massive hand to hold his weight from the bar while a free arm is used to choke Eliot from behind.

Androids peer out of their shanties as the train speeds above them. It winds along the river's contours, arcing over bridges and feinting toward the surface with the rescue drones following swiftly behind.

Eliot's ribs crack between the squeezing legs. A peaceful dizziness overcomes him as his throat is compressed by the hinge in the Russian's elbow. The lifeblood slows in his veins. But even as the breath bellows from his lungs, Eliot can sense that Slugger isn't as strong as he was in the pit. Oil bubbles in the bot's mouth, and there's a dampness by his right thigh from where a bullet penetrated his skin.

The train lowers; it wants to land but has too much speed. Eliot releases one hand from the undercarriage and rests his weight against the Russian's chest. He finds the wet spot on Slugger's leg and pokes his finger through the bullet hole in his jeans. The Russian growls beneath him. Sirens blare. The lights of the city blur past as the train gains altitude and loses the river below. Eliot hooks a wire with his finger and rips it out of the android's leg. As the limb flails uselessly beneath them, the enraged fighter clamps his teeth into Eliot's ear. Eliot turns his chin into Slugger's shoulder. He chews into a buckshot wound, and with his teeth, he rips out more wires from the android's arm.

The train rises. The bot's arm releases its grip. Eliot's ear tears off in Slugger's mouth as his body dangles over the river, his wires exposed, oil streaming from his wounds. He holds on to Eliot's coat lest he plunge into the dirty smoke of the city. Slugger needs Eliot now; the hunter clings to his prey. The train rises to clear a bridge. The fighter's weight stretches the seams of the coat as the train gains more altitude. The fabric rips, and the Russian's body falls from the sky. He howls and grabs in desperation at the air. With Eliot's torn coat in his hand and a bloody ear in his mouth, the fighter drops several stories until he lands atop a spire that pierces into his back and out his chest. Pinned and wriggling atop a bridge, the Russian fighter flails and punches as the oil pours from his body and the power drains from his limbs.

The train lowers. It finds a fast course against the eddies and turns with the contours of the river's path. Eliot crawls into the space between two cars and pulls himself onto the footplate as the train skims the surface of the water. He grabs for a handle and yanks an end door open and collapses his body inside. The door slams shut as the front car smashes against the shallows of the river. On impact, the train's safety-spray floods the interior with a deluge of heavy foam that expands into a rubbery shock absorber for Eliot's tumbling body.

The train twists and skids and caterpillars in the middle with cars springing into the air, erect, then falling with steel shards slicing through the metal in their path. The train tumbles to its side and floats atop the black-water sludge. The crash ends but the mangled iron rocks back and forth in the river like a fever-sick patient sweating in his bed.

Within the cars, the foam dissolves, and Eliot sinks in the white bubbles melting beneath him. Water rushes through the broken windows. Sirens sound above the din. Given his injuries, he crawls as best he can toward a crack in the fuselage. He grabs a sharp metal edge and allows the water to push him up through the opening. He emerges from the wreckage like a broken ghost climbing through the splintered planks of his casket.

Androids leave their homes along the banks and trudge out in the chest-high water to get to the fallen train. Some tear slabs of metal from the cars and rip the limbs off injured bots. Others steal wallets and watches from disabled heartbeats. Others still dive into the muck to pull survivors from the wreck. They form relay chains and move the victims to the riverbank where nurse bots treat wounds and administer CPR.

Gunfire explodes from a floater in the sky. Bullets sweep the river, cutting down the looters and Samaritans alike. The bots scatter and dive for cover but the gunfire persists.

Eliot kneels on the sinking metal and watches as a barrage of Molotov cocktails flies from beyond the shanties and smashes into the floater above. The craft bursts into flames and drops from the sky. It lands atop the train where it burns like a funeral pyre on a sacred river. Bots rush the downed craft and pull policemen from the wreck. They rip the dying heartbeats' limbs from their bodies in an orgy of revenge.

The flames ignite chemicals floating on the water's surface. From the west side of the river, a phalanx of officers strafe the tent city with machine guns. The bots retaliate with slabs of concrete launched from makeshift slings and catapults. They attack from the rooftops as the drones attack from the sky.

Covered in white foam, a Chug-Bot drifts by in the flaming current, and once again, Eliot remembers the girl. He tries to recall which car she was in. He leaps along the protrusions of the sinking train, looking for some sign of her between the cracks of the wreckage.

"Eliot," a voice calls from the shanties on the riverbank. "Get out of there!" His brother snaps a loop from his car before calling out again. "We gotta go!"

Black smoke rises from the river. Gunfire and screams penetrate the flames. Eliot hops along the sharp edges of a middle car crumpled like a sheet of paper. Deep within the crash, he sees a patch of pale white skin reaching upward from the darkness. He lowers his body into the twisted metal until he can discern the girl's form.

"Take my hand," he says, but the girl doesn't respond. He lies down against the hot metal and thrusts his arm into the void. "I won't hurt you," he tells her. "Take my hand."

Still, the girl doesn't respond.

Eliot extends his arm, his shoulder burning, until he has a grasp of the girl's wrist. He pushes himself up and plants his knees on the metal. Her body is weightless in his grasp. He lifts her easily, too easily; her uncanny lightness unsettles him. Standing on the fuselage, holding the girl in the air, Eliot can see that her torso is severed on an angle beneath her chest. Her parts spark and her wires sag beneath the clean shear that sliced her in half. Her open eyes are lifeless and blank, one with a little red fleck.

"Eliot," Shelley screams from a side of the battlefield. "Get out of there!"

Projectiles arc above them. The smoke billows. The train sinks into the muck. Eliot hears his brother screaming from the shore. He feels the river burning around him. He looks at the little red fleck in the dead bot's eye: so useless and intact.

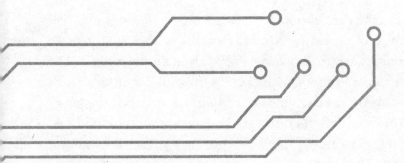

THIRTY-FOUR
Apocalypse

~~Left Arm—Uchenna~~
~~Right Pinky—Edmund "Pink" Spenser~~
~~Head—Jillian Rose Models~~
~~Legs—Tucson Metal Solutions~~
~~Torso—Chief Shunu/Joshua Dominguez~~
~~Right arm—Lorca~~
~~Eyes—Blumenthal Promotions~~

The police have a checkpoint on Crenshaw. Assault rifles across their chests. The car approaches. Inside, Eliot holds a rag to the side of his head. Behind the wheel, Shelley does the talking.

"I got to get him to a hospital."

Eliot shows the injury, and the cops wave them past. Blood drips down his neck. His clothes are soaked. The pain runs from the side of his head down his shoulder and into his busted ribs. He takes a vial from the glove box and pours a few drops in a rag. He takes a sniff then presses the cloth to where he used to have an ear.

"There's a first-aid kit in the galley," says Shelley

"I know."

"You got to take care of that."

Sirens flare around them. Armored trucks with SWAT teams race east through the city. Explosions blast through the night.

"I gotta get loops of this," says Shelley. "This could be my chance."

As they escaped the river, floaters and drones scorched the bots' tents and shanties with flamethrowers. Fleeing androids carried the fire to the warehouses and factories nearby. They smashed windows and flipped cars. They stole weapons from downed officers and shot back at the sky. Shelley drove with the current of the riot until he made it out of harm's way, but even now, in the car, they feel as if they're only inches ahead of the swell.

"Can you get to Avernus like that?" Shelley asks.

"I can get there."

"You'll need help."

"I'll have it."

Because he'll have Iris.

It wasn't pretty, it wasn't how he drew it up, but Eliot has her parts now, every damn one of them. Against all laws of probability, against all warnings and his own fears, he has everything he needs to put her back together again.

"You all right?" asks Shelley.

"I'm all right."

He's not all right.

The price was too high. It split him in two. Half of Eliot is in the car but the other half is kneeling atop the train with his fingers in a young girl's face.

"She was dead already," he says in the car.

"Who was?"

"The girl."

Shelley hasn't looked at him since the river. He aimed his loop-cam to take a picture when Eliot raised the bot out of the wreckage, but then he lowered the cam and looked away. Shelley, his flesh and blood, who has no quarrel with the ugliness of the world—shit, he revels in it—couldn't look at his own brother as Eliot removed the girl's eyes.

"There was no point in leaving them there," says Eliot. "Should I have just left them to sink in the river?" They drive past the pump jacks on the oil fields in Baldwin Hills. "She was a bot, for Chrissake. For all we know she was older than me."

"Who you trying to convince?" Shelley asks.

Throngs of androids drift onto the street to watch the fire from the hilltop. Shelley honks, but they're slow to get out of the way. Challenging and unafraid, they stare into the car as it passes.

"You can't tell Iris," says Eliot.

"Tell her what?"

"She'll never forgive me."

"All right."

"She'll never forgive herself."

A burning Dumpster blocks the entrance to the freeway. Shelley drives around it and merges onto the ramp. They head west toward the harbors, away from the riot, joining a stream of cars pouring onto the freeway. People headed for where they hope it's safe. Maybe Mexico, maybe the water, maybe south toward the desert. Somewhere they hope the bots won't follow.

"I fucked up," says Eliot.

"Only by your own terms."

"What other terms are there?"

The bridge to Naples Island in Long Beach is blocked off by armed heartbeats. They check pulses before allowing the car to pass. The island is arranged in concentric circles with canals that circumscribe the footpaths in front of the houses. Shelley's boat is tarped and moored in front of a vacant property that sits in the center of nine canals.

"I got it from here," says Eliot. "Go get your loops."

"I'm helping," Shelley insists.

They pull off the tarp and untie all but one of the ropes. They remove the bumpers. Eliot hands his brother the key to his apartment in exchange for the key to the boat.

"Call me when you get to Avernus."

"Of course."

"And do something about you ear," says Shelley. "It's really ugly."

The waterway is clogged with boats already leaving, headed to Catalina or a few days at sea until things settle down. If they settle down. There's no way to know.

"Come with us," says Eliot.

"You kidding? This is my chance!"

"But what if this is it?" Eliot asks. "What if the whole city goes up tonight?"

Shelley laughs. "And to think a schmuck like you was the spark."

The younger brother looks wistfully at the boat held to its mooring by one ragged piece of rope. This was his home, and now it's floating away. He puts a hand on Eliot's bad shoulder, above the wound that marks the day their family was separated into the living and the dead.

"You would have regretted it if you'd let her go," he tells Eliot. "For the rest of your life you would have wondered what it would be like if you'd taken those eyes."

"But do I regret taking the eyes?" Eliot asks.

"Not so much that you'll throw them in the sea."

A horn blasts as a tanker makes its way into the harbor. Smoke rises above the mountains and blacks out the moon east of the fires. A wave of hot air swirls all the way to the shore.

"Give my best to Mom."

The car door slams. The wheels screech as Shelley drives back toward the freeway. Eliot wonders if he'll ever see him again, wonders if he'll even survive the night. He probably will. His brother's the kind who always finds someone to take care of him. It just won't be me anymore, thinks Eliot.

He holds his side as he climbs aboard the boat drifting gently from the dock. He unties the last rope binding him to the land and tosses it onto the deck. Up on the bridge, he puts the key in the ignition and sets the throttle to neutral to keep the boat from drifting into the canal. He heads belowdeck for the first-aid kit so he can put something on his wound right away.

A man coughs as the lights come on. Eliot sees him on the portside couch in the galley. His clothes and skin are burnt. His eyes squint in the light.

"Good evening, Orpheus," says the old man, pointing his gun to urge Eliot's hands into the air.

"Good evening, Detective."

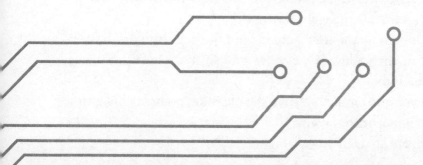

THIRTY-FIVE
The Canal

"We're adrift in the innermost circle," Flaubert says through his earpiece. "I need harbor police. I need a forensics team and a paramedic. Suspect sustained an injury."

What the old detective won't say in front of Eliot, cuffed and seated on the starboard-side couch, is that he has his own injuries to deal with as well. Second-degree burns and a broken leg from the blast didn't deter him from investigating the lead that came through on the drone feed. He was able to autodrive out to Naples Island; he was able to get himself into the boat and suck up the alcohol onboard to keep the pain at bay; but getting back onto the dock with a suspect in tow will be impossible without the aid of other officers.

"How long will it be?" he asks the dispatcher. Then after receiving his reply, "Very well."

Flaubert hangs up and activates his pocketbrane to record any ensuing conversation. He places it on a table next to Pink's laptop. The device glows green but will turn red if it detects anyone is lying. He finds the first-aid kit under the sink and opens it on the galley counter. Supporting himself on his less-injured foot, he dons a pair of latex gloves and goes to work on Eliot's wound.

"And that's the C-900 in the cabin?" he asks.

Eliot nods.

"And those are her eyes?" He gestures to the plastic bag on the couch. Eliot nods again, and the old detective tells him to hold still. He pushes aside the young man's hair and cleans the wound with a disinfecting pad. "She's beautiful." Eliot winces as Flaubert applies a layer of antibacterial gel. "Seeing her put together, I can understand your passion to save her."

With the old detective this close, Eliot can hear what a struggle it is for the man to breathe. Knocking on death's door but determined to see the job through—you have to admire the dedication. But why my case? Eliot wonders. Of all the open murders in Los Angeles, why was I so lucky as to draw this persistent bastard from the deck?

"We have time," Flaubert says as he stretches a bandage across the side of Eliot's head. "The department has more pressing concerns tonight." He tapes the bandage in place then steps away to evaluate the quality of his care. Back on the couch across from Eliot, he struggles to find a position that doesn't cause him pain. "Should you come clean, the courts might show leniency in their judgment."

Sitting in the boat's dark galley, the two adversaries face each other like weakened pugilists in the championship rounds of a fight. Each can hear the other's labored breathing; each can see plainly the other's wounds. Eliot is stiff, his neck bruised and swollen, an ear missing from his head. Opposite him, Flaubert's leg is compromised, his clothes charred, his eyelids drooping from exhaustion.

"Was it your hope," the old detective asks, "that Plath would take the rap for your crime?"

"I'm not the one who made her a suspect."

"Nor did you do anything to exonerate her. Did she matter less than your C-900?"

Eliot pulls at the restraints on his wrists. He looks at the curtain that blocks his view of the woman on the bed in the cabin. He looks at the eyes in the bag by the detective's side. A pair of handcuffs, a curtain, and a man stand in his way. And time, of course, of which Eliot has little left.

"How many were harmed as collateral in your campaign?"

"How many did Pink kill?" Eliot asks in response. "How many would he have killed were he to survive?"

Flaubert squints toward the stern of the boat as if the answer might lie somewhere near the bridge. "My feeling about Mr. Spenser is that he was a sociopath whose actions, though legal, were far from ethical. Nonetheless, it is my job to find his killer. It is the role I play in a process."

"A flawed process."

"The best process we have." His shoulders spasm as he coughs. "Democracy, capitalism, America—none of it is perfect, but we are always becoming, always improving toward an ideal. Call it an illusion, but it is a working illusion."

"Working for whom?"

"For those who opt in and play by the rules. Some of them anyway—you made a good living, did you not?" The old detective stifles a cough then clears his throat. He removes his pocket square but finds it charred beyond the point where it's useful. "Of course, if your quarrel was with the law, there were avenues open through which you could have attempted reform. You could have spoken out or offered financial support to a cause. With your famous last name, you could even have run for office if you had wanted."

The galley bobs up and down from the wake of a passing vessel. The curtain sways between the rooms. She lies a few feet away, thinks Eliot, fully assembled in the cabin except for her eyes. Just beyond the curtain, but completely beyond my reach.

"You played a role in this, too, y'know."

"I did," Flaubert agrees. "I should have done more to stop you."

"Or help *her*."

"Help *her*?" The old detective looks toward the curtain as if utterly confused. "They're here to serve us, not the other way around."

He wonders if Eliot's misunderstanding of that fundamental relationship lies at the root of his illness.

"Should we be indifferent to the suffering of those who serve us?" Eliot asks. "Why not treat them with dignity and respect?"

"But how much dignity and respect? So much that they drive us to extinction?" Flaubert wipes his mouth with the back of his hand. In his tattered coat and tie, he looks more like a rumpled professor tutoring after hours than a detective pushing for a confession. "Listen to my lungs," he says between breaths. "Look at the ash in the sky and the rioting in the street. Look at the newsbranes and what's happened to your own family. They're killing us, and you want to help them?"

"Not them," says Eliot. "*Her.*" He nods toward the curtain to indicate the body behind it as opposed to the abstraction about which the old detective speaks. A siren approaches. Pain sears into Eliot's shoulder and swells across his back. The sound gets louder then diminishes, promising Eliot a little more time.

"After I'm arrested," he asks the detective, "what will you do with her?"

The old detective squints an eye and shrugs. "The evidence room, I suppose. Then after your trial, those parts that were stolen will be returned. The rest will be given to Green Valley or sold off as scrap."

"And that serves your process?" Eliot asks. "That's fair to her even though she has done nothing wrong?"

"It's a great tragedy that there will always be victims. The state can enforce laws or regulations. It can settle disputes. It can prevent *some* tragedies, but certainly not all."

"But why not save a victim? If it costs you nothing—why not? All you'd have to do is give her her eyes back."

"And take them out again when I have to return her parts to their rightful owners."

"Or let her go."

"I need her body for evidence."

"Not if I confess."

Through the window, a shaft of light from a street lamp crosses the galley. The old detective sighs and shakes his head. "Eliot, this is not a negotiation. You have no leverage, and I don't require your confession. Sure, it would make things simpler; one might say you owe it to the city for the suffering you've caused. But as for any weakness in my case, make no mistake"—he gestures to Pink's laptop, to the eyes, to the C-900 behind the curtain—"I have you. Dead to rights. And I have no interest in aiding or abetting your perverse objective, which I advised against the night we met."

The feint cry of a siren sounds in the distance. The old detective checks his watch and guesses that the timing's right: this should be his men now coming to take the suspect away.

Eliot slouches on the couch as a sense of defeat drags down his chin and lowers his gaze to the floor. He sees Flaubert's shoes are covered with dust instead of their usual shine. He looks at his own shoes, too, and sees that red stain he picked up from the alley beside the *maquiladora* where Iris once worked. The stain is there from when the Disciples dragged him to the basement with Ochoa. Eliot remembers the smell, the block in Heron that Lorca must have chosen as a hiding place while she was affected by Iris's arm. He remembers how the security bot Uchenna said that smell was distinct to that street in Heron: No block in Heron smell anything like it.

And in that red stain on his shoe, in that sticky splash of color that reminds him of the flaw in Iris's eye, Eliot recognizes one last remaining chance to see his lover again—one last haymaker he can throw before quitting on his stool. To see her, hear her voice, bask in her aura one last time before the long humiliation of his trial and imminent sentence. His chin rises. His eyes are clear as he looks at the pocketbrane glowing on the table and softens to the old detective's gaze.

"What if I tell you where your partner is?" Eliot asks.

The curtain billows. The siren outside gets louder as it nears.

"My partner's dead," Flaubert responds.

"I know," says Eliot. "I was there when it happened."

The old detective glances at the pocketbrane and sees it's glowing green. So he *was* there with Plath and the others during the execution. Perhaps he also knew about the plan to bomb the precinct. A worse fellow than I imagined, thinks Flaubert. No court on the continent will show him mercy now.

"And what if I tell you where Lorca is?" Eliot asks.

Flaubert inhales, unimpressed, until he looks again toward the pocketbrane and sees it's still glowing green.

Hm.

Now, this he did not expect. If true, this changes his calculus a bit. But it can't be true, can it?

The waves lap against the hull of the boat. The nearing siren suddenly feels more like a threat than a rescue. The old detective could use another minute to sort this new development out.

"Let me and Iris go," says Eliot, "and I'll tell you where Lorca is."

Is it possible, Flaubert wonders as he watches the brane glow green, that here at the end of my career, after all the near misses and bum leads, on the night the city tears itself to shreds—is it possible that this turns out to be the big one?

The volume of the approaching siren increases. The boat rocks in the water. The old detective asks himself, why not this one? Haven't I always preached you work the file that comes to your desk? Small fish lead to bigger fish, shoe leather pays off? Why not this case, and why shouldn't it be me who brings it home?

"It's not in my authority to release you," says the detective. "But when my superiors arrive. . . ."

"Your superiors won't release me."

No, they won't, Flaubert agrees. Not after what happened to Ochoa. Not after the explosion at the precinct and the riot spreading from downtown. His tip will get lost in the hierarchy, or worse, in a rush to claim credit, someone will leak it to the newsbranes, the Disciples, or the Militiamen. The raid will be compromised, and once again, the terror queen will escape.

The boat sways in the current. The sirens stall. The old detective rubs the burnt stubble on his chin. He knows it should be he who brings her in; he'd do it right, even with his broken leg and his cough. And what a payoff for years of solid police work, what a legacy to the department, what a validation he thought would never come. He could tell Ochoa's children their father died for a reason, turn their daddy into a hero, strike a blow against the enemy, quell the rage on the street—but is the suspect telling the truth?

"She's in Heron," says Eliot, anticipating the question. Again, the pocketbrane glows green.

Flaubert taps his finger against his lip. He looks to the curtain then the eyes in the bag laying by his side. The young man's posture reveals the weight of his conscience. Lazar isn't looking to go free. He knows what he's done and the price he should pay. But it did all come from a place of love, did it not? As twisted and misplaced as his feelings were, from the beginning, all the young man wanted was the girl. Nothing more. And what a small price that is to pay for a prize as big as Lorca.

"If I put the eyes back in your girlfriend's head," Flaubert asks, "will you tell me then where Lorca is hiding?"

"I will," says Eliot, and the pocketbrane glows green.

The old detective inhales a big, thick lungful of sea salt air, and for the first time in years, the breath courses through his lungs without choking him at all.

"Well played," he whispers more to himself than to the suspect across the room. "Well played indeed."

So I'll see her one last time, thinks Eliot. I won't be able to spend the rest of my life with her, but at least for a brief moment our eyes will meet again. Like Orpheus before me, I will have my final glimpse, my last moment of love before an eternity of solitude.

The old detective picks up the bag containing Iris's eyes. He struggles to his feet and crosses to where he expects to find an android sleeping in a bed. But pulling back the curtain, Flaubert finds instead a blind foamer standing at the threshold with a flathead screwdriver in her fist.

"No!" Eliot yells, but with Lorca's arm protecting her, the raging bot stabs the screwdriver into the old detective's gut. The eyes drop to the floor as Flaubert reaches for his weapon. With a feral cry, the android stabs again and again until gunshots blast her atop the bed.

"Oh, God, no," Eliot yells as he passes the cuffs beneath his feet.

Oil and blood splatter the galley. Flaubert's body slumps to the floor. His lungs whistle as he strains to pull the weapon from his ribs.

Eliot seizes the bag from beneath the old detective. He pounces on top of the bot fluttering on the bed like a wounded bird. Oil gurgles from where the bullets struck. She swings her arms and bites. She claws at her own face as Eliot struggles to force her eyes into their sockets.

"Iris," he says as he pins her to the bed. He holds her face as the sirens near. "Iris, look at me."

The red-flecked eye connects with her brain. Her body calms. She blinks and takes a faltering breath.

"Eliot?" she asks as she looks at the bandage on his head. "Eliot, are you hurt?"

She looks down at her body and her wounds. She looks around the cabin, confused about where she is.

"My brother's boat," he tells her as he wipes the saliva from her lips.

The sirens near. A tear magnifies the little red fleck in her eye.

"Is this real?" she asks, her fingers touching his face. "Is this a dream or am I really here?"

"You're here," he tells her.

"And we're going to Avernus?"

"We are."

"And you've quit using drip?"

"Yes," he tells her even though it isn't true.

Red lights flash from the shore as a swell rocks the boat in the canal.

"Oh, Eliot, I'm so proud of you," says the bot dripping oil on the bed. "You did good."

EPILOGUE

Avernus

Eliot stands on the bridge maneuvering the ship out of the canal and into San Pedro Bay. It'll be an hour's journey before they reach the Catalina shoals, after which he has to clear San Clemente and San Nicholas Islands before he's past any threat from a patrol boat looking to haul him in.

"Eliot," her voice calls from the cabin. "I'm still bleeding."

"I'll help you once we're out of the harbor."

If the oil leaks into her works, it'll short her engine and she'll be damaged beyond repair. He has the tools to patch her up, but first he has to steer the boat out to sea. It's too risky to help her now. The police were at the dock as he was pulling out, and it's certain they've radioed ahead. He'll need to sail in the shadow of a tanker if he's going to sneak past the harbor police and the Coast Guard after that.

"I need you," she yells again.

"In a minute."

Who is this woman in the cabin of his brother's boat?

She was Iris first, then several other bots: a beauty, a martyr, a whore, a mother, a child, a murderer. Somewhere along the line she caught a virus that spread through her limbs. It must have been the foaming mouth that caused her to reboot and automatically power on. Thus it was a virus that saved me, thinks Eliot, that saved us both, but the fact that there's no antidote onboard means this is a problem that can't be remedied until we get to Avernus, if we get to Avernus. And who knows how they'll deal with it there? It's a week's time sailing and Eliot needs Iris as a shipmate, but a few more days of the foam expressing itself and the bot will be more dangerous than the sea. Eliot will have to pull her apart, drain her juice, and wait to reconstruct her when her system's clean. In other words, he has to kill her again just to save her.

"Sweetie, I need you."

"Can you hang on a little longer?" he calls back.

Orpheus never married. He never knew the day-to-day of a long commitment, only the fantasy of what life could have been with his deceased fiancée. If he had not looked back who knows what kind of husband he would have been, what kind of marriage they would have had, what kind of lives they would have lead? Would he have stayed faithful or run off with one of the goddesses that liked to sweep down from Olympus every now and then to fuck a mortal? Did Eurydice love him as much he loved her? The myth doesn't say.

"How you doing back there?"

"I'm trying to stitch myself up, but I could really use your help."

Who is this woman he's going to marry?

A pair of jets flies overhead on their way downtown. Could be posturing or it could be an actual bombing run. Hard to say how bad, how out of hand the riot is that he started. Will the city change after this? Is this a turning point or just another in a long line of incidents that will be subsumed by the status quo?

A line of ships heads west into the horizon. The radar shows light rain to the north. Flaubert's corpse lays in the galley where it fell. Eliot wants to give it a burial at sea. Make up a prayer and allow the man his dignity, he was a loyal servant who believed in the integrity of the state. It wasn't his fault the plates were shifting beneath him, and the man was too old and sick to adapt.

"Turns out you can bring back the dead," Eliot says to the corpse.

"Who are you talking to?" Iris calls from the cabin.

In the Greek's day it was impossible, but now mortality is conquered in the same way flight was conquered two centuries ago. Man never did learn to fly himself, but he built a machine that could carry him. In the same way, we have not learned to be immortal, but we have built machines that can carry life further into time than our fragile DNA would allow.

"A few more minutes," he yells toward Iris in the aft of the boat. "Then I'll come down and help, okay?"

"Okay," she replies quietly, in a way that expresses her frustration.

Who is this woman he's taking to Avernus?

Most of his description of the island was made up. He told her what she wanted to hear, but he has no idea what actually awaits them once they arrive. Will there be a place for them there, will they learn to fit in? He doesn't know. And their marriage, too, will depend on secrets. He won't ask how Pink came to be in her apartment that night, whether she was looking for work or something else. And why does she have to know about Martha and Titty Fat and the girl?

His head smarts, the pain in his shoulder is back. He sneaks another hit of drip. The clouds behind him reflect the fire across Los Angeles. Lives and fates welded together, metal contending with flesh, in a war against extinction. Eliot stands on the bridge adjusting the throttle and the angle of the rudder. Once he's in the open water he can allow the computer to navigate. He can put his faith in the machine, but first he has to steer out of port and select his destination.

The old detective did have a point, thinks Eliot. It's hard to argue I didn't transgress. The Universe speeds toward a greater complexity and our morality struggles to keep pace, but that's no excuse for not doing the work to figure out right from wrong. I have to redeem myself, thinks Eliot. I have to find the good and create new life from this flawed union that it might find a foothold in the sands of Avernus. I have to forge a new myth to replace the one that no longer applies.

"Eliot, I need you," she calls sharply from the cabin.

"All right." He looks back now that they're almost out of the harbor. "I'm coming."

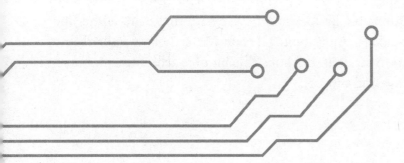

Acknowledgments

A couple of years ago, I was incapacitated by a painful injury in my lower back. Thankfully, my mother was kind enough to fly out to Los Angeles and look after me for the months it would take to recover. While bedridden, when I was unable even to pick up my head and see the screen on my laptop as it rested on my stomach, I somehow, through a fog of painkillers, typed out the first few drafts of this story. Without my mother's help, I never would have been able to manage the ordeal of my injury, let alone write a novel during that time.

Others were also extremely helpful in getting me back on my feet, especially Andrew McGlothin, Megan McGrath, Blake Lindsley, Christine Stauber, Dr. David Schechter, Arnold Bloch, Jake Goldberger, Jordan Ramer, Sandra Hoffman, Sagiv Rosano, Vanessa Coifman, the Schnur family, and my brother Jonathan. My ex-girlfriend Christina Blazek visited with her daughter Mekenna and their dog to cheer me up. My manager, John Tomko, read the initial drafts and showed confidence in the material. My agent, Ethan Ellenberg, gave invaluable advice as to how to bring the story home.

I'd also like to thank my editor, Brendan Deneen, for granting me this opportunity. Thanks to my copy editor, Jane Liddle; Nicole Sohl at Thomas Dunne Books; Shari Smiley; my attorney, Kim Jaime; and my secret weapons, Andy Nordvall and Marat Bokov. I thank my family and all my friends and hope this humble achievement is worthy of their love and support.